CHAPTER 1
A Truth Dying

ALBERT BROOKS WOKE UP ONE sunny morning to the sound of a lawn mower and a dog barking in the distance. Songbirds flitted about outside, singing just as they had when he was born that September day in 1934. Excited, Albert rolled over in bed to see if his wife was awake yet. She was still sleeping, so he went to the kitchen. Greeted by the congratulations banner his wife had put up over the big window by the kitchen table the night before, Albert smiled. He made himself a bowl of cereal and began to eat while watching the birds through a large window. He had glanced at a family photo sitting on the kitchen table when he heard his wife walking toward the kitchen.

"I hear my Empress Coney's approach," Albert said.

"Good morning, Mister," Coney said with a smile. She gave Albert a kiss on the cheek. "You're really excited about our family gathering."

"I am, and can I get more than a 'Mister' this morning?"

"I'm wearing this skimpy robe just for you."

"Hmm…you look good in silk."

Coney laughed. "The answer is no because, for one, our focus should be on celebrating our granddaughter's national junior volleyball game. Second, I need to get a few things together before our children show up, and you, my Mister, will get in my way."

"I will not."

"Yes, you will because you can't keep your hands to yourself, which brings up my third reason. My children and my grandbabies are not to see me in this robe. I won't traumatize them."

"Can I disagree with number three? You look fabulous. You look like you're forty."

"I know I look good, and that's why you're going to finish eating and get dressed."

Albert pouted. "Why was the answer no?"

Coney gave him a suggestive glare.

Albert sighed. "I want to make a dea—"

"There will be no deals, Mister. Behave and get dressed," Coney said as Albert took another bite of cereal.

"I love you too. We're doing a good job keeping the family close, by the way." Albert smiled, and Coney smiled back. He finished eating, got dressed, and gave Coney a kiss on the cheek before walking out to the porch.

Albert sat rocking in his favorite chair overlooking the large front yard he so carefully manicured each weekend. He saw his next-door neighbor and friend, Andre Ortiz, step onto his porch wearing a frown. Andre quickly walked toward the large, fenced garden sitting next to his house, pacing around the fruits and vegetables while he mumbled and stared at the plants.

Albert thought, *What has you frustrated, old friend?* Concern etched across his face, he asked, "What's going on, Andre? By this time, you would normally have started bragging about your prized tomatoes."

"These younger generations worry me, Al," Andre said with a troubled tone. "I spoke with Sean, my grandson, today over the phone, and I was so overjoyed that he's old enough to think to call me. I was so excited to hear his voice that I started speaking Spanish...and, Al, he didn't understand a word I said. He's only seven, but he thought I was talking gibberish, so I talked to my daughter. I asked Sully, 'Why isn't the boy learning his own culture? It's a rich culture.' So we started arguing, and she said that for now, he doesn't need to know." He bent over and checked a large tomato plant, his brown calloused hand rubbing his silver goatee. " 'All he needs to know is English because that's the language that will get him anywhere,' she told me!" Andre threw his hands in the air. "She said he'll learn Spanish in high school, but that's not the same as learning it from your own Mexican family."

Andre went out of the fenced garden, closed its gate, and sat down in a wooden chair on his front porch.

Albert exhaled and shook his head while he walked around his fence and sat down next to Andre. "That's why we have to keep enforcing things in our own families. The way our society is today, it's not so different from when we were young men of color. Assimilation, forget your culture, forget your heritage, and blend in with a society created by white men."

Andre sighed. "It's a shame. It *really* is a shame."

"I understand, but maybe you can negotiate with Sully so Sean can learn."

Andre nodded. "Maybe you're right, Al. Maybe you're right. I'll let her calm down and then give her a call later."

Albert could suddenly hear Andre's wife, Natalie, moving chairs around in their kitchen.

"Andre, are you coming in soon?" Natalie asked.

"Natalie, I'm coming in, honey. Just talking to Al."

"Hey, Al, how are you? The two of you aren't causing trouble now, are ya?"

"When have we ever caused any trouble?" Albert asked.

Natalie replied, "How about you try twenty years ago?"

"Oh! Now, woman, you're killing me." Andre was laughing as he spoke.

"She still talks about that?" Albert whispered.

Andre nodded his head while chuckling.

Albert heard a car drive up to his house. "Here are my troublemakers coming to my house." Albert gave a wave while he got up and headed home. He said, "Keep me updated. It's time for family."

"Alright, before I forget, let little Elisa know that Natalie has finished her dress," Andre said.

"I will. I'm sure that'll make her day."

Albert entered his house to see two of his granddaughters giving Coney a hug.

"Granddaddy!" the girls shouted.

"Hey, now, it's my unstoppable duo. Let me give you some sugar," Albert said. He gave each of his granddaughters a kiss on the cheek while Liz walked in. "Well now, my most challenging child returns to my house again."

"It's good to see you too, Daddy," Liz said as she grinned at her father and gave him a hug.

Albert said, "Well, everyone else should be coming soon. Where is Michael at?"

"He's coming, Daddy. He's getting something out of the car."

"Alright, well, I'm going to sit down in my living room and enjoy my sunroof so I can see these nice clouds we're getting today." The moment Albert walked into the living room, he couldn't help but think of what Andre was going through and how frustrated his friend must've felt.

Christina approached Albert with a big grin. "Granddaddy, can you watch me do my flips?" she asked.

Albert smiled as he sat down. "Of course! Go ahead and show me what you can do." Christina began to do flips as Albert clapped. "Impressive, Sugar. Keep it going!"

Elisa came up to Albert, grinning. "Granddaddy, why is Christina's hair wavy and straight like mine, but it doesn't grow long like mine?" she asked.

Albert replied, "For a six-year-old, you're so observant. Well, both of you are Cherokee, black, and maybe even have white blood. So the reason Christina has short hair is because of the African genes, which are just as special as the Indian, just different."

Christina came over to Albert with a surprised look on her face. "We're Cherokee, so that's our tribe?" Christina asked.

Albert's brow furrowed and the side of his mouth twisted while he looked at his granddaughter. Elizabeth, the second oldest of his daughters, knew they were Cherokee and looked more native than anything else. Albert called the whole family in the living room. "Elizabeth Sheena, you have to explain something to me," Albert yelled.

Liz replied, "Wow, Daddy. I haven't heard that since I was nineteen. What's wrong?"

"I just discovered that my eight-year-old granddaughter doesn't know she is of the Cherokee tribe. Now, I taught you and your brothers and sisters, and I expect it to be passed down. It's who we are, and we are fortunate to know that truth."

"I'm sorry, Daddy."

Noticing the rest of his children had arrived, Albert had Liz sit down. Once all of his children and his son-in-law, Michael, entered the living room to greet him, he asked, "Have any of you told my grandchildren in detail about their heritage. Or have you only told them they're black?"

The scared looks on their faces told Albert they had done the same thing Liz had.

Before Albert could say anything, Michael said, "My girls are black, so there's no point in them knowing more when that's all that matters."

Albert thought, *Boy, it's taking all of my strength not to throw my Bible at you, fool.* "So, are you trying to say that our Native American blood gets outdone by our African blood? Sit down, Michael," he said with a deep voice. "My family is one of the few that has held onto the practice of telling the truth instead of passing for just black and taking it for granted that we are of native blood. Your children are as much black as they're Native through me. Is that clear?"

Michael nodded. "Yes, sir, I didn't mean to offend you or make it seem like it was of no importance. It's just that people don't see a Native American girl when they see Christina. Liz and Elisa look far more like it than her."

"So, you're suggesting that because your daughter doesn't have longer hair, even though it's not coarse and curly, that she looks *blacker*? I guess the high cheekbones and those eyes don't count as far as you're concerned. So, I can safely assume that my daughter hasn't told you everything she knows. How about this? Do you think Tony, my great-nephew, looks more black or Native? He doesn't have the hair or high cheekbones, but he has the almond-shaped eyes and light complexion. So, does he have a right to claim his own bloodline?"

"Um…well, of course he does, but people don't see a mixed boy. They see a black boy."

"That's exactly my point. Why are you so concerned about what others think? See, that's the problem my family has fought against for a long time, and I'm not going to let this family break down on holding to the truth. It's wrong, and I see it to be cowardly."

Suddenly, Coney walked into the living room from the kitchen. "Al, are you giving these kids a rough time again?"

Albert replied, "No, they brought it on themselves. Besides, we haven't had story time in a long time. It's time they remember where they come from and who they are, not what society or the government wants them to be classified as." Albert reached for his large wooden chest of precious letters encased with plastic film—a burned book, pictures, and a diary from the past—and began to tell his family the truth about their heritage.

CHAPTER 2
The Beginning

"In 1828, my great-great-grandmother, Annabelle, was born into the Brown family on a plantation in Mississippi," Albert said. "The Browns' mansion was 110 years old; the white mansion was well-painted and cared for with its eight large pillars, supporting its enormous front frame, and three large staircases inside. Rows of aster and pasture rose went around the front of the mansion, which held twenty rooms, as large oak and bloomed magnolia trees outlined the land sparsely. Several buildings were on the property. A small slave house painted white and designated for house slaves was placed slightly behind the mansion, and a red-bricked cookhouse was connected to the mansion by a covered walkway.

"Annabelle began working as a house slave when she was eight years old, and she became a favorite of the master's daughters. Annabelle had her strongest connection with Master Brown's youngest daughter, Judy Mays. Their bond was so noticeable that when they were young children, Master Brown decided to label Annabelle as a house slave to please his daughters. Over the years, Annabelle was taught to cook, clean, serve meals, and care for children. It became harder for Annabelle, noticing the difference between her life and that of her owners. At times, her pride caused her to see herself in a higher status than the other slaves, even though her parents were field slaves.

"Judy Mays and her sisters treated Annabelle favorably for a slave, but their parents—especially their mother, Mrs. Regina—constantly reminded her of her status. Judy Mays encouraged Annabelle to always smile and speak softly to avoid her mother's wrath. Annabelle was a dark brown-skinned girl with an adorable smile. However, Annabelle was strong-willed, and one day when she was thirteen years old, she refused to work for the rest of the day. Mrs. Regina made Annabelle, wearing her brown cloth dress, stand in place holding a silver platter while she drank her tea..."

"Mrs. Regina, may I please sit for a moment? My feet are in pain," Annabelle begged.

Mrs. Regina, wearing a green plaid Victorian dress, glared at Annabelle from blue eyes and flicked her blonde hair behind her. "You will stand there until I say you may leave," Mrs. Regina said in her nasally, condescending southern voice.

Annabelle clutched the silver platter, wanting to throw it on the ground. Annabelle reached her peak of frustration and turned just as Mrs. Regina reached out to place the teacup on the tray. The teacup fell to the ground and shattered, spilling tea on the floor and over Annabelle's dress. Annabelle's eyes narrowed, and her teeth clenched as she felt the tea hit her dress. She thought nothing of the mess on the floor at first.

"Oh, no! My dress has tea all over it now!" Annabelle shouted in frustration.

Mrs. Regina rose from her rocking chair, her face a mask of rage and disbelief. "You little nigger! How dare you complain about your ugly rags when my carpet has been ruined by your stupidity!" Mrs. Regina shouted.

Annabelle looked down at the octagon-shaped carpet with white flowers. She began to back away as Mrs. Regina reached forward and slapped her. Annabelle placed her hand on her cheek and glared back at Mrs. Regina, her eyes narrowing.

An elderly slave, wearing a light brown cloth dress, moved toward Annabelle as though to remove her.

"Don't touch her, Ruth. It is clear what needs to be done here!" Mrs. Regina roared. "Go get Master Brown."

Ruth's eyes widened, and she gulped.

Staring down Annabelle, Mrs. Regina suddenly grabbed the girl's coarse, curly hair and turned her head toward Ruth, making Annabelle scream. Then Mrs. Regina snarled, "I said fetch him!"

Ruth jumped and left the mansion to look for Master Brown, returning with him shortly. While they waited, Annabelle stood in place as Mrs. Regina paced. Master Brown walked toward Mrs. Regina, wearing a high-collared white shirt with a blue cravat and brown trousers. He rubbed his brown hair, seeming quite agitated during Mrs. Regina's explanation of the incident.

With a steely glare, Master Brown marched up to Annabelle and smacked her, then he grabbed the back of her head and forced her face down on the tea-soaked carpet. "I think I know how to break you as much as it may disappoint my daughters," he said. "I cannot allow you to think you have any say-so." He released Annabelle, and she slowly lifted her head, holding back tears. "I think two days out in the fields will be enough to make it clear how good you have it here."

Mrs. Regina stepped in front of Master Brown. "Just two days?" Mrs. Regina asked. "You should have seen the look she gave me, a child with the thought of striking me back! I saw it in those devilish brown eyes of hers."

"Regina, I have set the terms, and that's final. I don't want things disrupted in this household over spilled tea. The girls are outside right now playing, unaware of this, and I won't over-punish her for spilled tea. That's irrational."

Mrs. Regina stormed upstairs as Master Brown stared back at Annabelle.

"Starting tomorrow, you will be seeing more of your parents, but not in the way you want. I guarantee it, little girl. Now, clean up this mess," Master Brown said in a calm, authoritative voice.

Annabelle knelt to pick up the pieces of the teacup before walking toward the kitchen. Body tremors ripped through her, and she took deep breaths to prevent herself from crying.

She entered the cookhouse just as Ruth started preparing supper. Ruth looked at Annabelle sympathetically from almond-shaped brown eyes before embracing the girl.

CHAPTER 3
Broken Rules

LATER THAT DAY, JUDY MAYS learned of Annabelle's punishment. Wearing her blue plaid dress, Judy Mays approached her father. He sat in his white rocking chair on the mansion's large wooden porch, watching the slaves work the fields.

Judy Mays sat in her father's lap, hugging him. "Papa, I don't want Annabelle out there with those dirty niggers," she said.

Mr. Brown stared into his daughter's pleading deep blue eyes and replied, "Judy Mays, my ruling on Annabelle stays. She spilled tea on the carpet, and she thinks too freely. I think she scared your momma too."

"Was it an accident? Did she say something, Papa?" Judy Mays asked.

Mr. Brown answered, "Your momma believes it was no accident, and she gave your momma a look of pure evil."

"That doesn't sound like Annabelle, Papa."

"It don't matter what it sounds like, Judy Mays. It is true." Mr. Brown could tell that frustration rose in Judy Mays, so he stroked her blonde hair.

Judy Mays stood and pouted. "She will come back to the house, right, Papa?"

"Yes, I have no desire to send her to the fields, but if she continues this behavior, she'll be out there with the others."

Judy Mays's face scrunched, and her eyes narrowed. She marched back into the mansion without another word. Mr. Brown sighed heavily and continued to rock in the chair.

Night came, and as Annabelle quietly entered the slave house, she thought of the terrifying struggles she would endure in the fields. The small white house had no beds, but wooden shutters covered the windows. The house slaves slept on the wooden floor next to Annabelle, and she stared into the darkness. The sounds of owls and insects usually helped her fall asleep, but she felt no comfort that night.

Mr. Brown and Mrs. Regina sat in their large bed, obvious tension between them.

"I can't believe you only gave that rebellious nigger two days out in a field," Mrs. Regina bickered. "She has been treated too well over the years."

Mr. Brown replied, "Regina, as I said before, I won't have disruption in this house over spilled tea. She is a child and a valued slave that does a better job here than some of the adult house slaves."

Regina became emotional. "Ethan, there's something different about her. Since she was a young child, we could tell she learned more easily than the other slaves, and it entertained our daughters to the point that they wouldn't take no for an answer about having Annabelle around. Annabelle's spirit is too strong. It must be broken now."

"Does she frighten you?"

"No! That child does not frighten me. I'm bothered that she has grown up with too much protection from the girls. She is more than a pet to them. I see it in all of them, especially Judy

Mays. We should have lent her away for a time to make her realize how good she has it here."

"I won't allow Annabelle's removal, Regina. There has been enough disruption, and I won't allow more to be added to the fire."

"Where is this sympathy coming from, Ethan? Surely you haven't let your emotions get attached because we have watched her grow."

"My mind is clear on how I see Annabelle, but I refuse to become a villain in my daughters' eyes," Ethan said in a troubled tone. "Sending Annabelle to the fields is enough stress for me."

Mrs. Regina sighed. "They would never choose Annabelle over you, Ethan. The girls love you more than any nigger."

"I know they love me, Regina, but I think you're right. Too much favor has been given to Annabelle, but we've kept it up for so long that ripping it away now would undermine us. You were surprised by the look Annabelle gave you. You could see she has no fear of you, and that's what bothered you."

Regina, in her white nightgown, scooted next to Ethan and embraced him. "I didn't know how to respond to her. I don't know why. With the other slaves, I would have felt more in control, but with Annabelle, I don't know what it was."

"I think it's because she looked at you with the same rebellious look that Judy Mays can show. You should have seen the look of disappointment on Judy Mays's face today. A bond has formed between those two, and even though we've taught Annabelle her place, a friendship exists between them."

"Then that relationship needs to be killed. Judy Mays and Annabelle are the same age, and the girls would carry them both around the mansion when they were babies. Annabelle needs to be taken away for a while. Ethan, what if you lent her to the Jacksons for a few years?"

"No, we will have to keep the laws in this house and allow nothing more. Judy Mays would hate us if we did such a thing. I don't want such a division to ever occur."

Regina caressed Ethan's face. "You mean it would break your heart for Judy Mays to hate you."

Ethan huffed while Regina continued to caress his face.

"Fine then," she said. "Two days in the fields, but don't expect me to show any mercy to that child."

"I want you to keep the peace and keep Annabelle in check when necessary. That's what I need from you, Regina."

Regina kissed Ethan and placed her head on his chest. "I understand."

The next day, Annabelle was awakened early by Master Coleman and taken out to the fields. Master Coleman was a shorter man than Master Brown. He had gray eyes and a stench to him. He wore a high-collared beige shirt with a loosened black vest and brown trousers. His brown beard, slightly untamed, was intimidating to Annabelle. He yelled at the field slaves with a bellow and was quick to use the whip in his right hand.

Claire, Annabelle's mother, approached Annabelle and gave her a hug and a kiss. "What you doing here?" Claire asked.

Annabelle switched to her colloquial style, replying, "I being punished for two days."

"Punished? I happy you a house slave. You sleep in a good house." Claire shook her head. "You not supposed to be here. Do as I do so Master Coleman have nothing to say to you."

Annabelle nodded and followed her mother, mimicking her.

Annabelle made it through the first day, exhausted and anxious to get back to the mansion. On the second day, Annabelle continued to work with her mother. Her frustration grew as she listened to Master Coleman's demeaning words. She pricked her hand on a cotton plant, and the pain was worse than other times she had pricked herself. Her pride took over as she put down the cotton basket and tried to nurse her finger.

Master Coleman noticed and approached Annabelle. "Annabelle Brown, you best pick up that cotton basket. Don't test me," he said.

Annabelle replied, "You can go feed yourself to the gators."

"What did you say, you rebellious nigger?"

Annabelle, tired and sore, stood. With a loud voice, she said, "You can go feed yourself to the gators. I'm tired!"

Claire stopped working and gasped while she stared at Annabelle.

Master Coleman kicked Annabelle, and she fell to the ground. "I'll make sure you get a good beating for that, you devil of a nigger!"

Claire ran to Annabelle, covering her daughter with her body. "Please, Master Coleman, she's young. She don't know what she say," Claire said.

Master Coleman replied, "Claire, you get off that rebellious little demon right now before I beat you too."

"Please, Master Coleman, I'll take the lashes for her. Please leave her be."

Master Coleman grabbed Claire's arm and threw her to the ground. "I said move it!" he yelled.

"Momma," Annabelle cried.

"Now stays back before I have her hanged instead of beaten, yah hear me?" Master Coleman said.

Claire cried uncontrollably. "Master Coleman, please don't do this. She only a child."

Master Coleman scoffed. "Well, by the words that's coming out of her mouth, I'd say she mighty close to becoming a woman, so I suggest she learn to shut her mouth like a woman. Otherwise, she may have to endure some womanly duties sooner than she wants."

Hearing the commotion, Master Brown rode toward them on his horse, holding the reins to keep the horse still. "What seems to be the problem here, Thomas?" he asked.

Master Coleman replied, "This here nigger has a strong mouth on her. I suggest we beat her or cut off a finger or toe to set an example."

Master Brown replied, "Now, Thomas, Judy Mays favors

this slave, and I would hate to see the look on her face if this slave were deformed."

"I understand, Mr. Brown, but she must be punished, sir." Master Coleman grabbed Annabelle's shoulders.

Annabelle shrugged, keeping her eyes on Master Brown. The smell of Master Coleman's hot breath disgusted Annabelle, but she tried not to show her nausea. She pouted and scrunched her nose, then attempted to walk toward Master Brown.

Claire looked at Master Brown, fear written over her face.

"She threatened to have me fed to the gators and laughed about it," Master Coleman said.

"I didn't laugh. You lie, Master Coleman!" Annabelle shouted.

"Annabelle!" Claire yelled.

"Hmm... Obviously, she does have a strong tongue on her, much like my daughter," Master Brown said. "I wonder who is learning from whom in this manner. Well, Thomas, I agree that she must be punished, especially with this most recent outburst. Have her tied and beaten, but not her face."

Master Coleman replied with a smirk, "Yes, sir. Do you want me to have the other slaves watch as an example?"

"Oh, no. I want them to continue working. I believe her wounds will be testimony enough to keep them in check. Besides, I want someone else to see her disciplined."

Annabelle was taken to a wooden post in front of a large green barn to be beaten, and Master Brown quickly rode back to the mansion. The barn was a few hundred feet east of the mansion.

Master Coleman stripped Annabelle naked vigorously. "Oh, you're on your way to becoming a woman," he grumbled.

Tears ran down Annabelle's face while she covered herself with her arms.

"Now, turn around."

As Annabelle turned, she squinted, seeing Judy Mays in one of the windows of the mansion, watching. She grinned, thinking maybe Judy Mays would come to her rescue.

"What are you smiling at, nigger?" Master Coleman grabbed Annabelle's face. "Let me tell you something, you unholy creature. When I get through with you, you won't be so quick to go against me, and you can kiss all that beauty away. Oh, yes. I've heard the others talk about you. 'Annabelle is such a pretty nigger.' I can't touch your face, but I can still take away the pretty."

He made Annabelle turn around and grabbed one arm. Scared, Annabelle crossed her legs as he tied her arm to the wooden post standing over a hundred feet in front of the barn. Master Coleman grabbed her other arm and tied it down.

In the mansion, Mr. Brown walked Judy Mays onto the porch in view of Annabelle. "Now, my dear Judy Mays, this is how you keep a nigger in check," he said.

"I don't understand, Daddy. What did she do?" she asked.

"She spoke back to Mr. Coleman improperly, so she must be punished."

Judy Mays glanced from the scene on the porch to her father. "Will it hurt her, Daddy?"

"No, sweetheart, she's a nigger. They don't feel like we feel. It won't bother her that much."

Master Coleman pulled out the strap and began whipping Annabelle.

Judy Mays watched in shock. "Daddy, are you sure? I can hear her screaming." She looked back out at the post, frowning as she put her hand to her chest.

Mr. Brown saw Judy Mays's frown and quietly exhaled while crossing his arms. "Sweetheart, go upstairs and play and stop worrying about a nigger."

"But Daddy, she's my nigger."

"I know, sweetheart, but you don't need to watch this. Now go upstairs and play with your toys. Go on now."

"Okay, Daddy," she said reluctantly.

She walked upstairs slowly, clutching her white bonnet, troubled by Annabelle's screaming.

Annabelle passed out from the pain. Master Coleman continued to whip her without interruption, but the last strike caused her to wake up. After twenty lashes, he called for Annabelle's father, William, to carry her away. She was weakened and bleeding badly.

William had dark brown skin, short coarse hair, and a slight build. He was taller than Mr. Coleman but shorter than Mr. Brown. He arrived, wearing a dirty white cotton shirt and beige trousers, and carried his daughter to a slave house.

As Claire cleaned Annabelle's wounds, William scolded her. "Annabelle, you cannot be so bold because it hurts all slaves, not just you. Next time you foolish, you may not be only one to get whipped, and sometimes, they sell us as punishment never to see family again," William said.

Annabelle frowned. "Yes, Papa. I won't do it again. I swear it."

The next day, Judy Mays separated from her sisters and secretly went to the slave houses to find Annabelle. Judy Mays replayed memories of them as little children to calm herself as she stood in front of Annabelle, wearing a blue bonnet to match her light blue high-necked dress.

"I'm so sorry about what happened to you, Annabelle. I've never seen nothing like it. It was scary," Judy Mays said.

Annabelle was still furious about her punishment, so she looked down and said nothing to Judy Mays.

"Annabelle Brown, you look at me when I'm speaking to you." Judy Mays frowned as she looked at Annabelle's expressionless face. "I'm really sorry."

"If you so sorry, why didn't you stop Master Coleman? You

saw him take me to the post, and you saw him tie my hands and take my shirt off. So why didn't you stop him?" Annabelle asked, tears filling her eyes.

"I didn't think... I didn't think he would whip you so bad. I mean, niggers are supposed to be whipped when they do something bad. It's punishment." Judy Mays shed tears and watched as tears flowed down Annabelle's face.

"We've been friends since we was children, and you watched me get beat from your house. I thought we were friends."

Judy Mays's heart beat faster. "I'm sorry. I don't know what I could've done. You were wrong."

Annabelle turned around, opened up her dress, and exposed her back to Judy Mays.

Judy Mays gasped and stepped back because she had never seen anything like it. She fell to her knees, looking at the dried blood and the size of the wounds on Annabelle's back. The sight made her nauseous.

"This is how bad he beat me!" Annabelle said tearfully.

Judy Mays sat on her knees and held her stomach before she vomited. Crying, she rushed toward the mansion.

As she approached the mansion, she stopped, weeping. The echoing voices of the overseers in the fields haunted her, the noise of them dominating the sounds of birds chirping. Judy Mays glanced up, noticing a bluebird with its bright blue plumage, orange collar, and white underbelly. She also noticed a chickadee with its black cap and beautiful gray and white plumage. Two birds she'd occasionally watched from her bedroom window couldn't be heard over the yelling and cracking of whips. Judy Mays dried her tears and marched toward the mansion. She realized there was something she could do. She searched for her father and found him in his study.

"Papa, may I may speak with you?" she asked.

Mr. Brown replied, "Why, yes, my dear. I have time to speak with you."

She walked into the room. Diamond designs stretched across olive green carpet, and oak bookshelves lined the white walls, covered by wallpaper that portrayed a lakeside. Judy Mays stood in front of the majestic mahogany desk as her father looked at her attentively.

"Papa, I spoke to Annabelle today, letting her know that she was wrong. I scolded her for being a bad nigger, and made it clear she must know her place. She has repented of her sins and apologized numerous times. The wounds on her back have tamed her dark nature. I ask that she be returned to the mansion. She has been punished and is in full submission."

Mr. Brown placed his hand on his mouth and looked into his daughter's blue eyes. "I've talked with Mr. Coleman. He has great concern about her obedience. He wants to tame her more and keep her a field slave temporarily. I have to give thought to this. Even though she was born here, she was placed as a house slave partly because of you and your sisters." He stood up and moved around the desk, sitting on it as he looked at his daughter. "Her quick-tempered moments of rebellion are dangerous and quite utterly disrespectful."

Mr. Brown continued looking into his daughter's eyes, watching her disappointment grow. He sighed and lightly tapped his finger on his desk. He noticed a silver platter sitting on his coffee table, an item Annabelle would've cleared if she had been in the mansion.

Mr. Brown exhaled as he placed his hands on his daughter's shoulders. "However, you say you have scolded her, and she has made numerous apologies, repented of her sins, and has had her dark nature turned." He touched his daughter's chin and kissed her forehead. "You may welcome back your nigger, but she must know her place. I won't tolerate more rebellion from a mere child. If she brings any more trouble to this household, she will be back in those fields for at least a year."

Judy Mays nodded her head. "Thank you, Papa. I will have her summoned back to the mansion." She left the study with a small smile on her face, keeping her head turned so her father wouldn't notice.

Mr. Brown sat back down at his mahogany desk and chuckled. "I'll have to keep watch on that clever daughter."

Judy Mays skipped to the outdoor patio where her older sisters, Sue Ellen and Scarlett, were sitting. She saw the blue-eyed teenagers grin the moment she neared.

Scarlett, who was taller than Sue Ellen, flipped her blonde bangs away from her eye. Sharing Judy Mays's southern accent, she said, "Judy Mays, you look very happy."

"I talked to Papa in his study, and Annabelle is coming back to the mansion," Judy Mays proudly said.

"Oh, so you had some words for Papa," Scarlett said. "Well, I'm glad Annabelle is returning. These other house slaves are a bore. I enjoy Annabelle's tirades."

"Why would you provoke such a thing out of Annabelle?" Sue Ellen asked, expressing her higher-pitched voice. "I love Annabelle. She's always been a great slave, and she always gets my hair right. She had one bad day, and Momma overreacted."

Scarlett giggled. "She told Mr. Coleman he can go feed himself to the gators. I wish I had been there to hear it myself."

"Mr. Coleman is an ugly man," Judy Mays blurted.

Gasping, Sue Ellen put her hand to her mouth. "Judy Mays! Little sister, don't say such things."

"I find it absolutely humorous, and being the second oldest, I say it's okay to be honest, Judy Mays," Scarlett said. "But not in front of that smelly man. Be polite."

"We all should've gone to Papa for Annabelle," Sue Ellen said. "I need my ringlets redone." She lightly tugged at a ringlet and accidentally pulled out one of her brown hairs. "Ugh! That's it! I want Annabelle back!"

"Go on, Judy Mays," Scarlett said. "Papa gave you permission to have her summoned back to the mansion now. I'm sure Genevieve will be excited too. She's hiding in the mansion somewhere."

"Okay, I'll have Annabelle brought back," Judy Mays said, leaving her older sisters at the patio.

Later in the afternoon, a slave named Bill approached Annabelle at a slave house. "Annabelle, Miss Judy Mays would like to see you right now," Bill said.

"So she sent a bloodhound to find me instead of coming out here herself?" Annabelle bickered.

"Those some mighty strong words for a nigger that just got beat."

Annabelle scoffed at Bill and left the slave house, returning to the mansion while trying not to show any anger due to the extra day of punishment she'd been given. She arrived at the mansion, dirty from being in the fields earlier that day, and opened the door.

"Now, hold it right there, nigger. What you think you doing opening that door being dirty as you is?" Master Coleman asked.

Annabelle turned around and saw Master Coleman on his horse. He chewed on sugar cane and carried his whip in his right hand.

He continued, "Now, you rebellious little demon, get back to them fields before I whip you again."

Annabelle replied, "I was told to come to the mansion by one of the slaves."

"Who in this home would want your presence?"

"Miss Judy Mays called for me, Master Coleman."

"Well, she's not here right now." Master Coleman held up his whip. "So I suggest you start backing up and go back to them fields like I said. It's a reason you was given a third day."

Annabelle's mouth curved downward in a pout as she sat down. "I'd rather obey her than obey you. You're nothing but a dirty white man that has a taste for Negro women cause you ain't never gonna get a white one."

Master Coleman snarled, "You truly are something. I will enjoy beating some more sense into you!"

"Don't you dare touch me, you snake in the grass!"

He got off of his horse and grabbed Annabelle by her hair. "Now come on, you rebellious nigger."

"Let go of me!" Annabelle screamed.

"Enough, Mr. Coleman! What do you think you're doing to her?" Judy Mays's voice rang out.

Mr. Coleman let go of Annabelle and turned his head slowly. "Miss Judy Mays, I thought you was your momma. I was about to teach this nigger some manners and wash her mouth out with soap."

"I showed up to the mansion as you requested, Miss Judy Mays," Annabelle said.

"Mr. Coleman, did this slave tell you that I called for her?" Judy Mays asked.

Master Coleman replied, "Yes, ma'am. She did say such a thing, but she has a mouth as poisonous as a snake. Nothing but lies."

"Mr. Coleman, if you ever handle this slave in the manner that you're doing right now, I guarantee you will be the one that gets whipped. Now get on to watching those in the fields like you're supposed to be doing."

"Yes, ma'am. I'm on my way...you spoiled little she-demon," Master Coleman murmured beneath his breath at Judy Mays.

"Well, Annabelle, follow me. How long has it been since you were allowed in the mansion?"

Annabelle replied, "I believe this be three days, Miss Judy Mays."

"Well, now you're always allowed back into the mansion." Judy Mays opened the door, and Annabelle walked in.

"Little sister, what are you doing with Annabelle?" a young woman with a more slender build than Regina asked, her voice a calm, mature alto. "Did Papa say she could come back?"

"Yes, Papa did," Judy Mays replied. "And I'm taking her to my room to get cleaned up. That's all, Genevieve."

Genevieve stood on the stairs with her long brown hair, blue eyes, and a beautiful red plaid dress. "Hmm...Annabelle, you truly are different from the other slaves," Genevieve said in an annoyed manner.

"Turn around, Annabelle," Judy Mays said. She then opened up the back of Annabelle's cotton dress. "This will never happen again."

Genevieve gasped, "Oh! Come on, let's go upstairs. Judy Mays, I'll take care of this—you can wait in your room if you'd like. Ruth, you come here."

"Yes, Miss Genevieve," Ruth said, coming out of a hallway.

Annabelle had never before noticed how long Ruth's hair was because it was always in a bun. She didn't understand how Ruth could have such long hair being a Negro woman.

Genevieve sighed. "Ruth, get a new dress for Annabelle. We need to get her cleaned up."

Ruth looked at Annabelle and beamed as she walked away.

Genevieve took Annabelle up to her room and cleaned the cuts on her back that her parents couldn't nurse. "My goodness. You sure have a strong spirit, especially for a Negro," Genevieve said. "Watch what you say, and I'm sure you'll do fine."

"Yes, Miss Genevieve," Annabelle said.

Ruth came to Genevieve's room. "Here is the dress, Miss Genevieve," she said.

"Thank you, Ruth, you may go now," Genevieve replied.

"Yes, ma'am."

Genevieve helped Annabelle put on the blue cotton dress with a white apron.

"You look mighty nice now, especially for a nigger. You're quite rare indeed," Genevieve said.

Annabelle smiled. "Thank you."

"Well, go on to Judy Mays. She wanted you in her room for whatever reason. She's hard to read, and I'm her sister."

Annabelle went to Judy Mays's room and knocked on the door.

"Come in and close the door, Annabelle, and have a seat on my bed," Judy Mays said.

Annabelle sat down on the soft pure white sheets next to Judy Mays.

"I'm sorry for not doing the right thing. You've been my friend since we were children. You have been a friend to me and not a slave. Never again will I let something like this happen to you, but you have to promise me you will obey the rules on this plantation so I can protect you."

Annabelle's eyes widened.

"What do you think?" Judy Mays asked.

"Thank you, Miss Judy Mays," Annabelle said.

"Don't you ever call me Miss Judy Mays in private ever again." Judy Mays smiled, and Annabelle smiled back. "You're my friend as far as I'm concerned, and you're family to me. Again, you will follow the rules. My papa said if you break the rules, you will go back to the fields for at least a year. Do we have an agreement?"

A joyful Annabelle answered, "Yes, I will follow the rules, I promise."

"Also, I've decided to do something that isn't so legal to show you that I'm serious about our friendship."

Annabelle's brow furrowed and her face twisted a little because she didn't understand what Judy Mays meant.

Judy Mays picked up a black-covered Bible, "I'm going to teach you how to read."

Annabelle was speechless, but joy filled her. "You gone to teach me how to read?"

"Yes, but you can't tell anyone about this because it's against the law."

"I won't tell nobody."

"Good. We both would get in trouble if someone ever found out. Well, let's begin."

CHAPTER 4
Powerless

EVERY DAY OVER THE NEXT three years, Judy Mays would call for Annabelle and teach her how to read. The more Annabelle read, the more she began to understand that many scriptures she had been told during her childhood by Master Brown were a lie. Master Brown had been making up scriptures, mostly about how a slave is supposed to serve. It hurt her greatly that the slaves were not being taught the truth about the Bible. Learning the truth over time that whites were not superior bothered her even more. However, to keep her family and the other slaves safe, she decided to remain silent though she wanted to speak the truth.

Therefore, Annabelle decided to pray every day. She asked God to give her strength and fill her heart with love. Her spiritual growth helped her follow the rules, along with her fear of being sent back to the fields. Her new resolve not only strengthened her, but it also strengthened her friendship with Judy Mays.

In March of 1844, Annabelle turned sixteen. To celebrate it, Judy Mays invited her to her room to try on her dresses as a present. She entered Judy Mays's room wearing her blue cloth dress and her hair in twin buns. Annabelle retained her soft-toned voice, nearly matching Judy Mays's. She stood almost eye to eye with Judy Mays, and both teenagers had an hourglass shape.

"Look at you. You've always been beautiful, especially for a Negro, and smart too," Judy Mays said. "Well, I have another party to attend with Edgar Reynolds, so put up the dress and let yourself out when you get done looking in the mirror. You never get to have a conversation with him. My momma always makes you work when he arrives. I hate it."

"Alright, have a good time."

"I will. He's wealthy." Wearing a green bonnet to match her green dress, Judy Mays smiled as she walked out.

Annabelle tried on a few more dresses, then as she headed back to the slave quarters, Master Brown called to her from the hallway.

"Annabelle, sixteen years old, and don't you look stunning?" he said.

Annabelle tilted her head. "Thank you, Master Brown."

"I want to see you in the guest room by the piano in ten minutes," he replied.

"Yes, sir."

Master Brown strolled down the low light hall, and Annabelle quickly went toward the living room, hoping to avoid him. She stared out a window and wished Judy Mays hadn't left. She went to the guest room, and Master Brown pulled her inside and closed the door. His aggressiveness caused Annabelle's heart to race.

The room had an eerie feeling to it. Two lamps sat on nightstands, illuminating the room, and a twin-sized bed was covered with white linen. The room itself held an atmosphere of fear, having no windows and low light. Master Brown would also eerily call an older house slave, Lanny, to the room when Mrs. Regina wasn't present. He commanded Annabelle to work upstairs when Lanny was called to the room. After Lanny would leave the room, she was silent for most of the day, and she never spoke about what happened. Annabelle stood petrified and refused to turn around.

Master Brown placed his hands on her shoulders, caressing them. His hands glided on her skin, and he caressed her neck while guiding her toward the bed. She felt his hot breath on her neck. It sent chills down her spine.

Annabelle slowly turned around, breathing heavily as her fearful eyes fixed on the door. "Master Brown?"

"You've never been bedded, have you? Smooth skin and a firm body, it's hard to believe you spent any time out in the fields," Master Brown said in a lustful tone. "Take off your clothes."

"Master Brown, you did not raise me to be that way. I'm a Christian woman, and I—"

"And nothing. You're my nigger, and I said take off your clothes. Don't make me repeat myself! This is my time. Mrs. Regina is at her sister's, and my sweet little girl won't be home soon, so don't make me wait."

"I'm sorry, master, but you'll have to knock me down before you can take my body," Annabelle murmured.

"Always the strong spirit. Quite different than any white woman I've met, and certainly any nigger woman."

Master Brown grabbed Annabelle by the neck, but Annabelle picked up a lamp and hit him with it, knocking him down. She ran to the door, but he tried to grab her by the ankle, causing her to stumble while he quickly stood up. The moment she reached for the door, he pushed her to the wall, punched her in the stomach, and then smacked her jaw. Annabelle fell to the ground, holding her stomach. He grabbed her and threw her on the bed, ripping the top part of her dress.

"I remember those scars on your back. Impressive how they look more like stripes, and your smooth and soft skin."

Annabelle cried, "Please don't, Master Brown. I'll do anything you want, but please don't do this."

"Don't cry. You're my special nigger now."

Master Brown then raped her. Afterward, Annabelle, shivering and hurt, headed toward the door. As she was leaving the room, he grabbed her arm and said, "Is it clear that I will make you suffer if you tell anyone?"

Annabelle sobbed. "Yes, Master Brown, very clear."

The next day, Annabelle went outside to sweep the porch after serving the Browns supper. She saw her parents at the green barn and quickly went to see them, but she froze when William saw her. William noticed she was quiet, so he asked her what was wrong.

"Nothing wrong, Papa," Annabelle said, switching to her colloquial style.

"What you mean nothing?" William asked, pointing at her arm. "Where you get bruises from?"

"I fell, Papa. I fell when I was walking down the stairs in Master's house."

William gave her a stern look. "What's the truth?"

"It won't matter what I tell you because you're a nigger. There's nothing you can do, and the best thing for me to do right now is to do what I'm told."

William looked at his wife, his eyes starting to shimmer with tears from his broken heart. He thought he knew what was going on between her and Master Brown.

"I have to go to the master's house."

At the distraught expression on Annabelle's face, Claire asked, "How about I ask to take your place, baby?"

"He won't allow that, Momma. You a field slave, and I scared." Annabelle began to cry. "I scared that if I don't do this, I'll never see you or Papa or Todd."

"Your brother only a child. Why he in danger?"

"All of you will be sold if I don't do as I'm told, and the master was serious about it."

Claire gave her daughter a hug. "My baby, pray to the Lord." Tears flowed down Annabelle's face as her mother continued, "Pray every day and do as you're told. It breaks my heart, but you safe as long as you do as you told. The master is smarter than us niggers, so be careful, baby."

Annabelle left her parents and went to the front porch, where she saw Judy Mays. She wore a dark red dress and smiled as though full of joy.

Running to Annabelle, Judy Mays shouted, "Guess what? I'm getting married! He asked me to marry him, so I'm going to be moving out very soon to live with Edgar. Oh, this is so exciting! I'm so happy! I asked Papa to give you one of the guest bedrooms before I move. Now, you won't be stuck out there with the rest of them niggers in that sweaty and nasty slave house."

"I'm so happy for you," Annabelle said hesitantly.

"What's the matter, Annabelle?"

"Nothing. I am a little tired from last night."

"Well, don't worry about that. The guest bedroom is where you will be staying, and it's comfortable. Now come with me so my hair can get prettied. I'm going to need help deciding what hairstyle I want to wear on my wedding day. It's so exciting!"

As Annabelle climbed up the stairs with Judy Mays, Master Brown entered the house. "Judy Mays, my little girl," Master Brown said.

"Hey, Papa. I was taking Annabelle upstairs to help figure out what hairstyle I'm going to wear for my wedding," Judy Mays said.

"My goodness! Isn't this exciting, Annabelle? Imagine, my sweet baby won't be over here so often anymore. I wonder how things are going to change around here."

Annabelle could feel her throat tighten. She grabbed the stair banister and squeezed it, keeping her eyes on Judy Mays.

"I may have to come up with some more work for you to do," he said.

Judy Mays pouted. "Papa, don't do that. She's not like the rest of the niggers."

"I know she's a bit different; I'll admit that." Master Brown looked at Judy Mays's undeniable happiness. "Well, go along and have some fun looking pretty, dear."

"I love you, Papa."

"I love you too. Annabelle, I'll see you later."

Annabelle walked up the stairs, feeling a cold shiver go down her back, dreading the night to come. She decided to focus on Judy Mays and help her pick out a hairstyle for the wedding. They talked for the next few weeks about what it would be like to be married and have children, but at night, Annabelle always prayed that she wouldn't have a child by Master Brown.

CHAPTER 5
Hidden Intentions

By April of 1844, the wedding planning continued. Annabelle had been moved into the guest room, enduring a month of being occasionally raped. One night during April, Master Brown welcomed himself again into Annabelle's room. He made her light both lamps and take off her white nightgown. During the time he forced himself on her, she held back her tears and didn't resist to avoid being forced down again. As he finished, Annabelle had her hand on Master Brown's sweaty neck to appease him. Her emotionless brown eyes stared at him.

"Am I a woman, a slave, or lover to you?" Annabelle asked.

Master Brown's mouth slightly opened as he stared into her eyes. "You do as you're told, and you will remain in my favor. Don't ever question me, or I will be quick to remind you of your place, and my daughters will have no say in that matter. I may show pity to a child, but not a grown woman."

Annabelle kept her hand on Master Brown's neck while she caressed it, afraid that removing her hand would dissatisfy him. "How can my master call himself a Christian man when he commits adultery by forcing himself on me?"

Master Brown smacked Annabelle's hand off his neck and put his hands on her breasts. "How can I be guilty of adultery when you're nothing but my property and a pet to my daughters?"

"Why do you continue to choose me?"

Master Brown propped himself up with one arm on the bed, looking at Annabelle unsympathetically. "You continue to test me, but I promise you, if you try me like this again, the next scars you receive won't heal over so smoothly. I may have particular tastes, but I will take what I want when I want, and that includes you. I suggest you learn to keep your mouth shut more often."

Master Brown's hand caressed Annabelle's cheek while his hand moved down her neck to massage her shoulder. "Your intelligence is a curse. If you continue this, I may sell those you care for most. They're nothing but expendable niggers that produced one rare nigger with stripes on her back."

Master Brown sat up and put on his white nightshirt. Annabelle slowly pulled the bed covers toward her to cover her body. He ignored Annabelle as he walked out of the room. Annabelle stared at the ceiling, exhausted, then put on her nightgown and blew out the lamps. While she lay in her bed, she crossed her legs and clutched the blankets, then rocked herself to sleep.

Three weeks before the wedding, Judy Mays asked Annabelle, "Have you decided who you like on the plantation? I can tell Papa, and he'll have it ordered for you two to be married."

Annabelle replied, "No, I don't. I've never been in love, so I don't want to marry and be a breeder for the master."

"Wow...I never thought of it like that. You sure are smart. Smarter than the others, that's for sure. I believe you're as smart as a white woman, and that's saying a lot."

"Oh, thank you."

"I'm sure Papa will be buying a few more strong males in a year or two, so don't worry about it. You're very beautiful. I can't wait to get this wedding started. Afterward, I'm going to get to be a woman, if you know what I mean."

They laughed.

"Oh, yes. I do understand completely," Annabelle said. The conversation gravely reminded her of what had been going on the past couple of weeks between her and Master Brown.

Judy Mays sighed while she stared at herself in the mirror. "I need you to stay here. I'll be right back."

"Okay, I'll be right here."

Judy Mays marched through the mansion, peeking into each room she passed before entering her father's study. Mr. Brown sat at his desk, but he put down the newspaper he held and smiled when she came into the room.

"Papa, I need to talk to you," she said.

"What do you need, sweetie?" Mr. Brown asked.

Judy Mays gulped and looked at her father. "I want permission to take Annabelle with me. I want her as my personal slave at my new home with my husband. Can I have her as a gift, please?"

Mr. Brown gave Judy Mays a concerned look as he rubbed his grayish-brown hair. "Why would you ask me this?"

Judy Mays frowned. "She's mine. I begged for her to be taken out of the fields. I took responsibility for her." She stomped her foot. "She belongs with me."

Mr. Brown sighed, rubbing his eyes. "I need her here."

Judy Mays's nose scrunched. "For what?"

"I hate to say this, but she's the best. I never would've guessed she would be so good. We need her here for when the old slaves die. I need Annabelle to teach the younger ones."

Judy Mays balled her fists and asked, "Why can't she come back when the others go into the dirt?"

"Judy Mays!"

"I'm sorry, Papa. I love Ruth and the others, but they are not Annabelle. Please, Papa. I don't care about getting a new carriage or new dresses or new whatever. Please let me take her."

"And what if one of your sisters had asked me this same request?"

Judy Mays scoffed. "Then we would have a problem. I played with Annabelle the most. We are the same age. Everyone else is older."

"Sweetie, that's not a good argument."

"If Annabelle had been given to one of my sisters as a wedding gift, I would've gladly gone over to my sister's with two slaves dragging behind me as gifts if it meant I could have her. She has always been *my* nigger, not theirs."

Mr. Brown stood from his desk and moved around it, giving Judy Mays a sympathetic look.

Judy Mays slowly began to shake her head as her lips started to quiver. "No, Papa."

"Judy Mays, I—"

"Momma can't stand Annabelle. Please, Papa, let me take her! She is the best, but you can get a slave or two to replace her. I know you can afford it, and Momma would be happy. She would stop whining about why we still have her." Tears fell down Judy Mays's face. "Papa, please don't say no to me."

"Sweetie, we will hold Annabelle for three years. After three years, you can have her."

Judy Mays, narrowing her eyes and curving her mouth downward, asked, "Why three years?"

"By three years, I'll have her paired with a strong male and she'll have a child bringing in more value."

"Papa, no. I won't allow it."

Mr. Brown raised his voice. "Who are you to say what's allowed?"

"She gets to choose."

Mr. Brown put his hand on his hip. "Oh, come on, sweetie. This is ridiculous, letting her choose."

"If she chooses someone here and if a child is produced, fine. But the child comes with her, and the male won't get sold, and Annabelle gets to visit him."

Mr. Brown's eyes widened. "I won't give her the option. The child will belong to me!"

Judy Mays gasped, "Papa, how can you say such a thing?"

"Judy Mays, you are testing me. I won't give up the child. Do you realize the child will be a new generation of profit?" He looked away from a tearful Judy Mays. "Fine. She keeps the child, but she doesn't get a choice."

"Papa!"

"No, it's her time to start producing babies. By three years' time, she should have one if not two, and I'm picking the male. Either that or I keep both the child and the male. Are we clear?"

Judy Mays frowned. "Yes, Papa, we're clear. She needs to like him."

Mr. Brown growled. "Judy Mays!"

"I'm not taking no for an answer. She needs to like him at least. She's my nigger, so I say she at least has to like who you pick. It'll produce a child quicker."

Mr. Brown sighed. "Fine, but don't try coming up with something clever to get your way. Annabelle has been given far too much. She's spoiled."

Judy Mays pouted as she looked away from her father.

"Don't give me that look. She is spoiled. We are done here."

She wiped her face. "Yes, Papa. The male...she still gets to visit him."

Mr. Brown gave his daughter a stern look. "Let me guess, you only want her to have children by the one."

"Yes, Papa. If you want him to lay with other slaves, I don't care. I only want Annabelle to experience him and for him not to be sold."

Mr. Brown sat on his desk while he looked at his daughter's demanding face. "Fine."

She smiled. "Oh, thank you, Papa!" She gave him a kiss on the cheek.

She immediately ran toward the door but stopped as Mr. Brown said, "Um, Annabelle...is not allowed to know about this. Matter of fact, no one but you and me. I will keep my promise. You know I will."

She smiled again. "I wasn't going to tell her anyway."

She quickly left the room as he scoffed. "I swear, my daughter is a swindler."

Going upstairs and into her room, Judy Mays smiled at Annabelle before grunting. "I need my hair combed again." She sat down in front of her dresser as Annabelle grabbed a comb and walked behind her. "I don't regret teaching you how to read," Judy Mays said with a grin. "I don't care what the law says about it. I think it's a wonderful thing between you and me." Suddenly, tears came into her eyes, and she said, "It doesn't matter to me that you're a Negro. You have always been a friend, and I'm going to miss you so much." She turned around and gave Annabelle a hug.

A tear traveled down Annabelle's face, "I'm gonna miss you too."

"Well, this wedding will be a celebration like nothing else, and I want you to wear this lovely dress." Judy Mays stood, opened her wardrobe, and pulled out a beautiful dress of light blue and white.

Annabelle said, "I don't know what to say. Will your papa approve?"

"Don't worry about him. If he says something, I'll throw a fit and he'll shut up. Besides, it's my day, and I want you dressed nicely—not like a slave. I also want you to meet Edgar. He is a nice man and is nice to Negroes. At his father's plantation, the slaves seem happier there than here, and maybe I could convince him to buy a nice man for you. You're so pretty, Annabelle. No reason for you not to get married like me."

Annabelle took a deep breath and gave Judy Mays a fake smile. "Thank you. I feel blessed."

The day before the wedding, Edgar arrived at the mansion for lunch. Being tasked with cleaning the upstairs prevented Annabelle from looking at the man Judy Mays spoke so highly of. Annabelle decided to go down the curving front staircase with its red oak banister. Suddenly, she heard Edgar's carriage take off and, gasping, she quickly turned to run back upstairs just as the mansion's front door opened.

"And what do you think you're doing, Annabelle Brown?" Mrs. Regina asked. "Were you downstairs spying on people when you were tasked with strictly being upstairs?"

"I was cleaning the banister, Mrs. Regina. I know how you like the wood to shine."

Mrs. Regina approached Annabelle, a malicious gleam in her eyes. "Do you take me for a fool?" she asked. Her blue eyes fixed onto Annabelle's anxious expression.

Annabelle felt the tension building as Mrs. Regina analyzed her.

"Your intelligence sickens me, even more so because of the fact that it may be more than my daughters' doing. You're different, but I will always take great pleasure in making sure you know your place. Are we clear, favored nigger?"

"Yes, ma'am, I understand."

"I know you do, sweetheart, but those eyes still tell the story of rebellion. I would gladly send you out to the barn to gain more stripes on your back right now, but Judy Mays would plead for you. When she leaves with my new son-in-law, I suggest you work to gain my favor and use that mind to keep me happy. Or I promise to make sure you will be the most decorated house slave on your back of any nigger in Mississippi. No child has ever looked at me like you. That will never occur again though, will it?"

Annabelle gulped as she looked at Regina. "It will never happen again, and I will do as you ask of me."

"I thought so. Finish up your duties. I know my daughter will continue to slow you down."

Later that day, Annabelle worked in the kitchen to prepare supper while Judy Mays's older sisters, Genevieve, Sue Ellen, and Scarlett, arrived to celebrate the last unmarried night of their younger sister's life. The daughters of Master Brown dominated much of the conversation at the table, and obvious favor was shown toward Annabelle.

The kindness Mrs. Regina's daughters showed Annabelle disgusted Regina. Regina felt she had been naïve and mistaken to believe that her daughters would view Annabelle as expendable as they got older. Regina now understood that her daughters viewed Annabelle more as an extended family member, a thought that angered Regina so much, she lost her appetite.

"Annabelle, bring me more turkey. I had forgotten what it was like having all my children here at the same time," Master Brown said.

Annabelle took the platter of meat over and stood next to Master Brown, placing the meat on his plate.

"Now, don't only give me the white meat—you know I like a little bit of dark meat too." Master Brown suddenly groped Annabelle's butt, an action that went unnoticed by Regina and the others, sending chills down Annabelle's spine. Master Brown chuckled as Annabelle gave him a few more slices of meat.

"Papa, make sure you don't eat too much. We don't want you falling asleep on the porch again," Sue Ellen said.

Master Brown laughed and replied, "Don't worry about me now. Your old man still has a younger side to him."

Annabelle's joy for Judy Mays was ruined by Master Brown's assault. She struggled to put on a smile for the other young women, but she later went to bed, exhausted and worried that she would be visited by Master Brown. However, he had indeed fallen asleep in his chair, so a pregnant Scarlett escorted her father to his bedroom, allowing Annabelle to rest peacefully and develop some excitement for Judy Mays's wedding.

On May 25, 1844, the wedding day arrived, and many guests appeared at the mansion. White tablecloths were put on the tables, and Annabelle noticed most of the other slaves were already awake earlier than usual. She rushed to put on her clothes, assuming she'd be reprimanded by Judy Mays's mother. Worried, she walked out of her room.

"Annabelle? Annabelle, why are you here?" Mrs. Regina said.

Annabelle turned around in the hallway to see Mrs. Regina standing behind her in a ruffled, dark green high-neck dress.

"I was getting ready to work, Mrs. Regina. I'm sorry I woke up late. It will never happen again," Annabelle said.

"Judy Mays must've been so excited she forgot to tell you. She wants you to be rested so you don't have to be up with the rest of the slaves."

Annabelle was stunned by Judy Mays's request. "Oh, my apologies, ma'am."

"That's not a big deal. You've always been a favored nigger, even after your one little outburst years ago. You know it has always surprised me how protective Judy Mays is of you. She treats you more like a friend than a slave. I guess it's normal. You're the same age as her. I expect to see you in an hour wearing the dress Judy Mays gave you."

"Yes, ma'am." Annabelle went back into her room, still trying to process what Judy Mays had done for her. She put on the light blue and white dress, which fitted her well, and began to pose in the mirror to enjoy the moment. She left her room only to be ambushed by Judy Mays.

"Annabelle!" Judy Mays shouted before running excitedly down the stairs. Her hair was in a ringlet style. "Today is the day. Isn't this so exciting? Now, what I want you to do is to just put the icing on my wedding cake. It's already done otherwise, and the rest of the day, I want you to be around the children. No need for you to do any real work today. It is my special day, and I don't want the dress to become dirty."

Annabelle smiled. "Thank you."

"Well, now, you go do that and then come help me put the dress on. Oh my God! I feel so happy! I can't wait until you can have a real conversation with him. My momma is an annoyance, sending you away any time he came over." Judy Mays ran back upstairs, screaming with excitement.

Annabelle felt happy for her and entered the kitchen building to put icing on the cake. When she had finished, she headed back to Judy Mays's room.

Mrs. Regina met Annabelle at the top of the stairs. "Hurry up. She refuses to put the dress on without your help," Mrs.

Regina said. With her hands on her hips, Mrs. Regina stormed off to Judy Mays's room, murmuring, "I can't believe we're waiting for a Negro girl. What is the matter with my daughter?"

Annabelle entered the room.

"There you are," Judy Mays said with a big smile.

Annabelle helped Judy Mays put on the white dress with its embroidered flower patterns and low-cut shoulders.

"You look so pretty, Judy Mays," Annabelle said.

Judy Mays gave her a hug. "Thank you. I do believe I may rival Queen Victoria."

"Get back, Annabelle," Mrs. Regina said.

"Yes, ma'am," Annabelle said.

"Now, Judy Mays, I must say you're the most beautiful bride I have ever seen. You make me proud, and I'm sure you will be the perfect wife for Edgar."

Judy Mays replied, "Thank you, Momma. Momma, do you mind stepping out? I'd like to just be with Annabelle for a minute."

"Sure, dear," Mrs. Regina said. As Regina began to walk out of the room, she glanced over at Annabelle. "Annabelle, I expect you to help in the kitchen during the wedding."

Annabelle replied, "Yes, ma'am, I will."

"Momma, she won't be doing that," Judy Mays said. "I told her to watch the children and sit down and enjoy my wedding."

"You told her what!" Mrs. Regina said.

"There are plenty of other slaves in the kitchen. I want Annabelle to see me get married, and I won't have it any other way."

Mrs. Regina grunted while she stormed off. "Judy Mays, you're truly more difficult than your sisters."

Judy Mays put on her yellow gold dangle earrings and giggled. "I think she's jealous of you, Annabelle."

"Don't say that," Annabelle replied. "I like to stay on your momma's good side."

"Don't worry about it." Judy Mays sat down in her white rocking chair with a puzzled look on her face. "Annabelle," she said, her voice soft, "does it bother you when I call you a nigger? I mean, does it hurt you or make you feel bad?"

Annabelle frowned, looking at Judy Mays, and she began to stutter.

Judy Mays continued, "Annabelle, tell me the truth."

Annabelle bowed her head, replying, "Yes, ma'am."

"Don't you ever say 'yes, ma'am' to me when it's just you." Tears filled Judy Mays's eyes. "Don't you ever call me that in private. You're no nigger to me. You're my friend, my best friend, even more than the girls in my wedding. Only my sisters come before you, so don't forget it. I don't care what Momma says. I can't treat you like property."

"Thank you so much."

As Annabelle began to sob, Judy Mays held her hands. "I guess with everything going on, all the questions I ever wanted to ask are coming out. I think a piece of me didn't want to believe I was still causing you pain after all these years."

"I'm afraid of what's going to happen to me when you go."

Judy Mays grinned and said, "Nothing will happen to you, I promise. Well, I have a wedding to get started, and you get to have a day dealing with children. Your favorite task."

Judy Mays, wearing a flowery veil with her white dress, walked downstairs with Annabelle following. Later, Annabelle watched the ceremony, smiling and imagining that maybe one day, she'd do more than jump a broom like the other slaves. A dress like Judy Mays's would be good enough for her.

After the ceremony, Annabelle was watching the children play. She noticed Judy Mays approaching her with Edgar holding her arm, and the joy on Judy Mays's face made Annabelle smile. Edgar was a tall and handsome man with blond hair and brown eyes.

Edgar wore a tightly tailored, navy-colored frock coat with a high-collared white shirt, a fancy blue vest, blue trousers, and a black cravat.

"Annabelle, I would now like to introduce Edgar Reynolds, my husband," Judy Mays cheerfully said.

"It is a pleasure to meet you, sir," Annabelle said.

Edgar replied, "I see you share Judy Mays's humor. She acts like we've never seen each other before. Judy Mays always speaks highly of you. It's obvious you have learned much from her."

"Thank you, sir. It's easy to see you make her happy."

Edgar smiled at Annabelle.

"Well, we must give time to the family and other guests. Annabelle, I'll be back to check on you later," Judy Mays said.

Annabelle nodded as the newlywed couple walked inside the mansion holding hands.

Suddenly, Genevieve's daughter, Lynne, her large brown eyes wide, came up to Annabelle. "My Auntie Judy said that you're a sweet Negro woman," Lynne said. "How did you learn how to have feelings? My papa said that Negroes don't have feelings like we do, but my auntie said you do."

Annabelle replied, "Lynne, your auntie is smart, and the secret is she is right. We do have feelings like you."

Lynne grinned. "When you get married, can you have a wedding like Auntie Judy?"

"I don't know, Miss Lynne. Who knows what the good Lord has for me."

"Well, I'm gonna go play now." The young brunette tossed her ringlets, then walked over to give Annabelle a hug—an action encouraged earlier by Genevieve.

"Annabelle, bring the children in for supper," Mrs. Regina said.

Annabelle took the children in for supper and sat in the cookhouse to eat her supper with the other house slaves.

Ruth looked over at Annabelle, smiling. "My word, Annabelle, you sure look mighty pretty in that dress," Ruth said.

Annabelle replied, "Why, thank you, Ruth. Miss Judy Mays insisted that I wear it."

"Now, be careful with it. You don't want to attract wrong men. They may treat us like animals, but when it come to wanting us at night, it different. I was fortunate. I didn't become a house slave until I was older, so I figure that how God spared me from being touched."

A light brown-skinned woman named Ada said, "Them young white men. They eyes always wandering. I ain't been touched yet, but I know the look when they think it."

"I wish I was lucky when I was younger," Alice, an older slave with silver hair, said. "I had a child by my old master. It was hard to accept. Life got much worse when Mrs. Jones caught me and my old master. That's how I ended up here when I was young, and they kept my son. Not a day goes by I don't wonder how he looks now. He came out very light-skinned. I think that was that Choctaw blood from my father why he came out so light. He only five when they sold me to this place. Now, he got to be about thirty years old. I pray to the Lord that he is kept safe and hope he not forgot he Choctaw too. I would always tell him when he was child, but they beat it out of us. It hard, Annabelle. Never let that happen to you. Do what you need to do to keep your family together."

Annabelle thought, *I never thought wearing this dress would cause Alice to talk about her son. I want to tell them what Master Brown is doing to me, but what can they do? She hasn't seen her son in years. I wish I knew looking nice would get Master Brown's attention. I would've covered myself in mud every day if I knew.*

As the ladies were eating, one of Judy Mays's guests—a skinny man—entered the kitchen drunk. He brushed back his brown hair and rubbed his sharp mustache. "There you niggers are. Oh, and Judy Mays's little pet," the man stuttered. "You three niggers, bring in the desserts."

"Yes, sir," the women said.

As the ladies carried the desserts down the covered walkway to the dining room, Annabelle began to follow them out of the kitchen. The man put his hand on the wall, blocking her. "I didn't say that you could leave, did I?"

Annabelle smelled the alcohol on his breath. "Why, no, sir,

I was going to the dining room to help the others," Annabelle said.

"I don't see a need for that. I see why Judy Mays has so much favor for you. I also heard that you'd been whipped for being rebellious at one time, and somehow those scars smoothed out like stripes. I'd like to see that."

"I don't think Miss Judy Mays would appreciate you talking to her slave like that, sir."

The man slapped Annabelle. "Don't you ever speak to me like that, nigger." The man stumbled while he took a step toward her.

"I'm sorry, sir, but I won't show you my scars." Annabelle backed into a wall.

"You're something, aren't you," he said with an annoyed tone, grabbing her arm.

"Let go of me!" she cried.

The man suddenly grabbed her right breast. "Don't you ever tell me no. I don't care how they treat you!" The man pushed Annabelle against a counter as she fought back. "Don't ever try to fight me," the man said in a belligerent tone. He pushed her against a wall again while his body swayed. "Now, you're gonna show me what's beneath that pretty dress."

Annabelle screamed, "Stop! Don't you ever touch me. Judy Mays!"

Judy Mays's eyes widened, and she stopped speaking with a guest on the lawn near the cookhouse. She excused herself as she rushed toward the cookhouse. Judy Mays aggressively pushed the kitchen door in, making a loud bang. She marched into the kitchen.

"What's going on in here?" she yelled. "Oh my God! Get off of her, you animal!"

Edgar rushed in the kitchen right behind Judy Mays. "Carl, what are you doing?" Edgar asked.

Judy Mays smacked Carl and pulled Annabelle away from him. Annabelle, crying and trembling, held onto Judy Mays.

"You animal, get out of my home!" Judy Mays yelled.

Carl replied, "Judy Mays, that nigger seduced me with her words and the way she walked. You need to teach that nigger how to act properly around a gentleman."

"How dare you! Get out of my home, and don't you ever come near this property again, or I will have you shot!"

Carl scoffed, "You're overreacting. She's just a nigger."

Judy Mays left the kitchen with Annabelle, who was still crying.

Carl turned to Edgar. "Edgar, that nigger seduced me. She thinks because she walks around in that dress, she's special like a white woman."

Edgar replied, "You have a problem. Judy Mays really values that slave."

Carl arrogantly replied, "There are plenty more where that came from. It may take a while, but she could find a replacement."

Judy Mays heard their argument, on her way out with Annabelle down the covered walkway, and became more enraged.

As the men continued to argue, Judy Mays, in her wedding dress, quickly escorted Annabelle into her room and angrily marched back downstairs and past guests who tried to greet her. She went into her father's study and grabbed a rifle off of a rack. She quickly loaded the rifle, and with her cheeks turning red, she marched toward the cookhouse. As she approached the kitchen, she could still hear the men arguing. She entered the kitchen with the rifle.

"Replace this, Carl," Judy Mays said.

Edgar leaned against the kitchen wall. "Judy Mays!" he screamed.

The gun went off while Judy Mays aimed it, grazing Carl on the shoulder, and Carl began to run down the covered walkway.

"She's crazy!" Carl yelled.

Judy Mays replied, "I told you to get off of my property, you bastard." She took another shot, just missing Carl as he ran into the mansion. Judy Mays ran after Carl as he bumped into several guests trying to escape through the main door.

"Judy Mays, wait!" Edgar yelled.

The moment Carl was getting in his carriage, Judy Mays pushed the main door open and took another shot, hitting him right in his buttocks.

Carl screamed in agony. "Please stop, Judy Mays!" Carl howled.

"Get off of my property!"

Guests watched in awe. Mr. and Mrs. Brown ran to the main door shouting, "Judy Mays!"

"What in God's name are you doing?" Mrs. Regina shouted.

"He tried to have his way with Annabelle in the kitchen, and he tried to lie about it," Judy Mays replied.

"Well, that's no reason to shoot him!" Mrs. Regina yelled.

"I don't care, Momma. He said I could replace her when I felt like it. So, I wonder if his momma can replace him. She's still in her thirties, so I'm guessing it's possible. You have till I count to five, Carl. One, two, three…"

Carl yelled at his driver, "Go, nigger! Get me back to the plantation before she shoots again!"

Carl's carriage took off toward his plantation, and Judy Mays smirked with great satisfaction. Her parents, shocked by her actions, were speechless, and Edgar's eyes remained widened as he watched.

As Judy Mays walked away to put the rifle up, Mr. Brown approached Edgar. "I hope you have the intention to always remain faithful to my daughter," Mr. Brown said.

Edgar looked at Mr. Brown with a shocked face and said, "Why, yes, sir. Of course I will."

"Good. That means we won't have to be planning a funeral anytime soon because it wouldn't be me to kill you, son."

Judy Mays entered Mr. Brown's study pouting, and she put up the rifle. Judy Mays turned around, and a pregnant Scarlett was standing in the doorway. The sisters stood eye to eye.

"What has gotten into you?" Scarlett growled. "The only excitement I should be experiencing any time soon is getting my body back."

"I—"

Scarlett grunted. "Wait before you say anything. Nod only if you didn't overreact." Judy Mays nodded as Scarlett twisted her mouth. "So it's half and half you didn't. What happened?"

"Carl tried to rape Annabelle."

Scarlett's jaw dropped. "He wouldn't."

"I saw it myself." Judy Mays frowned but held back her tears. "Annabelle was in tears, shaking like a small child. Did I overreact?"

Scarlett huffed, replying, "Between us, no. As far as Papa is concerned, I scolded you. Now this child won't stop kicking. You do know how to make life exciting." The sisters grinned at each other, then hugged, and Judy Mays felt the baby kick before leaving the room.

Judy Mays marched upstairs to her room, where she'd left Annabelle. Edgar followed her. Judy Mays walked into her room and gave her a hug.

"It is okay. He won't be back ever," Judy Mays said.

"Thank you," Annabelle said, her voice sounding troubled.

Edgar said, "Annabelle, I must apologize for Carl's actions. He was my guest at this wedding, and his actions were inexcusable whether you're Negro or white."

Annabelle replied, "Thank you, Master Edgar."

Regina rushed upstairs and entered the room. "Is Annabelle alright?" Mrs. Regina asked.

Annabelle looked at Mrs. Regina in disbelief as she heard the older woman ask about her wellbeing.

Judy Mays replied, "Yes, Momma. She's in shock, that's all."

"Well, that's good to hear. Judy Mays, there are other guests here, and besides the fact that you started shooting at someone in broad daylight, they still want to see you."

"Alright, Momma, I'll be down in a little while. Go on, Edgar, I'm coming."

Edgar left the room.

"Annabelle, I'm quite sorry about what occurred. Not even a nigger should experience what almost happened," Mrs. Regina said. "As a woman, I understand your pain. I'll leave it to Judy Mays to decide what you're to do for the rest of the day." Regina left the room, for the first time feeling guilty about something that had happened to a slave.

"I have to go downstairs to entertain the rest of the guests. I did just almost kill a man today," Judy Mays said.

Annabelle gave Judy Mays a hug. "Thank you. You really are my friend when it matters."

A tear glided down Judy Mays's face. "You stay here and rest. How about I send up little Lynne to keep you company? She always talks about you."

"That'll be fine."

"Alright, I'll send her up."

Judy Mays left and called for Lynne to go spend time with Annabelle.

Lynne went up to the room cheerfully. "Annabelle, are you okay?" Lynne asked. "You look like you have been crying a lot."

Annabelle replied, "Oh, no, little Lynne. I'm fine. It was something in my eye."

"Okay, let's play with my dollies. My papa got them for me last week."

Annabelle played with Lynne and thought, *It's so sad that they're taught to hate. So few of them think on their own or question what is right and what is wrong. I would hate to see Lynne grow up to be like most of these white people. Call us niggers, call us dumb, call us animals, and put chains on us like it is normal.* "Miss Lynne, I would like to ask you something."

"Yes," Lynne said with a big smile.

"Can you read already?"

Lynne beamed. "Oh, yes. I can read some words good because Auntie Judy was showing me."

"Can you read something to me?" Annabelle picked up Judy

Mays's Bible from one of the bookshelves. "Can you read a script from this Bible for me?"

Lynne began jumping up and down. "Yes, I can."

Annabelle opened the Bible. "Okay, can you read this here for me? I wish I knew what it said."

"Okay!" Lynne excitedly said, holding the Bible. "Okay, right here it says in Acts 17:26, 'And hath made of one blood all nations of men for to dwell on all the face of the earth, and hath determined the times before appointed, and the bounds of their habitation.'"

Lynne sat down with a confused look. "Do you understand it? It says of one blood all nations of men. I don't understand how it can say one blood all nations."

Annabelle sat down next to Lynne and touched her shoulder. "Miss Lynne, it took me a long time to figure out what that meant even when your Auntie read it to me. It means that all us people, God made us the same no matter what color we be."

"So we really do all have the same blood."

"Well, in a way, yes. We all come from Adam and Eve, so we all people."

"Then why are Negroes not as smart as us white people?"

"I don't know. I guess some time long ago, something bad happened, and that's why things are the way they are now."

Lynne frowned, then said, "I wish things were different because I saw my daddy whip a nigger one time. It looked like it hurt really bad, and I saw blood on his back. It scared me a lot, and I felt sad for him."

Annabelle gave Lynne a hug. "Now, Miss Lynne, I want you to make one promise for me. Never turn into a white woman like your grandma. Become someone more like your Auntie Judy. She is smart for a woman and kind, so you should try your hardest to stay that way."

Lynne grinned. "I will." She gave Annabelle a hug and ran downstairs to play with the other kids.

Annabelle looked out Judy Mays's window. *Oh, God, please save that child from the evil of this world,* Annabelle thought.

She noticed a robin and a sparrow in the same tree, and she thought, *If we were more like you two birds, I bet this world would be better.* She sat down in Judy Mays's bed, still trying to calm down from being attacked by Carl. *Thank you, God, for sending Judy Mays into that kitchen. You spared me from feeling more hurt.*

As the remaining guests dispersed around the mansion, Judy Mays approached Mr. Brown. "Papa, can I can take Annabelle with me?" she asked.

"Judy Mays, we have an agreement," Mr. Brown bickered.

"Papa, after what happened, can she come with me for only two or three days? You won't notice her absence."

"Annabelle stays."

"What about Annabelle?" Mrs. Regina asked, walking out of the dining room.

Judy Mays replied, "I only—"

"Judy Mays," Mr. Brown firmly said. "She stays here. We've had our talk unless you want me to change my mind."

Judy Mays bit her lower lip and exhaled. "No, Papa..." Raising her voice, she called, "Annabelle, come downstairs."

Mrs. Regina slightly frowned while she looked at Judy Mays's frustrated expression.

Annabelle came downstairs and saw Judy Mays's oak chest being carried out to a carriage by one of the slaves while Edgar came into the mansion. Annabelle saw Mr. Brown leave the mansion with Mrs. Regina following him.

Judy Mays turned to Annabelle. "There you are. I'm so sorry about what happened earlier today, but I can assure you that man won't be coming back. It's time for me to go. It's been a great time, and I promise to come back and visit when I can." Judy Mays wiped a tear from her eye. "After all, my parents do live here."

Annabelle grinned. "Yes, it has been a great time, and thank you, Judy Mays. You done more for me than anybody," she said.

Edgar approached Annabelle. "Annabelle, it has been a

pleasure. You're everything Judy Mays has said about you," he said.

Annabelle replied, "Thank you, Master Edgar. I'm sure you will treat her well."

Edgar smiled, wrapping his arm around Judy Mays's waist. "I'm looking forward to seeing you again, as I'm sure Judy Mays will be as well. Whenever you're ready, love." Edgar smiled once more and then went out to the carriage.

Judy Mays replied, "I'm coming, Edgar, honey." She nervously stared at Annabelle. "Well, Annabelle, dear, this is a new beginning for me, and I'm so happy. I'm going to miss seeing you every day and trying on dresses with you and reading with you." Judy Mays gave Annabelle a hug. "You're quite something special."

Annabelle said, "So are you." The women held hands one last time, and Judy Mays left the house for the carriage.

Annabelle took a deep breath, realizing that things might change for the worse now that Judy Mays was gone. She looked up into the sky, whispering, "God, please give me a way to get free from this place."

Later in the evening, Annabelle went upstairs to clean another staircase, and she could hear Master Brown and Mrs. Regina arguing. Annabelle was shocked to hear Mrs. Regina demanding a reason for Annabelle not being sent away with Judy Mays. Annabelle's heart raced while she eavesdropped on the conversation, but she missed hearing Master Brown's reason. Annabelle could only hear Mrs. Regina's angry disagreement with his decision to hold Annabelle. She leaned against the hallway wall and held back tears, realizing he was determined to keep her.

CHAPTER 6
Broken Chains

SIX WEEKS HAD GONE BY since Judy Mays had moved out, and things became worse for Annabelle. Instead of once or twice a week, Mr. Brown began raping Annabelle whenever he got her alone. This often happened when Regina left the property for a part of the day. Annabelle found herself praying twice or more a day not to become pregnant.

One day in July of 1844, Regina went to Annabelle, who was cleaning the patio. "I think my husband is having an affair with one of the women from town because lately, he's always leaving and saying he'll be right back," Mrs. Regina said. "I assumed he was walking around the porch, but when I would go there, he wasn't there. So, I thought maybe he was taking the horse for a short ride. When he comes back, it's always a little more than an hour later. Half the time, he shows no interest in me. Last week, I noticed a scratch on his back, and it didn't come from me. I can't help but feel that he's been with another woman. Annabelle, have you seen him leaving the plantation at night at all?"

Annabelle replied, "No, Mrs. Regina, he's never left the plantation at night. He goes out to the porch is what I've seen."

"Is that all? Weird. Anytime I've gone to the porch, he's not there. Well, I guess I must've been overthinking. You know us women."

Annabelle turned to Mrs. Regina. "Do you think Master Brown would bed a Negro woman?"

Regina abruptly smacked Annabelle. "How dare you, Annabelle! I could have you whipped like you were years ago for even talking like that! He would never touch a nigger. Never! He knows white women are the best, and if he was to bed another woman, it would be a white woman and not a nigger, so don't ever bring up such a crazy idea!"

"Yes, ma'am."

"Now, Master Brown has told me that he won't be back until tonight and to tell you that you are not to go to sleep until he gets home no matter how late it is. He wants his shoes cleaned when he returns."

"Yes, ma'am. I'll wait up for him just as you will."

Regina scrunched her face. "What did you mean by that, Annabelle?"

"Nothing, Mrs. Regina, just that I know you will be awake too, waiting for him to return."

"Actually, he has told me to go to bed, and he'll wake me in the morning. I expect supper at five today."

"Yes, Mrs. Regina, I'll have your favorite made today." *You deserve it, you fool,* Annabelle thought.

Annabelle later snuck behind the mansion to read the Bible Judy Mays had secretly given her. She began reading and came across a passage that touched her heart. Annabelle felt a change in her soul and spirit as she read in Psalm 136. "O give thanks unto the God of gods: for his mercy endureth for ever. O give thanks to the Lord of lords: for his mercy endureth for ever. To him who alone doeth great wonders: for his mercy endureth for ever. To him that by wisdom made the heavens: for his mercy endureth for ever. To him that stretched out the earth above the waters: for his mercy endureth for ever."

Annabelle believed that God's love endures for all. Not only white people, but for all people. It brought peace to her, something she hadn't felt in months. Tears spilled down her face, and she began to sing: "God, I've been through so much trouble, but I've done nothing to deserve it. Some days, I cry myself to sleep and pray for freedom. I feel my people's pain, and I see the hate of man. God, your love endures forever. You fill my soul with love, and you've shown me what others have tried to hide. It says that you're the Lord of Lords, so I ask you to please rescue me from this evil place. Lord, do you hear the chains they put on me? Please make me free as the birds, and bless me with a day I can smile into the sun. Your love warms my soul, so please give me a sign that I'll be free. Your love endures forever."

Six months of agony for Annabelle brought her to January of 1845. She had become the hidden trophy of Master Brown. She went out to her parents' shack to talk to her mother.

"Hi, Momma," Annabelle said.

"Annabelle, I so happy to see you. I worried. I haven't seen you in a week," Claire said.

"Yes, Master has kept me busy all day long, and at night, he makes sure I have a lot of chores that keep me in the house. I tried to tell Mrs. Regina about what has been going on because she feels he is lying with another woman. I tried to tell her it was me, but the thought of him bedding a Negro woman... She laughs at it. I see why he don't want her no more. She flat in the back, and she starting to get wrinkles."

"Don't say such things like that," Claire said as she tried to hold back her laughter. "Well, I pray to the good Lord every day you being kept safe from master's temper. Well, it be best if you get back to the house. I love you so much."

"I love you too, Momma."

Just as Annabelle was about to leave, Morgan—a middle-aged slave in a white cloth shirt and beige trousers—ran inside the shack.

"Oh, my Lord, Claire!" Morgan said.

"What is it?" Claire asked.

"Charles has run off again, trying to head up north, and they caught him."

They ran out of the house and saw the overseer, Master Douglas, pulling Charles by the hands. Then they saw the bruises on Charles's body.

Master Douglas took Charles to one of the barns and whipped him for over an hour until he passed out from the pain. As Annabelle heard Charles's screams, she realized that there was only Master Coleman, Master Ridge, and Master Jones watching the slaves. She realized this was her chance to finally run away and escape to the north because their entire focus was on the field slaves. In her experience, only the field slaves had tried to escape the plantation, making her believe her attempt to escape would be surprising. With Judy Mays and her sisters now gone and married, only Mrs. Regina was constantly in the house, and Master Brown was constantly in and out of the mansion.

"Momma," Annabelle said.

"Yes, Annabelle, what the matter?" Claire asked.

"This is our chance to run for the north and get away from here and Master Brown."

"Have you lost the little bit of sense you have? They'll send the dogs after you, especially with Master Brown liking you." Claire looked away with tears in her eyes.

Annabelle began to breathe anxiously, then said, "Momma, don't you see? The next time Charles or anyone tries to run, that'll be my chance to get away, and I want you, Papa, and Todd to come with me."

Claire looked at Annabelle, placing her hand over her heart. "No. We can't do it, baby. If we go together, we be caught, and we be sold by Master Brown. I fear he'll become more evil with you if that happens. You will have to go on your own and be quick about it when another slave gets loose."

Tears fell down Annabelle's face. "Momma, I really want y'all to come with me. Don't stay here. What if they sell y'all to punish me?"

"Girl, we'll be fine. Lord willing, we be fine. Now, get back to the house. You have to cook Mrs. Regina's dinner and stop spitting in that woman's food. If you get caught, I think she'd have you whipped like Charles. Ain't no mercy for a nigger, especially if you laying with the master...more than his own wife."

"I'll try to stop, Momma."

"Girl, not funny."

Annabelle walked out with a smirk on her face.

"Annabelle Brown, you better listen to me."

"I'll try, Momma. I guess today, I won't do it unless she calls me a nigger before I finish cooking her food."

As she went into the mansion, Regina was coming down the stairs.

"Annabelle, are you about to start cooking?" Mrs. Regina asked.

"Yes, ma'am, I'm about to start right now."

"Well, hurry up. I swear we treat you better than a nigger, and you take advantage of it."

"No, ma'am, I would never do such a thing. I'm a nigger. I have no thoughts."

"Well, that's true. Go now and get started. You said you were making chicken fried steak, mashed potatoes and gravy, with pecan pie...my favorite again."

As Regina turned to go back up the stairs, Annabelle murmured, "I'll make it real special this time."

Annabelle continued with her miserable tasks as time passed by, and she missed seeing Judy Mays every day. Judy Mays's visits were normally short and only two or three times a week.

Six months later, Charles escaped again and was gone for three days. Master Jones came back on the fourth day dragging Charles by a horse, but this time, they tied ropes on his arms and hanged him from one of the trees. Master Brown was greatly agitated, so he called all the slaves to the tree to watch him be beaten. Claire noticed all the overseers were at the tree, and she realized this was Annabelle's chance.

Claire slipped away into the mansion and pulled Annabelle into the kitchen.

"Annabelle, baby, it time for you to run and don't look back," Claire said.

"But Momma, I need to say bye to Papa and Todd," Annabelle said.

"No, baby. Now the time. We love you and hope you make it."

Tears flowed down Annabelle's cheeks. "It's not supposed to happen like this." She sobbed.

"I know, but I be damned before you be bedded by that man again or bear a child from him. It's been over a year."

Claire cried while Annabelle reached into a cupboard, pulled out a small sack, and started filling it with food.

"Now get out of here! Miss Judy Mays taught you directions. Now use them."

Annabelle frowned. "I love you, Momma."

"I love you too, Annabelle."

The second Annabelle started to run out of the cookhouse, Charles screamed like nothing she'd heard before. She turned around and saw the overseers had set Charles on fire.

Claire said, "Don't look back, baby."

Annabelle ran and didn't stop for some time. Tired from running, she ripped the bottom of her blue dress because it kept causing her to trip.

When the night came, it rained, and Annabelle heard so many different sounds she had never heard before. She began to pray, "Oh, Lord, please protect me and allow me to reach somewhere I won't be a slave but free and happy."

Early in the morning, Annabelle heard a carriage going past the small cave where she hid. She looked out and saw Master Brown with another white man. She leaned against the deepest part of the cave, holding her mouth to keep quiet. Annabelle felt tears traveling down her cheeks as the carriage stopped.

How did he find me with no dogs? she thought.

"It sure is hot today," Master Brown said.

"So you want this slave back in good condition, Mr. Brown?" the other white man replied.

"Yes, I want her back in excellent condition. She's of great value and an excellent cook, among other things. She's young, only seventeen, and I know she knows nothing of this land. Also, when you find her, keep in mind she'll fight you. She's not like the other niggers that'll run. I feel time is wasting away, so be quick about it and use the dogs if you have to, but I don't want her damaged. My daughter would never forgive me."

"Yes, sir, Mr. Brown. It will be taken care of immediately. By the way, why do you think this slave ran when she had the best living a slave could have?"

Master Brown replied, "One of my niggers, Charles, ran away again and almost got away. So instead of whipping him, we hanged him from a tree by his hands and burned him in front of the other slaves. He might recover, but he won't be able to run ever again. I believe she saw this, and it scared her, so she ran."

"I see. Well, we will get her back to you, and the dogs will be released as soon as we get back. It will only take us an hour to get back."

As they pulled off, Annabelle hurried to find a place the dogs couldn't get her. She ran in the swamp for a few hours but stopped when she heard another carriage approaching. The carriage came by with two women in it. While they passed, a chest on the carriage fell off, causing some of the dresses in it to fall out. The women stopped the carriage, and one woman with blonde hair got out and put the chest back on the carriage. "Now I have to buy new dresses. These are completely ruined," said the blonde woman.

"Well, forget it. We are on our way to Missouri. Just get in the carriage so we can get there," the other woman said.

As the carriage slowly began to move again, Annabelle thought, *The chest is almost empty. I can hide in it.* Annabelle ran after the carriage, hopped on, and quietly slipped into the chest. When night fell, she was able to slip out to clean herself and eat the little food she had taken with her when she ran.

Days went by, and Annabelle continued the cycle. She took some of the women's food when they weren't looking. One day, the women went past a man on a horse. "Sir, is this Missouri now?" one woman asked as she stopped the carriage.

"Yes, ladies, it is, but the two of you be careful. There are Injuns out here," the man said. "Don't y'all have a man with y'all?"

"Well, my cousin went ahead of us. He'll be back soon. I'm just slowly guiding us behind him," the woman said. "So as of right now, no, sir, we don't. We don't need a man with us."

"It's not right for women to be out here alone. I can accompany you ladies to the nearest town."

"There is no need. My cousin will be here soon, and we've made it on our own this far."

"Well, as a man, I have to say I'm uncomfortable with you ladies being alone, and your families would agree with me."

"Too bad our families aren't here to discuss this important topic. Thank you for your kindness. Like I said before, my cousin—who is a great man—will be here momentarily."

"He really is on his way back. He's only been away from us for a few minutes. Thank you, kind sir," the blonde woman said.

The man replied, "No problem, ladies."

The ladies waited for the man to ride far enough away that they couldn't see him, and rode away. A short time later, they came across a small pond, where they decided to take a break and sit under a tree to escape the heat.

"My goodness! It's as hot out here as it is in Mississippi."

"Yes, it is," said the other woman with a mature southern voice. "And it's humid, not just hot."

Out of curiosity, Annabelle lifted the chest lid a little and saw the two women sitting under a tree. The blonde woman had a skinny build compared to the other woman, and both were wearing turquoise pearl dangle earrings.

I bet it is cooler over there than it is in here, Annabelle thought.

The moment she closed the lid, one of the women noticed something move. She stood up and looked, trying to figure out if she was seeing things or if the lid of the chest had actually moved.

"What is it, Ruthanne?" the blonde woman asked.

Ruthanne looked back with a grin. "It was nothing, Elizabeth. I thought I saw a rabbit or something."

Elizabeth smiled. "That's nothing. We have enough of them back in Mississippi." She walked over to the pond to put water on her face. "I don't know how you convinced me to join you."

Ruthanne smirked. "You love me."

Elizabeth looked at Ruthanne, showing her lack of enjoyment. "I still don't understand. Why leave home?"

"I want to see more of the country. I won't sit around for a man to make me a wife."

"What's wrong with that?"

Ruthanne twisted her mouth. "I want to gain more education. Babies can come later, and I won't jump when a man says jump or bark when he says bark. If my daddy couldn't contain me, my husband won't either."

"You are so stubborn. Motherhood is a blessing."

"Of course, it is...not for me. Not right now, and you know I love children."

Annabelle continued to listen to the young women.

Elizabeth grunted, replying, "I feel like you tricked me."

"Possible...but I know you're curious about Missouri. We've got the money. We also ditched my sweet cousin, Harold, but you didn't complain."

Elizabeth stuck out her lips.

"Pout all you want. You know we wouldn't have gotten away without having a man with us some part of the way."

Elizabeth rolled her eyes. "You ready to go?"

"Sure, I'm ready to go. Let's go see one of the new towns. Hopefully, we don't run into any Indians."

"Yes, I'd rather not be seen by those savages. They scare me. I mean, what kind of a person wears feathers in their hair?"

"You know not all of them do that. Let's get going."

The ladies traveled down a trail made by previous carriages and went over a rock, causing the chest to bounce and Annabelle to hit her head on the chest.

Before she could cover her mouth, Annabelle said, "Ouch!"

Ruthanne stopped the carriage.

"What is it, Ruthanne?"

"You know, I never did get to show you my revolver, did I?"

"Oh, no. You keep bragging about what your daddy got you."

"I guess now is a good chance to show it off." Ruthanne casually pulled the revolver out of a small bag, then got out of the carriage, went to the chest with the revolver cocked, and shouted, "Whoever is in the chest, slowly climb out or I will shoot!"

"There's someone in the chest?"

"There sure is. I thought I saw something earlier, but I didn't want to seem crazy. Now, whoever it is, come out now."

"Please don't shoot," Annabelle said, slowly rising out of the chest.

Ruthanne's mouth dropped, and her green eyes locked onto Annabelle. "It's a Negro woman!" she said.

"What!" Elizabeth replied, her blue eyes widening. "There's a nigger in your chest!" Elizabeth hopped out of the carriage eagerly.

"What's your name?" Ruthanne asked in a deep voice.

"My name is Annabelle, and I—"

"She's a runaway!" Elizabeth shouted. "My daddy was just talking about a woman slave that had run away from Mr. Brown right before we left. She must be the slave they were talking about."

Ruthanne lowered the revolver reluctantly, asking, "How do you know?"

"It was said she was quite beautiful for a nigger and had scars on her back from being whipped. She has seven scars, and they're very smooth like they're natural patterns on her body, like stripes or stretch marks."

"Hmm...turn around and show your back," Ruthanne said with an authoritative tone.

Annabelle slowly turned around, starting to cry as she showed her back.

"Well, I'll be. Seven scars on her back looking like stripes instead of actual scars. How many times did they whip you for you to get those scars?"

Annabelle replied, "I was whipped twenty times for speaking my mind to my mistress and for spilling tea on a carpet."

"Well, I guess if I was to have been speaking my mind, I'd have scars all over my body too," Ruthanne casually said. "I've never been one to hold my tongue, not even to my daddy."

"So, what are we going to do with her. She's a runaway slave," Elizabeth said. "She's Mr. Brown's property, and he did have a high-priced bounty for her, especially for a woman slave."

"I'm not sure."

Annabelle turned around, sobbing. "Please don't turn me back over to Master Brown. I beg you to please take me at least to the town so I can travel on my own to the north. I don't ever want to see that man ever again."

Elizabeth stood eye to eye with Annabelle. "I've heard Mr. Brown takes good care of his slaves. Why are you so afraid of him?" Elizabeth asked.

"The reason he's offering to pay so much is because he beds me almost every night. More than he does his own wife, Mrs. Regina. I'm blessed to not have a child by Master Brown."

Elizabeth's face began to turn red with fury, and she abruptly slapped Annabelle. "I'm tired of hearing so many lies about good men! How dare you accuse him of lying with a nigger! You may have some beauty for a nigger, but you're no white woman."

"Enough! I believe her, even if your naivety finds it hard to believe. Think of all the obvious mixed-bloods," Ruthanne said. "Look at her arms—they still have bruises and scars from being grabbed and held. Besides, I've heard from my daddy that Mr. Brown was caught with a slave woman years ago on our plantation. You're naïve. He's a dirty man, and I've never liked him. You should see the way he looked at me sometimes, like if we were alone, he'd try to have his way with me."

"It wouldn't surprise me. He has taken my body since I was sixteen," Annabelle said as she wrung her hands. "On my birth month, he took me the first time and threatened to sell my family if I didn't do as he told me to. Do you know what it feels like to not be able to clean myself after it? It killed me every time. Mrs. Regina is such a fool. He's been lying with me more than her ever since Judy Mays moved out." Annabelle continued to wipe away tears while she looked at Elizabeth and Ruthanne. "It's such a disgusting life. I'd rather be hanged than to lie with him again." She sobbed.

As she continued sobbing, Ruthanne, with a heavy heart, was reminded of how easy a life she had compared to Annabelle.

Elizabeth, shocked by what Mr. Brown had been doing, broke out in tears and sobbed. "No woman should ever go through that. Please forgive what I said before. Being a Christian woman, I'm wrong, and I understand why you're so desperate to escape."

Ruthanne held back her own tears while she looked at Annabelle. "I've never let a man put his hands on me, and I would rather die myself than to go back to a place where a man can have my body like that," Ruthanne said. "You're very brave. I also must say we won't be going back to Mississippi for a while. We can get you up north so you can live where slavery is illegal."

Elizabeth smiled at Ruthanne through her tears. "I agree."

"So, Annabelle, how about you sit in the front with us? It

makes no sense for you to go back to lying down in a hot chest again."

"We can easily say you're with us, even though you don't have papers. Things are different in Missouri. There are more free Negroes there," Ruthanne said.

Annabelle replied, "Thank you so much."

CHAPTER 7
New Friends and New Faces

RUTHANNE'S RED HAIR, WHICH HUNG in ringlets around her face, began to blow with the wind as she approached Annabelle and gave her a hug. Ruthanne was as tall as Judy Mays, but she had a small mole behind her right eye.

"Well, now we have another person on the adventure with us," Ruthanne said. "I guess we're going to have to find a different city to go to." She smiled. "I'm guessing a small or medium-sized town with nice people."

"Y'all weren't sure what city y'all were going to?" Annabelle asked.

"Oh, no. It's that we were going to Jefferson City, and I'm not sure how they will treat a Negro woman. Missouri is still a slave state, but Negroes can also be free here legally, so as far as we are concerned, you were born free. Nobody will know you escaped from Mr. Brown."

Annabelle hugged Ruthanne. "Thank you so much. I'm sorry I ruined your plans. Why don't y'all have a man with y'all?"

"We did have a man with us. We may have purposely lost my cousin on our way out of Mississippi. My papa would've never allowed us to go on our own. Obviously, you know women are not supposed to travel alone. Anyway, let's see what we can find now."

"Is your cousin nice?"

"He's a good man. I love him. He's dumb as a rock, which is why I begged my daddy for him to go with us. We left him as soon he went into the supply store, so he'll be alright. Probably took him an hour to realize we were gone." Ruthanne chuckled. "I got tired of Mississippi and all its darkness, so let's keep it moving."

Annabelle frowned slightly. "So, I did ruin your plans."

"Oh, no. It was the Lord's work, I believe. If you had gotten out of that chest around here, you might have ended up in chains again."

The three women, who soon discovered they were all in their late teens, got into the carriage and rode through Missouri, sharing their stories.

In the early morning of July 24, 1845, the women arrived in a new town full of life.

"Oh, isn't this little town nice," Elizabeth said.

"It looks fine. I wonder how many men they have here," Ruthanne said.

"Ruthanne Williams, I'm surprised at you."

"What? I was curious. There isn't anything wrong with finding a good man in a town like this one. He'd better realize I'm not going to be slaving around for him all day long."

"I like the way you think," Annabelle said, smiling.

As they passed through the town, Ruthanne, who noticed nobody paid attention to Annabelle riding with her and Elizabeth, mumbled, "Oh, this may be the place for her to live after all. I know back at home, we would have gotten at least five stares by now." Ruthanne stopped the carriage and turned to Elizabeth and Annabelle. "I'm going to go ask someone if they have any places here that can be rented."

"Okay. Don't bring back any strange men now. You know

you not looking to get married yet," Elizabeth said as Ruthanne stepped out of the carriage.

Ruthanne huffed at her comment.

Elizabeth laughed and turned to Annabelle. "Truth is, she is looking for her Romeo, but she doesn't want to be thought of as stupid. She strongly believes a woman can be equally smart as a man, or even smarter."

"What!" Annabelle exclaimed. "I've never met anybody like that."

"She has definitely had some smart moments, and she is a good reader. She taught me words I had no idea existed, and it made me feel smart. Can you read, Annabelle?"

"No, I can't," Annabelle lied. Then she said, "Well, I can read some words because Judy Mays and I would always play together. I know the thing called the alphabet, and I know words like 'cat,' 'dog,' 'love,' 'God,' 'Jesus,' and some other words."

"How about we teach you how to read? But even here, you will have to keep it a secret. I'm sure that even though Negroes can be free, it is illegal for them to read."

"Why, thank you, Miss Elizabeth."

"Annabelle, that's Elizabeth. You're no longer a slave, so don't talk like one to me."

"Well, Elizabeth," Annabelle said with a smile. "I'm happy to have met you and Ruthanne. The Lord has been good to me, and I feel so good to be out here and away from the plantation."

As Annabelle and Elizabeth talked, a blond-haired man fixed his eyes on Elizabeth and came toward the carriage on a horse.

"Morning, ma'am. Anything I can get you?" he asked with a charismatic tone. "I was on my break from making another livestock pen. You look beautiful, especially with that lovely dress you're wearing."

"Why, thank you, kind sir." Elizabeth giggled.

"I can take your slave with me and get some water for you."

"Oh, no, she isn't my slave. She is a free Negro woman. We grew up together in Jefferson City."

Annabelle was shocked by how fast Elizabeth could tell a lie.

"That's right, sir. I'm a free woman," she said.

"My apologies, ladies. It's hard to tell the difference. My name is Jeff Taylor. May I ask your name?"

"Well, my name is Elizabeth, and this is Annabelle, my good friend." Elizabeth got down from the carriage. "Is this a nice town for Negro women?"

"Yes, it is. She's free, so she isn't to be treated as a slave. So, yes, I think it is. Honestly, it's the Injuns you have to watch out for because they come from the Indian Territory to get supplies from here."

"Well, I thought some Indians weren't so bad."

"Most are good, but I suggest you keep your distance from them, and they'll ignore you. Besides, most of them speak bad English or don't speak it at all."

"Well, thank you for your kind service. I'm sure we will see you around, Jeff."

Jeff beamed, staring at Elizabeth with his brown eyes. "It was nice to meet you, Miss Elizabeth."

"By the way, what is the name of this town?"

"Mercy is the name of the town."

"Why, thank you." Elizabeth turned to Annabelle with a big grin. "I think we might have found what we were looking for. Jeff said this town welcomes free Negro women, so I guess we will see what Ruthanne has found and go from there."

"That sounds great, Elizabeth," Annabelle replied. "I'm free, and now I may have found myself a home. This is turning out to be a special day today."

"Ladies!" exclaimed Ruthanne. "I found something! Annabelle, I talked to some gentlemen, and they told me about a man called Mr. Keys. He has two buildings he lets people live in as long as they pay rent to him. So how about we head over to those buildings, find Mr. Keys, and have a nice talk with him?"

"I met somebody," Elizabeth flirtatiously said.

"Is that right?"

"Yes, his name is Jeff Taylor. He said this is a nice town for a free Negro woman to live in."

"Wonderful to hear. How do you feel about it, Annabelle?"

"I feel good about it," Annabelle answered. "I just now wondered how I am going to pay Mr. Keys if he lets me stay? I don't know how to count, and I can barely read the words on money. All I know to do is cook, clean, sew, and work in a field. So, what can I do in this town to make money to pay him?"

Ruthanne turned to Elizabeth. "I guess now is the time to tell her. After all, you should know who your roommates are going be, don't you think, Annabelle?"

"You mean that y'all gonna stay here with me and not go back to Mississippi?"

"Well, in a way, yes. You see, we planned to be away for a couple of months out of Mississippi, even though we ditched my cousin. I'll write our families tomorrow so they know we are okay, and they're going to be really upset."

Annabelle gasped. "They're going to come look for you."

Ruthanne sighed. "They would if they weren't stuck managing the slaves. I'm sure they'll mail us back quickly, and I'll explain we have a safe home. They'll definitely come to see us, but by their arrival, I'll have a plan to keep you safe."

Annabelle smiled. "Oh, God bless y'all. But how we gonna pay rent when I have no money?"

"That's completely taken care of," Elizabeth replied, pulling out a purse, "We have more than enough to stay for a number of years. My daddy yelled at me for carrying so much money, but now it will come into good use. So, while I and Ruthanne will be paying the rent, you will learn more about how to read, write, and count."

Ruthanne scrunched her nose. "Since when did paying the rent become a part of the agreement?"

"Hush up, Ruthanne. Stop acting like you have no money. I swear, you're so cheap, and you have more money than I do."

"Whatever, I have my reasons for complaining. Who's buying the new dresses?"

Elizabeth turned her head slowly toward Ruthanne. "Well, not all got ruined, and they weren't my dresses mud ruined. Forget it. Let's go find Mr. Keys. I'm through talking to you."

Ruthanne jumped into the carriage. Annabelle, not sure what to say, sat in the middle, hoping the other two would stop fighting.

As the carriage took off, Ruthanne turned to Annabelle. "What's your favorite color?"

Annabelle grinned. "Well, my favorite color is blue," she said. "I guess it's strange for a girl to like the color blue more than pink, but I think it is a strong color."

"That's funny. Blue is my favorite color." Ruthanne laughed, enjoying the coincidence.

As Elizabeth fanned herself, she chuckled and said, "Both of you are odd."

"What is your favorite color, Elizabeth?" Annabelle asked.

"Red! Red! Red!" Ruthanne blurted.

"Ruthanne, Annabelle was asking me, not you," Elizabeth bickered. "Yes, she is right, Annabelle. I like the color red. It symbolizes love."

"Don't make me gag," Ruthanne said while she had the horse speed up.

I guess they're as good of friends as I'm gonna get, Annabelle thought. *I might as well get used to it.*

The ladies stopped at the next street, and Ruthanne said, "This is where that man told me the buildings were, so I guess we'll ask around for Mr. Keys and see what happens."

Ruthanne moved around boldly. The other two watched in surprise at how fast she asked complete strangers.

"I guess we should help Annabelle. Just walk with me so we don't have to worry about any trouble," Elizabeth said.

"Alright," Annabelle replied.

They got out of the carriage and joined Ruthanne. The ladies strolled around, asking anyone passing by if they knew Mr. Keys, but no one did.

Ruthanne huffed while she walked. "Come on. This town

isn't big. We should have come across someone that knows Mr. Keys." Ruthanne approached a man with a young girl. "Excuse me, kind sir, do you know a Mr. Keys?"

The sturdy brown-haired man wore a black frock coat, blue striped trousers, and a beige shirt with a deep blue cravat that was covered by a silk blue vest and held a gold pocket watch. He stopped, and in a voice that lacked a southern accent, said, "Yes, I do." The man looked at Ruthanne with jovial blue eyes. "I'm Mr. Keys—Allen Keys, ma'am. What is your name?"

"My name is Ruthanne Williams, and it's a pleasure to meet you finally."

Mr. Keys looked confused. "Finally?"

"Oh, yes. I was told you rent out two building, and I was hoping to rent out a room or two for some time."

"Well, that explains why you have been looking for me." Mr. Keys laughed. "Is it just you staying in the room, or will there be others?"

"There will be two other ladies staying with me for quite some time. I'll go get them. Please, stay right here."

"Alrighty, I'll be right here."

Ruthanne gathered Annabelle and Elizabeth. "Come on. Y'all move so slowly."

"Well, I shouldn't be surprised by your impulsive ways. You're the little girl that decided to cut up her dresses so she could run faster," Elizabeth said. "Your daddy never punished you."

"You said you would never bring that up again."

The ladies met up with Mr. Keys.

"Hello, ladies. So, these are your roommates, Miss Williams?" Mr. Keys asked.

"Yes, Mr. Keys. This is Elizabeth and Annabelle."

"Pardon me, but is Annabelle your slave, or is she a free Negro woman?"

Ruthanne's voice suddenly became strict. "She is a free Negro. Will there be a problem?"

"Blessed be the Lord!" Mr. Keys said firmly.

The ladies looked at Mr. Keys with wide eyes and raised eyebrows.

"You're the first white man I have ever heard praising the freedom of a Negro," Elizabeth said.

"I'm originally from Illinois, and I'm a Christian man. The Bible says all men are created equal, nothing more and nothing less. So, I'm pleased to meet you, Annabelle."

Annabelle stood slightly behind Ruthanne to hide her torn dress. "It's a pleasure to meet you too, Mr. Keys," Annabelle softly said. *Is this real? He's nicer to me than Edgar*, she thought.

"So, all of you must be good friends to be wanting to live together," Mr. Keys said.

"Yes, we are. Actually, her first name is Sasha not, Annabelle," Ruthanne said with a big smile as Annabelle gave her a confused look. "It's habit of mine. Sometimes I call her by her middle name."

"Oh, well, Sasha it is. Allow me to introduce you lovely ladies to someone quite special to me." Standing behind him, the little brown-eyed, brunette girl who wore a green plaid dress and a white bonnet stepped forward. "This is my little girl, Ashley."

"Hi," Ashley said, sounding shy.

"Hello there. You're so adorable," Elizabeth said, rubbing the girl's cheek with her hand. "How old are you?"

Ashley gave a big grin. "I'm four years old, and I will be five soon."

"Wow, turning into a big girl soon," Annabelle said.

"Yes, I am," Ashley replied, "and Daddy said he'll get me a beautiful doll to play with."

"Why, isn't that nice. I wish my daddy was as sweet as yours," Ruthanne said kindly.

"Your daddy did get dolls, but you either set them on fire or cut all their hair off," Elizabeth murmured.

Ruthanne slightly turned her head and whispered with a deep voice, "Are you really going to start something now?"

It looks like these two are going to start arguing again, Annabelle thought.

Right before things became more aggressive, an oblivious Mr. Keys invited the ladies over for tea and pie. Annabelle quickly accepted the offer.

Mr. Keys cheerfully escorted the young women to his brown-bricked two-story home to meet his wife, drink some tea, and eat some pie. A welcoming atmosphere greeted them. The walls were painted white. Two large windows with sandy-colored curtains allowed sunlight onto the wooden floors of the living room, which contained a fireplace with coal and a wooden coffee table surrounded by a few chairs and a sandy-colored checkered couch. A hallway leading from the living room contained three bedrooms. The dining room was segmented from the living room by an arch, containing a large burgundy carpet with diamond shapes, a fireplace, a large cedar table with several seats, and the kitchen doorway that connected to it.

When they'd gotten comfortable, he asked, "So where exactly are you ladies coming from?"

"We are coming from Jefferson City," Ruthanne said.

"Jefferson City. I've been there. It's not far from here. It's quite big for a Missouri city, but I guess the capital should be."

The ladies looked wide-eyed at Mr. Keys as they each forced a grin, hiding the increased pounding of their hearts.

"Now that's some excellent pie." Mr. Keys patted his stomach. "My wife, Rebecca, is an excellent cook. I'm truly blessed. Now, I do have a place for you ladies to stay…right above me. Only one person has lived there before you, and he was a clean fellow. Let me show you ladies around, and you can tell me how you like it."

Outside, the ladies climbed up to the second floor, and Mr. Keys opened the door. The upper quarters had a living room with a black couch and wooden coffee table sitting atop a wooden floor. Two large windows with beige curtains allowed the sunshine in. The living room led to a kitchen with a wooden table and stove. All of the walls were painted white, and the bedroom had a window and two twin-sized beds. A second set of outside stairs led to a well and an outhouse behind the home.

"Oh my God!" Annabelle exclaimed. "I thought this was going to be one or two rooms."

"Oh, no, it's almost as big as my quarters downstairs, and you ladies have your own stove to cook on. There are two beds already here. I can see if we can possibly fit in another bed, but it'll have to be purchased."

"We will take it!" Ruthanne blurted.

Elizabeth looked at Ruthanne and murmured, "We didn't even ask the price he wants us to pay. I guess some things will never change with this gal."

"In all the excitement, I didn't ask if you have a man present?" Mr. Keys asked.

"No, my cousin escorted us but had to return home. We are trying to be independent and not far from home. We do expect constant visits from our brothers, and we were hoping you would be comfortable with being the man of our quarters," Ruthanne said.

Mr. Keys smiled. "I think that'll work."

As they moved around, Elizabeth said, "Well, I guess it's time for us to find a nice supply store to get some food."

"There's one right around the corner, and I think that will fit best for Sasha as well," Mr. Keys said. "Mr. Boston's views are similar to mine, and he's friendly."

The ladies thanked Mr. Keys and went to the supply store on foot to buy some new supplies.

As the young women traveled, Ruthanne calmly grabbed Annabelle's hand. "I'm sorry for the name change, but it's to keep you safe, and it was the quickest name I could think of," Ruthanne said. "I hope you don't mind it. We should've talked about this earlier."

"Why is changing my name so important?" Annabelle asked.

"Mr. Brown will use your name to track you down, so it's

better if at least your first name is different. How about you take my last name?"

Annabelle's face expressed approval. "Okay...Williams is a nice name anyway."

Ruthanne smiled back at Annabelle, and the young women continued going through Mercy toward the supply store. When the ladies arrived at the brown wooden building, Elizabeth opened the door and a bell rang.

"This is a nice little supply store," Elizabeth said.

The store had wooden aisles barely taller than the women, and barrels stood in front of them. Some aisles were entirely made up of barrels, and the sound of chickens came out of a side door leading to a chicken coop.

A large, chubby, gray eyed, white-haired old man appeared behind the counter. He wore a blue high-collared shirt and a red cravat covered by a gray vest, and gray trousers

"Welcome, welcome. I'm Don Boston, so call me Mr. Boston or Mr. B." He laughed, his cheerful baritone southern accent less prominent than that of the women. "You ladies must be new here. I've seen most of the town's people, unless you've been going over to that snake—Mr. Hildebrand's store."

"Oh no, we don't know a Mr. Hildebrand. We are new here in town," Ruthanne said.

"Well, come on in and let me show you lovely ladies around."

Mr. Boston began to explain to the ladies where everything was, and Annabelle thought, *I've never been to a store or welcomed to one.*

Annabelle felt appreciated, something she hadn't felt in a long time, but she also made sure she stood behind Ruthanne, partly to hide the tear in her dress.

As Mr. Boston continued to show the ladies around, he turned around and asked, "Are you a free Negro or a slave?"

Annabelle said, "I'm a free Negro woman, sir."

Mr. Boston smiled. "That's what I like to hear in this town, improvement. You're not the only free Negro in town. There are thirty others for sure living in this town. Most of them married, as far I know, but there are two handsome young men I could introduce you to if you like," Mr. Boston said with a smile and a wink.

Annabelle giggled and answered, "Not right now. I'm not exactly looking for a man right now."

"Why not? You're a pretty Negro woman."

Ruthanne stepped behind Annabelle, touched her shoulder, and said, "Sasha just recently ended a bad connection. The man didn't treat her well like he should have."

Mr. Boston took off his glasses, then said, "I'm sorry to hear that, and I hope you recover. I know how you women are. I can tell you're one of the smart ones. Better to get out of a bad situation than letting it consume you. I've had some smart women in my life, and that's why I'm a single young man now, so if any of you ladies would like me to escort you out to the festival, I'd be glad to do so," he joked.

The ladies laughed, and Ruthanne's eyes widened.

"There's going to be a festival here?"

"Why, yes. It's the town founder's day. It will be the seventh time we've had it. Why, even a few of the Indians come from the Indian Territory to see the events."

Ruthanne smiled. "Wow, I guess it's a big deal if even the Indians show up to it. We will be there."

"That's the spirit! I have to pull out my good suit and hat now." Mr. Boston laughed. "Well, I'll let you ladies pick out what you need. I have to tend to Mr. Fluffs."

Annabelle had a confused expression because she'd never heard a name like that. "Who is Mr. Fluffs?" she asked.

He replied, "He's my cat. He keeps me great company. I'll call him." Mr. Boston pulled out a small bell from his pocket and shook it, and out came Mr. Fluffs. The large, green eyed, long-haired cat had a blotchy gray and white pattern.

Ruthanne's eyes widened. "Oh my God! I've never seen such a big cat in my life!"

Mr. Boston replied, "Well I might have spoiled him a little too much." He petted Mr. Fluffs as the cat rubbed him.

"You know, God has amazing power and timing. I found Mr. Fluffs behind this building, and nobody claimed him. He was a playful and carefree kitten. At the time, I was sad because my wife had gotten the smallpox and she didn't make it. I cursed God and said never again will I trust you, but what does he do? He sends me a companion who is keeping me company and doesn't eat all my food. Nobody could have timed that better than God. I was at the point of ending my own life, ladies, and God saved me from myself. You know, Mr. Fluffs may actually outlive me. Cats live much longer than dogs. Well, I'll leave you ladies to shop."

Mr. Boston returned to the counter while the ladies browsed around the store.

"He has some nice corn here," Annabelle said.

Ruthanne grabbed a bag of yeast. "I guess we can make some bread too."

"Oh, look, a chicken coop. I guess we can fry one up tonight."

Elizabeth looked confused and frustrated. "I'll grab some salt," she said.

The ladies went to the counter to pay for the supplies.

"Do you cut those chickens up yourself, Mr. Boston?" Ruthanne asked.

"Why, yes, I do," he answered. "How about I give you one of my extra roosters?"

"That would be mighty nice of you, Mr. Boston. You sure are a busy man."

"I find it's better to be busy than to grow old falling apart," Mr. Boston joked.

As the ladies gathered the groceries, Mr. Boston went to his chicken coop, grabbed a rooster, and butchered the chicken while the ladies finished their shopping. He brought out the butchered chicken, and Mr. Fluffs meowed from his spot on the counter.

"Wait, ladies, don't forget to give Mr. Fluffs his daily petting."

Ruthanne giggled. "I don't give free pettings to strange cats."

"He's not so strange. Introduce yourself, Mr. Fluffs."

Mr. Fluffs charmingly meowed.

"He's so cute!" Annabelle said. "Well, I believe in Ruthanne's idea of not giving free pets to a cat I don't know, so my name is Sasha Annabelle Williams."

"Well now, you big charming cat, I'm Ruthanne Matilda Williams."

Elizabeth stepped up to Mr. Fluffs. "I've met some spoiled pets over time, but you win by far, Mr. Fluffs. My name is Elizabeth Mariam Jones. His daily petting...this spoiled cat is something else."

The ladies giggled and petted Mr. Fluffs. Mr. Boston gave them the chicken as Ruthanne paid.

The ladies later left the groceries in their new home and explored around town, looking at all the different buildings. They came across a saloon, where a lot of commotion was going on.

Suddenly, three men walked out. They were so drunk, they could not stand up straight.

"Woo wee! Look at these lovely ladies and a Negro woman," one of them said.

"I know I'm drunk, but I've never seen such beautiful women in town," the other man said.

The third man, bigger than the other two, pushed them aside and belligerently said, "Now, look here. I'll take these two young ladies because I need two to satisfy me, and you fools can have the pretty Negro woman."

The women gasped, then their jaws dropped and their eyes bulged.

"Now, what do you think is going to happen between the two of us, big man?" Ruthanne asked, her voice harsh.

"This one is bold," the third man said, rubbing his dark brown beard and struggling to walk. "Well now, my bed has been lonely the past few weeks, and I'm sure you can keep it warm for me."

Ruthanne squinted and scrunched her nose. "Now, look here, you dirty, ugly, smelly drunkard! You'll never see me or any of my friends in your bed!"

The third man approached Ruthanne while the other two men watched. "Now...is that right? You, with your pretty skin and green eyes. You wouldn't be the first I'd held down."

Annabelle began having flashbacks of her first night being raped. She balled her fists and thought, *Never again will a man force himself on me.*

With a deep voice, Ruthanne said, "I suggest you step away. You wouldn't be the first man I put my fists on."

The third man turned his head, laughing. "Hey, boys, we have ourselves a fighter."

Ruthanne squinted and mumbled, "Here we go."

As the big man turned his head toward the women, Ruthanne punched him in his jaw, knocking one of his teeth loose. Unconscious, the big man fell to the ground, and the other two men looked on in shock.

"Mad Moe, is you okay?" one of the men asked. "He's not waking up."

Ruthanne turned her attention to the other two men. "So, do y'all want to try me too, or are y'all gonna show some respect?"

Annabelle's mouth dropped open, speechless. Elizabeth shook her head and murmured under her breath.

"Oh, no, ma'am!" one of the men shouted. "We respect you! We respect you!"

The two men dragged Mad Moe away from the ladies as some of the townspeople watched.

Ruthanne turned to the others, rubbing her hand. She ignored the townspeople and smiled. "Okay, are we ready to continue our tour?"

Annabelle, her mouth still open, nodded along with Elizabeth. The ladies walked around the town while Annabelle contemplated what had happened.

Annabelle turned to Ruthanne. "How did you do that?" she asked. "I've never seen a man punch that fast and hard, or even thought a woman could."

Ruthanne gave Annabelle a confident smile. "One day, there was a rattlesnake in one of our fields, and my daddy took me with him to kill it. The snake lashed out when it felt my daddy was in range. I learned how to be fast from watching the snake. It was so fast and aggressive, my daddy gave up and said that snake had the right to be there if it was fighting that hard. Then one day, one of my brothers stole one of my dolls and wouldn't give it back. I felt such a rage like nothing I've never felt. I balled my fist while they were laughing, and as fast as I could, I punched him in his stomach. He fell to the ground, crying in pain, and I never forgot how to do that. So, that's how I learned how to punch."

Annabelle was impressed with what Ruthanne had learned.

Elizabeth tauntingly asked, "Are you now proud of telling Annabelle how you became a brute?"

Annabelle laughed while Ruthanne looked at Elizabeth with an annoyed expression. "That doesn't make me a brute. That makes me hard to please, thank you very much."

The ladies arrived at a small red-colored store called Pots's Garments. It stood alone from the other buildings, with three dressed paper-mâché mannequins in a large window.

"Look at the dresses," Elizabeth excitedly said. "Let's go in."

Ruthanne rolled her eyes as they went into the store.

Annabelle was excited because she had never been in a store with clothes. The women walked around the sunlit room, surprised by how nice the few dresses were. Small wooden tables displayed fancy glass bottles of perfume. Men's clothing dominated the store displays. A dark brown-haired woman approached the ladies, wearing a low-shouldered, light blue floral dress, sapphire dangle earrings, and a flowery white hat. The young woman was shorter than the other three, having an average hourglass frame and a welcoming smile.

"Welcome to Pots's Garments, ladies. Is there anything I can help you with?" the woman asked.

"Who made these dresses?" Elizabeth asked. "They're gorgeous."

"Oh...why, I did. My name is Marilyn Pots, and who might you be?"

"I'm Elizabeth, that's Ruthanne, and this is Sasha."

"Nice to meet you, ladies. The dresses are mine. They're already purchased and on display until they can be taken home, but it's my daddy's store."

"This is such an amazing place," Annabelle said. "I've never seen anything like it. You're so talented."

Marilyn's emerald green eyes fixed on Annabelle. She grinned, exposing her dimples, and picked up a book. "I want to show you ladies something. It's what I call a dress book, and it shows all the different types I've made." Marilyn said happily. "I believe it will someday be a big deal to us ladies. Imagine being able to walk into a supply store and buying a book with different dresses in it, or even ordering from it? Aren't the possibilities exciting?"

Elizabeth seemed eager about the idea of ordering clothes from a book.

Ruthanne murmured, "I'd rather just walk in the store than spend money on a stupid dress book."

"Well now, what are you ladies looking for exactly? And don't worry, I sell to Negroes too…when daddy isn't here. I must apologize ahead of time. My views are not the same as his toward Negroes."

"Well, thank you for letting me know. If it's alright, I'd like it if you could tell me when you will be here instead of your daddy," Annabelle said.

Marilyn replied with a grin, "Of course. Besides, sometimes it gets boring here."

"Sasha," Ruthanne said, "what do you think of that blue dress?"

"It's beautiful," Annabelle replied, "and I think it would look lovely on you."

Ruthanne beamed. "Well, if you ask me, I believe it would look even better on you. What do you ladies think?"

"It would look lovely on her," Elizabeth replied.

Marilyn nodded. "I think it would make her stand out quite well."

Annabelle placed her hand over her heart and began to cry. "Thank you, Ruthanne!"

Ruthanne hugged Annabelle. "It's not a big expense. Besides, we need to replace your torn dress, and we need to look sharp for the coming festival."

Marilyn squealed and clapped her hands together. "Y'all gonna go to the festival? I'll be there too with a new dress."

"I'd like us to be scheduled for a fitting," Ruthanne said, giving Marilyn the money.

"Not a problem," Marilyn replied. "You will look great in them."

The women scheduled a time for the fitting, and Ruthanne smiled. "Why, thank you, Marilyn. Well, the girls and I need to get going. I'm so hungry, and we have food to cook."

"Alright, but stop by the store again soon, as it does get quite boring in here."

The ladies went back to their new home to prepare their food. Annabelle quickly noticed Elizabeth standing and watching as she and Ruthanne cooked.

"Is everything alright, Elizabeth?" Annabelle asked.

Elizabeth frowned and said in a soft voice, "I don't know how to cook."

Annabelle and Ruthanne looked at her with disbelief.

"What are you talking about?" Ruthanne scolded. "You made that pie for the picnic we had."

"Um, I didn't make it. Robin made it for me."

"What! I can't believe you made her do it. That child has always shown so much love, even for a slave."

Elizabeth started to sob. "I didn't make her do it. She volunteered to help me out because I was so ashamed."

"You big crybaby," Ruthanne said. She wiped the tears from Elizabeth's face, adding, "Well, there's nothing wrong with learning now, so let's get started."

"You said you want to teach me to read. I'll help you learn to cook," Annabelle said.

Elizabeth beamed and replied, "Okay, it's a deal. I'm going to learn how to cook."

The ladies spent the rest of the day teaching Elizabeth how to cook and bake. They laughed as they dealt with unexpected accidents while teaching Elizabeth different recipes. Flour spilled numerous times, Elizabeth cut herself, two fires got started, some of the food didn't taste very pleasant, and Ruthanne walked out once, screaming because of Elizabeth's lack of listening skills.

Annabelle spent more time comforting Elizabeth rather than teaching her because she would break down in tears. Night finally came, and flour and soot from the fires covered the ladies. Due to Elizabeth's constant mistakes, they ate the poorly cooked food because they were too exhausted to try again.

As the young women put on their nightgowns, Annabelle began to think about all the effort the young women had put forward for her and felt guilty about lying.

"Thank you for your extra nightgown, Ruthanne," Annabelle said.

"It's no problem. It would've been weird for you to sleep in your dress," Ruthanne replied.

Annabelle sighed while she looked around the bedroom. "I need to tell y'all a truth."

Elizabeth and Ruthanne gave Annabelle a concerned look.

"I can read and write. Judy Mays taught me, and I know I'm not supposed to know how."

"So, your promise," Elizabeth said.

"I'm keeping my word. I will help you learn. I was scared. I wasn't sure how y'all would act if you knew I could read and write."

Ruthanne gave Annabelle a slight smirk. "Judy Mays. I actually miss my conversations with her. It's okay. I understand being afraid, and you're smart to be afraid. When we go to the festival, we can't let you be alone. It's too dangerous, and you're still learning."

"Thank you for not getting mad at me," Annabelle said.

The two young women gave Annabelle sympathetic looks, and Ruthanne said, "Thank you for being honest."

Annabelle grinned at Elizabeth and Ruthanne. The young women continued to get ready for bed, and then they knelt together in front of Elizabeth's bed to pray.

Elizabeth got into one bed, and Annabelle and Ruthanne shared the other. As they rested, Elizabeth turned to Annabelle and Ruthanne with a smile. "I never guessed cooking was so hard and time-consuming. No wonder my Momma barely ever does it."

Ruthanne and Annabelle looked at each other. Exhausted and frustrated, they sighed deeply and shook their heads.

"So how about we do this again tomorrow?" Elizabeth asked.

"Oh, no," Annabelle said quickly. "You need at least two days of rest when learning."

"Really? Why is that?"

"Well, because we don't want our pretty hands to get any more scars, do we?" Ruthanne answered.

Elizabeth looked at her hands before looking at the ladies. "Oh, no, I guess that really does make a lot of sense. Men do like soft hands."

Annabelle whispered to Ruthanne," Good answer."

Ruthanne turned to Annabelle. "Trust me; after dealing with this girl for so many years, it comes naturally. I still wonder if she's this way from lack of experience or plain stupidity."

Annabelle quietly giggled. "Well, at least she's willing to learn."

"Yeah, that's true, but you're teaching her for the first thirty minutes. I never in my life thought I would see the day I would be forced to eat hard bread."

Annabelle sighed. "Me neither. Even as a slave, I've never had bad bread. I guess I can teach Elizabeth for thirty minutes instead of walking out mad like you did." Annabelle began to giggle as Ruthanne shook her head.

"I have dealt with her for eighteen years, and nothing has changed."

Elizabeth began to snore, and Ruthanne lifted her head with a frown. She shook her head and lay back down, giggling. "See? Nothing has changed."

Annabelle looked at Elizabeth and thought, *Elizabeth has no idea what it's like to live a rough life. She really had it easy living off of slaves and thinks it's normal.*

That night, Annabelle dreamed she was going through town as the sun began to set and the moon rose. She'd never seen the sun or moon move so quickly, and she felt herself starting to panic.

"Where is everyone? Why am I alone?" she yelled, running through the town to find someone. When she turned around, the moon and sun moved even faster.

"What's going on?"

The sun and moon moved so quickly that Annabelle couldn't keep track of what was happening, and she prayed, "God, please help me. Please send me help."

At the time Annabelle spoke, she heard Ruthanne's laugh as she said, "Annabelle, come on."

Annabelle turned around, seeing Ruthanne behind her. Shocked by Ruthanne's appearance, Annabelle hugged her, telling her the crazy things she'd seen.

Ruthanne grinned and laughed. "Follow me," she said before fading into the air.

"Ruthanne!" Annabelle screamed.

Annabelle heard Elizabeth's voice as the other woman appeared behind her. "There's no need to worry, Annabelle. Walk with me."

Annabelle grabbed Elizabeth's arm as the sun and moon continued their rapid progression throughout the sky. "We have to find Ruthanne. Something has happened to her."

"Oh, wait," Elizabeth said. "I know I saw Ruthanne over here just a moment ago."

Holding hands, they turned into an alley where they ran into Mad Moe and his thugs. The town suddenly began to shake.

Mad Moe gave a sinister laugh and said, "It's the blonde and the Negro woman."

"Leave her alone!" Elizabeth shouted.

Mad Moe and his thugs' eyes turned red. "You know, we can't get away with hurting a beautiful white woman. But a nice-looking Negro woman, nobody would care what we gonna do to her."

The ground cracked open, and tears flowed down Annabelle's face.

Elizabeth shouted, "Annabelle, run!"

"Get her!" Mad Moe hollered.

Annabelle ran and screamed for help as Elizabeth fell to her knees.

"Ruthanne, where are you?" As Annabelle ran, a part of the ground shifted up and pushed her into the air, causing her to fall. She stood quickly and was about to run when Mad Moe grabbed her.

Annabelle balled her fist and hit Mad Moe in the jaw, but he turned angry eyes on her.

"You have fight like the redhead. I'm gonna enjoy this one," Mad Moe said.

Annabelle kicked Mad Moe between his legs and tried to punch his face, but he caught her fist and laughed while his thugs watched.

"You got me once, but you not gonna get another hit like that." Mad Moe struck Annabelle so hard, it felt like all the wind in the town had combined with his fist.

Annabelle collapsed, and the sun and moon stopped moving. Tears flowed down her face because she couldn't tell if it was a dream or real anymore. "Please, somebody! Help me, please!"

Mad Moe stood over her, grabbed her neck, and ripped a part of her dress.

"Oh, you're nice." Mad Moe's thugs laughed as he whispered, "I tell you what. After I'm done with you, I gonna let them have some fun too. Just don't fight it."

"Please, don't do this! I'm begging you."

Mad Moe laughed, but the sound of banging drums filled the air, and the ground stopped shaking.

"What is that sound?" Mad Moe sneered.

Annabelle turned her head and saw a beautiful woman in white clothing. A golden aura surrounded her body.

"Annabelle, you're never alone. God is with you at all times and has seen your pain," the woman's voice echoed. The woman smiled, adding, "God has an appointed time for everything."

Annabelle noticed that Mad Moe and his thugs couldn't see the woman as she moved toward Annabelle. "It's almost time," she said before fading.

Mad Moe let go of Annabelle and balled his fists. "What the hell?" Mad Moe said.

Annabelle turned her head, watching as two tall beings moved in the fog, and the drums became louder. Out of the mist came two Indian men. She watched with wide eyes, having only seen Indian people a few times in the south, but none like these men.

Annabelle heard the drums even louder, and one of the men said, "Leave this woman alone."

Mad Moe gave a diabolical laugh, replying, "What right do you think you have here, Injun?"

"This is the last warning. Leave her or deal with us."

Mad Moe's thugs stepped back slowly, and the moment Mad Moe reached to draw his weapon, a gunshot echoed. Mad Moe fell to the ground, holding his shoulder and screaming in agony.

"I warned you."

Mad Moe's thugs grabbed him and ran away, and the sun began to rise again. Annabelle stood and approached the men.

"Thank you," Annabelle said, tears streaming down her face.

The lead man replied, "You're just as brave as you're beautiful," he said. "Never again will I let those men hurt you."

"I don't understand. You don't know me, and I don't know you, so why do you care?"

The man smiled, then he turned with the other man, and they faded from view as they walked away.

Annabelle, breathing deeply, turned her head to the right and saw the woman again.

The woman smiled. "Things are changing."

Annabelle woke up, breathing heavily as sweat beaded on her forehead. "Thank you, Jesus. It was a dream."

Ruthanne entered the room. "You're finally awake. It's nine o'clock."

"Oh, my! It's that late in the day already? I never get to sleep this late."

"It's alright. It's not like we had anything to do." Ruthanne noticed Annabelle's troubled expression. "What's wrong?"

"This dream I had. It scared me so bad because it felt so real."

Ruthanne gave a concerned look, then asked, "What kind of a dream?"

"Oh, where should I begin? The sun and the moon spun so fast I couldn't tell how many days were passing, and the Indians saved me from Mad Moe."

"That does sound serious." Ruthanne held her hand. "Tell me everything."

Annabelle explained the whole dream to her, and Ruthanne seemed alarmed by how detailed the dream was.

"It's not my dream, and I feel uneasy. Well, I suggest you pray about it, and I'll pray for you as well."

Annabelle felt some relief. "Thank you."

"Well, get cleaned up and dressed, and how about we explore the rest of town?"

"That sounds like a plan to me."

"Oh, before I forget, I have an extra dress you can wear. We're about the same size."

"Thank you so much."

"Bah, it's nothing."

CHAPTER 8
God's Appointed Time

AFTER GETTING DRESSED, THE LADIES strolled down the stairs and ran into Mr. Keys's wife, Rebecca.

"Hello there, you must be the new ladies living upstairs. I'm Rebecca. We didn't get the opportunity to speak yesterday."

The ladies were quite surprised by Rebecca's beauty when comparing her to Mr. Keys. She was Ruthanne's height, though marginally wider. Her black hair was styled into high twin buns, and her brown eyes were keen, while her ruffled red and white dress amplified her femininity. Unlike Mr. Keys, she had a minor southern accent.

While the ladies stood speechless, Rebecca gave a confused look. "Is everything okay?" she asked.

Ruthanne shook her head, replying, "Yes, Mrs. Rebecca, we are quite alright."

"Oh, please, call me Rebecca. You make me feel old by calling me Mrs. Rebecca."

Elizabeth, still trying to figure out how Mr. Keys ended up marrying Rebecca, said, "You sure are a beautiful lady. I'm sure Mr. Keys treats you well."

Rebecca grinned. "Well, yes, Allen has always treated me kindly since we were children. He has always made me laugh and feel good about myself."

Annabelle replied, "You two sound like best friends."

"He is my best friend. God brought us together. We always talk to each other about what's going on, and I think that's what helps us become even closer. Well, now, I guess you ladies are off to visit the rest of the town?"

"Oh, yes," Elizabeth said. "We are off to see where the festival is going to be held."

"That will be by the church. Just make a right and keep straight. There's no way you would miss it. Also, I'm making another apple pie if y'all would like to have some."

With a soft voice, Ruthanne said, "Of course, it would be our pleasure."

As Elizabeth heard Ruthanne's voice, her eyes widened. She slightly frowned and turned her head a little, trying to see Ruthanne's face, but she quickly looked back to Rebecca because she didn't want to upset Ruthanne by acting oddly.

Rebecca opened the front door with a smile. "Well, alright, I'll see you ladies later today."

"Goodbye, Rebecca," they replied.

They traveled toward the church, not saying a word. Annabelle thought Ruthanne was acting a little differently because she remained quiet for so long. With a perplexed look, Annabelle turned to Elizabeth, and she had the same expression. Elizabeth realized Annabelle had also noticed.

"Ruthanne," Elizabeth gently said, "are you okay?"

Ruthanne stopped walking and kept her head straight.

"Why wouldn't I be okay?" Ruthanne said with a minor crackle in her voice.

"Ruthanne?" Annabelle said.

Ruthanne inhaled and turned around with watery eyes, shocking Annabelle and Elizabeth. "The love she has for that man is... I've never... I've never heard a wife call her husband her best friend. That's amazing to me, and it makes me feel some type of hope. She reminds me how I feel about finding a man, and how I feel if I get married, my fun will be over. How this expectation of me not having a life and just popping out babies will be all I have. However, she mentioned how she believes God brought them together and how he is her best friend. I mean, how often do you hear a woman talk about how God set her up with her husband?"

A tear went down Ruthanne's face. "I'd rather be more like her than most of the women I have met in my life so far. She's free, happily married, has a life, and I can tell she's an amazing spirit. I want to explore at least some of the country, gain some more education, and be blessed with a man who supports me in that."

Annabelle put her hand on Ruthanne's shoulder. "I understand how you feel, and the way Rebecca talked about Mr. Keys definitely reminded me of my parents," Annabelle said.

Elizabeth began to cry and gave Ruthanne a hug.

"I don't want to get fat like my momma. I want to be like Rebecca too," Elizabeth said.

Annabelle and Ruthanne laughed as Elizabeth wiped the tears from her eyes.

"Well, girls, let's go see what this church looks like," Ruthanne said.

The women enjoyed the different sounds in the busy town, seeing the different people while they continued to explore and enjoy the late morning sun.

Out of nowhere, a man with a welcoming southern accent said, "Good morning, ladies."

The women stopped and saw a dark brown-skinned Negro man with welcoming round eyes brushing a horse.

"I wanted to ask if you ladies wanted some water. Y'all look hot over there."

"Why sure," said Ruthanne. "What's your name?"

"My name is Benjamin Moseley, ma'am, a free Negro."

"How nice your name is. This is Sasha, and this is Elizabeth."

Benjamin grinned and said, "Not that many Negro women in town. It's nice to see a new face." He turned to Ruthanne. "Ma'am, may I have the honor of meeting with her at the festival for an hour?"

Annabelle became angry by his assumption, and her eyes narrowed.

Ruthanne's mouth dropped open before she replied, "She's a free woman. I'm sure she'd prefer if you asked her yourself."

Benjamin's eyes widened as he took his straw hat off. "My apologies, Miss Sasha. Most Negroes in Missouri not free."

Annabelle crossed her arms. "Well, I guess I can accept your apology since you don't know me," she said with a stern tone.

Benjamin smiled and replied. "I'm mighty pleased to hear that."

Annabelle, still offended by his assumption, said, "By the way, I'm seventeen years old, and I say what I'm gonna do, so don't forget it."

Benjamin was quite surprised by her attitude. "I'm sorry. I was all wrong about you."

"Meh, you wouldn't be the first man to be wrong. I might see you at the festival."

"That's nice to hear. It was nice to meet all you ladies," he said, tilting his hat.

"You're the first Negro man I've met here, so it's nice to meet you, too," Elizabeth said.

"Nice to have met you, Benjamin," Ruthanne said as they walked away.

Elizabeth smiled at Annabelle. "So, he was pretty handsome for a Negro man, don't you think, Annabelle?"

"He was okay," Annabelle answered. "He assumes too much. I won't ignore him just yet. I did just meet him." *He was nice,* Annabelle thought to herself, *but I don't like how he assumed I was going to say yes, as if I don't have options.*

Ruthanne giggled. "Well, it's obvious he thought you were interesting. You were so anxious to leave, I forgot to get a drink of water from him."

"Sorry. Most men do find me interesting," Annabelle replied boastfully.

The ladies continued through town, and Ruthanne noticed Mad Moe and his men on the other side of the street. Not wanting to give Annabelle a panic because of her dream, she said nothing. Fortunately, Mad Moe and his men didn't notice the women walking by, and when the ladies had passed, Ruthanne gave a sigh of relief.

Annabelle turned to Ruthanne. "Is something wrong?" she asked.

"No, everything is fine. I was thinking of the next time we have to teach Elizabeth how to cook."

Annabelle laughed. "Yes, that will be hard to do."

Elizabeth, looking at all the different people and buildings, completely missed them talking. Ruthanne continued to dominate the conversation, cheerfully pointing at some of the buildings in town.

Jeff saw the young women and approached them. "Hello, Miss Elizabeth," he said.

The ladies stopped abruptly.

"Hi, Jeff," Elizabeth said. "How've you been?"

"I'm doing alright. I see you're moving through town with your lady friends. Hi, Miss Annabelle."

"Hello, Jeff," Annabelle replied. "And it's Sasha. Annabelle is actually my middle name."

Jeff gave Annabelle a perplexed look and said, "My mistake."

"This is Ruthanne, my best friend. We grew up together," Elizabeth said cheerfully.

"Nice to meet you, Miss Ruthanne," Jeff greeted.

Ruthanne smiled and replied, "Nice to meet you too."

Elizabeth was surprised Ruthanne smiled and didn't give him her usual disinterested greeting.

"Anyhow, we're going to go to the church. We will see you later," Elizabeth said.

"You ladies gonna be at the festival?"

"Why, yes, we will be there," Elizabeth said, her face showing interest.

"I will be looking for you. Y'all have a great day."

Jeff then left, and Elizabeth watched with a grin.

With a smirk on her face, Ruthanne turned to Elizabeth. "What was that?" she asked.

"What are you talking about?"

"What was with the quick hi and goodbye? That's not the Elizabeth I know."

"Well, it was nothing. I really want to see what the church looks like."

Ruthanne mumbled, "That little liar. I bet it's because I didn't give him my usual cold hi. This girl is truly special at times." Ruthanne whispered to Annabelle, "We're going play a little game with Elizabeth. Just follow along, okay?"

Annabelle, curious with what Ruthanne was up to, said, "Okay."

"That Jeff was so handsome." Ruthanne grinned. "I've never met a man like that. I wouldn't mind marrying after meeting him."

Annabelle's eyes got big, and Elizabeth's mouth dropped.

"Did you see the shoulders on him and his cute smile? Not to mention that nice blond hair and beautiful brown eyes. I think I may give him more than a dance at the festival."

Elizabeth couldn't tolerate Ruthanne's fake fascination.

"Ruthanne!" Elizabeth said. "How can you speak of behaving like a whore!"

Ruthanne irritably replied, "Are you calling me a whore, Elizabeth?"

"If you want to act that way, then yes, I am," Elizabeth answered, her tone passive. "He's a great man from what I see, and he does not need to be corrupted by such behavior. He was so nice to me and Annabelle. He's handsome and tall, and he has a nice voice. You can't behave like a whore to get what you want." Elizabeth frowned and crossed her arms. "No friend of mine should ever behave like that."

Ruthanne muttered, "Uh-huh, I thought so. So, are you saying there's a better woman out there for Jeff?"

With an uneasy tone, Elizabeth replied, "Well, not exactly. Maybe he's not the right guy for you. I mean, you're beautiful,

Ruthanne, but maybe if you feel so strongly about him, maybe that's a bad thing." Wringing her hands together, her tone became anxious as she said, "I don't understand why you would go so fast."

With the same grin as before, Ruthanne looked at Annabelle, and Annabelle figured out what she had done.

"For someone so interested in finding a man, you seem to have a rough time admitting that you like him."

Realizing Ruthanne had tricked her, Elizabeth stormed away, grunting and balling her hands into fists. "You, Ruthanne, are an evil-minded, twisted person. No wonder you can't get a man!" Elizabeth said.

Ruthanne laughed. "Wait, Elizabeth, it's not like I did let him have me."

Annabelle shook her head, trying not to laugh while Ruthanne continued laughing at Elizabeth's frustration. They followed after Elizabeth.

"Oh, slow down," Ruthanne said.

"Why should I? You don't really care. You just want to see if you can get a good laugh again."

"That's not true. Come on. I want to see what this church looks like. I'm sorry. I shouldn't have said what I said."

Elizabeth stopped and turned around, looking at Ruthanne's sympathetic eyes. "You're sorry...fine. Let's go to the church."

Ruthanne smiled. "Now, was it really that difficult?"

"Oh, shut up, Ruthanne. You're a difficult woman."

They strolled through town, looking at all the different people.

Annabelle thought, *If God brought me this far, surely he can bless me again.* Then she caught sight of the massive building. "That's a nice church," she said.

"For a town this size, that church is quite large," Ruthanne responded. "I wonder why they built it so big? There can't be more than eight hundred people in this town. Who else could they be expecting to fill it up?"

"Maybe a lot of people traveling from Jefferson City come through here," Elizabeth said. "That would explain why the church is so big."

"Hmm...maybe, but I think there is more to it than that," Ruthanne said.

With the sun at high noon, the ladies entered the building as if divinely guided to it.

"Wow, it looks even more magnificent up close," Elizabeth said.

"I'm afraid to touch the doors," Annabelle murmured, shaken by its presence. Annabelle grinned, adding, "I've never been in a church before, so I'm nervous."

While Ruthanne and Annabelle stood in amazement by the church's majesty, Elizabeth hurried to the doors and pushed them open.

"Oh my," Elizabeth said as she walked backward. "I've never seen anything even close to what this church is. It's like a small palace in here. There's even an upper level."

Annabelle and Ruthanne moved behind Elizabeth.

"Wow, who built it?" Ruthanne asked, looking at the brown pews and stained-glass windows depicting several biblical events.

"I don't know the word to describe it," Annabelle said, staring at the large pearl-colored angel statues sitting beneath the stained-glass windows. "Look at those angels. It's like they're just watching us, isn't it?"

"Only three of them. They look more like warriors than angels. Look at the muscles on that one! They really look like they could win a war if they had to."

"Well, that's the point," said a white man as he walked toward the women. His soft tenor voice was engaging. Tall and young, he had brown hair and brown eyes with a masculine physique, carrying a Bible in his hand. He wore a high-collared beige shirt and a green cravat, covered by a lavish green vest and navy striped trousers.

"You see, angels are not only God's messengers, but they're

warriors as well. So, I had the statues of the angels look more warrior-like, rather than peaceful. Some people object to the stained glass too, but I'd rather have them more realistic than idealistic. It catches people's attention more, and it encourages a curiosity for them to read the Bible."

"Wow, that's brilliant," Ruthanne said. "So, I assume you came up with the idea since you speak so passionately about it," she said with a smile.

The man tried not to smile and humbly replied, "Yes."

"Are you an architect?"

"Oh, no. I'm not an architect. I'm Pastor Avail. Peter Avail at your service, ladies, and this is my church."

"You look so young for a pastor," Elizabeth said.

"Thank you. Yes, I'm not that old. Some of the town's people have a problem with it, but age doesn't exactly determine your spiritual knowledge."

Ruthanne smirked. "I'm Ruthanne, and this is Elizabeth and Sasha."

"Pleasure to meet you," Annabelle said.

"The pleasure is all mine," Peter said. "By the way, when we are in the church and there is no church service, please call me Peter. I feel more comfortable that way. So, you must be free, Sasha."

"How did you know that?"

"For one, you feel free to speak to me; two, your clothes are nice; and three, the way Ruthanne introduced you to me was no different than how she introduced Elizabeth. You ladies must be good friends and new in town. We're having a festival soon in front of the church, and you ladies are welcome to attend."

"Yes, we've been hearing all about it from different people," Elizabeth said.

"Really, so are you ladies just passing through, or are y'all living here?" Peter asked.

"We'll be living here for a little while," Ruthanne said. "We're mostly getting Sasha on her feet so she can support herself."

"So is one of your husbands coming here soon as well?" Peter asked.

"Who said any of us were married?"

His tone showing concern, Peter replied, "It's unusual for women such as yourselves to be alone, especially if there isn't a man around to provide."

Ruthanne gave Peter an annoyed grin. "My father gave me enough money to pay for rent in this town. Also, we have the protection of Mr. Keys, as we are living in the upper quarters of his house."

"I see. Well, that's great to hear. New beginnings can be quite exciting as long you keep in mind that God won't let you go through something you can't handle. All things are possible through him, no matter how impossible they seem."

"Wow, did you practice that today?" Ruthanne said with a flirtatious giggle.

Peter gave an apologetic look. "Oh no, I guess it came out that way. My apologies. I didn't mean to preach."

"No, it's quite alright. Made me feel good," Annabelle said.

"Great! Well, I'm glad you ladies are staying with the Keys family. They're great people. If you can get ahold of Rebecca's pie recipe for me, I'd appreciate it." Peter laughed. "I hope to see you ladies on Sunday then."

"Of course. By the way, which angel is over there?" Ruthanne asked

"That would be the archangel, Michael. The other one over there would be the archangel, Gabriel. It brings great comfort walking in these front doors and seeing those two. It reminds me to be strong and remember who God is."

"I'm hoping to always have the same feeling when I walk in here. It was a pleasure to meet you, Peter."

"Yes, it was," Annabelle said.

"I look forward to hearing you preach on Sunday," Elizabeth said.

Peter replied, "I'm glad to have met you three."

The ladies left the church feeling excited to return.

"Oh my, I feel so free," Elizabeth said.

"Yes, I know what you mean. It feels like that place was filled with love," Annabelle said.

"I must say, I've never been to a church that I was excited to go to," Ruthanne said. "I mean, those statues were so realistic. It was like looking at the real thing. I felt closer to God just by being in the doorway of that church. I wonder how old Peter is."

"He can't be more than twenty, I'd say," Elizabeth said.

"I would say he is twenty-two. That would make him older than me," Annabelle said.

"Annabelle, I doubt it," Ruthanne replied as she smiled. "I think he's maybe twenty-five at most, especially since some of the people in town have a problem with his age, but he is quite handsome."

"You're walking a little faster than usual, Ruthanne. What's gotten into you?" Elizabeth asked, apparently unaware of Ruthanne's attraction to Peter.

Ruthanne slowed and thought, *Maybe I've shown that I've gotten too excited.* Turning, she replied, "Nothing. I was thinking about the festival coming up. It should be quite the experience, don't you think?"

"Oh...well, yes. I think it'll be quite a fun time. Annabelle, have you ever gotten the chance to leave the plantation for something exciting?"

"No, I'd never left the plantation until I escaped from it. Only thing exciting we'd ever see was the occasional Indian walking by. It was said they were taking in slaves, but Master Brown would say they would scalp us if they got to be alone with us, so we were scared of them."

"That bastard would make something up like that," Ruthanne said, her tone noticeably irritable. "Well, Annabelle, we'll make sure this will be an event you'll never forget. Elizabeth, I guess this is your chance to try on your new dresses when we get back home, isn't it?"

"I almost forgot about those dresses. Thank you, Ruthanne," Elizabeth said.

Ruthanne shook her head and thought, *This girl forgets about a huge chest full of clothes. How on Earth is she going to be a good mother?*

"I guess I can try on my other new green dress y'all bought me as well," Annabelle eagerly said.

"Look at you, so full of life," Ruthanne said.

Annabelle smiled. "I'm grateful for the new life God has given me and the people he has brought in my life."

Elizabeth grinned at Annabelle before turning her smile to Ruthanne.

As the ladies turned the corner, Marilyn grinned and called, "Elizabeth, Sasha, Ruthanne, wait! I'm glad I ran into you." Marilyn jogged toward the girls, exclaiming, "You must come to the store! I have some new perfumes you must try!"

Ruthanne gave Marilyn a blank stare, but Elizabeth smiled and squealed. Annabelle, on the other hand, was more interested in trying on the new dress waiting to be made.

Marilyn, with a huge grin, grabbed Elizabeth's hand. "Come quickly!"

Elizabeth ran off with Marilyn, calling over her shoulder, "Come on, girls!"

Ruthanne grunted, and Annabelle shook her head, thinking about the dress waiting for her back at their new home.

Marilyn rushed into the store. "Come on, Elizabeth."

Elizabeth quickly entered Pots's Garments after letting a carriage pass in front of her.

"We're here," Ruthanne and Annabelle said, breathing heavily while they entered the store.

"I'd never thought they'd run so fast to smell perfume," Annabelle said as she crouched.

Ruthanne, breathing heavily, replied, "They both have problems with their minds."

Ruthanne and Annabelle moved further into the store, still breathing hard. However, the aroma of perfume was so strong, they had to leave the store immediately.

"Oh my God," Ruthanne said, gasping for air.

Coughing with tears filling her eyes, Annabelle said, "How do they do it, Ruthanne? Judy Mays never used perfume like that. Was that a lot of different perfumes or just one?"

"I'm hoping that smell is from a lot of different perfumes because if that's just one, Elizabeth isn't taking that home with us," Ruthanne said, still struggling to breathe. "Are you ready?"

"Yes, I can breathe better now."

"Okay, let's go inside. Hopefully, the smell of perfume won't be so strong this time."

"I hope you're right."

The ladies walked in the store, "What took you two so long," Marilyn anxiously said.

Ruthanne answered, "We had to get some air, Marilyn. Annabelle and I do breathe air like normal people."

Annabelle and Ruthanne looked around with eyes wide, but they still had to wave their hands around and try to clear the smell of perfume.

"Goodness, where did you get all of these from?" Ruthanne asked.

"We got a shipment from Jefferson City. It's so exciting. Now, I can sell perfume and dresses. It's a dream come true for me."

Ruthanne looked at Marilyn sternly and thought, *Between Elizabeth and Marilyn, I might go crazy.*

"Well, I'm mighty happy for you, Marilyn," Annabelle said.

Maintaining her firm expression, Ruthanne rolled her eyes and waited for Elizabeth to finish looking at all the perfumes.

"Elizabeth, now don't you go pick something so strong our entire home is going to be smelling like it," Ruthanne said.

Elizabeth boldly replied, "Why not, Ruthanne?"

"Because I refuse to wake up in the morning smelling it, going into our home smelling it, or going to bed smelling it. The way you are, you would use it so much, it would kill a bloodhound's ability to smell."

Elizabeth gasped. "How dare you say that! I would never

use it that much. No matter how much I may like it, I do have my limits, thank you."

"Right..." Ruthanne said, her tone sarcastic.

Annabelle smelled the different fragrances.

"Wow, Marilyn," she said. "This one is so lovely. What's in it?"

"I'm not so sure, but I know it does have some lilac in there for certain," Marilyn said.

"What is a lilac?" Annabelle asked.

Marilyn cheerfully replied, "It's a lovely flower. I tell you what, since my pa hasn't come back yet, I'll give you this for free."

Annabelle gasped, "What!"

"No, really. I like you, and I think this will wear on you nicely, especially if you're trying to impress a man."

"So, you think this would attract a good man?"

"Yes, I believe it will. I can tell you're smart, so the perfume increases your power of control," Marilyn said as she smirked.

Annabelle recognized Marilyn's smirk as a friendly introduction to manipulation. "There's more to you, isn't there?"

"Well, I don't want to be dependent on a man, but I wouldn't mind the company of one. My papa has tried to have me married twice, but I didn't know one, and the other one was too controlling. He wanted a slave more than a wife, so I told him to go sleep with pigs."

Annabelle laughed. "You remind me of my friend, Judy Mays."

"Well, I'm sure. It's a good thing for there to always be a few smart women around. I can read, though my pa doesn't like it. He believes in old ways."

"Wow, you can read too."

"You can read, Sasha! That's exciting! You should read my Bible with me sometime."

"I'd like that."

"We'll have to keep it our secret, especially since you're not supposed to be reading. I learned how to read by listening to my pa read the newspaper to himself while I stood behind him, pretending to play. Then I'd have him read the story over to me. I've only become good at reading for about four years now."

"Ruthanne and Elizabeth know I can read."

"Oh, well then, we'll keep it a secret still from my Pa. As I said, he holds strong to the belief that no Negro or woman should be able to read."

Annabelle smiled. "Alright, sounds fine with me."

Ruthanne, curious about the conversation Annabelle and Marilyn were having, walked up. "What did you find?" she asked.

Annabelle answered, "Marilyn is giving me this lovely perfume. Smell it."

Ruthanne looked back to see if Elizabeth was paying attention.

"I'll try it for you, Sasha. That smells lovely."

"Well, it's hers now," Marilyn said, smiling cheerfully.

Ruthanne thought, *If Elizabeth sees Annabelle getting this perfume, she'll buy ten more.* "I don't think I could take it," Ruthanne abruptly said.

"Take what?" Annabelle asked.

"Let's keep this a secret that you were given the perfume. If Elizabeth sees you have something, she's sure to buy ten or more perfume bottles, and I think that would drive me crazy."

Annabelle grinned. "Alright, I'll walk out the store now."

"Good thinking. We'll be out in a minute."

The women heard a backdoor close just as Annabelle was about to exit the store. A white man with grayish-brown hair, standing slightly taller than her with a slow and confident walk, came from the back of store.

With a little rasp in his voice, he asked, "Who are you, nigger?"

Annabelle froze and slowly turned around. As her eyes locked on the skinny man, she saw him pull out a revolver and aim it at her.

"Oh no," Marilyn said.

"The name is Mr. Pots. This is my store, and I don't allow niggers in here. So give me one good reason why I shouldn't pull the trigger, you thieving nigger?"

Marilyn stepped in the way of the gun her father held.

"Marilyn Alice Pots, you let this nigger in here, didn't you?"

"Pa, I won't let you treat her like that. She purchased the item she is holding and behaved like a good free nigger should," Marilyn calmly said as Mr. Pots put his revolver down.

Mr. Pots replied with a frustrated tone, "Well, what could a nigger afford 'cause she sure the hell couldn't afford a dress unless she stole the money."

"She bought one of them new perfumes, Daddy. It doesn't even smell nice. I just wanted to get rid of it because I didn't want the other ladies to find it."

"Well, I guess that'll do. What's your name, nigger?" Mr. Pots calmly asked as he rubbed his short grayish beard.

"Her name is Sasha, old man," Ruthanne bickered.

"Old man, old man," Mr. Pots angrily said. "Listen here, you redheaded devil with your deceitful green eyes—"

"Deceitful green eyes? How you dare say such a thing? You obviously bring misery into people's lives with your rudeness. You're a depressed bastard!"

Mr. Pots's wrinkles tightened around his brown eyes. "How dare you say such a thing to me! I could have you hanged. And I'm not depressed. I work hard every day for my daughters... that makes me happy."

"And there is only one here!" Ruthanne arrogantly said.

"My other daughters like to live on the other side of town, and Marilyn is my youngest jewel. She makes me proud. However, now that she's letting niggers in here, I have to rethink my policies. Sasha seems like too nice of a name for a nigger. Tell me something, can you read, Sasha?"

Marilyn shook her head, implying that Annabelle should lie.

"Why, no, Mr. Pots. I can't read at all," Annabelle said.

"Good. At least you know your place," Mr. Pots said in an assertive tone. "Well then, I guess I can at least like you enough to let you come in the store. You know, Marilyn can't read that good, but she can count well, so no nigger is gonna be surpassing my sweet angel."

"Yes, Mr. Pots. I would be happy if I could count correctly."

Mr. Pots looked up with a smirk on his face. "Well, that's not gonna happen here, little Sasha. Niggers don't have the smarts us white folks have, and you never will. Best you can do is please a man or maybe make nigger babies, but since you ain't a slave, the best you can do is please a man."

"That's enough, you old bastard. We're leaving," Ruthanne said.

Marilyn forcefully smiled and whispered, "I'll have to thank Ruthanne for giving me a new name to call my father." She then reverted to the daughter Mr. Pots expected. "Alright, ladies, that's fine. Come back anytime," she said. "You're welcome too, Sasha."

"Only if she comes with one of these two lovely ladies is she welcome here!" Mr. Pots hollered.

"I'm sure at least one of us will come back with her, you old bastard. This is the only fabric store in town," Ruthanne said.

"I'd prefer if it wasn't the red-haired devil," Mr. Pots uttered.

Ruthanne stalked toward Mr. Pots. "Look here, you old perver—"

"Now, Ruthanne, we have an appointment to keep," Elizabeth said, placing her hand over Ruthanne's mouth.

Once Elizabeth took her hand off Ruthanne's lips, Ruthanne muttered, "I guess you're right."

Annabelle, still upset with her confrontation with Mr. Pots, said nothing.

"We'll see you later, Marilyn," Elizabeth said, forcing herself to smile.

The ladies left quickly, avoiding any more arguments with Mr. Pots.

Mr. Pots left the store, muttering, "Crazy, rebellious women. They've got some nerve to even consider talking to me like that.

Those ladies must be new here in town. What do you think, Marilyn?"

Marilyn replied, "Well, Pa, I'd say they may be new here, but either way, they're fun customers."

"You can't allow disrespectful behavior. I taught you better on how to handle customers like the redhead.

"You're not up here enough to show me how."

"Hmm, that reminds me... I need to find you a husband. I won't be around forever, and God forbid I leave you alone."

"Pa, I wouldn't be alone. I do have my sisters to help take care of me."

"Yes, but they all live on the other side of town, and you know they can't be there all the time for you. You know Anne is expecting to have that baby soon, and the others... Well, they should be giving me some grandchildren soon."

Marilyn, aggravated by her father's views, rolled her eyes and went back into the store, mumbling, "You old bastard."

Annabelle and the other women made it back to their home, and before they could walk up the stairs, Rebecca came out with a grin.

"Ladies, come inside and have some pie," she said.

They gladly accepted her offer and came inside the house, excited to try some pie at the dining room table.

"What kind of pie did you make?" Elizabeth asked eagerly.

"I've made my best today, blueberry pie," Rebecca said.

"Oh my, blueberry pie! I haven't had that in such a long time!"

"I've never had it before," Annabelle said.

Rebecca smiled at Annabelle. "Prepare to be amazed and enjoy," Rebecca said. "I believe it's only right that you get the first slice, Sasha."

Rebecca cut a nice big slice of the pie and put it on Annabelle's plate.

"This does look good."

"That looks so delicious," Ruthanne said.

Annabelle stuck the fork into the pie and took a bite. Her eyes filled with satisfaction and joy. "Wow, this is amazing," she said. "I could eat this all day! It's so good."

"Why, thank you, Sasha," Rebecca said with a warm smile.

Rebecca handed Ruthanne and Elizabeth their plates, and they immediately took bites of their pieces.

"This is unbelievable," Elizabeth said. "You should be teaching me how to do this instead of these two."

Annabelle giggled while Ruthanne gave Elizabeth a humorless gaze.

Rebecca sat down with the ladies and helped herself to a piece of pie after looking outside at Ashley. "It is quite nice to have the company of other women around. It's a lot easier than to deal with a child and a man."

"Is everything working out alright?" Ruthanne asked.

"Yes, things are actually great. It's really a matter of me having some alone time so I can gather my strength back. Ashley is such an active child. I mean, I'm grateful for it, but my goodness. She is completely incapable of sitting down for ten minutes. Other than that, things are great for me. I'm a blessed woman. How about you all? You've had to have met some new people besides Mr. Boston."

Ruthanne smirked. "You've talked to Mr. Boston?"

"No, Allen did. He stopped by there to pick up some food for me, and they had a nice talk. Mr. Boston is quite pleased to see some new faces in town, and he even offered to take all of you to the festival." Rebecca chuckled.

"Yes, Mr. Boston is quite something, but I think I could go for Mr. Fluffs before Mr. Boston," Ruthanne joked.

Rebecca laughed with the women. "I could see that."

Rebecca continued, "So, Annabelle, tell me something. How do you think you're going to fit in this town? There's few people here that are for you."

Annabelle was hesitant to answer, but she replied, "Well, I

believe God can provide me with what I need, and I'll have to pray to him for guidance."

"Well now, that's the best answer any woman has ever given me. People truly have the uncanny ability to make situations worse. Most people who have a serious problem only go to God when things are bad or when they think there's no other way. People don't take the time to pray to God, to casually speak to God, or to simply thank Him. We try to live our lives to not need God. Some people treat others in that fashion, living their lives while trying to achieve a goal, and not realizing there are plenty of opportunities for God to put what they need right in front of them. It's an unstable way to live, and it leads to unhappiness."

"How so?" Elizabeth asked, captivated by Rebecca's wisdom.

"Did you know in Luke 11:9-10, it says: 'And I say unto you, Ask, and it shall be given you; seek, and ye shall find; knock, and it shall be opened unto you. For every one that asketh receiveth; and he that seeketh findeth; and to him that knocketh it shall be opened.' That means don't complain to God about something you didn't ask for. He'll say, 'But you never asked for it,' even though he knows that's what you want or need. It is more like a term of an agreement. You acknowledge God by asking him for things, and he'll be happy to bless you if it's meant for you at the right time."

Annabelle smiled while she listened to Rebecca's wisdom.

"I have a question that seemed to escape the minds of many people," Rebecca said. "How is it that you women were able to travel alone without a male relative or at least a male friend?"

Ruthanne was stunned by Rebecca's question. Annabelle had nothing to say, and Elizabeth couldn't think of anything. Rebecca looked at the women's expressionless faces.

"My father was quite fine with us coming here. My cousin, Harold, escorted us. We have plenty of money to take care of ourselves," Ruthanne said.

"Yes, that's quite true," Elizabeth said.

"What about you, Sasha?" Rebecca asked.

"Well, my family is free and was actually pleased for me to

have the chance to go with them. You know...find something good for me and live peacefully. There's not many places for a Negro woman to go and live peacefully, so my family didn't mind me leaving as long as I'm with Ruthanne and Elizabeth."

Rebecca looked at the girls, judging the expressions on their faces. She gave a slight nod as she ate the last piece of her pie before lightly tapping her fork against the table. She then grinned at the women. "Woo! I feel so full from that pie."

"It was mighty good," Annabelle said.

"I'm glad you enjoyed it, Sasha. Elizabeth, so tell me how it was growing up in the capital?"

"I didn't grow up in the east," Elizabeth said convincingly.

Ruthanne slightly bit her lip as her grip tightened on her plate out of Rebecca's sight.

"No, silly. I meant Jefferson City, not the capital of the country." Rebecca chuckled.

Ruthanne mumbled, "Please don't realize how stupid Elizabeth is at this moment."

Elizabeth laughed. "My goodness. Silly me. Well, it's a nice city. I love it."

Rebecca smirked, asking, "How did you come to befriend Sasha? It is quite rare for white women to be allowed to befriend a Negro woman, even in this state."

Elizabeth suddenly looked uneasy. "Why, my parents were quite different than other white people. They were always strict with me as to how we would treat others. It didn't matter what color they were. We are all God's children."

"That's great you were raised in such a manner. So, again, how long have you ladies known each other?"

"Since we were children," Ruthanne said.

"That's a long time. So, when is your birthday, Sasha?" Rebecca asked.

Elizabeth replied, "Well, it's—"

"Oh no, Elizabeth, my apologies. I was asking Sasha."

"In the month of May," Annabelle answered without hesitation.

"In the month of May?"

Ruthanne tightened her grip even more as she tapped her foot. "God, I know most slaves don't know their birthdate, but please let her know," she whispered to herself.

Rebecca glanced at Ruthanne, asking, "Did you say something, Ruthanne?"

Ruthanne smiled and shook her head.

"Oh, okay. Sorry." Rebecca smiled at Annabelle, asking again, "So, what's the date?"

Unprepared for such a question, Annabelle blinked quickly and dropped her gaze downward. "Oh, the date of my birthday." She gave a nervous laugh. "My momma always would say it's when the birds sing the loudest."

"When do the birds sound the loudest?" Rebecca asked in a curious manner.

"They always sing the loudest on the seventh."

"Is that right? I'm quite impressed with that. I'm born on May eighth, so isn't that nice?"

Annabelle's throat tightened and she wiped her mouth. "Wow."

"I'm quite pleased to have met someone else born in May. It's such a lovely time of year. You know, my mother always said that May is lovely because it's the time of the year when you can really see parenting at its best. Look at the birds, for example. The male sings his heart out all throughout late March and April to prove himself to the female. He finds a mate, and they raise helpless little hatchlings usually starting in May. So, I do find it quite interesting how you were told May is the time when birds sing the loudest."

Ruthanne and Elizabeth started to become uncomfortable while Rebecca picked up their plates, went into the kitchen, and set them on a counter. Rebecca came back into the dining room and sat down.

"So, Ruthanne, when were you born? You seem like a summer baby, as feisty as you present yourself."

Ruthanne tried her hardest to smile when Rebecca returned to the table.

"I was born in August. August 24th of 1827," Ruthanne said.

"That makes a lot of sense," Rebecca replied with an innocent smile. "So, Annabelle, tell me about your parents. They must've had a hard time raising you in this state since it's a slave state. Why didn't they go up north?"

Ruthanne slightly sighed as she stared at the table.

"It was hard growing up," Annabelle nervously said. "I really didn't have any friends except Ruthanne and Elizabeth. So, to have them here with me makes me feel pretty good about my past."

"Well, I'm surprised a beautiful woman such as yourself isn't married by now. It's quite shocking to me. Even for a Negro woman, you're quite beautiful."

"Oh, well I've...just not found the right man. I... I don't want to marry a man I don't love."

Rebecca looked at Annabelle's face and saw her resolve. Ruthanne began to twiddle with her fingers underneath the table.

Rebecca smirked. "I completely agree with that approach."

Elizabeth remained seated quietly.

"I'm sure we've all experienced spoiled little boys," Rebecca said. "If I saw one in particular today, I'd give him a punch in the nose."

Annabelle suddenly became fired up.

"I'm with you there," Annabelle said. "Men really only think about one thing anyway, from my experience. It makes me feel so disgusted and powerless."

Ruthanne gave Annabelle a concerned look, but Annabelle was focused on Rebecca, and she continued, "I could go another year or two without a man touching me at all, as far as I'm concerned. No seems to mean nothing when it comes from a woman."

"Well said," Rebecca enthusiastically responded.

Elizabeth began to feel awkward.

"But what if you find a good one?" she asked.

"Elizabeth, I think Jeff is fine for you," Annabelle said. "You clearly like him, but as for me, I really don't need a man right now. I'm still young, and I'm beautiful."

Rebecca stood up with her hands on her hips as she laughed, seeming to acknowledge Annabelle's determination to be independent. Ruthanne giggled.

"Keep telling the truth," Rebecca said.

"Show me a man who can cook besides Mr. Boston, who lives alone," Annabelle said firmly.

The women laughed.

"Show me a man who realizes the amount of work it takes to raise a child and says thank you," Rebecca said. "Show me a man who realizes that just because you say 'howdy, ma'am,' I'm not impressed."

The women continued to laugh.

"Show me a man who realizes that I do have intelligence," Ruthanne insisted.

"Show me a man who knows how to clean a baby," Rebecca said.

"Well, show me a man who doesn't mind that I can't cook," Elizabeth said.

The others looked at Elizabeth and laughed out loud.

"That may take you some years," Rebecca said.

"At least that skill I do possess," Ruthanne said, holding her stomach to contain her laughter.

Rebecca quickly looked out the window at Ashley as the others continued laughing.

"You know what? I was going to tell you ladies something," Rebecca said. "I honestly wish my husband knew how labor pains feel."

The women gasped, but Ruthanne suddenly began to laugh and almost fell on the floor. Rebecca and Annabelle also began to laugh, while Elizabeth looked at the others, confused.

"Why wish such a thing?" Elizabeth asked.

"So he would appreciate me, Elizabeth. I mean, I'm surprised after long nights of nursing Ashley, I didn't kill him for leaving everything on me, including cooking while she cried."

"Did you ask him to help?"

"The one time I did, he frowned and said that he thought all of it was my responsibility. The nerve. That conversation went on for almost an hour about our responsibilities. Now, he's much better, but I wish he knew what I went through," Rebecca admitted.

"You're good. I've heard stories from my cousin. She's been married for seven years." Ruthanne snickered.

"There are days that it becomes more of a job than enjoyable, like I'm taking care of another child."

"Yeah, tell me about it," Annabelle blurted.

Rebecca's eyes widened, "What!"

Ruthanne gasped, "Oh no!"

"How much do you know of it? Have you had a child?" Rebecca asked.

"No, she was talking about Mr. Brown," Elizabeth blurted.

Ruthanne smacked the back of Elizabeth's head. "You're unbelievable!" she snarled.

Rebecca folded her arms. "Well now, who is Mr. Brown, Sasha?" she asked.

Ruthanne stood up quickly. "Look at the time. I believe it's best we go now."

"Have a seat. I knew something was quite unique about you ladies ever since you came here. I was trying to see if Sasha was going to be the one to crack since she doesn't exactly fit the picture with you two."

"How so?" Elizabeth asked.

"Two wealthy, young white women befriending a Negro woman as structured as this country of ours is? I have a hard time believing wealthy white people in this state would be so freely open to their daughters befriending a Negro girl. Even in the free states, it's a rarity. Sasha being with the Indians is far more believable. So, be so kind as to tell me who this Mr.

Brown is? I have no intention of telling anyone else. Something I truly believe is nothing happens by coincidence, and God has his ways of having the truth come out. I truly believe he has brought you three here for a reason, and I want to be a friend and a guide for you ladies, so let's start at the mystery behind this Mr. Brown person that Sasha clearly feels strongly against."

CHAPTER 9
Truth Revealed

ANNABELLE BOWED HER HEAD, CLENCHED her hands, and in a monotone, said, "Mr. Brown was my master in Columbus, Mississippi. That's all I know is we were in Columbus, Mississippi. I've never left the plantation, so I don't know much."

Ruthanne exhaled, then said, "We are all from Columbus, Mississippi. Elizabeth and I were traveling up to Missouri to explore the cities. We don't exactly have permission from our families. We came across Sasha, or should I say, Annabelle, when she was running away."

Rebecca glanced at Annabelle with a smirk and said, "So, it's Annabelle and not Sasha. Besides being a slave, why were you running away. Do you have family?"

"My momma pushed me to run away when another slave was caught," Annabelle answered. "All the overseers were gathered and setting him on fire. I was Mr. Brown's bed slave almost every night. It started when I was sixteen." She frowned, then continued, "It got to the point that I would keep the light on and lie in my bed, waiting for him. During the first year, he started touching me more than Mrs. Regina, his wife. I got tired of being woken up to please that man. I saw no end to it, and my parents... It was killing them that they could do nothing. I couldn't tell Judy Mays, my best friend. How would she feel to find out her daddy was forcing himself on me, her best friend, not to add that I'm a slave." Annabelle began to become more upset, wiping a tear from her eye. "It was such a horrible feeling every night, not knowing if that man was going to touch me." She began to sniff, trying to hold in her tears. "Forgive me. I shouldn't be crying about this. It's done and over with."

Rebecca placed her hand on Annabelle's hand. "No, don't apologize for having feelings. I can't imagine what it must've felt like being forced by that man," she said. "It breaks my heart to hear of such a thing. It is sad the hypocrisy that goes on in our country. These men call themselves Christians but commit adultery. In addition to that, they commit rape and act like it is a normal part of life. You're an amazing woman, Annabelle."

Annabelle beamed at Rebecca. "Thank you."

"As for you two... For y'all to break the law and help a runaway slave come this far."

Elizabeth bowed her head, and Ruthanne unremorsefully folded her arms.

"I congratulate you for doing a remarkable and bold thing. If only more people were like you two ladies. I really admire that."

Ruthanne and Elizabeth smiled at Rebecca.

Elizabeth let her breath out while her smile faded.

"I almost did the wrong thing," she said. "And I just can't imagine what you would've gone through if I had turned you in, Annabelle."

Annabelle touched Elizabeth's hand and replied, "But you didn't."

Elizabeth wiped a tear from her eye and grinned. "You're a stronger woman than me, and I don't think I could have made it as a slave. The things you had to do, and to be treated so badly... I feel horrible that I never paid attention to my own slaves back at home."

"So, your family owns slaves?" Rebecca asked.

Elizabeth answered, "Yes, we have about forty slaves on my family's plantation. I've never noticed all the things they do. Most of my time was spent in the house or in town, so I never really noticed them out in the fields. My daddy kept me away from a lot of how things were run. As he would say, it's not a woman's place."

"Well, I bet if you'd seen everything, it would've changed your mind a long time ago," Ruthanne said. "I saw everything that was going on, even as a child. I would see slaves get beaten, have their fingers or toes cut off, get dragged by horses, and even hanged and burned. The truth is that I've always had plans to leave Mississippi, Elizabeth. I hate every bit of it. How can we call ourselves Christians but support such an evil way of life? It's so hypocritical!" Ruthanne said with a firm voice.

"You have strong words of wisdom," Rebecca humbly said. "I see this country of ours getting closer to having a major outburst over what is right and what is wrong. Some people may even lose their lives standing up for the right thing. There are times when God calls on us to do the right thing unexpectedly and not at a moment of our choosing. Many times, it's hard to do the right thing. You ladies may not realize it, but our country is divided. I've listened to Allen have talks with the other men in the city, and it is serious. There are people who have purposely moved here to vote and keep slavery in the state of Missouri."

"But how can them moving here keep slavery in the state?" Annabelle asked.

Rebecca replied, "The men vote on it and decide what law is and what law isn't."

"So do y'all get to vote too?"

"No, women are not allowed to vote, something else I wish would change."

Annabelle folded her arms and cynically responded, "So, not even a white woman can vote at all. I guess a Negro woman will never have the chance if y'all can't even vote."

"It's a serious thing, and you will find plenty of men who don't think we should vote."

"I never really saw it as a problem," Elizabeth said.

Ruthanne rolled her eyes and slapped her hand on the table.

"My goodness, Elizabeth, you can't be so slow to think about this type of stuff!" Ruthanne yelled. "Learn to question some things at some point in your life. They are not God, the laws are not perfect, and they certainly are not fair. We are only a few steps above a slave. Think about it. Some men still don't like women to even read. How stupid is that, Elizabeth?"

"Ruthanne, calm down," Rebecca said. "I understand the frustration you feel, but Elizabeth is an example of what they have been molding women to be. So, I do see it being a while before we can vote like men."

Elizabeth gave an apologetic stare at everyone while she took a deep breath. It had been a long time since Ruthanne had shown so much anger toward her. She frowned at the other women.

"I remember my father telling me all I needed to know was how to cook, clean, and provide children for my future husband," Elizabeth said. "I never thought of it limiting what I could do with my life." Elizabeth sighed and balled her left hand into a fist, adding, "He would even take books from me."

Ruthanne had never seen such an expression on Elizabeth's face before. "Are you okay, Elizabeth?" she asked.

"I'm mad that I never really thought of the roles of a woman like that. I mean, I just... I can't believe it took me this long to really see the only things that were expected of me. It makes me feel so stupid for living my life that way and not following anything I really liked to do."

"I completely understand. I felt the same when Judy Mays taught me how to read the Bible," Annabelle said. "So much we were told by the master wasn't true, and it made me so mad to learn the truth. It's hard to accept, but I've learned to try my best to not follow everything. If you go against everything, your life will be sad and lonely."

"Yeah, I guess you're right, Annabelle, but I certainly don't feel like being bothered by any man for a while," Elizabeth said.

Rebecca giggled and stated, "My goodness, at the rate you ladies are going, you'll be lucky if you get married by the time you're thirty years old."

"I probably do need that long to give a man a chance in hell," Ruthanne said.

The women laughed.

"Ruthanne, whoever you marry will have to have the patience of Job," Annabelle said.

"Whatever, I'm not that difficult. I did smile for Jeff."

"That's right," Elizabeth said. "You did that just to see me react."

"It's not like I like the guy anyway. Blond hair isn't exactly an attraction for me," Ruthanne said.

Rebecca asked, "Which Jeff?"

"He's some guy Elizabeth met the first day we got into town," Ruthanne sarcastically said.

Elizabeth's nose slightly scrunched while she gave Ruthanne an aggravated stare.

"Jeff Taylor is not just some guy!" Elizabeth yelled. "He's sweet and kind and handsome. He even treated Annabelle nicely, and he didn't even know who she was to me."

Rebecca beamed, replying, "Well, I've heard he's a nice man."

"Why, thank you, Rebecca. At least somebody has some confidence in my man-picking abilities."

Ruthanne erupted with laughter. "Really! Would you care to talk about the ones before Jeff?"

Elizabeth's eyes became big and filled with embarrassment. "No, that's not necessary," she said.

Ruthanne smirked. "We'll start with Robert, who had the dreamiest blue eyes you had ever seen. That's until you caught him and Jean Johnson in his barn getting a little more than comfortable. Or how about Jonathan, who seemed liked such a good gentleman until he told you that you couldn't even talk to me anymore, then you found out he was married to a woman in

New York. And my favorite, Billy from Birmingham, Alabama. What a man he was."

Elizabeth shouted, "Now, there's no need to go there!"

"Hush, it is old news."

Elizabeth folded her arms, frustrated with Ruthanne's pursuit.

"Now, Billy seemed like a nice guy. However, after courting this man for two months, Elizabeth finds out he has not one child, but four other children by a married woman."

Ruthanne began to hysterically laugh as Annabelle's and Rebecca's mouths dropped. Elizabeth sat, angered by Ruthanne's amusement.

"So, are you telling me that man was having an affair with a married woman?" Rebecca asked.

Ruthanne answered while she continued to laugh, "Yes, ma'am, that's what I'm saying."

"How do you know the kids were his?"

Ruthanne cleared her throat. "Well, she had been married to her husband for how long, Elizabeth?"

Elizabeth murmured, "Eight years."

"Eight years!" Ruthanne shouted out, laughing.

"Oh my," Rebecca said, giggling while Annabelle shook her head. "Do you think the man knows that the children are not his?"

Ruthanne replied, "Well, when both of you are blondes, and your kids come out with red hair, it should make you wonder."

"Wow, how sad is that," Annabelle said.

Rebecca stood up and sighed. "That must be a hard thing to live through. Do y'all want some tea?"

"Thank you, Rebecca," Elizabeth said. "I need something to calm my nerves since Ruthanne can't keep her mouth shut."

Ruthanne placed her hand on Elizabeth's cheek and said, "I'm just explaining why I lack faith in your man-choosing abilities." She gave Elizabeth an unapologetic smile, adding, "And who are you to talk about people who can't keep their mouths shut?"

Elizabeth rolled her eyes. "You don't have to make me appear incompetent in the process."

"Annabelle, did you want some tea?" Rebecca asked.

"I'll have some, Rebecca," Annabelle said.

"Not a problem." While Rebecca started to go toward the kitchen, she asked, "How did you find out about his children?"

Elizabeth answered, "When I was walking through town one day with my sisters, she approached me and talked to me alone. She explained the whole situation to me. It was quite hard to hear, but I could see she wanted him involved in their lives, and if we were to have wed, it would have made things more complicated. So, I ended the relationship between us and moved on."

Ruthanne chuckled. "You mean for a moment, you didn't have the words of a Christian woman."

Elizabeth turned to Ruthanne with a stern look. "You really find that one funny," she said.

"Maybe just a little," Ruthanne sarcastically said.

"It was better for you to have done that than to deal with the drama that would have come afterward," Rebecca said. "Just think of it this way: God has someone more worth your time waiting for you."

Elizabeth replied, "Thank you, Rebecca."

After heating water for tea, Rebecca sat down at an oak rocking chair in the living room while the young women followed her. Annabelle and Elizabeth sat in chairs while Ruthanne stood in front of the wooden coffee table.

"There will always be some form of drama that enters our life. We have to hold on and not lose faith. There truly isn't anything in this world that God won't let us go through that will destroy our destiny. It may hurt, but in the end, things will work out."

"Well, I'm going to head upstairs to imagine my new dress," Ruthanne said.

"Since when are you excited to put on a dress?" Elizabeth asked.

As Ruthanne was about to say something sarcastic, Mr. Keys opened the door and came in.

"Good afternoon, ladies," he said.

"Hi, Mr. Keys," the young women responded.

"Hello, honey," Rebecca said.

Allen smiled. "I hope I wasn't interrupting anything you ladies were talking about."

"No, you weren't. I was heading upstairs for a moment to think about my dress, Mr. Keys," Ruthanne said. "I will be back a little later for my tea."

"Getting ready to show off your dress?" Mr. Keys asked.

"No, I won't show it off until the day of the festival. There is no need to shock the world yet."

Ruthanne headed upstairs.

"She makes me so mad at times," Elizabeth said, folding her arms.

Mr. Keys chuckled. "Well, she is certainly confident in herself." He sat on the sandy-colored checkered couch and continued, "The festival looks like it's going to be even better than last year."

Rebecca replied, "That sounds wonderful, Allen."

"Hildebrand is causing a little bit of a problem though." Sitting back on his couch, Allen sighed deeply.

"What is it that he's stirring up trouble with?"

"Mr. Hildebrand wants there to be no Negroes or Indians to be allowed to come to the festival. He has a few of the other business owners on his side. However, Mercy doesn't have any laws stating Negroes and Indians are not allowed at the celebration."

Annabelle sighed, and she began to feel uncomfortable, wondering if she'd have the chance to experience a town festival. Mr. Keys placed a hand on her shoulder.

"I don't want you to worry about this situation. I promise I will fight this issue to my best ability if it comes up again, Sasha. Makes no sense to have no rights to even show your face at a public event. That's too extreme. Who knows what new laws that man will try to create?"

Annabelle beamed and replied, "I believe you, Mr. Keys. It must be hard, even as a white man, to stand up against someone like that."

"There are some men in this world of ours that seek to gain positions of power by being appointed by God, but there are others that go out to seek it for themselves. The people that seek out power for themselves have no interest in truly improving our society or following the teachings God put forth. Jesus talked to both the Jew and the gentile. He connected with both, and we should follow such an example of how to live. Mr. Hildebrand is an unfortunate example of a hateful man."

Rebecca moved from the rocking chair to the couch to sit next to Allen. "That's what we're supposed to stand up against, right?" Rebecca asked, giving him a reassuring kiss.

"Sure, dear," Allen said, smiling. "Sasha, have you and the others had a nice tour of the town so far?"

Annabelle answered, "Yes, I've had a great time so far meeting a few new people. Some are quite different, like Mr. Boston."

Allen laughed, replying, "Ah, yes, Mr. Boston. I do enjoy his company. Have you met Mr. Fluffs?"

Annabelle and Elizabeth laughed.

"That's the biggest cat I have ever seen," Elizabeth said.

"And we stopped by that nice store, Pots's Garments, with all those clothes in there," Annabelle said. "We've met Marilyn Pots, and I have a feeling that we'll become good friends."

Rebecca giggled and said, "Oh, yes, I bet the two of you would make great friends."

"Yeah, I believe it can be a great friendship there, but my goodness, there is one problem."

"What would that be?" Allen asked.

Elizabeth sighed. "Her father, Mr. Pots, came in from the back of the store when all three of us were there. He was a nasty old man, or as Ruthanne said, an old bastard."

Rebecca began laughing hysterically. "I can't help but to laugh at that," she said.

Allen also laughed a little. "It sounds like you lovely ladies will do fine here in Mercy," he said.

"If Ruthanne doesn't make any more enemies here, I believe we will," Elizabeth joked.

"What enemies has she made?" Allen asked.

"Well, Mr. Pots. He calls her the redheaded devil, and there's Mad Moe."

Allen and Rebecca stared with blank looks and bulging eyes.

"You ladies ran into Mad Moe?" Rebecca asked.

"What happened?" Allen questioned.

"Well," Elizabeth said, "he and his men came up to us drunk."

"Okay, and what happened?"

"Mad Moe said some inappropriate things, and Ruthanne gave him a nice hit to the face. She hit him so hard, he didn't get back up, and his men carried him away."

Allen and Rebecca looked at Elizabeth, dumbfounded.

Allen stuttered, "Ruthanne knocked out Mad Moe with one hit?"

"Yeah, one hit and he was lying on his back," Annabelle said.

"Oh my," Rebecca said.

"What's wrong?" Annabelle asked.

Allen stared at Annabelle and Elizabeth in disbelief as he shook his head. "You ladies will have to avoid that man for quite a while, Elizabeth," Allen said with a fretful tone. "Mad Moe is actually a very dangerous man that's suspected of more than one murder, and I'd hate for any of you to become a target of his."

Elizabeth replied, "Well, we'll have to make sure we stay clear away from those men, won't we, Sasha?"

Annabelle gave Elizabeth a concerned look.

"Of course we can stay away from them," Annabelle said.

"I'm sure you ladies will do fine once the whole incident is completely forgotten about," Allen said.

The talk of Mad Moe did nothing but remind Annabelle of the dream that had troubled her so much.

Annabelle stood. "I guess I should also go and imagine the dress Marilyn will make for me."

"Well, I'll stay here. I'm enjoying the conversation," Elizabeth said.

"So, it seems you're going on the same trail as Ruthanne," Rebecca said.

"What do you mean?" Annabelle asked.

"I guess you're not letting anyone see you in the dress until the day of the festival."

Annabelle giggled, replying, "I guess I can copy Ruthanne in that way. She has some habits that I really like." Excited, Annabelle left the house and headed for the outside stairs that led to the second floor.

"That Sasha is truly something special, I have to tell you, Allen," Rebecca said.

"Yes, I think you're right. I think God has a funny way of bringing people into your life," Allen said.

Elizabeth beamed and said, "I think that as well."

"Well, come help clean these plates," Rebecca said.

"Of course, Rebecca," Elizabeth replied.

As Annabelle climbed the stairs, she had flashbacks of the dream. She began seeing the beautiful woman she'd seen in her dream. Annabelle held her head anxiously and thought, *I can't be losing my mind now. I need to go inside so nobody can see me like this.* She went inside, breathing heavily and attempting to calm herself down.

"Who is that?" Ruthanne asked.

"It's me, Ruthanne," Annabelle said.

"Hey, stay out there for a little bit longer so I can take this dress off."

Annabelle sat on the couch. "Are you sticking to your word about not letting anyone see you in your dress?"

"Of course, I have to keep my word to the best of my ability. I'm going to be too beautiful. Can't wait until Marilyn makes it. Elizabeth better tie Jeff down if she wants to keep him, and Mr. Pots won't be calling me a redheaded devil. Trust me; that old man is going to feel young again in more than one way."

Annabelle laughed. "Ruthanne, you're something."

"I promise you that I'll have Mr. Pots asking me to give him more children," Ruthanne said, chuckling.

"Trust me; you'll be doing all the work with that man."

Ruthanne stuck her head out of the bedroom door. "Annabelle, that was quite a dirty thing you said."

Annabelle crossed her legs and replied, "Meh, it's the truth."

Ruthanne chuckled. "I'm going to remember that one. I can see it now. I'm sorry, Mr. Pots, but I need a man who won't have me doing all the work."

Ruthanne laughed hysterically, and Annabelle joined in.

"Now, Ruthanne, I didn't say it like that."

"It's okay, Annabelle. I give you full credit for the idea." Ruthanne walked out of the room in her dress. "What's on your mind? I can see something is bothering you."

"Mr. Keys mentioned that we need to stay away from Mad Moe when Elizabeth told him about you knocking him out. They think Mad Moe may be responsible for a few murders in the town, so he wants us to be extra careful not to run into that man."

Ruthanne frowned. "I guess I do have a special ability to attract the wrong kind of attention. Is that all that's bothering you?"

"I had a flashback of the glowing woman like I fell asleep standing up. It was really scary. I thought I was going crazy."

Ruthanne sat down next to Annabelle and held her hand.

"Don't worry about it so much. If you worry, it will drive you crazy. Now maybe you were just daydreaming to get Mad Moe out of your mind. I mean, there's much more to think about, like how you're going to look in that dress."

Annabelle felt relieved by Ruthanne's assurance.

"Well, go ahead and try the dress on that I told you about earlier. I'm sure you'll look rather wonderful."

Annabelle went into the bedroom, excited by the thought of looking more valuable than a slave. She began to close the door.

"Wait, I want to help put it on," Ruthanne said.

"Oh no, that's okay. I like your way of thinking, and I want to try to get it on myself."

Ruthanne smirked and said in a manipulative tone, "Well, alright. I guess I'll have to be patient like you'll have to be patient to see me in my dress."

Ruthanne was about to turn the doorknob, but Annabelle's head suddenly poked out the door, and she looked at Ruthanne.

"That was a nice try. You know I want to see your dress on you too," Annabelle said before closing the door again.

Ruthanne stomped her foot and folded her arms. "Ugh, I guess I'll have to wait."

Annabelle put the Victorian green dress on, looked in the mirror, and placed her hands over her mouth. Her heart filled with joy as she thought, *I look just as beautiful as Judy Mays. I'm no longer a slave.*

Continuing to look in the mirror, she couldn't stop smiling at herself. She turned toward the door, wondering how Ruthanne must look in her dress. Annabelle looked back into the mirror, twirling around to see how it felt to be in an elegant dress and imagining it was hers.

"Annabelle, are you alright in there? You know it's not healthy to get stuck looking in the mirror, honey. You'll end up with Elizabeth's intelligence if you keep it up."

Annabelle stopped looking at the mirror and began taking off the dress. "That's not funny at all, Ruthanne."

Ruthanne laughed. "But it's true."

Ugh, Annabelle thought, *I can't believe I feel like taking this dress off because of Ruthanne saying something like that.* She put on her blue dress again and left the room, trying not to appear in haste.

"Wow, you came out of the room faster than I thought you would once I said that," Ruthanne shrewdly said. "And with no help."

Annabelle went into the kitchen, frustrated that Ruthanne could read her actions. "I wanted to get something to eat and didn't want to ruin the dress."

Ruthanne giggled. "Okay, if you say so, Annabelle. So, do you feel like you will have the men staring at you?"

"I don't know. I'm not really thinking about looking good for the boys, but I think the dress looks great on me. Thank you for letting me try it on."

Ruthanne smiled at her. "It was nothing. I know the dress Marilyn will make you will also make a great impression. Besides, we all need a new beginning at some point in time."

"I guess you're right. So, what did you think of Rebecca's story about Mr. Keys?"

Ruthanne crossed her legs and sat back on an old oak couch. "Well, it does make me think twice about not pushing every single man away. Even though I'm not in a rush to get married, I guess it would be foolish to pass up a good-hearted man because he appears sooner than I wanted him too. Honestly, I hate it in a way."

"Why can't men wait and relax? We're not going anywhere."

"Trust me; I bet for most of those men, it's about the sex and them thinking they'll have someone to control." Ruthanne folded her arms and deeply exhaled. "I'm jealous of what Rebecca and Mr. Keys have. It's quite something special, isn't it?"

"Yeah, they have something special between them," Annabelle reluctantly said.

Ruthanne slightly pouted while she looked out the window. "Anyway, the day is almost over, and the sunset is in full bloom."

"This day did go by quite fast, didn't it?"

Ruthanne nodded and asked, "Where did Elizabeth go?"

"She's still downstairs with Rebecca and Mr. Keys."

"She's still down there talking, eh? I guess some things won't ever change." Ruthanne stood up and stretched her arms. "We can get supper ready. Elizabeth still can't cook anyway."

As Ruthanne and Annabelle prepared their supper, Elizabeth came in. "Something smells mighty good. Can I help?"

Annabelle and Ruthanne looked at each other.

"Umm, you can set the table," Ruthanne said.

"Okay."

After preparing everything, the ladies sat down, prayed over their supper, and enjoyed their meal. Afterward, Annabelle began cleaning the dishes and was still thinking about the glowing woman she thought she'd seen.

Ruthanne asked her, "You still thinking about the glowing woman?"

Not wanting to worry Ruthanne Annabelle lied, "Oh no I'm not thinking about that I'm tired."

"Well just remember I'm around to talk."

Annabelle smiled at Ruthanne, saying, "I won't forget to say something if I'm worried."

Ruthanne smiled, "Alright I'm off to the bedroom to read."

"I'll be there soon, once I finish cleaning up the kitchen."

"I'll get Elizabeth in here. She's only messing with her hair."

"You don't have to do that."

"Ha, trust me Annabelle I do. The last time Elizabeth probably cleaned anything was her shoes when she stepped in mud."

Ruthanne went into the bedroom and hit Elizabeth with a pillow. "Go help Annabelle clean the kitchen."

Elizabeth bitterly replied, "Ugh, why don't you?"

Ruthanne sharply answered, "I know how to clean a kitchen. You, on the other hand, only know how to wipe yourself down and dishes."

Elizabeth grunted and walked into the kitchen. "Hey, Annabelle, what do you need help with?" she asked.

"Just a few things," Annabelle said.

"So, are you excited about the upcoming festival?"

"Well, yes, I'm a little excited. I've never been to one, so I guess I should be a little more excited than I feel now."

"Don't worry about it. I'm sure you'll feel full of excitement on the day of the festival. There will be so much to do that you'll have a hard time choosing what to do first."

"Wow, it will be that exciting? What's there to do?"

"Yes, it will, and a lot of people will be there. Some have competitions for best livestock. Some have acrobats and tricksters. It will be hard to not have a great time and enjoy the day. With all the different food and fun games that will be going on, I'm sure it'll be a little overwhelming for you."

"What do you mean by overwhelming?" Annabelle asked.

"Your mind will have a hard time thinking of what to do because you feel so good."

"That does sound like a fun time."

"Well," Elizabeth responded, "everything here is cleaned up and ready to be used tomorrow, so let's go to bed."

Elizabeth and Annabelle went into the bedroom, only to find Ruthanne passed out on her bed with a book on her chest.

"She likes to think she's so tough." Elizabeth snickered, putting a blanket on Ruthanne. "Well, Annabelle, I guess we should join her."

Annabelle yawned and raised her arms. "Yeah, it has been a long day today."

"You have a good night, Annabelle," Elizabeth said, lying in bed and blowing out the lamp.

"You too, Elizabeth, have sweet dreams."

Elizabeth smiled and fell asleep.

Annabelle turned on her side and thought, *I hope I have sweet dreams.*

After Annabelle fell asleep, she heard her name being called, so she opened her eyes and saw nothing but light. She squinted, noticing that she was outside her home and sitting in the middle of the street.

"What's going on?" Annabelle asked. She called for Ruthanne and Elizabeth, but there was no reply. All she could hear was the wind blowing. *This must be another dream*, she thought. She ran to Mr. Keys's door, but when she tried to open it, the door was locked. She began to panic and screamed as she fell to her knees. "Why can't I wake up?"

"Annabelle, don't be afraid," a woman said with a soft voice.

Annabelle turned around, only to see the glowing lady with a face like lightning. She stood in beautiful white clothes with a gold aura. She moved toward Annabelle, and Annabelle scrambled to get up.

"Don't come any closer to me," Annabelle nervously said.

The glowing woman stopped walking. "There is no reason for you to be afraid. I'm not here to hurt you."

"Who are you?"

The glowing woman smiled at Annabelle. "I'm a messenger and a guardian sent from the Father."

"So, you're an angel," Annabelle apprehensively said.

"Yes, I am, and I'm here to guide you."

Annabelle knelt.

"Please stand. I'm not the Father, so please don't bow to me."

Annabelle stood, shaking. "What would an angel want with a Negro woman like me?"

"All of God's children are beautiful and capable of great things in this world, so the color of your skin is of no matter."

Annabelle gave a cry of frustration. "It matters in this world!" she yelled.

"It will change at its appointed time, and nothing can stop that."

"What is your name?"

"My name is Constance."

Annabelle's eyes widened. "I've never heard of a name like that one. Why have you come back to me in my dream when you could have come to me when I'm not sleeping?"

"Because you would have run away out of fear, and talking to you in your sleep allows me to talk without you running."

"So, in other words, you would rather talk to me in my dream when I'm unable to wake up and forced to listen to you."

"You can look at it that way if you want." Constance put her hand on Annabelle's shoulder. "Would you prefer it if I were to wake you up?"

Curious as to what the angel had to say, Annabelle seriously thought about it. "I'll agree to stay asleep."

"Very well. Now, let's change the scenery a little."

Constance waved her hand, causing the bright noon sky to change to a sunset. Annabelle looked around in awe to see that instead of being in the town, they were now standing on a mountain.

"It's so beautiful, Constance. How did you do such a thing? I've never seen anything like it."

Constance replied, "Feel the presence of the Lord. With your spirit and heart, listen."

Tears ran down Annabelle's face. "What is the purpose of this?" she asked.

"There will be a brief period during which you'll face giants who have become accustomed to destroying lives."

"Giants? Do you mean Mad Moe?"

"Yes, and others," Constance said.

"Please don't allow them to harm me."

"Annabelle, the devil walks the Earth like a prowling lion looking to devour anyone that he can. This is also true for the demons that are under him, and unfortunately, you find evil humans. So don't be afraid, for the Lord is with you, and I'm here to give you the message to help strengthen you. The Bible that Judy Mays gave you, continue to read it." Constance wiped the tears from Annabelle's face and gave her a hug.

"Never in my wildest dreams would I have ever expected to receive a hug from an angel," Annabelle said.

"Even the wildest dreams can come to pass no matter what the world says."

Annabelle glanced at Constance. "I have questions. Who were those Indians that were in my dream?"

Constance moved away from Annabelle. "Walk with me."

Annabelle joined the angel, and an eagle flew down to perch

on Constance's shoulder and spread its wings. Annabelle gasped and stepped back while she looked at the large bird.

"There's no reason to be afraid," Constance said.

"That's a huge bird! I've never seen anything like it."

Constance grinned. "This is an eagle."

"So, that's what an eagle looks like!" Annabelle looked at the bird, astonished by its beauty and size.

"I've read about them in the Bible when I was with my friend, Judy Mays."

"Yes, Judy Mays took a large risk for you. The eagle is mentioned twenty-three times in the Bible, and its time you began to prepare to spread your wings like the eagle."

"Who were the Indians in my dream?"

"I can't tell you right now who the men are, but they're meant to be in your life. In the coming future, you will face some troubling things, but the Lord thy God won't allow you to go through anything that will kill your destiny."

Annabelle exhaled deeply. "God thought enough of me to send me an angel." She looked up into the sky and shouted, "Thank you, God, for showing your love!" She gave the angel a hug.

"Thank you for coming to me."

Constance smiled at Annabelle. "I'm more than happy to do the Lord's will."

Annabelle felt the spirit of God descend on her and give her strength she had never felt before. She became filled with so much joy, she began dancing and shouting out thanks to God.

Constance sat down on a rock, observing. "This is the presence of the Lord you're feeling."

Annabelle was so overjoyed, she didn't know how to stop, and tears of joy fell down her face. She finally stopped dancing but couldn't stop moving, still overwhelmed by what she felt. "I gotta do something. I gotta sing something."

Constance replied, "Okay, sing out with your soul."

"Will you sing it with me?" Annabelle asked.

"Of course. Whenever you're ready, let's sing to the sunrise."

Constance raised her hand to the sky, and the sunset became a sunrise.

"It's beautiful." Annabelle smiled. Looking at the astounding scenery, she began to sing, and Constance sang with her.

"God, thank you for showing me your love, and thank you for not letting me go! I'm so blessed. Your love is more than I imagined, and I must say, I'm more than thankful. You sent me help when I felt so lost and gave me strength when I was weak! I must shout it out that you're more than amazing, your love endures forever, and I must sing of our great God. You saved me from the chains and have blessed me with more than enough. Just as you rescued Daniel from the lions, and just as you rescued the Hebrews from Pharaoh, you rescued me. So I say thank you for changing my life."

"What a lovely song."

"Thank you. I sang what was on my mind and in my heart."

"It's a good thing you're learning to let go and let God work things out. There are many people that learn this and forget this the moment their trial has passed. Be careful not to make this mistake. Tomorrow will be a new day for you. My message has been given."

Constance began to walk away.

"Please wait. Who are the Indian men?" Annabelle asked.

Constance turned around. "Well, if you really want to know, Annabelle..." Constance raised her hand and snapped her fingers.

Annabelle woke up, realizing that she had been released from the dream. She sat up in the bed, disappointed. She exhaled and looked to her left, and there stood Constance. "You stayed," Annabelle mumbled in disbelief.

Constance sat down on the bed and smirked. "So, I'm thinking this time, you won't run from me."

"The dream was real."

"Not really. Our talk was real, but the rest was in your dream. Now, as for those Indian men that you're so interested in, those men are meant to be a part of your life. So when you meet them, don't be quick to judge them. There's more to come, and that's why you must not see with your eyes but with eyes of faith for what God is promising you."

"So, I'm not to be quick to judge the new people I meet?"

"There will be new people that you meet, some good and some bad."

"Well, that seems to be the pattern that has been going on lately. Mr. Pots isn't exactly the nicest person by far, and he doesn't even like Ruthanne, and she's a white woman."

"Mr. Pots is lonely. He's a depressed man who doesn't know how to handle the pain of loss. Unfortunately, as time has gone on, he has learned to push people away with no interest in learning how to love again. His daughters are the only thing he's living for, instead of turning to God to help him heal. He has been on a dangerous road for a long time, but his heart isn't as cold as he believes it is. Unfortunately, some of the bad people you will encounter are quite different than Mr. Pots and truly are evil, so don't lose faith when you encounter these heartless people."

Annabelle nodded her head. "So this is only the beginning."

"Don't be afraid. God will bless you with someone quite special. Everything has an appointed time, and God forgets none of his promises," Constance firmly said.

"I want to thank you for appearing to me while I'm awake. I feel so honored and blessed to speak with you outside of my dreams, and I don't know how to thank you enough. Can I wake Ruthanne and Elizabeth so they can also see you?"

"Not this time. Their faith will have to continue to grow differently than yours."

"When will I meet the Indian men?"

"You will meet them at the appointed time. No matter how much time goes by, don't lose faith in what you have been told. I believe that it's time for me to go and take care of some other tasks."

"Before you go, can you promise me that you will visit me

again? I don't mind having an angel as a new friend in my new life."

Constance happily looked at Annabelle and gave her a hug.

"I will be around when I'm needed, so no matter how bad things seem to be going, remember that."

Annabelle disappointedly huffed. "Well, alright. Thank you again for doing this for me."

"It was my pleasure, Annabelle." Constance's aura suddenly became brighter, and she disappeared.

Annabelle sat back in her bed, filled with joy and excitement. *God is really thinking of me*, she thought. While the moonlight shined through the window, she looked over at Ruthanne and wanted to tell her what had happened. She took a deep breath to try to calm down from the excitement because she couldn't stay still. *Annabelle, get ahold of yourself. You can't tell Ruthanne or Elizabeth,* she thought. *They will think you've lost your mind.* She struggled not to shout out with joy, and she felt such a relief, even though she'd received a message that there would be a time of struggle. All she could think of was that God thought so much of her that he sent an angel to her. Annabelle calmed down and smiled as she lay in her bed, falling asleep.

"Annabelle! Annabelle! Annabelle!" Ruthanne shouted at the top of her lungs, causing Annabelle to fall out of her bed.

"What's going on? Did something happen?" Annabelle asked.

Ruthanne laughed. "Good morning, Annabelle."

"Ugh, I can't believe you did that."

"Aw, no worries. It's 9:00 a.m. We have things to do before the festival."

"Did Ruthanne wake you up?" Elizabeth asked.

Annabelle yelled, "Yes, she did. She scared the life out of me, screaming in my ear."

"Get used to it. That's what I had to tolerate."

Ruthanne giggled. "So, we're getting fitted by Marilyn today, and how about we go check out the rest of town?"

"I think that sounds like fun," Annabelle said.

"Let me help you up since I did scare you out of the bed."

Annabelle held out her hand, and Ruthanne grasped it. Ruthanne tried to pull her up, but instead, Annabelle tugged Ruthanne over the bed.

Ruthanne screamed, "Annabelle!"

Ruthanne fell over to the other side of the bed, and Annabelle laughed.

Elizabeth rushed into the bedroom. "What happened?" she asked.

Ruthanne sighed. "Well, she got the best of me and pulled me on the other side of the bed."

Elizabeth began to laugh. "Don't be a sore loser, Ruthanne. You had it coming."

"Whatever, I always win in the end," Ruthanne said.

Annabelle looked over to Ruthanne. "I'll be ready soon."

"That sounds good to me." Ruthanne said, standing to stretch her back.

"Before I forget, Elizabeth cooked the eggs, so I'd be careful of eggshells if I was you."

Annabelle gulped and thought, *I think I'll skip breakfast today and take an apple with me.* She washed up and left the room, planning to grab an apple and walk downstairs. With her hand stretched out, Annabelle thought, *I'm so close to it.*

"Annabelle, there you are," Elizabeth eagerly said.

Annabelle thought, *How did she do that? I didn't make a sound.*

"Guess what I made?"

"What did you make?" Annabelle asked with a fake smile.

"I made scrambled eggs, and I've been waiting for you to test them out. I did break a shell, but no worries. I did get the shell out."

Annabelle became frustrated and thought, *How Ruthanne got out of this mess amazes me.*

"Come on. Have a seat."

"I'm sitting. Can you please calm down? I'd hate to see how you would act if you got a present."

"I'm sorry. I'm so excited! Ruthanne got up a little earlier and said she ate some apples, so she wasn't hungry when I got done making the eggs."

Ruthanne is too smart for her own good, Annabelle thought.

"Well, lucky me. I'll be the first person to test this, right?"

"Yes, you will!"

God, Annabelle thought, *you send me an angel at night but let me go through hell during the day. This is too much.*

Elizabeth placed a plate of scrambled eggs in front of Annabelle.

Annabelle looked at the scrambled eggs. *Oh...the eggs look a little more like soup.*

Elizabeth sat down, waiting for Annabelle to take a bite.

Annabelle nervously took the first bite of the runny eggs and shrieked in her mind. *Oh no, she didn't check to make sure they're cooked all the way.*

"So, how is it?"

Annabelle struggled to swallow the first bite. "I can tell you put your heart into this."

"Yes, I did. This is the second batch. The first somehow turned black, and I know that's not right."

Great, she didn't season the eggs. Annabelle cleared her throat and asked, "Could you pass me the salt?"

"Sure thing! Here you go."

To season the eggs, Annabelle put three teaspoons of salt on them. She decided that she could handle taking a few more bites, but there was something different about the second bite. She began to chew and felt something crunch. Elizabeth was still looking at Annabelle, excited that she was eating the eggs she'd made.

Okay, Annabelle thought, *I'll have to do something crazy.* She forced her small bit of food over to the side of her left cheek.

"Not too bad once you put salt on them, eh?"

Annabelle struggled to smile with the food in her mouth, "Oh no, it's not too bad since you only learned just now."

Elizabeth stood up with a big grin and her hands on the table. "I'll put up the saltcellar."

Annabelle reached the saltcellar and said, "It's okay."

"I insist. You're kind enough to sit down and try my cooking. It is the least I can do."

"Well, alright." Annabelle picked up the saltcellar, and a brilliant idea came to her. She began to hand the saltcellar to Elizabeth and then let it slip and fall on her plate, spilling salt all over the eggs.

Elizabeth gasped. "I'm so sorry."

"It's quite alright, Elizabeth, everyone makes mistakes."

"What a mess!" Elizabeth picked up the saltcellar. "I ruined the food. I'm so sorry."

"Don't worry about it. I wasn't that hungry, so don't worry about it. I know Ruthanne must be waiting for us anyway. We should get going and get fitted, then see the rest of the town."

"Actually, I'm going to stay when we visit Marilyn and see if she's made anything new. You and Ruthanne have a good time and stay away from Mad Moe."

"Trust me; I don't plan on seeing that man."

"I believe you, Annabelle. It's Ruthanne I'm a bit worried about."

"Yes, she does have a weird way of attracting attention," Annabelle said, standing.

"I'll be down in a little bit," Elizabeth said.

"Okay, we'll wait for you."

Annabelle went outside, spit the food out, and headed downstairs to join Ruthanne in getting fitted and touring the rest of the town. As Annabelle climbed down the stairs, she witnessed Ruthanne eating an apple. Annabelle stopped on the last step and stared at Ruthanne angrily.

"You have a lot of nerve leaving me alone up there to test Elizabeth's cooking," Annabelle said.

"I wasn't going to eat that stuff," Ruthanne said with a full mouth.

"So you left me to suffer instead!"

"I'm sorry. Was it that bad? The whole thing didn't have eggshells in it, I hope."

"No, just my second bite had eggshell in it. To spare Elizabeth's feelings, I had to trick Elizabeth into thinking she spilled the saltcellar on the eggs so I could leave. I just spit out the food, but you were too busy enjoying your apple."

Ruthanne laughed. "That was smart. That's quick thinking."

"When you work for crazy people for most of your life, you learn a few things. So, which way are we going today?"

"I think we can go explore the west side of town. It is the only part of the town we haven't walked through yet, so let us see the glory of the west side."

"Alright, when Elizabeth comes down, let's go and hurry back before it becomes hotter."

Elizabeth soon came downstairs, and the young women traveled to Pots's Garments. Marilyn took their measurements for a dress. During the fitting, the young women had a fun conversation. After Marilyn finished, Elizabeth decided to stay, but Annabelle and Ruthanne left. Annabelle and Ruthanne strolled for several minutes and passed by Mr. Boston.

"Hello, ladies," Mr. Boston said.

"Hi, Mr. Boston," the women said.

"I haven't seen you ladies for a few days now. Has everything been working out?"

"Yes, Mr. Boston, things have been going good for us mostly," Ruthanne said.

"Mostly? Why only mostly? Have you ladies experienced something unpleasant?"

Ruthanne exhaled. "We had a nice encounter with Mr. Pots yesterday."

"Mr. Pots, that miserable old man."

Annabelle and Ruthanne snickered over Mr. Boston considering Mr. Pots old and not himself.

"That man hasn't been the same since his wife, Emma, passed away. How sad it is to see a once happy man become bitter and cold."

Annabelle chuckled. "He named Ruthanne the redheaded devil."

"My goodness, Ruthanne, you made an impression already," Mr. Boston joked.

"I do seem to have a talent," she replied.

"Now I have something to laugh about with Mr. Fluffs. So, I assume that you ladies are going to the west side of town?"

"Why, yes, we haven't seen anything over there yet."

CHAPTER 10
Shadows of the Darkness

Mr. Boston frowned, realizing that Annabelle and Ruthanne might soon see the ignorance and racism in the town.

"Mr. Pots is nothing but a grub compared to some of the monsters you might meet walking into this side of the town," Mr. Boston said. "Especially you, Sasha. Do you remember the man I told you to stay away from?"

Annabelle replied, "Yes, I do. His name is Mr. Hildebrand."

Mr. Boston nodded. "The supply store on the right side of the street belongs to Hildebrand, so don't even bother going in there at any time."

"So, this is where the town becomes ugly," Ruthanne said.

"My dear, calling it ugly isn't even close to the best description of this side of town," Mr. Boston said. "You would even have difficulty with some of the people on this side of town, Ruthanne."

"Let me guess. My red hair and green eyes."

"You amaze me with your sense of humor and sarcasm."

Ruthanne replied, "It helps keep my day brighter, Mr. Boston."

"I bet it does, but the two of you must stay together. Nobody will care about something happening to a Negro woman."

"Has something happened before on that side of town?" Annabelle nervously asked.

Mr. Boston answered, "Yes, a few years ago, a murder happened on that side of town. It was Mad Moe and his thugs who were involved. Unfortunately, the investigation did not go on for long because a weapon couldn't be found. The investigation was also discontinued because the man that was murdered was a Negro. He was unarmed, and the few witnesses that were around said he was returning to the east side of town, and they heard a gunshot. The problem with most of their stories is Mr. Kennedy, who owns two of the saloons on either side of town, said the man was in his saloon getting a drink when Mad Moe and his thugs surrounded him. He stated that they threatened the man, and to avoid a fight, the man left the saloon. Unfortunately, the man never made it back to the east side of town. So, we have a murderer roaming free in this town of ours, and it sickens me."

Ruthanne held Annabelle's hand and said, "We'll be quite alright, Mr. Boston."

"Well, alright. You ladies come right back to this side of the town though," Mr. Boston reluctantly said. "I have to get back to the store and open it up, and I'm sure Mr. Fluffs wants some company."

"Well, have a good day," Annabelle said.

Reluctantly, Mr. Boston walked away, praying, "God, please protect them, especially if they choose to go on that side of town."

"Should we go there?" Annabelle nervously asked.

"I think we'll be fine," Ruthanne said. "Besides, we need to be familiar with the whole town. Who knows, we may have to go to that side of town. So, you ready, Annabelle?" Ruthanne nervously asked.

"Yeah, we're looking around town. No need to go into any stores," Annabelle said.

The ladies explored, looking at the buildings, houses, and stores.

"It's not so much different than the east side of the town," Annabelle noted.

"All except one thing. For the past five minutes, we've been walking through town, and people have been staring at us."

"What? How can you tell?"

"I can tell because I see people whispering to themselves, and back one block, this woman dropped her groceries. That woman was more than shocked to see you, and maybe even me. I see what Mr. Boston was talking about now. I can see how dangerous this area can be, even at high noon."

The ladies strolled past a saloon when a man wearing a purple vest, which complemented his white high-collared shirt, purple cravat, and beige trousers, stumbled his way through the doors.

"Woo wee! I love my off days," he said.

"Oh my God! Is that Jeff?" Ruthanne asked. She whispered wittily to Annabelle, "He's taken in more than he can handle. He hasn't even noticed us yet."

Annabelle giggled, and Jeff turned his head awkwardly toward them.

"You're Elizabell's friend," Jeff said, tilting over.

Ruthanne and Annabelle laughed out loud.

"What is so funny? Did I miss something?" he asked.

Ruthanne replied, "No, you didn't miss anything. We were just talking about a joke."

Jeff staggered and slurred, "Well, ladies, don't stop the jokes because I'm here. Where is Elizamabeth?"

"Elizamabeth?" Ruthanne began to laugh again. "You mean Elizabeth, right?"

"Well, damn it. That's what I said, isn't it?"

"Not really. You added a few more letters to the name, Jeff," Annabelle said.

Jeff turned to Annabelle. "Are you mocking me, nigger?" Jeff asked.

Annabelle was surprised and began to feel uncomfortable.

"Nigger!" Ruthanne snarled. "Jeff, don't you ever call her that."

Jeff stumbled toward Annabelle. "Now, you listen here. Just because you're free don't mean you have value."

With a nervous expression, Annabelle backed up because he smelled so bad, and she wanted to be out of his range.

"You sure are pretty for a nigger. Thought maybe I can have some time with you before I deal with Elizamabeth."

Ruthanne stepped in front of Jeff. "I don't think Elizabeth will be speaking to you again. It's the middle of the day, and you're drunk," Ruthanne said with an unforgiving tone.

Jeff put his hand on Ruthanne's shoulder. "Now, honey, if you feel so left out, all you have to do is tell me. I wouldn't mind getting time from a redhead. I like the curve on your rump anyway."

Ruthanne smacked his hand off her shoulder. "I'd live in the Sahara before you would even have a chance."

"Well now, you don't have to say it like that. I'm sorry if I seemed rude to Sash." Jeff gave Ruthanne a hug. "I'm sorry. I don't mean any disrespect."

Ruthanne frowned in disgust while she put her hand over her nose.

Jeff stretched down Ruthanne's back and began feeling her butt. "It's so firm and hard."

Ruthanne pushed Jeff back. "Get your hands off me!"

A few townspeople noticed the commotion and began to watch.

"My God, it's the firmest thing I've felt in a long time."

Annabelle's mouth dropped in disgust and shock.

Ruthanne balled her fist. "It's going to be the last thing you will get to feel." She took a swing and punched Jeff in the nose, causing him to bleed and fall.

Jeff whined, "Why in the hell did you do that!"

"Now you will think twice before doing that to another woman! I doubt Elizabeth will want to be speaking to you after this."

Drunk and dazed from Ruthanne's hit, Jeff struggled to get

up. "I'll teach you a lesson, you redheaded whore," Jeff said, holding his nose.

Ruthanne's eyes widened while her mouth slightly dropped. "Whore! Did he call me a whore!"

Struggling to stand while holding his nose, Jeff began to laugh. Ruthanne marched up to Jeff with her fists balled and kicked him between the legs. Jeff yelled in agony and began coughing on his own blood.

"I won't forget this, you witch," he said.

"Okay, it is time to go, Sasha."

"I agree," Annabelle hastily said.

Ruthanne grabbed Annabelle's hand, and they began to jog back to the other side of town.

"Now, hold on a minute, ladies," a man said. He had a deep voice and southern accent akin to Mr. Boston's.

Ruthanne and Annabelle turned around and saw a tall, older white man staring at them with his glacial blue eyes. He wore a black top hat that partly hid his grayish-brown hair. A black frock coat covered a high-collared green shirt, and a marvelous red cravat wrapped around it. His gold pocket watch complemented his fancy, dark green vest. He walked forward in his black trousers, clutching his black walking cane.

"I'm not sure if I can let y'all walk back without giving you a warning."

"I'm sorry, but this woman and I are going back to the other side of town," Ruthanne said.

The man helped Jeff get up, and Jeff limped away, howling in pain.

"That's quite impressive to cause a man so much pain. You must have quite a temper on you, pretty lady."

Ruthanne smirked and replied, "Actually, I'm not so quick to act, but a man can't touch me and expect nothing to happen to him."

"I admire a woman that treasures her body. However, I don't appreciate the presence of the nigger that you have walking around with you."

"Well, I suggest you get used to it. So, what is your name since you seem so interested in my business?"

"The name is Victor Hildebrand, but in this case, I'd prefer it if you called me Mr. Hildebrand."

Annabelle's eyes became bigger, and her grip on Ruthanne's hand began to tighten, realizing who this man was. Ruthanne's grip tightened as well. She understood that he was one of the landowners she had been warned about.

"That's nice, but we will be off now," Ruthanne sarcastically replied, turning away from Mr. Hildebrand.

"Now, hold on. I gave you my name, so what is your name?"

Ruthanne let go of Annabelle's hand and turned. "It is none of your concern, Mr. Hildebrand."

She quickly turned around again, grabbing Annabelle's hand, and they began to head back to the other side of town.

"Now, hold on, ladies. He asked you a question," a young, brown-eyed white man said.

Annabelle and Ruthanne slowly turned around to see another man standing by Mr. Hildebrand. The young man had an average build, hairless face, curly brown hair, and a confident posture.

"The name is Casey Bones, ladies. Now, what are your names?" he demanded with his arrogant southern accent.

"Now, if you wanted to ask so plainly, I may have been more open to giving you my name," Ruthanne said. "However, I have a little bit of a temper compared to most women, if you don't mind."

"I like a little fight in a woman, but showing such disrespect to Mr. Hildebrand isn't tolerated."

"By all means, let me make it more clear for both of you then."

Ruthanne let go of Annabelle's hand, reached into her brown purse, and pulled out her small revolver. Annabelle's eyes widened as Ruthanne cocked the gun and held it at Casey, causing some of the townspeople who noticed to stare in disbelief.

Casey pulled the revolver from his holster and held it to his side. "I like you more already."

"Now, here is your option. Lower your weapon and kick it over here, or take a bullet for a man who would probably push you in front of the bullet anyway."

"You wouldn't dare pull the trigger," Mr. Hildebrand said.

Ruthanne pulled the trigger, shooting at the ground.

"What the hell!" Casey said, feeling the wind off the bullet go past his leg.

Ruthanne replied, "This is your last warning, Casey. Give me your gun."

Casey looked around, noticing that the gunshot had attracted the attention of some of the townspeople. Not wanting to get shot by a woman in public, he placed the gun down on the ground and slid it to Ruthanne.

"What are you doing?" Mr. Hildebrand asked.

"Some of the people are watching what's going on."

Mr. Hildebrand sighed. "Well then, we will have to continue this conversation some other time, ladies."

"Not likely," Ruthanne said, picking up Casey's gun and dropping it in her purse.

Ruthanne grabbed Annabelle's hand and held her revolver in her other hand before running to the other side of town. With the townspeople confused by what had happened, they slowed to a walk and continued as if nothing happened.

"It is far from over, you clever girl," Hildebrand said.

Mr. Hildebrand and Casey went his store, both bitter about the incident and ignoring the townspeople that began to ask questions.

Annabelle and Ruthanne finally stopped to rest once they had reached one of the streets close to the church, and Ruthanne put her revolver back into her purse.

"Oh my God," Annabelle said. "I'm burning up in this hot dress."

"Me too. These things were never made for moving around," Ruthanne said.

Annabelle was still trying to gather her thoughts. "Ruthanne, what happened?" Annabelle said, gasping for air. "I mean, is it normal for you to attract crazy people?"

Ruthanne, still wheezing, laughed. "That was a rush, wasn't it?"

"How can you laugh at something like that? And you keep the gun in your purse!"

Ruthanne sat down, exhausted from running. "Well, it was my daddy's, but I took it once he kept leaving it on the table at home. Come over here."

Annabelle followed Ruthanne.

"Here is where we need to be right now."

"I don't understand," Annabelle replied. "Why are we sitting by the horses' water trough?"

"We need to loosen up." Ruthanne reached for the ladle hanging over the water.

"Ruthanne, there is no way I'm drinking that water. I've eaten leftovers from the masters, but I refuse to drink water for horses."

"Whoever said we were going to be drinking this water?"

Ruthanne dipped the ladle in the water and tossed it on her chest. "Oh my God, that felt so good. Now it's your turn, Annabelle."

"I'm not going to toss water on me like a crazy woman."

"Is that right?" Ruthanne dipped the ladle in the water again. "Now, Annabelle, you can do it yourself, or I'll do it."

Annabelle squinted. "You wouldn't dare."

Ruthanne smirked and tossed the water on Annabelle's chest.

Annabelle gasped. "I don't believe you!"

"Calm down. You're making a big fuss about nothing."

"About nothing? I'm soaking wet now, and what was the point of your tossing the water there!"

Ruthanne poured more water on her chest and began to jump up and down. "Wait and see, Annabelle. I'm going to open your eyes to something."

Ruthanne began to return to their home, and Annabelle followed. When she stopped walking, Annabelle stopped next to her.

"What are you looking at, Ruthanne?"

"I'm looking at those boys over there," Ruthanne boastfully said.

"Why would you, of all people, even care about that right now?"

Ruthanne giggled and answered, "Come on, follow me."

Annabelle gave Ruthanne a suspicious look and followed her.

Before they were in view of the young men, Ruthanne turned around. "I almost forgot. I'm going to need you to jump up and down like I did earlier."

"Why would I do that? That's so childish, and I'm not a child."

Ruthanne placed her hands on Annabelle's shoulders. "Trust me; there's nothing wrong with having a little bit of fun."

Annabelle sighed. "Well, I guess." She jumped up and down. Her breasts poked out more, and she quickly put her hands on top of them. "I don't want those showing."

Annabelle tried to adjust herself in the blue dress, but Ruthanne smacked her hand.

"Don't you dare, you look great. Now we're matching," Ruthanne arrogantly said.

Annabelle's eyes got big, realizing Ruthanne's bust was showing a lot more.

"You troublemaker. You're always finding a way to attract attention," Annabelle muttered.

"Please, Annabelle, I just feel like making heads follow me."

Ruthanne grabbed Annabelle's hand, and they approached the young men. Annabelle noticed two young women sitting down next to the men, and she halted Ruthanne.

"There's two women sitting there. Should we really walk past them, Ruthanne?"

"Oh please, ignore those two, and let's have two seconds of fun."

They went up to the young men.

"Well, hello there," one of the men said.

"Why, hello," Ruthanne flirtatiously said.

"Hello," Annabelle shyly said.

"You ladies must be new in town," one of the other men said.

Ruthanne replied, "Why, yes, we are. We were just going home to rest. I mean, I'm just feeling nearly overcome by the heat!"

The men stared at both Ruthanne's and Annabelle's breasts lustfully.

"By all means, feel free to come by anytime," another man said.

Ruthanne beamed and giggled. "By all means, we might just do that. Well, we're off, boys."

As the ladies began to leave, Ruthanne turned around, eyeing one of the men. One of the men whistled at Ruthanne and Annabelle, causing one of the nearby women to hit him.

"I don't believe you," the young woman angrily said. The woman stood up and walked off, the other woman angrily following her.

"Now, just hold on a minute. That didn't mean nothing," the man said.

As Annabelle and Ruthanne passed a few buildings, they began to laugh.

"I cannot believe that fool actually whistled at us," Ruthanne said. "Anyhow, now you just received a lesson on how easily distracted men can be."

Annabelle shook her head in disbelief while she laughed.

"Let's go see what Elizabeth is up to," Annabelle said.

"Yeah, that girl will get lost in her wardrobe if you let her, but I love her anyway. She's always been there."

Annabelle grinned and said, "Getting those men to look actually made me feel good."

"Well, that was the point. Sometimes, it takes a little extreme behavior to make the day better."

While Annabelle and Ruthanne were returning to their home, Mr. Hildebrand and Casey were riding to the other side of town.

"How dare those two witches disrespect me in such a manner, especially that nigger!" Hildebrand said.

"I kind of like the redhead, though she's crazy," Casey said.

"Don't lose your focus, Casey. We cannot allow such disrespect. If we see them, they'll have to answer to me. That redhead won't be bold enough to pull the trigger against two armed men."

"I don't know about that," Casey sarcastically said.

"For her to be disrespectful and stand up for that nigger is too much, and it cannot be tolerated. If one begins to defend a nigger, then another and another will do the same, causing the state to eventually become a free state. I won't allow such blasphemy to appear while I'm around."

"How much of a threat do you honestly see those two women?"

Hildebrand turned to Casey angrily. "This is how garbage, such as the so-called right to freedom, comes about. All it takes is one person, just one, to stir the pot and cause anarchy in our land. Those Injuns didn't know what to do with land, so we took it from them. Those grass niggers and the niggers in chains are the low ranks of humanity. How do you control two things that are barely human?"

"I'm not sure what you mean."

"We've done it for hundreds of years. We take what belongs to us. The Injuns don't deserve the land. They're an uncivilized and savage race that would rather play in mud and let trees grow instead of building wonderful cities. Indians would rather chase buffalo and deer instead of raising animals on their property like a civilized man. Indian women have political power, and even some of the women are considered soldiers. Few can read or write, and they speak gibberish. The niggers are no different than Indians except they're dumber. God forbid they find an Indian village. I've even seen them take in the niggers, then lie and say that the nigger is their slave. In a couple of weeks, you see the niggers working the land just like the Indian. The nerve of those savages. Even when a few of them tried to be civilized and bought a few slaves, they comforted them. You see them mixed breeds in the deep south still, but they're different than the others out here in the Indian Territory."

Casey gave a confused look and said, "What do you mean by different? Those mixed breeds are at least as human as them full bloods from either breed."

"No, those mixed-blooded niggers in the south. Half of them don't even realize they grass niggers too. They can't even speak that gibberish Indians speak anymore. They as dumb as a normal full-blooded nigger. But the women, when they're mixed just right, come close to the beauty of a white woman. It's a few of them left that ain't slaves and living with them Indians that are still there, but they speak their language and speak English. They still can't read or write like them savages even out here, but sometimes, you can't tell the difference between the master and the slave because they all dress the same. Every year that I've gone out to Indian territory, we've seen more mixed-bloods, so I'm going to educate you, boy. One thing we do is take the manhood from the niggers and Injuns. You do that by killing them all or making them subordinate to our rule. You kill the structure of the families, but that don't really work too well with the Injuns. Sometimes, you gotta kill some of the women because they'll lead like the men. I've never seen that in niggers though, but with them Indians, it depends on the tribe. Some are more savage than the others. The next step is take away the land and don't allow them to own a damn thing. The moment you let them own something, the more knowledge they gain, and they'll find some fool that'll teach them too."

Casey sighed. "Yeah, I can see some of the people in town wanting to show a nigger how to read."

Mr. Hildebrand grunted. "We must keep them chains on

them. Even in the south, I know some men that will still take some Indians for their plantations. Besides, there's no real difference between Negro and Indian. One is just darker than the other with nigger hair."

"Yeah, my daddy always would say them niggers and Indians really ain't no different at all."

"Well, your daddy taught you right. However, at the same time, we can't allow them to work together. That's dangerous."

"Why is that?" Casey curiously asked.

"Because if the two come together in a bond stronger than the one that exists between them niggers and some of the tribes, it'll create another war in this country of ours. It'll be like nothing we have never seen. There are already tribes favoring Negroes, and they've been doing it for a long time. Those Seminoles, Delaware, Pequot—and I even heard that Shawnee—was taking them in. There are almost none of them left, but they have the audacity to take in those niggers. Seeing the redhead protect the nigger reminds me of what the abolitionists are doing."

"I think some states not allowing slavery is the problem," Casey surmised. "Slavery should be in every state so we can stop these abolitionist groups, and I don't see a problem with correcting those women."

"Indeed, a wrong is only set right when a punishment is given. Never has a nigger disrespected me by refusing to give me her name. I know the place we need to go in order to find out some more information about this situation."

"Where would that be on this side of town?" Casey asked.

"We're going to visit one of the eyes of this town, Mr. Pots."

"I look forward to this ride. His daughter is a mighty fine single woman."

Mr. Hildebrand smirked. "Well then, today may be a special day for you."

Casey grinned. "I'd be more than grateful."

The two men then calmly rode their horses to Pots's Garments.

During this time, Annabelle and Ruthanne arrived at their home, smiling and laughing.

"Elizabeth, where are you, girl?" Ruthanne called before walking into the kitchen. "Elizabeth, where are you?"

"Wow, is she still with Marilyn?" Annabelle asked.

"Hmm...I think she is. Follow me." They left their upper quarters and went down the stairs, looking for Elizabeth.

"Hey ladies, how has your day been going?" Rebecca asked when they approached the store. She stood in her doorway, wearing a ruffle-shouldered green dress and a white bonnet.

"Hello, Rebecca, we were looking for Elizabeth. Have you seen her return?" Annabelle asked.

"I saw Elizabeth leave about two hours ago. I'm not sure where she went, though. She was smiling, so I assume she was in a good mood. Is everything alright, Annabelle?"

"Yes, we were trying to see what she was doing."

"I'm sure she's out enjoying herself," Rebecca said.

"Yeah, every now and then, she goes off on her own," Ruthanne said.

"Surely, you're not worried about her," Rebecca asked, her tone tranquil.

"Why, of course I'm not worried about her. She's grown and can do whatever she wants," Ruthanne said, her tone guarded. Ruthanne folded her arms irritably and asked, "What are you doing, Rebecca?"

"I'm preparing to plant these wildflower seeds out here so the place looks more welcoming."

Ruthanne said, "Well, I'll be glad to help you."

"Are you sure? You seemed so focused on finding Elizabeth a moment ago."

Ruthanne convincingly replied, "She can handle herself. Besides, I don't know if I can do another shopping day with her."

Rebecca laughed. "You really are not the type to do all the typical things of a woman."

Ruthanne gave a prideful smirk. "I do tend to have a rebellious side to me every now and then."

"What about you, Annabelle? What are you going to do?"

Annabelle answered, "I guess I'll stay here and help. It will be nice to do something else for fun. I've never planted flowers before. Are they like cotton?"

"Well, yes, they are similar to cotton, but I promise you won't have to pick them," Rebecca said.

"Picking a flower is much more enjoyable than picking cotton from the fields, trust me."

"Well, ladies, let us begin our journey to making the outside seem more pleasant."

They began planting the flower seeds as Elizabeth was making her way back to the Potses' shop. On the way, she stopped by Mr. Boston's store, smiling.

"Good day, Mr. Boston," Elizabeth said.

"Hello, Elizabeth," Mr. Boston cheerfully said. "Let me introduce you to someone quite important. Mrs. Davis, please allow me to introduce you to Elizabeth Jones. She is new here in Mercy."

"My word, she is quite a lovely young lady," Mrs. Davis said.

Mrs. Davis was an older short brunette with stripes of white hair running through her twin bun hairstyle. She wore a dark red ruffled dress.

"Thank you, ma'am, it is a pleasure to meet you," Elizabeth said.

"Where are the other lovely young ladies?" Mr. Boston asked.

Elizabeth replied, "Sasha and Ruthanne walked over to the other side of town because they wanted to see it."

"That's right. I did see them earlier today." Mr. Boston huffed. "I hope those two managed to stay out of trouble. Well, Mrs. Davis is a wise woman with a lot of fire, much like Ruthanne."

"Stop it, Mr. Boston," Mrs. Davis said, giggling. She looked at Elizabeth with her welcoming brown eyes and smiled. "Anyhow, I do look forward to meeting with you again, Elizabeth."

Elizabeth replied, "I'm sure Ruthanne and Sasha would be pleased to meet you as well, Mrs. Davis."

Mr. Fluffs suddenly strutted down the counter and meowed.

"My goodness, Mr. Fluffs. My apologies. I almost left without saying goodbye to you," Mrs. Davis said. "You adorable cat."

Mrs. Davis picked Mr. Fluffs up and petted him, then put him down while he purred.

"Well," the older woman said, "I'm off now to take care of some other business. The two of you have a blessed day."

"You as well, Mrs. Davis," said Mr. Boston. "Now, what can I do for you, Elizabeth?"

"I was just stopping by, Mr. Boston. I was in the area on my way to the Potses' store," Elizabeth answered.

"I'm assuming you're going there to buy a new dress."

"I got fitted for one already, but I'm really going by to see Marilyn."

"The youngest daughter of Mr. Pots," Mr. Boston said in a meditative tone. "She is quite something special. She is talented when it comes to making things—dresses, perfumes, hats—and the girl even knows how to weld, even though she learned that against her father's will. I'm interested in seeing what will become of her in the coming years. Marilyn is only seventeen years old, but you would never think it while having a conversation with her. No different than Ruthanne. I bet she is quite the reader."

Elizabeth's eyes widened slightly. "How did you figure that out?"

"Ruthanne carries herself in such a carefree manner that her confidence shines without effort. Elizabeth, you know her better than anyone here in the town. When have you ever known Ruthanne to chase after anyone?"

"Well, never. She always says it is their loss, and they're not worth a minute of her time."

Mr. Boston smiled. "That's exactly how you need to carry yourself as well. Even though right now, a lot of people would disagree, a woman that can speak her mind is priceless. A woman who can think for herself is able to be a great wife because she is able to help support her husband and her family better than a woman who is just playing a role and won't say anything."

Elizabeth looked down, doubtful of her ability to be bold like Ruthanne.

"What's wrong, Elizabeth?"

"Nothing. I was just thinking."

"People who have great potential to do things in life are the people who ask God for help and never give up."

"Thank you, Mr. Boston."

"Trust me on that. I know I'm an old man, and that gives me the advantage of experience, but there are even old fools in this world."

"Well, I'm off to go visit Marilyn. I'll see you later."

"Alright, take care of yourself now."

Mr. Fluffs came up to Elizabeth tactfully and meowed. Elizabeth giggled.

"You're going to make sure I give you attention, Mr. Fluffs." Elizabeth reached over and petted him. "Oh, you supersized cat, I can't help but enjoy you."

Elizabeth waved goodbye to Mr. Boston and left the store, feeling more confident about herself because of Mr. Boston's words.

"This heat is no joke out here. It's almost as bad as home." Elizabeth went over to Pots's Garments, humming to herself elegantly.

"God, thank you for another day of happiness," she murmured to herself before she entered the Pot's store joyfully. "Marilyn, are you still here?"

"I'm back here, Elizabeth," Marilyn shouted.

Elizabeth went to the back of the store. "What are you doing back here?"

"I'm just bringing out some new perfumes that just arrived this morning from New York City," Marilyn excitedly said.

Elizabeth's blue eyes widened. "From New York City! Oh, we must try a few of them."

"Elizabeth, we can't try that many. I'm supposed to be selling these for other customers that come in. However, I don't see the harm in doing a few test sprays."

Elizabeth squealed. "You're so much fun."

The women began testing the different perfumes, sometimes pretending to be rich women.

Marilyn sprayed herself with perfume and said with a fake British accent, "Oh, my dear, that's simply lovely. It tickles me."

Elizabeth sprayed herself but coughed, then said with a fake British accent, "How dreadful is this odor! It is an insult to the crown."

The women laughed, enjoying their time while they tested the different fragrances.

Marilyn suddenly heard the door open and rushed to the front of the store,

"Good evening, ma'am," Marilyn said.

"Why, good evening, dear. I heard you recently received some new perfumes," said a pale-skinned woman.

"Yes, ma'am, we got them from New York City."

"I must say that does sound exciting, and how many variations do you have?"

"We have ten different new types of perfumes, ma'am."

The woman beamed. "What a great day this is turning out to be."

Elizabeth walked to the front of the store to see who sounded so cheerful. It was an older woman with a pea-green dress, puffed sleeves, and a green hat with flowers. The plump woman noticed Elizabeth behind the counter.

"Hello, dear. I had no idea there were two of you working here."

Marilyn replied, "Oh no, she is a friend of mine. She doesn't work here, ma'am."

"How nice it must be to have a friend come by and spend time with you while you watch the store for your family."

Marilyn gave the brunette a fake smile, trying not to be insulted by the woman's assumption.

"No, ma'am. Remember? I actually work here. I introduce clothing and perfumes, and I count the money, so I do most of the work here."

"What a pioneer you are, trying to be independent in this world of ours," the woman methodically said. "There isn't anything wrong with learning how to do things in this world. Just remember your place, dear. You need a man in your life to provide for you and the family you will give him. Most men don't like a smart woman, so it's okay to lower yourself in order to get a good one. That's what I did," the woman said in a prideful tone. "My choice gave me beautiful dresses and jewels, not to mention my four lovely children. From the day I got married, I was known as Mrs. White, and it is a wonderful experience I hope you girls get to have soon."

Marilyn scoffed. "I'm sorry, but I'm in no rush to be married. I'm only seventeen years old, and I haven't met a man that I'm interested in. I feel so pressured half the time by my father and the other half by the people in this town. I won't be handed off to a man I barely know because people want me to!"

Mrs. White replied, "My dear, I didn't mean to make it sound that way. I mean, there are women who have that opportunity, but you take what you can get. You don't pass up the offer of a high-ranked officer in our military or from a successful plantation owner. Then you will never have a full life."

"I'd rather live happy making a little money with a man I really love. I mean, I could only imagine lying on my back for a man I don't even love like those harlots in the saloons. I can't do it because of a man's status. My sisters did that, and I can't bring myself to do the same."

Mrs. White shrugged. "How improper of you to speak of it in such a manner. Those harlots have no hope of becoming married and are the lesser examples of being a woman."

Marilyn folded her arms. "Even if that's true, I won't settle for a man that thinks he owns me. My mother did it, and my sisters have copied her." She said daringly, "So tell me, do you know the difference between being a submissive wife and being a slave?"

Mrs. White's blue eyes began to blaze like torches. "Are you suggesting that because I made a choice to marry my husband to gain social status, that makes me his slave?"

"Tell me, Mrs. White, has there ever been a young beautiful woman like myself that ever seemed to catch your husband's eye for more than a moment?"

Mrs. White began to turn red in the face and clutched her white gloves. "I know nothing of the sort. Now, I have more errands to run today. I'll take the new perfume that smells like jasmine."

"Yes, of course, Mrs. White. Time is valuable, especially to such a busy woman as yourself," Marilyn sarcastically replied. "So tell me one thing. Does your husband send you out at certain times of the day when he says he's having business partners over, or do you leave when you want some alone time?"

Mrs. White sharply replied, "None of your concern. I'll return sometime later to see what else you have."

"Of course, Mrs. White. Time is short. And certain things don't take much time at all," Marilyn said with an instigative tone.

Mrs. White rushed out of the store to her carriage, each of her footsteps becoming heavier. She stepped inside so fast that she scared her driver. He turned around, frightened.

"Who is you?" he said.

"Billy Jo, shut up and drive. We need to get back home as quickly as possible!" Mrs. White yelled.

"Yes, ma'am," Billy Jo replied, "but it will be mighty hard with some of these people in the way."

"You get us back home in a reasonable time, and you can eat some of that steak at the table!"

Billy Jo's eyes widened while he pressed the two horses to move faster, almost running over a clumsy man.

"If you don't mind me asking, why are we rushing so much?"

"I have a feeling that Mr. White may be getting into something he has no business getting into."

Billy Jo grinned and mumbled, "Woo! It looks like I'm gonna hear some action tonight. Mr. White may be sleeping in the slave houses tonight."

Elizabeth approached the store's door with a confused look on her face. "Will she come back?" she asked.

"She always returns, even though I'm snippy with her."

"Why did she leave so suddenly, Marilyn?" Elizabeth asked.

Marilyn grinned at Elizabeth and chuckled. "You really are naïve, Elizabeth. Learn the silent language of a woman, and you will understand a lot of things in life. I'll explain it to you. When the time comes that you find yourself a married woman, and you ignore signs or put your marriage in a certain position, you will find out what it really means to have your heart broken. Never allow a younger, single, beautiful woman to spend a lot of time alone with your undisciplined husband. Even if he is a good man, that's asking for trouble letting a man be in a situation like that."

"Not every man can possibly be that disloyal."

"Elizabeth, you still don't understand, dear. It's not always the man that you have to keep an eye on, but some of these women that have no problem with stealing a husband."

"So, you're saying that Mrs. White's husband is having an affair?"

"He sends her off to go shopping while the kids are not home, and he isn't having business partners over. What more of an opportunity to have a little extra fun on the side?"

Elizabeth sighed. "My goodness. I would have fallen for the same thing."

"You see, there is a difference between a husband wanting his wife to have some free time and him sending his wife away almost every day."

Elizabeth frowned a bit. "That poor woman. What a horrible thing to realize."

Marilyn walked over to the counter, closing up the bottles of perfume Mrs. White had been sampling. "It's a sad thing to realize, and that's why I won't marry to gain social status. Maybe we are less likely to deal with a man that commits adultery when we marry for love."

Elizabeth looked at Marilyn happily. "Maybe you're right, Marilyn."

"Well now, what are you doing for the rest of the day?"

"I guess I'll go back and find Ruthanne and Sasha. They're probably returning from exploring the rest of the town."

Marilyn smirked. "Those two are definitely special. The way they carry themselves as women is quite amazing. I consider myself confident, but those two take it to a whole different level. I will certainly come by and spend more time with you ladies."

"That sounds wonderful," Elizabeth said. "It will certainly be a great time. I guess I'll go back and see if they have returned yet."

"Sounds like it will be a good time. And I will see what day I can leave the store and let my father have it for a day." Marilyn giggled and continued, "It will also show him how much he really needs me around."

Elizabeth beamed and said, "I can't wait for you to come. I will see you later."

Marilyn waved, "Alright, bye."

Elizabeth waved back and left the store, still thinking about what Marilyn had said. Elizabeth was bothered that she didn't understand the hint Marilyn was giving to Mrs. White.

"Well, God, I guess there are things I still need to learn." Elizabeth began humming as she walked back to her home.

When Elizabeth arrived, she noticed the new flower boxes on the outside of the house full of dirt.

"What a change," she said.

Laughing, Ruthanne left the house with dirt stains covering her dress.

"Well, look who it is!" Ruthanne joyfully said.

Elizabeth looked at Ruthanne unenthusiastically.

"What's with the face, Elizabeth? You haven't seen me for a few hours."

Elizabeth smirked as her eyes examined Ruthanne's dirty dress. "I guess some things never change, no matter how old we become."

Ruthanne looked down and lifted the dirt-covered dress slightly. "Yes, I guess some things will never change."

Annabelle came out of the house, looking as dirty as Ruthanne.

"Hi, Elizabeth, we were about to finish planting the rest of these seeds if you want to join us," Annabelle said.

Elizabeth began to giggle as Rebecca, as dirty as Annabelle and Ruthanne, came out of the house with a small bag of seeds.

"Looks like we have another hand to help out," Rebecca said.

Elizabeth replied, "I don't see myself saying yes to this at all, seeing all three of you covered in dirt."

Annabelle and Rebecca laughed, but Ruthanne grabbed a chunk of dirt and put her hand behind her while she marched up to Elizabeth. Then she quickly plopped the dirt on Elizabeth's dress.

Elizabeth's mouth dropped while she stared at the dirt on her dress.

"Yeah, some things really don't change," Elizabeth said in an aggravated tone.

"Don't be so sore about it, Elizabeth, it's just dirt," Ruthanne said. "We'll wash afterward, even though it'll take a while."

"Guess I was going to get dirty anyway."

"Now that's the spirit, Elizabeth," Annabelle encouragingly said.

Elizabeth picked up a piece of dirt and tossed it on Ruthanne's dress, laughing. The other women gasped when they watched Elizabeth's childish actions.

"Well now, how unladylike," Ruthanne joked.

"Ladies, let us finish the job so we can enjoy a piece of pie afterward," Rebecca said.

"Sounds like a plan to me," Annabelle replied.

The ladies continued planting the flowers as a hairy blond man walked up behind them, wearing gray-striped trousers, a gray vest covering his white-collared shirt and red cravat, and a gray frock coat. He stood behind the women, examining what they were doing.

"Now, I know good and well I'm not witnessing such beautiful white women digging in the dirt with a nigger," the man said, revealing his harsh authoritative southern accent.

Annabelle's heart dropped as she and the other women turned around, alarmed by the tone of the man.

"Well now, Sheriff Shepard, what a surprise," Rebecca formidably said.

"It's not a good surprise for me to find three white women digging in the dirt next to a nigger."

Rebecca and Ruthanne stood up firmly.

"Sheriff Shepard, I would appreciate if you could show me respect by not calling my resident a nigger," Rebecca firmly said.

"Resident!" Sheriff Shepard replied.

"Yes, she is paying rent upstairs and hasn't missed a payment yet."

The sheriff approached Annabelle, glaring at her with his callous gray eyes. "I find it hard to believe that she can afford to pay you unless she's robbing people," Sheriff Shepard boldly said. "What is your name, Negro?"

"My name is Sasha."

"She does not live alone, Sheriff Shepard," Rebecca said.

"I'm living with this Negro woman, Sheriff Shepard," Ruthanne said cautiously.

"I'm also living with Sasha," Elizabeth boldly said.

"A redhead, blonde, and a nappy-headed Negro. How did you three get together?"

"We all come from Jefferson City, and we grew up together," Ruthanne said.

"Hmm...another free nigger," the sheriff irritably said. "How are y'all paying Mr. Keys rent with no man present?"

"Our fathers have given us money, with the exception of Sasha, whose family has no means of giving her much. But Mr. Boston pays her to clean his store."

"Well, I guess there's not much I can do about that right now. I suggest you stay on this side of town and consider yourself lucky that there are few here that would welcome a Negro to live in the same building as them. Now, you let me know if they miss rent, Rebecca. Can't be letting these Negroes feel comfortable."

Annabelle nodded her head and said, "Yes, Sheriff Shepard."

"I suggest you continue to know your place, and I may come to endure your presence. Be glad you're not one of them Injuns. I only feel comfortable with them attending the festival, church, and Mr. Boston's supply store. Even though it is beyond me why Mr. Boston continues to allow them godless savages to come in his store, I guess money is money."

Rebecca pursed her lips and gave Sheriff Shepard a blank stare.

"Anyhow, the day goes on. Good day to you ladies, and you as well, Negro."

"Good day, Sheriff," Rebecca agitatedly said.

Sheriff Shepard strutted toward his horse.

"Well, Annabelle, there's another enemy for us," Ruthanne said.

"Another enemy?" Rebecca asked.

Ruthanne calmly replied, "Yes, we ran into Mr. Hildebrand and Casey Bones. It all started because of Elizabeth's drunken lover boy, who offered his body to me as Annabelle stood right next to me. I may have gotten a bit too physical with Jeff and attracted more unexpected attention."

Rebecca sighed. "I see things became rough in one day."

Annabelle noticed Elizabeth turning red before she tossed dirt onto Ruthanne's back. "What do you mean, my lover boy?" she angrily asked.

Ruthanne turned around with a perplexed look on her face while scraping the dirt off her back. She replied, "Throwing dirt...how childish. And yes, the dog named Jeff that flirted with me and spoke his warm words to you."

"How can you say he was my lover boy, Ruthanne!"

"You were the one falling for him."

Elizabeth put her hands on her hips. "Ugh, how dare you say that! It's not like I started courting with the man."

"Okay, girls, enough of this bickering," Rebecca said. "The issue I see here isn't Jeff, but the other two men you encountered today."

Ruthanne exhaled and nodded. "Yes, that was not the greatest experience."

"Ruthanne pulled a gun on them," Annabelle abruptly said.

"You pulled a gun on them!" Rebecca said. She put her hand on her head.

Ruthanne replied, "They were scaring us, so I made things even."

"It was exciting but scary," Annabelle said.

Rebecca crouched down, holding her stomach and closing her eyes.

"Are you okay, Rebecca?" Elizabeth hesitantly asked.

"I'm sorry if I upset you," Ruthanne sympathetically said.

Rebecca said, "By no means have any of you made me upset. I'm just going through a stage."

Ruthanne folded her arms. "Cramps. Yeah, I get those too in that messed up time of the month."

Rebecca smiled at Ruthanne. "Oh no, I'm not going to be having one of those for quite a while. I'd say I won't be having one of those for another seven months."

Annabelle, confused by Rebecca's words, asked, "What will happen in seven months?"

Rebecca stood up and said, "Well, Annabelle, I'm going to have another baby in about seven months."

The women jumped up with excitement and shouted with joy. "Congratulations, Rebecca!" they said.

"So, have you told Allen the good news yet?" Ruthanne asked.

Rebecca rubbed her hands together. "I'm going to tell him tonight after dinner," Rebecca said.

The women rushed toward Rebecca and gave her a hug.

Annabelle couldn't stop smiling for Rebecca. The thought of bringing a child into this world seemed almost impossible to Annabelle. She thought, *Should I even consider having children with all the hate in this world?* However, the expression of joy on Rebecca's face weighed on Annabelle's heart.

"Is something on your mind, Annabelle?" Rebecca asked.

"Oh no, I'm really excited for you," Annabelle answered.

The doubt in Annabelle's eyes was noticed by Rebecca, but she decided to ask Annabelle later, when Elizabeth and Ruthanne were not present.

"What's everyone so happy about?" Ashley asked. The women turned around to see little Ashley beaming with excitement. "Mommy, I want to know why everyone is so happy," she asked.

"Ashley, darling, you will find out soon. Come say hi to Miss Williams, Miss Sasha, and Miss Jones," Rebecca said.

Ashley skipped toward the women. "Hello, I'm Ashley."

The women giggled.

"Honey, I'm sure they remember your name. You're the only daughter I have."

Ashley blushed and reached for Rebecca's hand. Rebecca held it while welcoming the other women to come inside for some lunch after changing clothes.

As the women changed their clothes and regrouped, Mr. Keys was on his way back home after talking with a few other businessmen.

On his way home, he passed Red Maple, a saloon where many of the top officials of the city assembled.

"I haven't been to the Red Maple in a few days. I should go there and see what the main talk in town has been this week," Allen said to himself.

He entered the Red Maple. The saloon was large, having several wooden tables and chairs out on the main floor, a second floor, a black piano in the corner, and a large bar with shelves covered in bottles of alcohol.

"Allen, it's been a few days!" said a short bald man. He wore a white collared shirt, a brown vest, and black trousers.

"How are you doing, Scott?" Allen replied as he stepped up to the bar.

Scott replied with his nasal voice, "I'm not doing bad at all, Allen. It's actually been a little slow the few days you haven't been in."

"How slow has it been?"

"Slow enough that the sheriff has only been here twice this week, and I've only seen the mayor once this week."

Allen looked confounded. "I wonder if something is going on."

"I'm sure we'll hear if something big is happening. We both own property, so we have to be informed if something serious is going to occur."

"You're right. I guess I worry a little too much sometimes. I swear, ever since Ashley was born, I've been more cautious than ever."

Scott chuckled. "Allen, daughters tend to do that to us no matter how tough we are in our younger years."

Both of the men laughed, though Allen believed something wasn't right.

"What did you want?" Scott asked.

"Glass of whiskey—I haven't had it in a while."

Scott poured him a drink while Allen put down his money. Scott handed Allen the drink, and Allen took a sip, just leaving enough for one more drink.

The saloon doors opened up slowly, and the men turned their heads.

"Hello, Mr. Keys and Mr. Walker. May I come in for a glass of water?" Benjamin asked.

Scott replied, "I guess, if it is of no problem for Mr. Keys here, I see no problem in you coming in for a glass of water, Benjamin."

"Come on in, Benjamin, it is mighty hot today," Allen hospitably said.

"Why, thank you, Mr. Keys," Benjamin respectfully said.

Scott poured Benjamin a glass of water while Benjamin stood by the door and waited.

"Come sit down, Benjamin," Allen invited.

Scott's brown eyes looked up to Allen, and he yelled, "Now hold on, Allen! I don't mind a Negro coming in, but I can't allow him to have a seat."

"Scott, almost nobody is here at the moment. Let the man sit down."

"Well, there are no administrators here at the moment. I suppose you can have a seat this one time. Go ahead and have a seat, Benjamin. Thank Mr. Keys while you're taking a seat, Benjamin. If it wasn't for him, you'd be standing."

"Thank you very much, Mr. Keys," Benjamin said.

"It's not a problem at all, Benjamin," Allen said. "So, are you excited about the coming festival?"

"Yes, sir. I'm looking to see all the people there in their nice clothes. If you don't mind me asking, will Sasha be there too?"

Allen grinned at Benjamin. "I'm sure she'll be there."

"That's nice to know, Mr. Keys."

"So, do you find Sasha to your liking?"

Benjamin grinned. "I think that she may find a liking for me as well, sir, but I wasn't sure when I would see her again."

"Don't worry yourself a bit, Benjamin. I know for a fact Sasha will be at the festival, and you will have your chance."

"Why, thank you, Mr. Keys. That has made my day." Benjamin finished his glass of water with a smile and stood up. "Thank you, Mr. Walker, for allowing me to have a drink of water."

Scott replied, "Don't mention it, Benjamin. Just remember your place, and you'll do fine here."

"Thank you, sir. I will, and I look forward to coming to the festival this year."

"You have a good day, Benjamin," Allen said.

"I thank you, sir," Benjamin said as he left the saloon.

"Allen, explain to me who this Sasha woman is?" Scott asked.

Allen replied, "Sasha is one of my new residents that came into town a couple of days ago."

Scott picked up the glass Benjamin had used and threw it in the garbage.

"Why did you throw the glass away? It was perfectly fine."

"I threw it away because now it has Negro germs on it. Even though I don't mind Benjamin, I have to think of the rest of my customers, Allen."

Allen shook his head. "Scott, that's ignorant of you. That boy don't have any weird Negro diseases."

"I'm not going to risk it. What more do you want? He was allowed to get his drink of water and left peacefully, and far as I'm concerned, he's a little spoiled. Not to mention you encouraging that boy to even have the nerve to talk to a white woman. That's in no way okay."

"Sasha is a free Negro woman. She came here with her two other friends that are white women."

"How could a Negro woman have enough money to pay you rent, Allen?"

"She's from Jefferson City. She's not from around here. I'd imagine her family are blacksmiths, tailors, or traders who have done mighty well for themselves. Not to mention that she is living with two white women. The way they dress, I would say that they come from wealthy families or families that are doing mighty fine. All three of them are prime pickings, so whatever men end up marrying any of those women will be quite blessed."

"Even the nigger?"

"Yes, even Sasha is quite beautiful."

Allen gulped his drink, masking his agitation toward Scott's persistence in questioning Annabelle's origins and his use of the word "nigger." Allen stood up and stretched his arms. "Well, Scott, I'm off to see my lovely wife and my little girl."

Scott smiled. "Well, alright. I'll be looking for you to come by tomorrow since I haven't seen you for most of the week."

"I'll try to make sure I stop by, Scott."

Before Allen could reach the saloon doors, they slowly opened.

"I'll be damned, Allen Keys, it's nice to run into you today," said Sheriff Shepard.

"Sheriff Shepard, it's good to see you also, but I'm in a bit of a rush to get home to my wife," Allen said. "I'm sure I will probably see you tomorrow."

Allen began to go past the sheriff, but Sheriff Shepard grabbed his arm.

"Now, hold on a minute, Allen. We have a matter to discuss that involves your wife."

Allen somewhat narrowed his eyes, asking, "What do you mean by that?"

"I witnessed your wife digging in the dirt with a nigger this afternoon. And I must say I was quite disgusted with how your wife was working so hard to plant some stupid flowers when the only one that should have been out there working was that nigger. Not to mention that two new white women were also digging in the dirt with the Negro. So, tell me, what do you think of that?"

Allen shrugged. "I'm surprised that Rebecca didn't toss any dirt on you, to be honest, but I can't monitor my wife's every move throughout the entire day. Sheriff Shepard, if my wife wants to plant flowers outside of our home on our property, I won't be able to stop her. She's never been a passive wife."

"Well, sheriff, I'd say it's nice for the women to learn something productive from the nigger. It's not like she was the one whipping them," Scott said.

Sheriff Shepard replied, "Shut up, Scott. This doesn't concern you unless you want to explain to me why you let that nigger, Benjamin, in here."

Allen responded, "If you must know, Sheriff Shepard, that was my doing, not Scott's. Scott wouldn't even allow Benjamin to sit down next to me."

Sheriff Shepard crossed his arms. "What did he come in here for?"

"Sheriff, the boy only wanted a glass of water, and he ain't got any real money. The only thing he's able to do for money is give water to the horses and clean them."

"Huh...and that's the only thing even close to a job a nigger deserves besides washing clothes and cleaning out buildings. Anyway, I better not ever see that nigger sitting down at this bar. He's a good nigger, and I wouldn't want to have to display my authority on him anytime soon. I'm talking to you, Scott! This is your saloon, fool."

Scott jolted and dropped a glass while Sheriff Shepard's tone rang out. "Why, of course, Sheriff Shepard. He won't be taking any seats at the bar," Scott nervously said. He bent down to clean up the glass off the floor.

"While you down there, fix me up a shot of rum," Sheriff Shepard said.

"No problem, Sheriff Shepard."

"Allen, I believe I have made my point here. Don't mistake me letting you go as me not seeing your true colors. I suggest you make sure that nigger is paying her rent. Otherwise, there will be trouble. She seems like one of the smart ones, so I'm sure she'll make a good servant. I wouldn't mind if you sent her my way to help my wife cook."

"I'll look into it, Sheriff," Allen respectfully said.

"I look forward to seeing you all at the festival then," Sheriff Shepard mockingly said.

"Same to you, Sheriff Shepard. See you later, Scott."

Scott replied, "Have a good day, Allen, and tell Rebecca I said hi."

Allen exited the saloon grumbling, and he rushed home to feel comforted.

Allen entered his home, still bothered by the sheriff's rants.

"Hey, honey, how was your day?" Rebecca asked.

"Oh, not too bad, Rebecca. I'm a little bit tired dealing with the town hall," Allen replied.

"Good evening, Mr. Keys," Annabelle, Ruthanne, and Elizabeth shouted.

Allen replied, "Oh, well...hello, ladies. It's nice to see all three of you here today."

"I've decided that we're having a special dinner today, Allen," Rebecca said.

"Sounds good to me," Allen said.

Allen heard fast footsteps coming toward him, and he turned to see Ashley smiling and running toward him.

"Daddy, Daddy, I watched Mommy plant flowers today," Ashley said.

Allen replied, "Now, that sounds exciting, my little princess."

"Go on, Allen. The two of you go and play for a couple of minutes," Rebecca said.

Allen and Ashley went outside while the women set the table.

"This is so exciting. I can't wait to see the look on his face, Rebecca," Elizabeth said with a big smile.

"He'll probably look stupid for about five minutes before rejoicing in having another child on the way," Rebecca said. "He wants a son. I can see it in his face sometimes that he desires to have at least one boy."

"Well, this may be the son that he wants. Imagine the joy on his face when you have the baby," Annabelle said. "One of the happiest things that happened in the slave homes and the mansion was the birth of babies. New life was something Master Brown couldn't control. It was given to us."

The women listened to Annabelle as she continued.

"It is amazing how a child can bring such strong joy into our lives. Children ain't born with hate or anger. They are brought into this world full of love and curiosity. Not one of the white babies I was told to hold pushed me away or called me a nigger, and that's what helped me realize how God's love has no limits."

Rebecca placed her hand on Annabelle's shoulder. "You're loved here, darling."

Annabelle placed her hand on Rebecca's and smiled. "You're so blessed that it amazes me. I'd like to come at least halfway to where you are."

"It isn't everything, girl," Ruthanne arrogantly said.

Elizabeth crossed her arms and looked at Ruthanne irritably, and Rebecca shook her head casually.

"You all are too serious." Ruthanne laughed.

"Ugh, Ruthanne, you're a pain in the rear," Elizabeth said.

"Please, it was beginning to get too mushy for me. By all means, I can understand, Annabelle. But this is a new beginning, girl. Let's enjoy it and get ready to celebrate the new addition."

"You're right. I guess I was having some memories come back to me," Annabelle said.

"Sometimes, you need to remember the past to be grateful for what you have now," Ruthanne said.

The women finished setting the table while a spirit of love and grace filled the air. The women then began cooking, enjoying each other's company, before bringing the food to the dining room table. Rebecca anxiously exhaled with the news she had withheld from Allen.

"These are the moments making me second-guess not wanting a maid. Come in, you two," Rebecca yelled.

Allen and Ashley came inside the house, excited for their meal.

After everyone was seated, Allen prayed over the food. "Father God, thank you for your continuous blessings not only to my family, but also to our new friends who were guided by you to our door, amen. I must say, I'm quite excited to have all of you here at the dinner table. What a glorious day it is."

The three young women smiled at Allen with honor and humility. Rebecca placed her hand on Allen's shoulder calmly and smirked at him, barely able to contain the surprise.

Allen turned to Rebecca and gazed at her while his eyebrows lifted. "Is there something you want to say? You've always been quick to speak before."

"You're going to be a father again!"

Allen stared blankly into Rebecca's bright brown eyes. He looked at Annabelle, Ruthanne, and Elizabeth, and he saw them all smiling at him.

"So this means I'm going to be a big sister?" Ashley asked.

Rebecca replied, "Yes, it does, my little flower."

Allen, still speechless, grunted, then he shouted with a big smile before wrapping Rebecca into a clutching hug.

"To say this day is glorious isn't enough." Allen exhaled. "You all knew about this?"

"Well, Ashley knew nothing of it," Rebecca said.

"I know she didn't know. She's my eyes and ears." Allen laughed. "What an enormous blessing. I don't even have an appetite anymore."

Rebecca laughed. "You have to calm down, Allen. You do know you're free to breathe. You've always been quick to breathe, Allen."

The women laughed hysterically while Allen continued to grin.

"Thanks be to God." Allen grabbed his cup and raised it in the air. "A toast not only to the new addition to my lovely family, but to friends who are more than welcome in my home."

Everyone, including young Ashley, raised their cups in the air in agreement. The night was filled with laughter, hope, and love as they shared their dinner together. Annabelle, Ruthanne, and Elizabeth said good night to Allen and Rebecca before going upstairs to their quarters.

Sitting in his chair, still overwhelmed with joy, Allen turned to Rebecca, smiling.

"Come here, my queen of the day and night."

Rebecca sat in Allen's lap, and Allen held her hand soothingly.

"Every day I wake up," he said, "I thank God for you and Ashley, and it makes my days so much sweeter."

Rebecca placed her forehead against his. "And every moment I have, I thank God for showing me what a wonderful man you are."

"Your eyes are like an ever-burning sunset that gives hope of another day to come."

Rebecca beamed. "Careful now, that kind of talk is why we have another one on the way."

Allen laughed and said, "So, you know it helps when you're the mastermind at times."

Rebecca laughed and replied, "I initiate for us to have fun on occasion. Did you forget your birthday?"

Allen giggled. "Not one moment of it, my dear."

The two kissed each other passionately, stood up holding hands, and went to their bedroom as two soulmates.

Upstairs, Ruthanne lay in her bed and stared at the ceiling. The amount of joy present during the dinner was a feeling she hadn't had since she was a pre-teen. She looked at Annabelle.

"Hey, Annabelle, you feel like talking?" she asked.

Annabelle turned over to face her. "Ruthanne, how did you know I wasn't asleep?"

Ruthanne smiled. "Because you're like me, and I bet you're thinking of how much love was going on downstairs."

Annabelle irritably huffed. "I guess there's no point in me even acting like you're wrong. Is Elizabeth awake too?"

"Ha, she's been asleep for the past fifteen minutes. I'm surprised she hasn't started to snore yet."

"She seems to have no worries in this world. Sometimes, I wish I was more like that."

"Annabelle, my mother was twenty-five years old before she

married my father, and she ended up giving him five healthy children."

Annabelle's eyes widened somewhat, "My goodness, I would've thought she'd be younger when she met your father."

"Me too, but she was still a beautiful woman."

Annabelle lifted her head and asked, "Why wasn't she younger when she met your father?"

"My grandparents wanted her to marry this really wealthy guy, but my mother didn't love him at all. He treated her like she was lucky to have his attention. So three days before they were supposed to be married, she ran away for a month and returned to my grandparents' plantation in time for my grandfather's birthday."

"Your mother is a brave woman to do something like that. My parents were two of the few slaves that got to choose. My pa had to ask Master Brown if he would allow him to be with my momma."

"Wow, Annabelle, I'd say to be a Negro woman, you would need to be as brave as a white woman. I'm glad my father didn't force me to marry anybody. When I was younger, I'd look into the sky and wonder if the light coming from the sun was really God's light. Those are some of my best memories as a child—looking up into the sky and watching the sun break through the white clouds with a warm summer breeze. I believe that's what helped give me strength in my faith in God. Looking into the sky and seeing all the different clouds reminds me of all the different people in our world. There's somebody for everybody, so don't worry about finding love. God will send it to you."

Annabelle happily looked at Ruthanne and said, "You always know what to say."

Ruthanne shrugged. "I guess in a way, I've developed some of my mother's personality."

"I'd say that's a great personality to have."

Ruthanne gave a joyful smile and said, "I glad you think so, Annabelle. My father says I'm a bit too much like my mother." Ruthanne giggled. "I think if you and me are able to even have half the love Rebecca and Allen have for each other, we'll do fine."

"It is something special to watch, isn't it? Seeing the two of them heals my heart in a way I didn't think was possible." Annabelle lay back down in her bed, staring at the ceiling with a smile on her face.

Ruthanne lay down and exhaled, then whispered, "I guess I'll keep some of my hopes to myself so I can stay strong for all of us."

Ruthanne suddenly felt herself become heavier. She grunted and attempted to sit up, but she couldn't. Her eyes dilated, and she began to breathe heavily as she attempted to move. The room filled with light, and suddenly, she could sit up as she felt a change in the air, which became calm. Her mouth dropped open as she looked around with eyebrows raised and eyes wide.

"Where am I?" she asked, watching in awe while the room turned into a coniferous forest. "I was just looking at the ceiling of my room, and now I'm in a forest. What is going on?" She stood next to her bed, looking into a sky filled with stars, and saw a great, calm river reflecting their light. The warm air made Ruthanne feel at peace as her green eyes slowly scanned the forest.

"Quite beautiful, isn't it?" said an angelic voice.

Ruthanne turned around slowly and asked, "Who are you?"

A tall, beautiful woman with a face as bright and startlingly beautiful as lightning, wearing golden armor, and surrounded by a golden aura walked toward Ruthanne. "Don't be afraid, Ruthanne. I'm not here to harm you."

"Is this a dream?"

"Yes, this is a dream. However, this is unlike any dream that you have ever had," the angelic figure said as she smiled.

"This makes absolutely no sense. Am I dreaming? Why can't I wake up and stop this if this is my dream?" Ruthanne angrily said.

"Patience, Ruthanne. I have an important message for you, and that's why you can't wake up."

"A message? Who do you have a message from?"

"I have a message from the most high God, your Father in heaven."

Ruthanne looked at the woman, slightly shaking her head as her eyes began to dilate again. "I must've eaten something bad, or I must be thinking of what Annabelle was talking to me about."

"This isn't your imagination. There is no trickery here, and I have truth to be spoken to you."

Ruthanne scoffed, "I'm sorry, but I don't believe you."

"Ruthanne, you believe in God, and I'm a messenger. Now is the time to have faith in the Lord."

"I don't understand why God would bother sending me an angel."

"Ruthanne, every day you pray and say, 'Lord, thank you for another day, allow me to see the real evil in the shadows and the real love in the light.'"

A tear suddenly traveled down Ruthanne's cheek, but she wiped it away, holding back her tears.

"Ruthanne, even the strong shed tears. It does not make you weak. The strongest spirits are those that seek and speak truth. They love, show kindness, forgive, help the weak, are patient, and are humble. It is time for you to let go of your doubt and seek God's kingdom. I'm not here to judge you, but I'm here with a powerful message."

Ruthanne began to shake while tears covered her cheeks. "Please forgive me for my doubt, beautiful creature."

"There's no need for that. You're to be a pillar for someone who will go through trials when she has done nothing wrong."

"Who am I to be a pillar for when I doubt myself at times?"

"You will have the right words to say when the time arrives."

Ruthanne exhaled, asking, "Will I remember this dream?"

"You will remember what you need to know. Anyway, now

is the time for me to go, and from this point on, there will be changes. You will see shadows of the evil in this land."

Ruthanne's eyebrow lifted, and her mouth slightly dropped. "The shadows of the evil in this land? What does that mean?"

"The time for me to leave is now. I have delivered the message you needed to hear. As a favor, to end any doubt about this dream, Ruthanne, I will have two bundles of the mountain mint placed on the supper table. Your favorite flower—you won't find them everywhere. Now keep on smiling, Ruthanne," the angelic figure said with a warming smile.

"What is your name, angel?"

"You will know my name at the appointed time. Believe in what I have told you."

The angelic figure faded away in the moonlight, and Ruthanne suddenly woke up, looking around the room and breathing heavily. As the faint moonlight shone into the room, she looked at Elizabeth and Annabelle and saw that they were asleep. She remembered that the angel had told her that her favorite flower was to be placed on the dinner table.

Ruthanne slowly entered their kitchen, shaking a little with each step, to look at the table. She began to shake even more as she stood in the doorway of the kitchen. She turned her head to the left, and she saw nothing on the table. She walked up to the table to make sure nothing was there.

She huffed and said, "I must be losing my mind."

Ruthanne turned around to go back to bed, but then the Earth shook, causing her to fall to her knees. The quake lasted for two seconds while Ruthanne stared at the bedroom doorway, but Annabelle and Elizabeth slept through the shaking. She stumbled back into the kitchen and saw two bundles of the mountain mint. Ruthanne gasped, putting both of her hands over her mouth to stop herself from screaming.

"What is this!"

Ruthanne put her back against the wall. She slowly approached the table, grabbed the flower bundles, and snuck outside with the full moon guiding her. She dug a hole with a trowel as quickly as she could, placed the flower bundles in the hole, and smoothed out the dirt so nobody would know something was buried. She walked back upstairs, still shaking.

Ruthanne sat in her bed, unable to sleep, and mumbled, "What am I supposed to do?"

Ruthanne fell into a light sleep, feeling the rays of the sun getting stronger while it rose. She awoke before the others so she could clear her mind. She got dressed in the kitchen to avoid waking the others. She took an apple with her and forced herself to eat. As she walked down the stairs, she saw Rebecca.

"Good morning, Ruthanne. Today is a good day," Rebecca said.

Ruthanne apathetically replied, "Good morning, Rebecca."

"You seem a little distracted this morning. Did you sleep well, Ruthanne?"

Ruthanne forced a smile. "Yes, I'm fine. Just a little blinded by the glare of the sun."

"Alright, as long as nothing is wrong. I know what's like to wake up with something still on the mind."

Ruthanne continued to smile at Rebecca. "Thank you for your concern. Did you feel the earthquake last night?"

"Earthquake? Why, no. I was up a bit late last night, but I felt nothing like that."

Ruthanne exhaled. "I guess it must've been a dream of mine."

"I've had dreams like those. Don't let them bother you too much."

"Thanks, Rebecca. I'm going to take a short walk and enjoy the cool morning air."

Rebecca asked, "Alright, are the others up?"

"No, sleeping as usual, and Elizabeth is snoring as long as she can."

Rebecca laughed. "So, Elizabeth is the loud one at night. That's quite funny. The two of you are as opposite as day and night."

"I'd like to think so. I know I can seem a bit snobbish to

certain people, while Elizabeth has this ability to treat everyone as important and fun."

"We all have strengths and weaknesses. Otherwise, why would we need God or each other?"

Ruthanne grinned, finding Rebecca's comment strengthening. "I guess I'll go now and enjoy my short walk before the girls wake up."

"Trust me; I understand wanting some time to yourself quite well. Wait until you have kids! Then time alone will be a necessity in life."

"I'm sure it will be."

Ruthanne went toward the back of the building to reach the other side of the town faster. She stopped halfway to see if Rebecca was watching her. Not seeing Rebecca, she quickly ran over to where she'd buried the flowers.

"It looks like nothing is here," Ruthanne said. "I couldn't have buried those flowers that well in the night."

Strangely, the wind began to increase as if a storm were coming. Ruthanne looked down and saw her handprint next to her foot. She grabbed a trowel, knelt down, and began to dig vigorously. She tried to avoid getting dirty so she wouldn't be questioned. While she was digging, she felt something go in her nail and looked at her hand. The soft leaf of the mountain mint was partially stuck in the tip of her fingernail. She took the leaf, smelled it, and gasped, looking down to see a few of the flower petals exposed. She panicked and reburied the flowers.

"God, I don't understand why I must go through this." Ruthanne calmed herself down and wiped the tears from her face.

She took a deep breath and began to leave the yard, but she heard a voice from the house.

"Ruthanne, where are you?" Elizabeth asked.

"Is it possible for that woman to survive without me in the morning?" Ruthanne whined. "I'm coming, Elizabeth!"

Elizabeth poked her head around the corner. "Why are you back there?"

"Mind your own business! Did you even eat?" Ruthanne asked, her tone irritated.

"Well, no, I didn't eat. I was waiting for you."

"Go eat! I already ate my breakfast." Ruthanne went to the front of the house.

The town had begun its regular routine. Carriages rolled by, and children played outside.

"Considering I just pulled out flowers from the ground that miraculously appeared on a table, I guess my dreams have more meaning than I wanted to believe. God must really care to tell me to be on guard," she said to herself.

She sat down on a bench and closed her eyes, trying to clear her mind of the worries. A horse neighed, and Ruthanne opened her eyes to see Victor Hildebrand on his horse.

Mr. Hildebrand's blue eyes glared at Ruthanne.

"Well, if this ain't pure luck for me to find the troublemaker when I had given up hope," Mr. Hildebrand said.

"Look, it's the crippled wolf with his tongue hanging out," Ruthanne snarled.

"You arrogant woman! How dare you speak to me with such disrespect? I'll teach you what your father should have taught you."

"My apologies, Mr. Hildebrand. I have a habit of speaking the truth, as harsh as it may seem."

Mr. Hildebrand adjusted his black top hat snobbishly. "Stand up and give me your respect. I'm a representative of the town of Mercy."

Ruthanne looked at Mr. Hildebrand while she pursed her lips and raised an eyebrow. "I'm sorry, Mr. Hildebrand, but I seem to have forgotten how to stand at the moment."

Mr. Hildebrand sneered as his eyes narrowed after hearing Ruthanne's tone. "Where is that Negro woman you were with?"

"If you must know, I don't know, and she is none of your concern."

"Keep counting your blessings. I see it in your keen green eyes that you're a man-killer."

Ruthanne sarcastically replied, "Why, Mr. Hildebrand, you flatter me. If you really want to know, yours wouldn't be the first life I've taken."

Mr. Hildebrand glared at Ruthanne as he began to turn red, and he shrugged within his brown plaid frock coat. "You watch the words that come out of your mouth, you redheaded demon."

"Same to you. I suggest you leave now because there ain't nothing here for you."

Mr. Hildebrand snarled, "It's women like you that create disorder in our country." Hildebrand snapped his horse's reins and rode off to the west part of town. Ruthanne watched him ride off, eager to see him disappear.

Rebecca came out of the front door. "Well, wasn't that exciting?" she said.

"You heard all of that?" Ruthanne asked.

"No, I didn't. Just the part when he called you a green-eyed man-killer and a redheaded demon, which I found flattering too."

Ruthanne laughed. "You made my day." She stood and gave Rebecca a hug.

"I try, my dear. Mr. Hildebrand is a typical man of today, believing women have a set role in life. It seems you have also gotten on that man's bad side. Good for you."

The women laughed while they looked at the morning sun.

Suddenly, Allen rushed out of the house. "I'm running a little late for work, Rebecca. I'll be back in time for supper," he said.

Rebecca replied, "Alright, honey. I'll tell Mr. Boston you said hi."

"You ladies stay out of trouble."

"Go on, Allen. We'll do fine here."

Ruthanne sat down and huffed.

"Are you going to be alright out here?" Rebecca asked.

Ruthanne answered, "Yes, I'm waiting on the girls to see if they had any ideas for us to do today."

"Anyway, I'm going to go back inside. I can't leave Ashley alone for too long. And before I forget, the festival will be in two weeks, so I hope you have a nice dress for the occasion."

Ruthanne gave a big smile. "I didn't realize it was so soon. It's a blessing we went to Marilyn when we first arrived in Mercy. Annabelle will have a lovely new green dress."

Rebecca beamed as she nodded her head. "This is starting to become a special time. Well, I will let you have your day."

"I'm sure I won't be going far today. I'm waiting for the girls."

CHAPTER 11
Unforseen

"Sounds to me like you're waiting for them to come up with an adventure instead," Rebecca calmly said.

Ruthanne smirked. "It amazes me how well you can read me."

"Great minds tend to think alike, my dear. Wait until you become a mother, then other amazing instincts kick in."

Ruthanne giggled. "Not anytime soon. I'm getting to enjoy this life of freedom."

"Nothing wrong with that thought. Just don't pass up a good man because the timing didn't match up to when you believed it should happen." Rebecca returned to the house to watch Ashley.

Ruthanne sat back and felt the calmness of the day to come.

Despite the worry she had felt over her dream, a calm warm wind came through. Ruthanne thought, *God, is this your love because there's never been a time I needed it more.* The wind calmed down, and Ruthanne beamed. "Thank you, God, for never abandoning me," she said. She closed her eyes as the rays of the sun warmed her.

"We're ready for the day now, Ruthanne," Elizabeth said.

Ruthanne glanced up at Elizabeth and saw she had put on one of her newer dresses.

"You know you love those dresses, Elizabeth," Ruthanne said.

"It looks elegant, doesn't it?"

"If you say so," Ruthanne murmured.

"You say something?"

"I said it doesn't look bad on you at all."

As Elizabeth climbed down the stairs, she cheerfully replied, "Why, thank you, Ruthanne. I thought you made one of your demeaning comments."

"Well, not this time. I'll save that energy for later," Ruthanne sarcastically said.

Elizabeth glared at Ruthanne while her smile dropped. "Annabelle loves my dresses, don't you, Annabelle?"

Annabelle came outside and closed the door, starting down the stairs in a green floral dress Elizabeth had given her.

"I think it looks lovely, Elizabeth," Annabelle said.

Ruthanne squealed. "Look at you, Annabelle! You're adorable."

Elizabeth rolled her blue eyes. "So, she looks adorable, and I don't look bad," Elizabeth growled.

Ruthanne smacked her lips and replied, "Hush, Elizabeth, you wear those dresses all the time. You're nothing new."

Elizabeth folded her arms. "Anyway, at least you're right about Annabelle. She is adorable in that dress."

Annabelle blushed. "Thank y'all. I feel so good."

Ruthanne replied, "You should feel good. So what did you have planned, Elizabeth?"

Elizabeth answered, "Well, I say we go see Marilyn and see how her work is coming along. I especially think she'll be thrilled to see you, Annabelle."

"Sure, I'd like to see Marilyn," Annabelle confidently said.

"I'll come along with you two since Rebecca is with Ashley. No sense in me sitting around here on my own," Ruthanne said.

The women went toward the store to surprise Marilyn.

The women arrived at Pots's Garments with smiles on their

faces, ready to show Marilyn the dresses. Ruthanne entered the store first.

"Marilyn, are you here?" Ruthanne shouted.

Marilyn anxiously walked from the back of the store.

"It is great to see you! Are you here to get something else new for the festival?" Marilyn asked.

"I have something better in mind," Ruthanne said. "Ladies, you can come in now!"

Elizabeth and Annabelle entered the store with their dresses.

"Oh, my word! The dresses look gorgeous on you girls. I can't believe they fit that well."

Marilyn began to lightly jump, her eyes widening as she smiled, looking at how well-fitted the dresses were on the two women. Marilyn approached Annabelle and Elizabeth, smiling.

"The fact that the dresses look so good on the two of you is enough to bring me joy for the rest of the year."

Ruthanne replied, "They do look cute, Marilyn. It makes me excited to try on the blue dress you're making."

Marilyn grinned. "I'm sure it'll look as lovely as these dresses look on them. That red dress glows on you so well. I never imagined it would look so good!"

Elizabeth replied, "Why, thank you, Marilyn. I must say, I'm excited to see what you will be wearing at the festival."

"I will have to show you ladies that surprise." Marilyn locked her eyes on Annabelle. "You're the first Negro woman that'll wear my work." Tears started to flow down Marilyn's face, and she gave a big smile. "You wear it with such grace, Sasha. I feel words can't even express what I feel right now." Marilyn hugged Annabelle. "I have to work on not being so emotional. It is just a dress."

"Nonsense. This is your passion, and so few of us have something like this," Ruthanne encouragingly said.

"I must say, the dresses you made certainly look like the best. It's like what my friend, Judy Mays, would wear," Annabelle said.

"I honestly didn't think I would look so good in red, Marilyn. It's so exquisite," Elizabeth said.

Marilyn replied, "I must show you ladies what I have. I finished it two days ago. Follow me. I've been keeping it upstairs."

They went upstairs, anxious to see Marilyn's new dress.

"Look at that!" Elizabeth shouted.

Ruthanne and Annabelle gasped when they saw the beauty of the dress.

"I don't think I've ever seen a dress so white in my life," Annabelle said.

"Why, thank you, Sasha," Marilyn said, smiling.

"Marilyn, you really outdid yourself with this dress," Ruthanne said. "Can we trade?"

Marilyn laughed. "I may consider that after the festival."

"It is truly a work of art. I wouldn't mind wearing such a thing on my wedding day," Elizabeth said.

"I think you're thinking too far down the road, Elizabeth. You first need to find a man because the things you've struck gold with are losers," Ruthanne said.

Elizabeth glared at Ruthanne, and she scrunched her nose.

"Of course, crush all my dreams with one statement, Ruthanne!"

"Well, it's the truth. Would you prefer for me to lie to you?"

Elizabeth snarled, "At this point in time, a lie would make me feel so much better."

Marilyn began to laugh. "I didn't mean for this dress to start an argument."

"She's jealous that I try to find a good man," Elizabeth said.

Annabelle sighed and asked, "How did you get the designs in the arms so well, Marilyn?"

"Jealous!" Ruthanne shouted. "Why would I be jealous of deplorable trash like Jeff?"

Elizabeth angrily replied, "Why are you bringing up Jeff? That was so mean of you to act like you liked him."

"If you would have admitted it, I wouldn't have acted like I cared about that failure. Jeff is so handsome, blah-blah-blah."

Elizabeth pointed her finger at Ruthanne as her eyes dilated. "You've got some nerve, Ruthanne, you agreed with me on that!"

Ruthanne folded her arms. "Good looks and money are not the only things that matter."

Ruthanne and Elizabeth continued to argue while Marilyn inched toward Annabelle. "Is this a normal argument for them?" Marilyn asked.

"Yes," Annabelle answered. "I think it was an argument that never got finished."

Elizabeth bickered, "How dare you keep bringing up my past failures, Ruthanne? Just because I'm not afraid to keep trying, it doesn't mean I'm stupid."

Ruthanne replied, "No, but the men you pick, like Jeff, think women are trophies to be won over with ease."

"Why do you keep bringing up Jeff? Did something happen?"

Annabelle murmured, "I don't think now is the time to tell her, Ruthanne."

"Well..." Ruthanne said, but she stopped when they heard a thump.

The women looked downstairs to see who was down there. Marilyn began to go downstairs, and the others followed her.

"Who's there?" Marilyn asked.

"Marilyn, dear, do we have appointments coming in here anytime soon?" Mr. Pots asked.

Marilyn sighed. "Daddy, it's only you. I thought you were a customer."

"Why no, my sweet angel, I'm excited about the festival coming up. We're bound to have a nice boost of customers."

Marilyn walked up to reorganize the perfumes on the counter, and the other young women walked behind her.

Mr. Pot's eyes narrowed. "You've been kept busy by company, I see."

"Yes, Papa, I was showing them my new dress."

"How nice, and I see the Negro woman came as well. Your name was Sass, wasn't it?"

"My name is Sasha, Mr. Pots."

Mr. Pots replied, "Well, Sass was close enough, and what do you have on? How do you have such a beautiful dress?"

Annabelle replied, "Lovely, isn't it. Like it's one of Marilyn's makings. We bought a design she's already making."

Mr. Pots frowned and shook his head. "You must not leave here with that dress."

Annabelle's eyebrows shot up. "What— What do you mean I can't leave with this dress? The dress is mine, Mr. Pots."

Mr. Pots tightened his jaw. "Excuse me, nigger?"

"Mr. Pots, the dress has already been paid for," Elizabeth shouted.

"You stay out of this, Miss," Mr. Pots said. "Marilyn, give this beast her money back. She cannot leave here with a dress."

"Daddy, why are you making such a big deal of this? She'll look wonderful," Marilyn said.

Mr. Pots replied, "That's exactly my point, Marilyn. If some of the officials in this town find out that we helped this woman look as she does now, that will be the end of our business."

"We didn't help her, Daddy. I'm making the dress, and if someone has a problem with it, they can talk to me about it."

"I won't allow such a dangerous decision to even come to your mind." Mr. Pots approached Annabelle. "Now, I'm gonna ask you one more time not to take the dress."

Ruthanne stepped in front of Annabelle. "And what do you propose she wear?" Ruthanne sarcastically asked.

"She can walk in the town naked for all I care, you rebellious redheaded demon," Mr. Pots said.

"Look here, you coward—"

Mr. Pots's eyes got big. "Coward! How dare you! I can't stand to see my daughter's work being worn by a Negro. It's beneath her."

"Father, she is welcome to wear the dresses I make as much as Mrs. White is," Marilyn said.

"How dare you say such a blasphemous thing!" Mr. Pots said. "If you say such a thing in front of anyone with power, you will ruin your chances of ever leaving this town and making dresses for important people."

Marilyn frowned as she looked at her father.

"Now, for the last time, you won't leave with that dress."

Annabelle began to back away from Mr. Pots. "I'm sorry, but I can't lower myself anymore to make you feel comfortable, Mr. Pots," Annabelle said. "You have raised a lovely daughter, and I hope that you can learn from her. Her mother must've been a strong woman to deal with a man like you."

Mr. Pots's mouth dropped while listening to Annabelle's harsh tone. Abruptly, Mr. Pots pushed Ruthanne out of the way and grabbed the green floral dress. Annabelle grabbed Mr. Pots's hand, but with a cry of outrage, he ripped Annabelle's dress. She screamed in terror while Ruthanne and Marilyn pulled Mr. Pots off her. In the struggle, Mr. Pots stumbled and fell to the ground, knocking over a table with several perfumes placed for customers.

Annabelle began to hyperventilate, and Elizabeth's eyes widened as she covered her mouth. At this time, the perfumes shattered on the floor, cutting Mr. Pots's hand.

"Are you okay, Daddy?" Marilyn asked.

Mr. Pots slowly picked himself up. "I'm alright. I... I just need to go to the back room," he said.

Marilyn frowned, watching her father struggling to stand up. Mr. Pots looked at his hand, noticing the deep cut from the glass, and walked to the back room, shaking his head.

Marilyn, ashamed of her father's assault, went to Annabelle and held her hands. "Words cannot even express how sorry I am for what my father did."

Tears began to run down Annabelle's face. "Now what am I supposed to wear for the festival?" she asked.

Marilyn hugged Annabelle. "Don't you worry about a thing, Sasha. I'll still finish the dress."

Annabelle wiped the tears from her eyes. "But your father," she objected.

Marilyn boldly replied, "I will deal with that old man, so don't worry about it."

"It is truly a good thing that you're doing, Marilyn, but are you sure your father won't get in the way? Or ruin it?" Ruthanne asked.

"I have just enough time to finish making her a new dress for the festival," Marilyn said. "It took me eight months to make the other dresses, and none are labeled. I'm the only one that knows each dress's owner."

Elizabeth exhaled and asked, "What if your father was right?"

Marilyn answered, "I would rather take the risk instead of continuing to be passive."

"How about we get the dress out of here without anybody noticing, and that way, they would never know Sasha got the dress from here."

"That's ridiculous for Marilyn to make such an effort to hide the truth from these people," Ruthanne unsympathetically said.

"I agree with Elizabeth," Annabelle said. "I'm more than grateful that you would do this for me. But I see this putting all of your work into danger, all for a Negro woman. Please, listen to Elizabeth. I'm afraid of what the people of this town would do to you if they found out you made a dress for me."

Marilyn frowned as she looked at Annabelle, but she boldly said, "I'm making that dress for you, Annabelle. However, Elizabeth is right, so I guess that means we'll have to make it a night delivery."

"If you want to do it that way, fine, but I will be the one to pick up the dress," Ruthanne firmly said.

"I could pick up the dress. You don't have to do that for me," Annabelle said.

"There's no telling what could happen to you at night. Don't forget, not everyone is this town will welcome a Negro woman, especially at night. It is far too dangerous to even consider.

We'd have to go with you, and what if Mr. Pots learns of this plan?"

Marilyn shook her head in agreement. "Well, I believe it is settled," Marilyn said. "In two weeks, I will be able to have the dress made for Annabelle. Ruthanne will come to pick it up."

Elizabeth beamed, having done her part in helping make a serious decision. Annabelle took a deep breath and forced a smile while looking at the others.

Marilyn gave Annabelle a hug. "It's going to be quite alright."

Annabelle replied, "I'm sorry I've become a burden."

"No, Annabelle, you helped me see even more how much of a fool my father really is. Even the elders in our own families can remain fools, full of pride and unforgiveness. Oh, and before I forget, I have something for you, Elizabeth."

Marilyn went to the back table behind the counter and picked up an oval-shaped bottle.

"This is a new perfume that I'm sure you will like, and it is enough for all three of you."

Elizabeth smiled, clutched her hands, and quickly reached out for the perfume. "Thank you, Marilyn. I'm too excited for this festival now," Elizabeth said.

Marilyn replied, "I figured since your last trip was interrupted by Mrs. White, I could at least make up for it in some kind of way."

Ruthanne raised an eyebrow and asked, "Who is Mrs. White, Marilyn?"

Marilyn answered, "She is a rich, very powerful woman that didn't realize she has an adulterer as a husband."

"Now, that sounds interesting."

"Yes, I became annoyed with her talk of how I'm getting old and I should be married, so I told her in my own way about something I may have seen."

The women hysterically laughed, which released the tension they were all feeling.

"I guess we should get going. I believe we have had enough drama for today," Ruthanne said.

"I completely understand, Ruthanne. I think I will take the time to forget a part of this day."

"Ruthanne, wait, what were you going to say to me about Jeff?" Elizabeth asked. "You never told me what happened besides that he was drunk."

Annabelle looked at Elizabeth with pity, knowing the truth would only disappoint her.

Ruthanne replied, "I think we should talk about this at home."

"No, Marilyn is a friend, and I don't hide things from my friends, so what is it?"

"Sasha and I ran into Jeff on the west side of the town, and you know he was drunk. Well, he couldn't even say your name right, but he also said a lot of improper things to us. He has no good intentions for you, Elizabeth."

Elizabeth frowned, and her eyes shifted toward the ground.

Marilyn said to Elizabeth, "I know how you feel, but don't let one man ruin things for the one God has for you," Marilyn said. "One of the worst things we can do is hold onto that anger so much that the next man catches our wrath."

"Don't think too hard on it, Elizabeth. You know the right man will find you. It's just that sometimes, we find trash before treasure," Ruthanne encouragingly said.

"It's not like he was courting me, so I shouldn't be so down," Elizabeth said.

"Now that's the way to look at this," Marilyn said. "You met a dishonest man, but fortunately, God showed you his true personality before you became involved with him."

Elizabeth grimaced. "Yeah, you're right. Both of you are right. Well, now that I know the truth, how are we going to cover up the tear on Sasha's dress?"

"I have that covered. I have some other dresses she can wear, and you can just bring it back later, Sasha."

Annabelle replied, "Thank you, Marilyn."

"No problem. It was my father that tore it, after all."

Marilyn selected one of her dresses and gave it to Annabelle.

"Where can I change?" Annabelle asked.

"There's another room in the back you can change in, and that way, you can avoid my father too."

With her eyes wide, Annabelle slowly entered the room, hoping to avoid Mr. Pots. The other women watched carefully to make sure she made it to the room. Marilyn turned to Ruthanne and Elizabeth.

"I'm still in shock about what my father did, and I don't know how else I can apologize. It's like these past three years, he has become more racist, and it scares me."

"Our fathers are slave owners, so we both grew up with this. I must say that your father is a crumb off a loaf of bread," Elizabeth said, crossing her arms as she looked at Marilyn. "I've seen my father whip slaves, so it bothers me very little because I became used to it. I've seen some of the slaves who escaped become captured. Their hands and feet were bound, and they were dragged by a horse back to the plantation. We even have an older slave with one hand. The other hand was cut off for him punching an overseer. I thought it was normal until one day, my favorite house slave, Robin, accidentally dropped some of our dinner, and my father hit her.

"When Robin came to our plantation, she was only two years old and without a mother. I wasn't sure at the time if her mother had died or if they took her away from her mother. She's very light-skinned, with long wavy sandy-brown hair, and as a seven-year-old child, I didn't understand why she looked so different from the other slaves. As she got older, I realized she had brownish-green eyes, but I know Negroes don't have green eyes. It then occurred to me she wasn't just Negro, but she was part white. At eleven years old, I realized a dark truth. Her father must've been white. She's a smart girl, and as she became older, she started to remind me of my own family. At thirteen years old, I realized my cousin, Jennifer, always came over, even when there were no family gatherings."

Elizabeth gave a slight grin. "Jennifer is one of my favorite older cousins. However, I never understood why she would come over so much when she lived fifteen miles away. Jennifer paid close attention to Robin, and she never really commanded her. She always held more of a disciplinary tone with Robin and would even play with her. As Robin became older, she was trained to hold herself higher than the other slaves, and she almost never left the mansion unless my mother took her to town. She was always a house slave and never given leftovers like the other slaves. I always thought it so odd that my father avoided Robin at times, and he preferred the other house slaves to bring him his meals. I couldn't figure it out as to why she was treated so differently. I even caught my own mother reading to Robin when she was a young child."

Elizabeth slightly shook her head. "Why would my mother do such a stupid thing? She taught me it was against the law for Negroes to learn how to read or write. I think that entire week, I couldn't let it go, and I gave Robin such a hard time the entire week. I finally let it go, believing maybe my mother needed to teach Robin a little so she could cook or know how to organize something in the mansion.

"One day, when I saw Robin sleeping, she was in the most peculiar position. Her arms were over her head, and her eyes were cracked open. I found it funny because I know I've seen someone else who slept like that. I went through the hallway, wondering to myself why that was so familiar. When I went downstairs, one of our house slaves came up to me panicking, apologizing for waking up late since we were expecting Jennifer early that morning for breakfast. The shock came to me that Jennifer sleeps like that. I was so shocked, I told the slave it doesn't matter. She'd be patient. That morning, the more I looked at Jennifer, the more I saw Robin. It took everything I had not to break down in tears because of the possible shame.

"Jennifer noticed something was wrong with me, and she asked if I was alright. I told her I was fine and hadn't slept well, so she let it go, and everything continued as normal. Jennifer continued to treat Robin with such kindness, and it seemed like a hidden love. Every time Robin walked away, carrying a tray back to the kitchen, it seemed to disturb Jennifer in some small way. Amazing how I'd just began to notice after all those years of having Robin. However, I remember seeing the same expression on Jennifer's face when she was married, and Robin was six years old. Robin was allowed to hold Jennifer's first-born, my little cousin, Isabelle. That was peculiar to me that Jennifer was so willing to let a young Negro child hold a newborn immediately after her."

Elizabeth shrugged her shoulders, looking at Marilyn and Ruthanne. "Not even my mother objected to her great-niece being held by a Negro child before her. I began to believe that this slave was more than a slave. I prayed to God because I began to become so confused. It was hard for me to dislike Robin because from the day she was brought to the mansion, she was welcomed. I also noticed a few of the slaves didn't like her for some reason. Oddest thing happened as Robin became older. She started to look like an exact copy of Jennifer, especially when she had ringlets in her hair, to the point that the only difference between them was the little bit of color Robin has." Elizabeth took a deep breath, and she began to sob.

Ruthanne placed her hand on Elizabeth's shoulder. "Elizabeth, what is wrong?" Ruthanne asked.

Elizabeth replied, "When Robin turned twelve, she was carrying a tray to my father. She accidentally dropped it, spilling drinks on the carpet. I remember it like it happened yesterday. My father reacted so badly. He went toward Robin and smacked her hard. He called her a luxury nigger, and I saw the look on my mother's saddened face. Something came over me, and I stepped in front of him with tears running down my face. I asked him, 'How can you treat your own niece like a dog?'

"My mother was heartbroken that I not only figured out the truth but spoke it. My mother broke out in tears and ran to Robin and gave her a hug. My mother helped Robin up and took her to the well to clean the tea off her dress. My father asked me how I knew that. I told him because they look so much alike, and the love that Jennifer showed for Robin was undeniable. It takes a lot for a mother to deny her own child. I even said to him that Isabelle looks like Robin...what a rage that brought out of my father. My father came to me like I was a little girl, telling me that even if someone else figures it out, not to say anything. I told him it was a foolish thing to hide the truth from her and her younger siblings."

Elizabeth sighed.

"Unfortunately, my father believed it was the right thing to do then. He believed it would be easier for them to learn this when they're older. I felt hurt holding such a secret, and my father was clearly angry at me for yelling the truth in front of Robin. God must've been at work that day because in the middle of my father trying to explain why it was right to keep it a secret from Robin's younger sister and brother, Jennifer walked in. I remember the happiness on her face, but I couldn't help but frown because I felt in a way, I'd failed her.

She noticed the look of disappointment on my father's face, and she asked what was wrong. I told her that her daughter needs her now. She thought I was talking about Isabelle and said she left her back at the plantation. I told her, 'No, your oldest daughter.' She shouted at my father with such a rage, asking how he could tell me the truth as tears started to run down her face. I told Jennifer I had figured it out on my own. She asked me how I could possibly tell, and I told her what I told my father. Love is a powerful thing, and it is hard for a mother to deny her children, especially when a daughter begins to look like and act like her mother.

"I've never seen Jennifer cry like that, so I gave her a hug. It was such an enormous amount of shame I was feeling from her. I asked her about the father, but she wouldn't tell me much, only that it had only happened a few times and that he was no longer alive. She asked where Robin was, and I told her my mother was cleaning off her dress, so she went upstairs like she was a nervous child going to a school. I remember it like it was yesterday. She walked up to Robin and gave her a hug. She told Robin she had loved her from the moment she gave birth and had refused to give her up, so she was forced to send Robin here. Knowing Robin for most of her life, I'd never seen that girl cry out of pain until that day. Robin truly believed she didn't have a mother, but that day, all the pieces came together. I could see it touched my mother, but I felt like my father still had regrets about the reunion.

"So that's my family secret, and now, Robin is being put in an arrangement when she is of age. Robin will be given to a northern white man who will tolerate a half-blood. My family feels that's best for Robin, and it helps hide the shame of my family. My mother feels that it will help Robin live a more normal life and that it's a blessing she is as light as she is."

Elizabeth frowned while she huffed. "Ruthanne, that's part of the reason I decided to leave Mississippi with you. I couldn't stand being around with them dictating who Robin would be with, but their minds have already been made up. My only hope is Robin does fall in love with that man, and the man who takes her will love her back."

Ruthanne and Marilyn looked at Elizabeth with big eyes as they slightly frowned.

"It makes so much sense though, Elizabeth," Ruthanne said. "When I really think about how Robin was treated, she is treated differently than the others. Your parents surprise me. All this time, your mother and father have been protecting Robin while keeping her a secret."

"That must be an intense feeling, Elizabeth," Marilyn sympathetically said. "I couldn't imagine a secret like that in my family, and I can't imagine my family handling it that well."

Elizabeth pursed her lips, and her eyes shifted away from Marilyn.

"Some secrets are not meant to be kept. That took a lot of courage," Ruthanne proudly said.

Elizabeth's eyes fixed on Ruthanne and Marilyn. "I'd like to keep this between us though. I don't even want Sasha to know of this part of my life," Elizabeth said.

Marilyn and Ruthanne nodded their heads at Elizabeth. The

young women heard Annabelle opening the door and turned their heads anxiously. Annabelle came out of the room. The new green and white dress fitted Annabelle as if it had been drawn for her body.

The women looked in awe as Annabelle approached them.

"Are y'all ready to go?" Annabelle asked.

"Look at you! I should use you as a live model the way you wear that dress," Marilyn said.

"Why, thank you, Marilyn. I feel so good in this dress you made."

"I think we're ready to go. Are you ready, Elizabeth?" Ruthanne asked.

Elizabeth replied. "Yes, I'm ready for the rest of the day that's still to come."

Ruthanne gave Marilyn a hug. "I guess that means we're to do some other things, Marilyn. Besides, I'm sure you'll have some customers to deal with soon."

Marilyn giggled. "Well, yes, but not as interesting as you all."

The women giggled and said their goodbyes to Marilyn. Marilyn watched them walk away while she picked up a perfume bottle and sighed. She went to the back room once she couldn't see her friends anymore. She saw her father sitting down in his chair with a bandaged hand, staring at the cuckoo clock.

"You always seem to adore that clock so much, Papa."

Mr. Pots replied, "I admire the bird, Marilyn. Even though the bird in the clock isn't real, it is reliable and incorruptible. I wish I was more like that cuckoo bird. Maybe I would have been a better husband for your mother if I was more like that cuckoo bird."

Marilyn knelt down next to her father and held his hand. "Daddy, nobody is perfect, and I don't know what to do with you. Each year, you seem to become a more bitter man. Daddy, I'm afraid for you because bitter people are miserable people, and nobody wants to be around a miserable person. That includes me."

Mr. Pots turned his head to his daughter, noticing her creased forehead and sad eyes. "I'm sorry for everything that I have done wrong. You and your sisters are all I have, and I don't want any of you to experience the regrets I have."

Marilyn scowled, and her eyes narrowed. "Daddy, you have to stop feeling sorry for yourself. I can't stand to see you becoming less of a man each year."

Mr. Pots patted his knee as he pursed his lips. "You have so much wisdom for such a young woman, and I'm proud of you. Marilyn, Anne isn't the oldest child. You had a brother, Andrew, who was such a happy child, but he was killed by a runaway horse. The horse was not tied down properly by a Negro man, and I never did forgive that man. Your mother managed to forgive that man. How she had so much love for people, I will never understand. I'm happy you're more like your mother." Mr. Pots wiped a tear from his eye. "He's buried at the cemetery behind Pastor Dawson's church. We decided to never bring it up, and we never brought you or your sisters to his grave. It was too painful. Anne was one when he died. I've let Andrew's death turn me into a hateful man. How can God forgive me of my past crimes? I deserve to burn in hell for all that I have done and said."

"Nobody deserves to suffer for an eternity. Papa, I've learned how to read, and I've been able to read good for the past four years."

Mr. Pots looked away from Marilyn while he shook his head.

"I know you don't approve, but I've been reading the Bible. It says all you have to do is ask God for forgiveness and forgive those that have done wrong against us. Love and forgiveness are freedom, Papa, no matter how much the past hurts."

The cuckoo clock struck 1:00 p.m., and the cuckoo came out of the door, making the call of the bird.

Mr. Pots looked at the bird, then turned his head toward his cut hand.

"God bless you, my youngest daughter. Even now, because of your words, I know what I must do."

"I love you, Daddy."

Mr. Pots calmly put his hand on Marilyn's hand. "And I love you as well."

He let go of his daughter and went upstairs.

Marilyn smiled as heart beat faster. "Wow, so I had an older brother," she said, frowning. "I guess I'd change too if I'd lost a child."

Marilyn went to the front of the store, then looked at the clock, and her emerald green eyes widened.

"I need to get started on Sasha's dress. God, bless me with your strength so I can complete this dress in time," Marilyn murmured.

She gathered supplies and entered a back room to get started on a new design.

Annabelle, Ruthanne, and Elizabeth arrived back home and stood in front of the stairs, still shocked by Mr. Pots's outburst.

"I'm done exploring the rest of this town for the rest of the week," Annabelle said. "I would rather help Rebecca continue planting her flowers than take another risk like that."

"I understand, but don't let that crazy man discourage you," Ruthanne said.

Elizabeth replied, "I agree with Annabelle a little though, Ruthanne. I really think it would be a bad idea for her to ever go out in this town alone. It feels like we've met more people that hate her than those that like her."

"She can't hide in the shadows the rest of her life, Elizabeth," Ruthanne griped. "That's enough to make anyone miserable."

Annabelle replied, "Elizabeth, Ruthanne is right, as much as I hate it. I can't go on living my life in the shadows because people hate me for being a Negro woman. I also think you're right too. I don't think it's a good idea for me to ever walk alone in this town. I feel scared sometimes. Only you, Ruthanne, and Rebecca know who I am. I'm scared that they'll find out where I'm really from."

Rebecca stepped up behind Annabelle from inside the

house. "The people of this town will never know where you originally come from, Annabelle," Rebecca said.

Annabelle turned around and grinned at Rebecca, feeling Rebecca's genuine words. Ruthanne also smiled. The women spent the rest of the day with Rebecca, enjoying each other's company.

A week passed into August of 1845, and the women continued their usual routine. They often sat in a hammock in the yard that Elizabeth had brought from Mississippi. Marilyn worked vigorously on the new dresses, excited to finish them. Rebecca had begun knitting new baby clothes, and Ruthanne watched her intuitively. Ruthanne began to wonder how Peter was doing. She hadn't seen him in over a week, and she hadn't visited the church to avoid the possibility of Annabelle being rejected. However, she couldn't help but daydream about him and wonder how good of a pastor he might be.

Five days before the festival, Ruthanne became aggravated that she hadn't seen Peter. She stood up calmly from the hammock in her orange and white dress.

"I'm going to explore the town a little," Ruthanne said.

"Well, alright, stay out of trouble. Allen still worries that Hildebrand will do something crazy," Rebecca said.

"I'll be super nice today. I just want to see something."

Ruthanne quickly traveled toward the church to get away from Elizabeth and Annabelle. She reached the church and stared at the amazing architecture. She took a deep breath and headed toward the church doors, unsure if Peter was in the church. She stopped at the doors and turned around, suspicious that one of the other women might have followed her. After checking, she felt comfortable and walked inside, still amazed by the three angel statues.

"They look so real. It is amazing to me," Ruthanne said.

She noticed five other people in the church praying silently. The beauty of the sunrays shining through the stained-glass windows of the church made it seem as if God himself was there personally. Ruthanne felt such a strong presence of peace that she almost forgot she'd originally come to look for Peter. She strolled down the aisle, realizing she should have been more patient.

She turned, intending to return home, when Peter moved around a pillar with his Bible in his hands.

"Ruthanne, it's great to see you," Peter said. "How are you doing?"

Ruthanne, caught off guard, stuttered, "I'm quite fine. I was on my way out."

"Are you sure? You clearly haven't been here long. Is everything okay?"

"Oh no, everything is fine. I've done what I needed to do here." She reached for the door handle anxiously.

"Wait! Are you sure everything is okay? I haven't seen you or the others in any of the services. Allen and Rebecca have both been to the service, but I didn't get the opportunity to ask them how you all are doing."

Ruthanne held on to the door handle. "All is well. I wasn't sure if it was safe for Sasha to come here, pastor. There is no Negro church here. I don't worry about Rebecca's or Mr. Keys's treatment of Sasha. However, I cannot say the same of the rest of your congregation. I have already seen some of the evil in this town called Mercy, and I refuse to put Sasha in any danger, especially in a church, the most sacred ground out here."

"I'm sorry for what you have experienced here in Mercy," Peter said, "but it is something I'm trying to eliminate in this town by showing love to all. I wish it was far easier to reach the hearts of men, but a closed ear usually means a closed heart. The only way I know how to open ears is by being an example of what it means to truly be a Christian."

"It's nice to hear that you're aware of the problem, Pastor, but that does not guarantee Sasha's protection," Ruthanne replied. "I will admit that in my own personal time, I spend much time praying to God, and I have asked him to change my heart. Even though I have become better over time, I must admit that an inappropriate approach against Sasha by one of the members of this church may cause me to revert for the moment. I promise they will see the wrath of a woman who would barely make it into the gates of heaven."

"I understand the seriousness that you speak of. I do ask that you give these people a chance. Sasha won't be the only Negro in the church. There are twelve others who normally come here."

Ruthanne let go of the door handle and looked into Peter's comforting brown eyes to assess his intentions. She looked away from his face and exhaled.

"I know hate only creates more hate. You promise me if I bring Sasha here, she'll be welcomed."

Peter nodded. "I will promise you she'll be welcomed with open arms. If anyone mistreats her, then I will deal with them appropriately."

Ruthanne opened the door and grinned. "Don't disappointment me, Peter."

He smiled at Ruthanne.

She continued, "I will see you at the festival, Pastor Avail."

"I will see you as well, Ruthanne."

Ruthanne returned to her new home, hoping Peter would keep his promise.

He watched Ruthanne while she headed away.

"What a brave, crazy, and loving woman."

An old man calmly came up behind Peter. "Pastor Avail, please help me finish reading the book of Psalms," he said.

Peter replied, "Mr. Jefferson, there is no way we are going to get through the whole book of Psalms together today. That's 150 chapters."

"Please, as if you have plans today, Pastor Avail. With me being the treasurer, I know your schedule." Mr. Jefferson gave an instigative smile, adding, "I must admit, though, that was a pretty young lady."

Peter pressed his lips together. "Mr. Jefferson, the conversation between that young woman and me was professional and pure."

"I believe you. Take it from an old goat like me not to be so serious. Otherwise, you can miss out on what God is putting in front of you. Professionalism also includes recognizing miracles and divine connections. Don't ever forget that."

Peter began to return to the pews with Mr. Jefferson and mumbled, "I'm the one that's supposed to be giving biblical advice, but this old man seems to have a good point."

Mr. Jefferson smiled at Peter and patted him on his back. "Well, now that this old goat has made a point, let's get to reading." Mr. Jefferson went to the front aisle, excitedly laughing.

The other four people in the church looked at him snobbishly as he moved down the aisle.

"Don't you old goats look at me as if I'd lost my mind. I'm sanctified."

Peter shook his head and apologized to the other members while he approached the front of the church to sit with Mr. Jefferson.

Mr. Jefferson looked at Peter and chuckled. "Pastor Avail, maybe you need to take up the habit of running if you're having trouble keeping up with me."

Peter chuckled, responding, "I may have to try that, Mr. Jefferson. Now, let's get started."

Ruthanne arrived at her new home with a feeling of calmness and reassurance. The second she began to go up the stairs, the front door opened.

"Where did you go, Ruthanne?" Annabelle asked.

Ruthanne answered, "Hey, I went for a quick walk. What have you been up to?"

"I've been playing with Ashley to let Rebecca focus on her knitting. She seems to get more excited every day about the baby. I guess I would too if I were in her shoes."

"Anyway, I'm going to rest in the kitchen for a while. Is Elizabeth upstairs?"

"No, she took off not too long after you to go see Marilyn."

Ruthanne smiled and said, "It's nice to see that she has become quite the socialite."

Annabelle's eyebrows slightly rose. "What's a socialite?"

"A socialite is a person who tends to seek out people, and in turn, becomes influential or—in other words—important. In a way, kind of like me, she may meet more people by being around Marilyn. Because she is around Marilyn, people may trust her faster, and she may gain respect faster from other people in the town. That respect can equal a form of power, making her important to the people of this town. That's the simple way of putting it without using fancy words."

Annabelle giggled. "All of this talking to people is what can get people to like her."

"Yes, that's how it sometimes goes in our lovely society. Talking will either get people to love you or hate you."

"I guess it is best I don't talk unless I'm spoken to."

Ruthanne replied, "You don't have to take it so seriously."

"I'm used to people first looking at me and thinking, 'It's a Negro woman.' Not, 'oh, she speaks well' or 'she's a nice person.'"

"I understand what you mean, Annabelle. Hopefully, things will change fast."

Annabelle pursed her lips slightly. "How long do you think it will be before our country changes?"

Ruthanne's eyes quickly shifted away from Annabelle and then back. "If we're lucky, I'd say fifty years with a lot more laws in place."

Annabelle sighed. "So, we might not even live long enough to see such a change."

Ruthanne walked down the steps and sat in the hammock, looking at the sunrays breaking through the clouds. "I hope we do get to see something so spectacular, Annabelle. For such an enormous change to happen would bring me so much joy,

I wouldn't mind living to a hundred to see what other changes would ensue."

Annabelle sat down next to Ruthanne. "I wouldn't mind making it that long with you."

Ruthanne smirked at Annabelle and looked back at the clouds. She wondered, *Is this what perseverance is, God? Looking at clouds, knowing that the sun is on the other side, and that its rays will eventually come through?*

The front door slowly creaked open, and a small hand appeared on the post.

"I see you, Miss Sasha!" Ashley said.

"I see you too, little Ashley," Annabelle said as she and Ruthanne giggled.

Ashley smiled at them, holding her long curls and twirling anxiously.

"Are you going to play with me too, Miss Ruthanne?"

Ruthanne replied, "Well, why not? I have no other plans today."

Ashley excitedly pulled off her green bonnet and ran to the side of the brown-bricked house.

"Now you've gone and done it, Ruthanne," Annabelle said.

"What do you mean?" Ruthanne asked.

"Come on! It is time to race me!" Ashley shouted.

Ruthanne looked at Annabelle and slightly drooped as she heard Ashley's demand.

"Oh no, she's one of those little girls," Ruthanne said. "I thought she was more like Elizabeth. You know, dolls and combing hair."

Annabelle replied, "Since you started this, I think it is only right that you be the first to go."

Ruthanne looked at Annabelle while she exhaled and slightly grimaced.

"Alright, I'll go first. There's no point in arguing about it." Ruthanne went over to Ashley promptly. "All right, little Ashley, where are we racing to?"

Ashley twisted her body side to side in her puffy yellow

dress as she beamed. "From here to the horses' water trough," she said.

Ruthanne put her hands on her hips. "All the way over there?"

"Are you scared, Miss Ruthanne?"

Ruthanne thought, *This child is almost like me. I'd better watch myself.* "Okay, you have a deal, little Ashley."

"Great!"

Ruthanne pulled her dress up to her knees so she could run.

"Go!" Ashley yelled with all her might.

They raced all the way to the horses' water trough. Ruthanne managed to beat Ashley, but she was breathing hard.

"That was great! Let's do it again!" Ashley exclaimed, grinning.

Ruthanne frowned and walked back with Ashley. "How about we let this be Annabelle's turn this time?"

"Okay, I'll go get her right now!"

Ashley jogged to Annabelle and pulled her by the arm. Annabelle glared at Ruthanne with her eyebrows scrunched while she pouted. Annabelle raced, though Ashley beat her in the race, and they came back with Annabelle breathing heavier. Ruthanne was expecting Ashley to be tired, but Ashley convinced her to race her again. Annabelle and Ruthanne raced Ashley six more times, to the point that their legs tired out and their sides were hurting. Ashley was breathing hard and smiling because she won the last four times.

"That was so much fun!" Ashley said. "Do y'all want to race one more time?"

The women looked at Ashley with big eyes, struggling to stand upright.

"Ashley, dear, I think Annabelle and I are too tired, but we are happy to have played with you."

Ashley frowned. "Well, okay. We can do it tomorrow then!" Ashley ran off to the house.

"How does she still have so much energy?" Annabelle asked.

Ruthanne replied, "Okay, Annabelle, I thought there was nothing to motivate me to get married soon, but that girl has done it. If I have kids like her, I have to have them soon."

Annabelle sighed. "I agree with you there. We need to ask Rebecca how she does it. This is madness."

"Not only is it madness, but she made us look like a couple of fools in front of the other townspeople that saw us racing a five-year-old. I think she made you look like the bigger fool since you almost tripped on your dress the last time," Ruthanne said.

"I didn't almost trip. I was just tired. We're certainly not telling Elizabeth about racing a five-year-old."

"That's the last thing I need is her bringing up in the future that I got worn out by a five-year-old," Ruthanne replied. "I guess we should walk back before she comes back from Mr. Pots's store."

Annabelle replied, "You can walk?"

"I'm hoping I can, but don't tell my body that." The women stumbled back to the yard of the brick house. They sat down in the hammock, staring at the beginning of the sunset.

"This feels so good right now. I don't think I'll be able to move to make it upstairs for supper."

Ruthanne looked over at Annabelle. "We must before Elizabeth attempts to make dinner again."

The women sat in the hammock for two hours, watching the townspeople pass by. They then decided to go upstairs to start making supper.

Suddenly, the front door opened, and Rebecca walked out. "Hello, girls. I must ask you what you did to my little Ashley. She's napping early," Rebecca said.

Ruthanne and Annabelle looked at each other with tired eyes and then looked at Rebecca.

"Do you see the expressions on our faces, Rebecca? Your daughter wore us out and almost caused Annabelle to trip over her own dress," Ruthanne said.

Rebecca asked, "What do you mean?"

"Ashley asked us to play with her, but I didn't know her version of playtime was running."

Rebecca giggled and shook her head. "So, she wore the two of you out?"

"Ruthanne now wants to hurry up and have children to get it over and done with," Annabelle said. "The whole time I've known her, she's wanted to wait until today."

Rebecca laughed. "I'm sorry, but that's too funny. I will admit, Ashley does have a lot of energy. I'll let the two of you recover on your own."

"How do you do it, Rebecca?" Ruthanne asked.

Rebecca answered, "Well, at first, it was exhausting, but over time, I believe my body became used to the challenge. I hope my body can keep up better than it did today. Well, tough it up, ladies. It's the joy of motherhood."

Annabelle and Ruthanne looked at each other with pursed lips as they huffed and climbed up the stairs sluggishly. Rebecca chuckled and returned to the house to check on Ashley.

Elizabeth returned from Mr. Pots's store and saw that Ruthanne and Annabelle had cooked dinner already. She was perplexed because both of them were fast asleep.

Elizabeth poked Ruthanne, and she awoke, dazed.

"What on earth is the matter with you and Annabelle?" Elizabeth asked.

"Elizabeth, it's you," Ruthanne said. "You have no idea what we went through today watching Ashley. That child was something else. I guess we both passed out from being so tired."

"A five-year-old exhausted you and Annabelle?"

"Oh no, that's not what I was saying. I was saying that cooking supper today was exhausting. How ridiculous, Elizabeth, for you to think I said a five-year-old was too much for two grown women to handle."

Elizabeth's blue eyes widened. "Calm down. You're always in an irritable mood after waking up from a nap."

Ruthanne grumbled, "That isn't true. You always ask me stupid questions when I'm waking up from a nap."

Elizabeth rolled her eyes and entered the kitchen to check on the food.

Ruthanne rubbed her eyes and poked Annabelle. "Annabelle, wake up. Elizabeth is back."

Annabelle sat up, stretched her arms, and moaned. "I guess it's time to have supper then," she said

"Y'all should have waited for me to return. Annabelle, I still need to get my cooking skills sharp," Elizabeth said.

Ruthanne looked at Elizabeth with a conceited glare and narrowed eyes, and Annabelle gave her a concerned look. They walked over to their dinner table, blessed the food, and ate, enjoying each other's company.

That night, Annabelle gazed at the wonder of a full moon.

"Ruthanne and Elizabeth can't support me forever. What happens when they get married?" Annabelle said to herself.

Ruthanne noticed Annabelle staring at the moon and came up to her, placing her hand on Annabelle's shoulder. "So, what's on your mind? You're staring at the moon like it shouldn't be there," Ruthanne said.

Annabelle turned to Ruthanne. "Oh, nothing really. Thinking about what the dress will look like," Annabelle said.

Ruthanne beamed. "I'm sure it will be the greatest wonder of the festival."

"You always seem to know what to say. How do you do that?"

"A lot of experience and a lot of pain—some not worth mentioning, and the rest is worth forgetting."

"I wonder if there are women as messed up as we are."

Ruthanne giggled. "Trust me; there are women with far more depressing lives. Don't stay up too late. Who knows what tomorrow holds."

Ruthanne entered their bedroom, noticing Elizabeth was already asleep. She smirked and lit an Argand lamp.

Ruthanne whispered, "Annabelle, don't take too long watching that moon."

"I'm going to sleep soon, Ruthanne."

"Okay, see you in the morning." Ruthanne lay in her bed and fell asleep quickly.

Annabelle walked around the room and grinned at the other two women. She whispered, "I would never have thought I would meet friends like you two."

She put on her nightgown and lay in her bed.

"Even with the visit from Constance, I still lack faith. God, please forgive me for not trusting you. I've come so far. I hope something truly good does come from our going to this festival. God, whatever good thing you're bringing in my life, please bring it fast."

CHAPTER 12
Perception

Two weeks passed, and Rebecca's pregnancy was now slightly obvious. Marilyn also finished Elizabeth's and Ruthanne's dresses, and the young women picked them up. An anxious Ruthanne was ready for the festival, which finally came on August 25, 1845.

"It is the day of the festival, and we have another new dress to get!" Ruthanne whispered. "Rise and shine, Elizabeth, a new and exciting day is here!"

"Why on Earth are you up so early, Ruthanne? The festival won't begin until noon," Elizabeth whined.

"Hush, you're always the early bird. This shouldn't bother you."

Elizabeth frowned, replying, "You have some nerve to say what doesn't bother me."

"Well, I know you quite well, Miss Elizabeth. If you lie back down in your bed, then I will know for certain that I disturbed your sleep."

Elizabeth glared at Ruthanne, got up, and went into the kitchen, murmuring to herself while Ruthanne watched her.

Ruthanne giggled to herself and mumbled, "She tried to act grown. That was cute." Ruthanne glanced at a sleeping Annabelle and left the bedroom, walking toward Elizabeth with an excited smile. "Marilyn is bringing the dress over here."

"Wait, I thought you were going to get the dress from her."

"Marilyn changed her mind. She really wants to see Annabelle's face when she shows it to her."

"Now you have me excited. It's too early for this much fun."

"Hush, it's never too early."

The doorknob turned. Ruthanne and Elizabeth turned their heads excitedly when it opened, and Rebecca walked in quietly.

"Rebecca, we thought you were Marilyn," Ruthanne said.

"I'm sorry I ruined the excitement. I didn't want to miss this either," Rebecca replied.

"Wait a minute, you knew?" Elizabeth asked. "How long have you known Marilyn was bringing the dress here?"

Before Rebecca could answer, Ruthanne stepped behind Elizabeth, waving her hands and shaking her head at Rebecca. Elizabeth felt the wind come off Ruthanne's hands and turned around.

"What are you doing?"

Ruthanne replied, "What are you talking about?"

Elizabeth glanced at Rebecca and turned to Ruthanne. "You pain in my side. You told her a long time before you told me."

Ruthanne scoffed. "That's not fully true."

Elizabeth scowled. "How is that not fully true? You told me a few minutes ago, but Rebecca came knocking here knowing Marilyn would be here, and our door was unlocked."

"Okay," Ruthanne admitted, shrugging. "Maybe I did say something to her before you, but that's because I knew she would probably have something to do."

"So you mean I don't have a life now?" Elizabeth asked.

"No, I don't mean that at all. I just meant that I figured you wouldn't be planning anything before the festival."

Elizabeth smacked her lips. "You're such a trickster, Ruthanne."

"I beg your pardon?" Ruthanne growled. "Elizabeth Jones, are you calling me a trickster?"

"Did you hear me stutter, Miss Williams?"

"Ladies, that's enough, or you'll ruin the surprise for Annabelle by raising your voices," Rebecca said.

Ruthanne grunted and looked away from Elizabeth. She sat on the couch, crossing her arms.

Marilyn soon arrived, and the three women became ecstatic when they saw the dress she had made.

"Marilyn, this dress is astounding! You have truly shown your talent!" Rebecca said.

Marilyn replied, "Why, thank you, Mrs. Rebecca. I hope it's to Sasha's liking."

"Well, if she doesn't like it, I wouldn't mind having it," Elizabeth said.

"Elizabeth, you should be ashamed of yourself," Ruthanne said.

Elizabeth scoffed. "Hush. You were thinking the same."

"The dress is truly wonderful, Marilyn. I'm glad we had you come over instead of my picking it up. I think it will mean the world to Sasha, and I think you'll want to see her reaction."

"Why, thank you, Ruthanne. I guess it's time to wake her up," Marilyn said.

Elizabeth opened the door slowly and entered the women's room. "Annabelle, it's time to wake up!" she said.

Annabelle rolled over and stretched her arms.

"Good morning, Elizabeth. What's going on?" Annabelle asked.

"It's the day of the festival, so let's have some breakfast together," Elizabeth said.

"Let me put my gown on."

"No need for that. Ruthanne will be back with your new dress soon."

Annabelle's eyes became bigger, remembering that Ruthanne had made an agreement with Marilyn to pick up the new dress. Annabelle followed Elizabeth out of the bedroom only to see Rebecca, Ruthanne, and Marilyn standing in their kitchen.

"Surprise, Annabelle, it's time for the festival!" Marilyn said.

Annabelle gasped when she saw the dress Marilyn was

holding. The elegant dark blue and white colors of the dress almost brought her to tears. The white was designed into thin vertical stripes on the entire dress.

Annabelle ran to Marilyn and gave her an overwhelming hug. "I don't know how I could ever repay you, Marilyn. Thank you," she said.

"Your smile is your thanks. Now, let's make this a wondrous day we will never forget."

"What do you mean by wondrous?" Annabelle asked.

Marilyn replied, "Oh, it's another word for amazing, that's all."

Annabelle beamed, and Marilyn handed the dress to her. She took the dress back into the bedroom and lay it on her bed.

Annabelle left the room, beaming while she thought about her new dark blue and white dress. "Well, will you ladies join me for breakfast?"

The women began to cook and set up the table. The moment was a joyous occasion. After cooking, the women sat down at the table to enjoy breakfast together. Ruthanne and Annabelle finished their breakfasts anxiously, and Elizabeth went into the bedroom to change into her ruffled yellow dress Marilyn made. Annabelle came into the room as Elizabeth finished putting on her dress and put her own new dress on. The two women looked at each other and how the dresses fitted them perfectly.

"Elizabeth, you look so beautiful," Annabelle said.

"Why, thank you. You look quite beautiful yourself," Elizabeth said.

They went out of the bedroom and posed for the other women. Each of them had their hair styled in twin buns. The women laughed as Elizabeth and Annabelle made goofy poses.

All the women were later prepared to leave for the festival. Ruthanne, with her ringlet-styled hair, wore a white dress with light blue trimmings and a white bonnet. Marilyn had her hair styled in ringlets too, and she wore a ruffled white dress with her white bonnet. Rebecca, with her spaniel curls, wore a solid yellow dress and a white bonnet. The young women walked down the stairs, excited for the events to come.

Allen was happily waiting at the bottom of the stairs, Ashley standing by his side. He stood, looking sharp in a black frock coat, black trousers, and a black walking cane to match. His high-collared white shirt had a red cravat tied around it, and he wore a green silk vest with a gold pocket watch in it.

Ashley began jumping up and down in her red dress the moment Rebecca came down the stairs. "Mommy, everyone looks so pretty today!" Ashley said.

"I'm glad you noticed today is a special day," Rebecca said.

"Today is the festival, and I get to play games."

Ashley gave her mother a hug. Everyone then began to travel to the center of the town, excited to spend time with one another.

As they started, Allen nudged Rebecca, and she turned to him.

"What is it, Allen?" Rebecca whispered.

"The rules for the festival haven't changed from last year. The motion to change it failed," Allen said.

Rebecca frowned at Allen, causing him to look away. "I'll tell her the rules to keep people from thinking that we've been socializing with her," she said.

Allen nodded in agreement. When they arrived at the festival, signs were posted everywhere. Allen immediately picked up Ashley without saying a word and greeted another man.

Rebecca held Annabelle's hand compassionately and looked at her with sympathetic eyes and a frown. "Sasha, there is something you need to know. There are certain areas of the festival and certain events that you cannot participate in because they're only for whites. We had recently put in a new vote on the matter to allow everyone to participate in everything this year, but we were outvoted."

"So what are you saying?" Ruthanne abruptly asked.

"We can go to any part of the festival and participate in all the events, but Sasha must be on the west side of the festival, and she is only allowed to participate in a few events. I'm sorry. We've tried to change the law for the past three years. It was a war to allow Negroes and Indians to even come here peacefully."

"It's okay. I'm grateful to be able to even come here with all of you," Annabelle said.

Ruthanne balled her fist as she grunted and shook her head. "Annabelle, go show off your dress to the other Negroes. We will come to you and spend the rest of the festival on the west side, so you're not alone," Ruthanne said.

Annabelle looked at Ruthanne. "I will see all of you in a little while then."

"Don't forget how to twirl that dress like I showed you," Elizabeth encouragingly said.

"Okay, well, I'll see all of you soon. I'll be good," Annabelle said.

She calmly left while the other young women watched, and Allen came back with Ashley.

Ruthanne tapped her foot. "I don't feel comfortable letting her walk around on her own like this. She is still naïve," she said.

"I agree, Ruthanne. I will follow her closely with Ashley since we didn't spend much time looking at the different shows on that side of the festival," Rebecca said.

"Rebecca, are you sure you want to do this? I could do it myself," Allen said.

"Allen, I will be fine. I'm a grown woman and pregnant. I don't think anyone is going to give me grief. Nobody likes to get in the way of a pregnant woman."

Allen nodded his head in agreement as he lightly pursed his lips. The group agreed to the arrangements and separated.

The festival was crowded with families who participated. Rebecca and Ashley hurried to follow Annabelle from a distance. Ruthanne left on her own to search for Peter, but she did try to keep an eye on Annabelle from a distance. Allen and the other two women looked in awe at how fast the others left them.

Elizabeth and Marilyn paired off to look at the different events. Allen took his time to socialize and build political connections.

Ashley tugged on her mother's dress irritably. Rebecca turned around attentively and said, "What is it, Ashley? We're trying to catch up with Sasha."

"Mommy, am I going to have the chance to see some stuff?" Ashley asked. "I would like to try to win a toy this year."

Rebecca kissed Ashley on her cheek. "Of course, you will get the opportunity to play at the events this year. I promise you that. Just for right now, we need to see where Sasha is going to."

"Why do we have to follow Miss Sasha. Isn't she a grown-up too?"

"She is a grown-up, but she also is new to the festival. I wanted to make sure she was okay, so can you be my big helper today?"

Ashley smiled while she listened to her mother. "Yes, I can help find Sasha with you, Mommy."

"Well now, that sounds like a big girl. You make me happy."

Rebecca reached for Ashley's hand, and they continued their search for Annabelle.

Annabelle was mesmerized by the different things that were occurring. During the time she went through the crowd, people were shocked by the beauty of her dress. The white women whispered as their eyes focused on her dress. One drunken woman standing outside of the saloon stumbled and fell to her knees when she saw Annabelle passing her. Her friends came up behind her to help pick her up.

"Don't touch me! Did you see that nigger?" the drunken woman said. "Where did she get the dress from?"

Her friends looked in awe at the dark blue and white dress.

As Annabelle continued to stroll through the festival, oblivious to the attention she was attracting, a little girl approached Annabelle. She tugged on Annabelle's dress, and Annabelle slowly turned around.

The little girl gave a snaggletooth smile. "That's a pretty dress, lady," the girl said.

Annabelle smiled and knelt down. "Why, thank you, little girl. That's a pretty little yellow dress you have too," Annabelle said.

The adulated little girl grinned and ran off, giggling. Annabelle stood up and noticed that some of the white women were watching her. She wanted to avoid any confrontation, so she continued to go to the side of the festival Negroes could stay in and enjoy what was occurring.

As she hastened herself to enjoy the day, she felt another tug on her dress, but this was different. She stopped to see the shoe of a woman standing on her dress. Annabelle grabbed the skirt of her dress and tugged it from under the woman's foot.

"That's some good strength you have in those arms of yours. Is that from picking cotton or carrying your master's supper?" the woman said, exhibiting the same voice pitch as Annabelle.

Before Annabelle stood a bold, blue-eyed, blonde-haired woman in a yellow and white ruffled dress, wearing gold diamond dangle earrings on her ears. She had a small gap in her front teeth that was barely noticeable.

"You speak English, don't you? You're not one of them Indians."

The blonde stood eye to eye with Annabelle, and her demeanor was identical to Ruthanne's but with a far darker inception. Annabelle gulped as she took a breath, and her brown eyes locked with the woman's eyes.

"I was never a slave," Annabelle said.

The woman put her hands on her hips. "So, let me guess, sugar cane or South Carolina picking indigo, or did you come with the Indians? Or better yet, are you a side dish some pathetic white man is using because his wife ain't good enough?"

The woman stepped on the dress again, and Annabelle abruptly tugged the dress from the woman.

The woman stumbled back and giggled. "I like you already. That must take a lot of courage, defying a white woman like myself in public. The name's Sierra Nicole Cruise, you ignorant nigger. So, who did you steal the dress from, Delilah?"

Annabelle's forehead creased while she scowled, and her eyes narrowed. Sierra quickly slapped Annabelle in the face, and a crowd of people stopped to watch the disturbance.

Annabelle looked around, noticing the eyes of the town watching her.

"You don't understand who Delilah was, do you, nigger?"

Annabelle glared at the woman, and she pressed her lips together.

"Delilah was a whore and manipulator of men, which is what I imagine you'd be, wearing that dress. A nigger couldn't afford such a fabulous dress."

Annabelle inhaled as her eyes shifted away from Sierra Nicole's eyes. "What is a manipulator, if you don't mind me asking, ma'am?"

Sierra Nicole scoffed. "I guess to help your tiny mind understand, a manipulator is a trickster and a liar. They use their words and their body to get what they want."

"I'm sorry to disappoint you, Miss Cruise, but I'm no manipulator, and my name is Sasha. A white woman wants what belongs to a Negro. Who would have ever thought a day like this would come?"

Sierra Nicole turned red in the face and raised her fist. "Look here, you nappy-headed whore, how dare you say I would want what a nigger has!"

Annabelle turned from Sierra Nicole.

"Don't you turn your back on me, nigger! You heard me, didn't you?"

People began to look at an agitated Sierra Nicole while she looked back at the people with her twisted face.

"What are you self-righteous fools looking at?"

Sierra Nicole stormed off as she grunted, looking back to see if she could see where Annabelle was heading, but she couldn't see her.

"Next time, you won't be able to walk away, Miss Sasha."

Annabelle continued through the festival, desperate to avoid any more attention. As she proceeded, she realized there were a lot less booths set up on that side. She realized why Negroes were allowed on this side of the festival. Only white people willing to let Negroes participate were in the area. She frowned, seeing there was little to do. She sat down on a bench with a frown, looking at the other side of the festival.

"Enjoyable sight, isn't it, Miss Sasha?" Benjamin said.

Annabelle shrugged and rolled her eyes, turning her head toward Benjamin with a forced smile. "Well, hello there. It is Benjamin, right?"

"Why, yes, ma'am. That's my name, and I must tell you, you speak so much like the white people."

"Well, it is called English," Annabelle gruffly said.

Benjamin slightly bit his lip as he heard the serious tone in her voice. "Would you be interested in meeting the other Negroes in town, or I can show you what they have for us here."

Annabelle continued to force a smile while she looked at Benjamin's nervous expression. "You can take me to the others."

Benjamin's eyes widened as he grinned at Annabelle. "You is going to like them, I promise you."

Annabelle stood up and walked with Benjamin as she quietly exhaled. Benjamin hummed as they went.

"Please don't hum. It is a bit annoying."

Benjamin asked, "What is it you mean by annoying?"

Annabelle inclined her head. "Wow, clearly you must be joking that you don't know what that means."

"Why, no, ma'am. I was a slave, but I was rescued when I was a child. I was Timothy Benson, and I never looked back."

"Which state were you a slave in?"

"I was in Georgia and went through Alabama, and I almost got caught in Mississippi. I tell you, it was the Lord having mercy on me. Who would ever think the Lord would care about a nigger?"

Annabelle looked away from Benjamin and slightly cleared

her throat. "Well, that must've been a bad life to have been a slave and to have to change your name."

"Yes, them white people beat us, sell us, breed us like cattle, and sometimes, you see them masters that like Negro women."

"That's sad, Benjamin. I'm sorry that you lived that life."

"Yes, well, I'm grateful to the Lord now for saving me. The Lord saved a Negro."

They continued to stroll through the festival while Benjamin excitedly explained the events at the different stands to Annabelle.

"Now, who is that you with, Benjamin?" a woman said with a conceited southern accent.

"Ah, hush up, Sally. You knowing my business too much," Benjamin said.

Sally replied, "Excuse me, Benjamin, but you can't walk here with someone new and not be nice. What your name?"

"My name is Sasha. I'm from Jefferson City."

Sally replied, "So you is free, is you?"

"Yes, I'm free, but I'm still a slave with these laws."

"You got a strong tongue. I surprised they haven't killed it yet."

Annabelle smirked. "They tried to, but they failed. So, your name is Sally?"

"Yes, that's it, and I proud of it."

"Why you taking up all our time, Sally?" Benjamin whined.

"Benjamin, you shut your mouth and keep your eyes on what's really important," Sally said.

"Maybe you should listen to Miss Crazy Sally," a hazel-eyed man said with a smooth southern accent.

Annabelle turned her head tentatively.

"My, what beauty in the state of Missouri, I must say. By the look on your face, I know you must be thinking about what his name is."

Annabelle apathetically giggled at the man's boldness. The olive-skinned man approached Annabelle. His trousers and vest were beige, and they held a silver pocket watch that covered a dirty, high-collared brown shirt.

"The name is Daniel, and I'm sure such a rare beauty as you will love me."

"Daniel, all you did was embarrass yourself, you no-common-sense fool," Sally said.

"Sally, you angry woman, you mad 'cause now we have more choice besides you, Esther, Cecilia, Jean, and Ruth."

Sally put her hands on her hips. "You forgot Margaret, fool!"

Daniel scoffed. "I didn't forget Margaret. Nobody wants her unless she shrunk to one man size."

Benjamin shook his head while Annabelle's mouth dropped.

"That was rude and in front this new Negro in this town. She already think you a fool," another woman said in a southern accent as she approached Annabelle. "I'm Esther." Esther looked at Daniel and pursed her lips as she shook her head. "Shame on you, Daniel, talking about Margaret like that. I should tell Mary."

"Please don't put words into this beautiful young woman," Daniel said. "It's not rude speaking truth."

"Actually, I somewhat agree with her, Daniel," Annabelle said.

Sally and Benjamin began laughing.

"You didn't even ask me what my name was. How rude of you to think I would be interested in someone like you, and my name is Sasha."

The others gasped, and their mouths dropped open.

"You speak like a white woman!" Daniel said with his eyebrows raised and eyes wide.

"I never thought of it that way. I do have white friends. My entire life, I've had white friends, and I learned from them—not my parents—how to speak."

Sally's eyes fixed on Annabelle, and she scrunched her face and pressed her lips. "Yeah, but you still a nigger in their eyes," she said.

"Sally, that wrong," Benjamin said.

Sally replied, "Hush it. She a grown woman."

"Yes, I'm a grown woman, but I can see that you're still a child," Annabelle said.

"Look here, you new here," Sally snarled. "You must've come with your white friends, 'cause ain't no nigger going to be able live here alone."

"You're right, but I'm still a grown woman under no white man's foot. But I see you still think like a slave even with the shackles off."

Daniel and Benjamin looked at each other with wide eyes while the argument escalated.

"You have no idea what it is to be a slave. You were born free, weren't you, like this fool Daniel? I been beat by my parents and my masters, and watched my masters beat my parents. My momma couldn't even choose who she make children with. My momma didn't even know how children came. She was fifteen. My pa was twenty-nine or thirty years old and only there for one month, and my masters called him a good stallion. What you know of it but nothing?"

Annabelle clenched her teeth. "I'm sorry your momma never had a chance, but did you have a chance?"

"What you mean?" Sally asked.

"I mean, do you have children?"

"No, I got away before the masters gave me a man. I've never known a man."

"Then be happy you were never forced to be taken by a man. I'm done here, Benjamin. I need to find my friends. Nice to meet you, Daniel. I'm sure I will see you around."

"The pleasure is mine, beautiful Sasha," Daniel said.

"Ah, hush, Daniel. If you keep it up, you won't be a mulatto dog no more. You be a wolf, and wolves get shot," Sally said.

"Oh, you hush. You jealous of her, and you only met her today."

Sally slapped Daniel in the face and left. Annabelle shook her head and began to return back to the events as Benjamin followed her.

"I'm sorry for Sally's behavior. She was wrong," Benjamin said.

Annabelle replied, "No, she was right to feel hurt. She can't help but compare herself to me. The thought of a Negro born free bothers her."

Benjamin replied, "But that her problem. She can't change you, and she need to let go."

"I know her issues, and I understand them, so I'll take them as they are."

"Okay, don't be mad at me, but what you mean issues?"

"I mean problems, Benjamin."

"Oh, well, I think that's a nicer word for problems. What else white people teach you?"

Annabelle glanced at Benjamin. "They taught me a lot of things, but I was mostly taught by one friend. It is against the law, so I don't show everything I can do, or it will bring me trouble. White people don't like a smart Negro."

"So can you read?"

Annabelle lied, "No, I can't read, but my white friends can read even though they are women."

"You must be special for them to like you."

"Well, Mrs. Keys is my friend, and I adore her little girl."

Benjamin looked at Annabelle with a raised eyebrow. "What you mean adore?"

Annabelle rolled her eyes, but she felt sympathetic because of his lack of knowledge. "It means I like or love her being around me."

Benjamin grinned while he slightly cocked his head and looked at Annabelle. As they explored the festival, they stopped at a few of the stands. Annabelle began to enjoy Benjamin to the point that she ignored the white people.

She held back her smile as she listened to Benjamin's interest in learning and his kindness. She watched him and would move further away if she felt he was too close. Benjamin blushed as she responded to him, but he didn't notice when her smile started to fade.

"Sasha, there you are!" Rebecca said.

Ashley ran up to Annabelle and gave her a hug. Rebecca came up behind Ashley, noticing Benjamin with Annabelle.

"We got tired of the events occurring on the other side of the festival, so we decided to look for you."

"I'm glad you and Ashley found me," Annabelle said.

Rebecca replied, "I hope we didn't interrupt anything."

Annabelle went up and gave Rebecca a hug. "Actually, no, you're welcome. I would enjoy having you and Ashley with us."

"Good afternoon, Mrs. Keys and Miss Ashley," Benjamin said.

Rebecca replied, "Hello there, Benjamin, were you showing Annabelle the different events of the festival?"

"Why, yes, ma'am. I have, and it been my pleasure."

Rebecca smiled. "I'm glad to hear so. How about we walk around some more?"

Benjamin replied, "Please lead the way, Mrs. Keys."

The women began to move as Ashley skipped next to them, and Benjamin followed behind them.

Rebecca leaned over covertly to Annabelle. "Is he bothering you, Annabelle?" she whispered.

"Well, no, he has been a nice man to me, and he even introduced me to the other Negroes in town, but I feel a little too comfortable with him," Annabelle whispered.

Rebecca giggled and gave Annabelle a smirk. "So, you feel like you're beginning to like him then?"

Annabelle shook her head and grimaced. "I shouldn't feel that way. I barely know him."

"You should give him a chance. There really are not a lot of Negro men in this city. Even though I would support you with a white man, the idea of it could get you or even the man you fall in love with killed. Why not give him a chance? He is a handsome man."

Annabelle's eyes narrowed. "Ugh, I want to feel like I have options. Instead of just giving him a chance, what about me?"

Rebecca tilted her head toward Annabelle. "Well, dear, I'm trying to get you to give yourself a chance."

"But I already know that he likes me, and that bothers me so much."

"Well, why not? You're a beautiful woman. Why wouldn't he be interested in you?"

"He doesn't even really know me. Me saying yes so fast makes me feel like I'm like the white women I've mocked. I've seen those rich white girls get told who to marry. The only joy those women even have are their children that they reluctantly gave their husband."

"Annabelle, I'm not saying you need to take him in and marry him. Spend time with him and at least try to be a little open, and if you want me to watch, I will."

"What do you mean that you're going to watch?" Annabelle asked.

"Invite him to the house and spend time together on the hammock."

Annabelle looked back at Benjamin and saw him laughing with Ashley. "I'll give him one chance for me to even consider, Rebecca," she reluctantly said.

"Give him two chances, and I won't bring up Benjamin ever again."

Annabelle pouted, asking, "Why two chances?"

"Trust me, Annabelle. With men, the first time doesn't always go so well."

"Okay, so two chances, but only if Benjamin asks to spend time with me. That's the only way."

"Sounds good. I'm sure he'll be excited."

Annabelle exhaled as she looked away from a smiling Rebecca.

"Anyhow, we need to find my husband and the other girls. I get tired easily carrying this baby."

Annabelle replied, "I agree. I'm starting to get hot. The sun is strong today."

Benjamin caught up to them. "Mrs. Keys, with your permission, may I come along?" he asked.

"Why, of course, Benjamin. We could use the presence of a man while we search for the others. Besides, Ashley needs someone else to put all her energy on," Rebecca said.

They moved toward the eastern part of the festival with Ashley, who occupied Benjamin while Annabelle and Rebecca continued their conversation.

Marilyn and Elizabeth had their fill of adventure and began to look for Ruthanne. While they passed one of the events, they heard a crash by one of the saloons. Stumbling out of the saloon was Mr. Pots with two other men, so drunk he didn't even realize his own daughter was staring at him. Marilyn's jaw dropped as her eyes narrowed, and she turned away hastily as Elizabeth followed her.

"How embarrassing that he has become for me to be a drunkard in this town," Marilyn said.

"I'm sorry you had to see that. I know the feeling of having some embarrassing family moments," Elizabeth said.

"I shouldn't be complaining. It could be worse. He could be gone from my life. How crazy it is that life can change things so quickly." Marilyn put her hand on Elizabeth's shoulder. "Well, that's enough of that. I refuse to be one of these women living in self-pity. Let's find Ruthanne."

Elizabeth's eyes opened wider while she listened to Marilyn's quick resolve. "I guess you and Ruthanne have more in common than I expected," she murmured.

The women continued to explore the festival in search of Ruthanne. The excitement of the festival could be heard throughout the town, and joy was in the air.

Ruthanne constantly sighed and kept her lips pursed as she searched for Peter. She heard laughter by one of the stands and saw Peter with the old man who had been in the church.

"Hello, Pastor Avail, it is a pleasure to see you here," Ruthanne said.

"Ruthanne, it is a pleasure to see you today, and as you can see, I have kept my word," Peter said.

"You have kept part of your word so far, Pastor. We'll see what happens in due time."

Mr. Jefferson noticed the shyness between the two and smiled. "I will excuse myself so the two of you may continue your conversation, Peter," Mr. Jefferson said. "Miss Ruthanne, it is a pleasure to meet you. My name is Mr. Jefferson."

Ruthanne replied, "The pleasure is all mine, Mr. Jefferson, are you also a pastor?"

"By no means, ma'am. I'd be a horrible pastor. I'm the treasurer. I tell the truth people don't want to hear." Mr. Jefferson chuckled and tilted his black top hat.

Ruthanne smirked. "I do appreciate a good sense of humor. It is greatly appreciated."

"A woman as beautiful as a diamond is great to see, along with a strong essence in character." That said, Mr. Jefferson walked off cheerfully, leaving Peter and Ruthanne alone in the crowd.

"What an entertaining little old man he is! How did you ever come across such a man?"

"He supported me when most of the congregation didn't. The majority of the town originally didn't believe I could be a pastor because of my age," Peter said. "Without people like him in my life, who knows if I would have been shunned away from God's calling in my life."

Ruthanne sarcastically replied, "And here I thought you were a secure man that knew what he wanted in life."

Peter's eyes widened slightly. "Please don't be confused. I'm human, and I do make mistakes, and I—"

"I'm joking with you. You must really come across some interesting characters to be so defensive," Ruthanne said.

"Actually, I'm amazed I have any energy left after dealing with some of the people of this town, but that's the price of being a disciple of God. How about we walk around and talk about you more. I was hoping this conversation would also involve things about you that I don't know."

"In due time, or do you not have the patience of a godly man?"

Peter snickered, but he quickly covered his mouth to force himself to stop laughing.

"There it is, a laugh. I think this might work out after all."

"What will work after all?" Peter asked.

Ruthanne smirked. "Nothing for you to worry about, I promise. Now let's go enjoy some of the events these nice men put up for the town."

The two of them traveled to different events, enjoying every moment of the time they were spending with each other.

A little girl came up to Ruthanne and smiled at her. "What a pretty dress you have! Where did you get it from?" she asked.

Ruthanne replied, "My friend, Marilyn, made it for me. She works at Pots's Garments. Do you know where it is?"

"No, I don't know where it is."

As Ruthanne explained to the little girl where she needed to go to find the Pots's Garments store, a woman came up to Peter.

"Hello, Pastor. It is a pleasure to see you today, looking so handsome," Sierra Nicole said.

"Why, Miss Cruise, how nice it is to see you again."

Sierra Nicole approached Peter, placed her hand on his shoulder, and began to caress it. "Now, Pastor Avail, I told you to call me Sierra Nicole. No need to address me so formally."

Ruthanne turned around after giving directions to the little girl and saw Sierra Nicole. She walked toward Sierra.

Sierra Nicole leered and said, "Is there something that you want, dear? The pastor and I are quite busy."

Ruthanne giggled with a fake smile. "Actually, Peter was with me, and we were just leaving," she said.

Sierra Nicole took her hand off Peter's shoulder and antagonistically approached Ruthanne. "Now, what would the pastor want with such a child who clearly doesn't know her place in the world?" she asked.

"How outlandish you are for insulting my maturity. I assure you I'm more of a woman than you."

"Look here, I'm quite sure you know nothing."

Peter attempted to walk in between the two women, but Ruthanne pushed him out of the way.

"It's quite clear to me that you think of him as more than your pastor, and I'm quite sure the feeling isn't mutual," Ruthanne said.

Sierra Nicole gasped. "How dare you speak to me in such a way, and in front of the pastor!"

"Ha! He isn't oblivious to your approach. I can tell by the look on his face." Ruthanne took off her bonnet and valiantly smirked at Sierra Nicole. She flung her bonnet in Sierra Nicole's face and put her arm around Peter's arm. "I'm sure this isn't the first time you have attempted to seduce the pastor. Ugly women in the pursuit of a man are equally pathetic to a woman who has the intelligence of a sheep."

Peter's eyes widened, and his jaw dropped. "Ruthanne, that's enough," he said. "That's beneath you. Please apologize to Miss Sierra Nicole." Then he looked at Sierra Nicole and said, "The same goes for you. Ruthanne is new to the town and a kind woman, when she wants to be."

Ruthanne crinkled her nose as her green eyes narrowed and locked on Peter. She unlocked her arm from Peter's while she glared at him. "You can have the witch, Peter, or should I say...Pastor," Ruthanne said.

"Hold on, Ruthanne, don't be so angry. Both of you were wrong."

Ruthanne scowled and began to leave when Annabelle and the others saw her.

"Hey, Ruthanne! Wait!" Annabelle shouted.

Ruthanne turned around, moved toward Annabelle, and said, "Sasha, I thought you were on the other side of the town,"

Annabelle replied, "I was, but I'm done there. We were going back to the house."

"You look bothered. Is everything okay?" Rebecca asked.

Ruthanne replied, "I'm quite alright. I was having an interesting conversation with Pastor Avail."

Rebecca glanced at Peter, noticing Sierra Nicole glaring at Ruthanne with furious blue eyes.

"Well, let's go back to the house then. Benjamin, are you joining us?" Rebecca asked.

Benjamin answered, "Why, yes, ma'am. It would be my pleasure."

Annabelle rolled her eyes as she stared at Ruthanne.

"Hello there, Delilah. How interesting it is that you and this redheaded charmer know each other," Sierra Nicole said.

"I told you, my name is Sasha."

"The nerve of calling me a charmer, Sierra Nicole. I suggest you keep your words to yourself. Otherwise, I might have to temporarily suspend my ladylike behavior," Ruthanne said.

"Ruthanne, there's no need for such aggressions. Please behave as a Christian woman should," Peter said.

Ruthanne glared at Peter with her narrow eyes while he attempted to be neutral in the confrontation.

Rebecca noticed Annabelle giving the same look to Sierra Nicole as Ruthanne.

"Anyhow, ladies, that's quite enough. I think we need to find the others and return home," Rebecca said with a nervous tone. She stepped in front of Annabelle and Ruthanne and put her arms around them, prompting them to turn around. "Good day, Pastor Avail. We look forward to seeing you on Sunday."

"Good day, Mrs. Keys, Ruthanne, Sasha, and Benjamin," Peter said.

Ruthanne turned her head irritably and said, "Yes, Pastor Avail, I look forward to it."

Sierra Nicole scoffed as her mouth curved into a leer. "I will be looking forward to seeing you ladies again," Sierra Nicole said. "The sooner the better, I say. Keep on walking, redhead and nigger."

Then a few strangers passing by began to mock Annabelle as she walked with the others, and she heard them.

"Hey nigger, how did you get a dress like that?" one woman said.

"She thinks she's one of us," another woman griped.

The comments greatly upset Annabelle, even though she kept a blank face, but Ruthanne noticed the change in her stride. Rebecca had covered Ashley's ears until they traveled far enough away from the women. They were so repulsed that they didn't notice Elizabeth or Marilyn. Ashley saw them and tugged her mother's dress.

"Mommy, there's Miss Elizabeth and Miss Pots," Ashley said.

"Elizabeth, Marilyn, we're over here," Rebecca said as she waved.

The two women walked over to the others, slightly smiling.

Elizabeth replied, "I hope you all have had a great time here. I know Marilyn and I, for the most part, had a great time."

"Not really, but let's not let the day be spoiled," Ruthanne said.

"Well, what's the matter, Ruthanne?" Elizabeth asked.

"I'll discuss it later. Now isn't the time. Let's go home."

Elizabeth frowned at seeing the frustration in Ruthanne's face. The group began to return to the house, cheerfully talking among themselves.

"Hello, Benjamin. I didn't realize you knew these ladies," Marilyn said, smiling.

Benjamin nodded his head and replied, "Hello, Miss Marilyn. And yes, ma'am, I do know these good people."

Marilyn continued to grin.

"Yes, they are good people, and thank you for the work you did on Hansel. I know he can be a difficult horse."

Benjamin smiled. "It always my pleasure. He a good horse

with me, but I think 'cause I give him a little hay or carrot. And you good owner, Miss Marilyn."

"Why, thank you, Benjamin. I'll make sure to keep bringing Hansel back to you. I'll even make my papa bring him when he's in a good mood. Years of good service should be rewarded."

"That sounds good to me."

Benjamin and Marilyn continued their small talk, unaware that Annabelle was listening with her eyes pointed straight ahead.

As Ashley began to skip with her bonnet in her hand, a strong wind took it.

"No, Mommy, my bonnet! It flew away," Ashley cried.

The others tried to retrieve it, but it landed in front of Mr. Boston and his black cane. Mr. Boston looked prominent with his top hat, fancy blue vest and cravat, high-collared dark blue shirt, dark blue frock coat, and striped blue trousers. He hadn't noticed the bonnet in front of him.

"Mr. Boston, please grab that bonnet," Rebecca yelled.

Mr. Boston tried to grab it, but the wind carried it away, and it landed on the foot of a man walking by. The man stopped and grabbed it from the ground.

"You seem to be chasing this, Mr. Boston," the man said with a different southern accent.

The man handed the bonnet to Mr. Boston after he'd hobbled over to him.

"Why, thank you, John. You Indians always seem to have great reflexes," Mr. Boston replied. "I'm glad to see all of you here."

The ladies and Benjamin approached Mr. Boston to retrieve the bonnet, and Mr. Boston excitedly turned around.

"John, I'd like you to meet some good people in this town. This here is Mrs. Keys and her young daughter, Ashley. This is Mr. Pots's youngest daughter, Marilyn, who I'm sure you know, and this is Miss Ruthanne and her good friends, Miss Sasha and Miss Elizabeth. Also, our best horse caretaker in town, Benjamin."

"It is a pleasure to meet you all. I'm from the Cherokee Nation in Indian Territory many miles away from here," John said as a man, a teenage boy, and a woman joined him. "This is Samuel, my wife, Camille, and Michael. We are glad we came today, Mr. Boston."

Mr. Boston grinned. "Well, I'm glad you're having a splendid time, John."

Annabelle was intrigued because they were dressed like white people, like the Indians she had seen in her dream. She was also fascinated by John's southern accent, but who the Indians were took priority. She approached with a smile.

"Are both of these Negroes free?"

"I'm happy to say that I'm a free woman," Annabelle said.

"It's funny how different you are from our slaves. You speak out," John said.

Annabelle gasped. "Slaves! You have slaves!"

"Yes, my tribe has both Negro slaves and those that are free. Largely, the ones who are free are also of our blood."

"So, you mean they also Indian?"

"Yes, but they're the lesser members of my tribe."

"I know some people who are Negro and Indian, but they never mentioned anything about Indians having slaves."

"Only four other tribes besides my own have slaves."

Annabelle thought, *Wow, even the Indians take Negroes as slaves, but do they treat slaves like the white people do*?

John smiled a little, "It has been interesting seeing a Negro born out of slavery and not of mixed blood. Quite different than a runaway. Isn't that right, Benjamin?"

Benjamin nodded nervously.

Annabelle frowned, and she shook her head. "And I thought Indians were different than white people, but you sound more like the white people who kicked you out of your own land."

Camille unfolded her arms as she glared at Annabelle in disbelief. Samuel and Michael also looked at each other in disbelief.

John stepped over to Annabelle. "A little education means

nothing. Don't ever compare my people to them. We took care of the land, but they cut down every tree they see and shoot every animal they see. My ancestors went to war against the white man, then chose to try to live like them. We started to farm like them, to keep our land, and decided to take slaves to show that we can live as equals. But what happens? They find gold. They tell us we have to leave with rifles pointed at our faces. You have no idea how many of us died walking to this fruitless land. You haven't even seen our slaves. They live in the same state that we do."

"But does it make it right for you to hold them?"

A tear fell down Annabelle's face. Ruthanne stepped up to Annabelle, placing her hand on her back, coaxing her to turn away from the Indians.

"I'm sorry you feel that way, Sasha, but we are not cruel like the white men."

"Good day, John, it was a pleasure to meet you," Rebecca said. "Goodbye, Mr. Boston."

"Alright, take care, everyone," Mr. Boston said.

"It was nice to meet all of you," John said.

The ladies and Benjamin left, with Ruthanne continuing to coax Annabelle away. The other Indians watched timidly as they went.

"Mr. Boston, we will stop by later for supplies. It was good to see you again."

Mr. Boston replied, "I will look forward to seeing you under less stressful conditions. Please excuse Sasha. She is a strong spirit and intelligent. I feel she has learned much from Ruthanne and Elizabeth, which has caused her to be quite outspoken at times."

"The last thing we need is another one like her in Indian Territory," Samuel said.

"What do you mean by another like her, Samuel?" Mr. Boston asked.

"Our mixed Negroes feel that they should have the same rights as others in the tribe...the ability to vote for chiefs and other privileges. The mixed-bloods are our people, but if we allow it, I feel we will be looked down even more by the United States."

"The Cherokee seem to become more complex every year, Samuel. My advice to you all is don't push away your own kin, even the ones with Negro blood. You never know what a child could grow into."

"Interesting, Mr. Boston. Again, we will stop by your store later this month," John said.

Mr. Boston smiled. "Sounds good, John. I look forward to seeing all of you again. Michael, Samuel, Camille, take care of yourselves now."

The Cherokee got into their carriage to return to Indian Territory. Mr. Boston watched them ride away as the sunset began. He exhaled and frowned, holding his black cane.

"The more I see them, the more they're becoming like us. How sad it is to see a noble group of God's children adopt the policies of the ones who hate each other." Strolling back to his store, Mr. Boston greeted those he passed on his way home. He watched the sunset and saw a slave loading a wagon, saying to himself, "How much harder will the nation fall before it realizes how wrong it is?"

Annabelle and the others arrived home, exhausted from their day.

"What a relief this day is over, and I'm ready for supper," Rebecca said.

"I agree, between this weather and all this walking, I'm tired," Elizabeth said.

"Well, ladies and gentleman, I will wait out here for the sunset to end, then call it a day," Ruthanne said.

"Why?" Elizabeth asked.

"I guess the one thing I can say I've learned so far is to take nothing for granted."

"I agree with Ruthanne. I think I'll sit on the hammock and enjoy what God has given me," Annabelle said.

Ashley tugged on her mother's dress. "Mommy, can I sit outside with Miss Sasha and Miss Ruthanne?" Ashely asked.

"No, Ashley, I think they need some adult time. Besides, I need your skills in the kitchen. You ladies are welcome to join us tonight," Rebecca said.

"Thank you for the invitation, Rebecca, but I think I need to work on my own time," Ruthanne said.

"Yes, I think I need a little time alone," Annabelle said.

Benjamin inhaled, keeping his hands in his pockets as he stepped toward Annabelle. "If you want, I'd be pleased to keep you company, Miss Sasha," he said.

Annabelle replied, "I'm sorry, Benjamin. I appreciate it, but I meant I was going to spend time with Ruthanne. Maybe some other time."

"Well, if that's what you want, I will listen. I guess it is about time I go home, y'all. Have a blessed day."

"Bye, Benjamin," the ladies said when he walked away.

"I agree with you, Ruthanne," Marilyn said. "Ladies, it has been a pleasure today, but I think it's time for me to return home."

Elizabeth hugged Marilyn. "We will see you later on then," she said.

Marilyn beamed. "I look forward to it."

The women said goodbye to Marilyn as she went home, glancing at the architecture of the town. She playfully spun around a few times when the sidewalk was clear of people.

"Well," Elizabeth said after Marilyn left, "I will go upstairs now and see what supplies we have since we need to shop later."

"It would help if you paid attention," Ruthanne mockingly said.

Elizabeth put her hands on her hips. "Good day, Rebecca; little Ashley. I have to go prove someone wrong."

Rebecca chuckled at the time Elizabeth marched up the stairs.

"Anyhow, ladies, Ashley and I need to go before Allen returns from the festival," Rebecca said, escorting Ashley inside the house.

Annabelle and Ruthanne sat down in the hammock, showing signs of exhaustion. Ruthanne looked at Annabelle and nudged her.

"What was that for?" Annabelle asked.

Ruthanne answered, "You're such a liar, Annabelle. You completely lied to avoid Benjamin."

"What else was I supposed to do? I needed some time away from him. He acts like I'm the only Negro woman and he is the only Negro man in this town."

"Annabelle, there are not a lot of options for you out here. Benjamin is a free man, and you're a free woman, and if you don't mind my saying so, he is quite handsome."

Annabelle scoffed. "Don't you dare try that. Don't go that far into trying to get me to give him a chance."

"You said you would give him a chance, Annabelle. That's what you told Rebecca."

"Okay, I will give him a chance, but don't lie and say that you find him handsome."

Ruthanne smirked. "Actually, I do think he is a handsome man."

"Now I know you're crazy. I have never in my whole life heard a white woman say that a Negro man could be handsome."

"Well, you heard it directly from me. I think he is a handsome man, and I think you should let your guard down a little and see how it works out."

"But you can't say things like that. You calling a Negro man handsome can get him killed. I've seen death happen over lesser matters, or at least leading slave masters to give beatings to a slave or give a slave cuts."

Ruthanne frowned. "I'm sorry I upset you. I don't have that experience in life, but I've had some experiences with men, and I'm telling you that Benjamin is a good man. Do I know if he is the one for you? I don't know, but you can't hide forever and expect to be happy."

Annabelle began to remember what the angel had told her and felt afraid that Ruthanne was right. She exhaled as fear crossed her face, and she looked toward the sunset. "If something special does happen between us, I don't think I will ever tell him that I was a slave, Ruthanne. That my family was left behind."

"Annabelle, if that's what you want, I'll support you in your decision." Ruthanne grabbed Annabelle's hands. "That's what real friends do. We support each other in the good times and the bad times."

Annabelle shrugged. "I don't know what scares me more—letting another man into my life or the fact that I'm still in a slave state."

"I think the scarier thing would be to live in a hole from this point on. God set us up. Think about it—what are the chances of running into white women from the south who don't support slavery? The thing my family has benefited from, and I'm against it. I couldn't tell you how many slaves my family has had over the years. So the next time you see Benjamin, no matter how pathetic his words may sound, give him some time to get to know the man better."

"I guess I have to work on my smile a little more," Annabelle sarcastically replied.

Ruthanne lightly chuckled. "That would be a good start, Annabelle. A smile goes a long way."

Annabelle tilted her head as a grin formed, then she asked, "Are you going to tell me how things between you and Pastor Avail went?"

Ruthanne quickly stood up. "I think it is time we went inside to help Elizabeth before she burns down the house, don't you think?"

"You cannot give me advice and then ignore my question as to how well things went at the festival! I saw how you looked at him. I'm not stupid!"

Annabelle followed Ruthanne upstairs, harassing her about details on Pastor Avail.

Ruthanne replied, "Some details are best-kept secret for the time being."

"Ruthanne! You can't be serious about keeping all of it a secret."

They entered the kitchen, ending the conversation to help Elizabeth. The women continued talking about the festival, laughing and enjoying each other's company.

CHAPTER 13
Agendas and Commitment

Two weeks passed, bringing in September of 1845. Mr. Boston had offered Annabelle to be a clerk in his store once he learned she didn't have a job. Ruthanne also decided to take a clerk position in Mr. Boston's store, intending to see Peter when he needed supplies and to protect Annabelle. Elizabeth began to help Marilyn in her store, even with Mr. Pots's objection to a woman having a job. Marilyn rebelled by refusing to cook for her father for two days straight, leading to her negotiating with her father to make an exception for Elizabeth. As the women worked, the possibility of Elizabeth and Ruthanne returning to Mississippi began to dwindle, even with their families demanding their return.

Elizabeth had begun to grow fond of doing things for herself, but she felt she would eventually need to return to Mississippi. Robin was in her heart constantly. Because she was responsible for Robin discovering the truth, Elizabeth felt even more accountable for her. Elizabeth was also divided on returning because of her new friendship with Marilyn and the fear of what might happen to Annabelle if she returned to Mississippi.

Ruthanne was still driven by her ambition to escape the reins of the south. Her feelings for Peter had also grown, making her uncomfortable. The presence of racism in Mercy made her more determined to guarantee Annabelle's freedom. Years ago, Ruthanne had witnessed a runaway slave being skinned alive and saltwater poured onto his open wounds. The cruelty she witnessed that day haunted her. She knew Annabelle needed to be careful her entire life, and she believed that in time, Annabelle would have to move further north.

One night, a nightmare filled with screams startled Ruthanne. The sound of a gunshot and the laughter of a man were all she remembered when she had awoken in a cold sweat. Ruthanne glanced over at Annabelle and Elizabeth as she breathed heavily, lying in her bed. She stared at the full moon, wondering if the dream meant anything. The week after that, Ruthanne watched the sunset, and in her heart, she realized that even if her true love was not Peter, she didn't want to return to Mississippi. She loved her family, but their morals clashed with hers. The evil intentions of Mr. Hildebrand were obvious, making her feel the need to be committed for the first time. A commitment to make sure Annabelle achieved happiness while maintaining her own.

During this time, Annabelle gained a new perspective on life. It was the first time in her life she had the opportunity to work and be paid for it. She felt comfortable under Mr. Boston's leadership and having Ruthanne with her. She thought about Ruthanne's words and how to heal. Even the kindness of a few customers encouraged Annabelle.

Mr. Boston employed her to care for the chickens and to keep products organized. Working in Mr. Boston's store also kept her out of sight of Mr. Hildebrand and Sheriff Shepard. Mr. Boston was pleased with both of the women, and he received many compliments from customers. One September day, Mrs. Davis, in a green and red ruffle dress, walked into the store, causing the bell to ring.

"Hello, Mr. Boston and Mr. Fluffs," Mrs. Davis said.

Mr. Boston replied, "Good day, Mrs. Davis. It is a pleasure to see you. What can we do for you today?"

Mrs. Davis smiled. "I need some oats, wheat, flour, and eggs for the week, Mr. Boston."

"I can get those for you, Mrs. Davis," Ruthanne said.

"Hello there, Ruthanne, it is always a pleasure to see such a beautiful young lady," Mrs. Davis said.

Ruthanne beamed. "Why, thank you, Mrs. Davis. I'll get those supplies for you, ma'am." Ruthanne went to the chicken coop after she grabbed the other supplies. "Sasha, I need some eggs up here for Mrs. Davis."

Annabelle replied, "Okay, I will bring them in a minute."

Ruthanne advanced to the front of the store with the other supplies and put them on the counter.

"Sasha is bringing up the eggs for you, Mrs. Davis. Is there anything else you need today?" Ruthanne asked.

Mrs. Davis replied, "Oh, no, dear. That's all that I need for this week."

The bell rang while the door opened. Ruthanne looked, and to her surprise, it was Mrs. White, wearing a blue dress and dark blue bonnet to match.

"Hello, everyone," Mrs. White said.

"Hello, Mrs. White," Ruthanne said.

"Welcome, Mrs. White," Mr. Boston said, putting on an obligatory smile.

Mrs. White walked through the store, looking at supplies while the others watched apprehensively.

Annabelle marched to the front of the store with the eggs in a small woven basket.

"Mrs. Davis, here are your eggs. A nice size too," Annabelle said.

"Why, yes! They're quite lovely, Sasha," Mrs. Davis said.

Mrs. White noticed Annabelle giving the basket to Mrs. Davis and approached the counter maliciously. "After you're done serving, nigger, I will need your assistance with a few groceries. I have no intention of getting my dress dirty," Mrs. White said.

"No need for that type of talk here, Mrs. White. Sasha does an exceptionally good job here," Mrs. Davis said.

"Mrs. Davis, your tone is quite irritating. Why are you defending a slave?" Mrs. White asked.

Mrs. Davis scowled, replying, "She is no slave. She is a free Negro, not bound by the ignorance of the law."

"Ignorance? You call the richness of our culture ignorance? Why, that's our lifeblood. Mr. Boston, please clarify that this Negro isn't your slave."

"Mrs. White, I have no slaves, nor will I ever accept the lifestyle," Mr. Boston said. "Now, Sasha has been working here and has done an exceptional job."

"Well now, giving a Negro woman a job over a white woman is quite repulsive. I must say I'm disappointed. I may let Sheriff Shepard know."

Mr. Boston sighed. "Mrs. White, she was not selected over any white woman in this town that I can assure you of."

"What an empty threat. How sad you are, picking a fight in a supply store," Mrs. Davis said.

Mrs. White replied, "How dare you try to belittle me! I assume there must be good reason."

"Sasha, dear, thank you for the eggs. You may go back to tending the chickens," Mrs. Davis said.

Annabelle returned to the chicken coop, avoiding eye contact with Mrs. White as Mrs. Davis faced Mrs. White.

"Lucille, what makes you so vindictive nowadays? Is it your unhappy marriage? Or are you still mourning the loss of your first two children?" Mrs. Davis frowned. "You have truly changed since we were children. Sad to see that you prey on the weak. I wonder how you react to your two young children when they try your patience. I do sympathize that you have experienced some horrible things over time, but did you ever consider that God wouldn't bless you with more children until you learned to love again?" Mrs. Davis then turned to Mr. Boston and Ruthanne. "Thank you for great service, Ruthanne. Mr. Boston, I will see you within a week or so. I will pray for you, Lucille. My heart breaks for you."

Mrs. Davis exited the store while Mrs. White watched her leave. A shallow tear went down her face, and Mrs. White wiped it away.

"Mr. Boston, I'm here for some flour and beans, then I will be on my way."

"Sure, I'll grab those for you," Mr. Boston said.

Ruthanne suddenly noticed Mrs. White's lips beginning to quiver before the older woman's face went blank, clearing her throat.

Mr. Boston brought her supplies to the counter. "Is that all Mrs. White?" he asked.

"Yes, that's all. I think my time here has expired." Mrs. White paid for her supplies and nodded to Mr. Boston before exiting the supply store.

"That was unexpected. I didn't know what to say to her," Ruthanne said.

"There are some pains in life that are so deep, people do either of two things. They either heal and move on from the pain, or they latch on and let the pain corrupt them," Mr. Boston said. "In worse cases, people lose faith in God and stay angry with unforgiveness in their hearts. There is no poison like unforgiveness. Unforgiveness is bondage. It isn't power over the past. Sadly, Mrs. White is a hurt woman."

"How sad it must be. I couldn't imagine losing two children."

Mr. Boston nodded, and he frowned for a moment. He turned around and gasped. "Look at the time! All that drama, and time went by with it. You and Sasha are done for the day."

"Mr. Boston, are you trying to get rid of us?" Ruthanne lightheartedly asked.

Mr. Boston laughed, answering, "Of course not. I figured you two ladies had plans."

"Well, as a matter of fact, we do have plans. Sasha, it is time for us to go home."

Annabelle left the chicken coop and cleaned off feathers from her dress.

Mr. Boston grinned. "Well, ladies, I will be looking for you tomorrow, and under less dramatic conditions."

The ladies laughed while they walked to the door.

"Enjoy the rest of the day, Mr. Boston," Annabelle said.

The ladies left the supply store and headed home.

"So, are you excited for another cooking day?" Ruthanne asked.

"I believe I'm more excited since Elizabeth's skills have gotten better, and she has stopped crying when you yell at her," Annabelle said.

Ruthanne laughed, shaking her head. "That isn't fair. It is like the woman is unable to count or measure. However, I believe it is your patience that has caused Elizabeth to bloom."

Annabelle's eyes gleamed. "Why, thank you, Ruthanne! I believe my past experiences have taught me that Elizabeth's lack of talent is a minor problem."

As the ladies approached their home, Benjamin noticed them walking by as he gave water to a horse. The palms of Benjamin's hands started to become sweaty as he approached Annabelle and Ruthanne.

"Good evening, ladies, how's y'all doing this day?" Benjamin asked.

The women turned around.

"Well, hello, Benjamin. How nice to see you, isn't it, Sasha?" Ruthanne said.

"Nice to see you, Benjamin," Annabelle replied, her tone unreceptive.

Benjamin replied, "Since I finished giving water to horses for the day, would it be alright if I walk Miss Sasha home, Miss Ruthanne?"

Ruthanne kindly giggled while looking at Benjamin.

"Excuse me," Annabelle irritably said. "You ask her if you could walk me home. I guess you're still thinking I'm a slave."

"Sasha!" Ruthanne said. "Don't belittle his politeness. It took a lot for him to even ask such a question. Benjamin, you have my permission to accompany Miss Sasha. Just make sure she is back before sunset."

Annabelle put her hands on her hips. "Excuse me, how are you giving him permission on my behalf?"

"I'm clearly making a good decision for you since your pride continues to sabotage efforts."

Ruthanne began to walk off as Annabelle scowled and crossed her arms.

"Remember, Benjamin, she needs to be back before sunset."

"Yes, ma'am. I make good on my word," Benjamin said.

"Ruthanne, you can be sure I won't forget this," Annabelle bickered.

Benjamin looked at Annabelle and frowned. "Is there something wrong, Miss Sasha?" he asked.

Annabelle sighed. "No, Benjamin, my friend is holding me to my word."

"Well, I say honesty keeps everything clear, even if it hurts."

Annabelle scoffed. "I'd say some things you can't be honest about because you can't trust people."

"I guess it changes on who you honest to. Not everybody wants to cause pain."

"So, how was living in Georgia?"

"From what I remember, it was good but scary. I remember my pa. He always say do what master say, and you live happy. One of my masters lay with my momma, and I saw them. He told me leave and that I got no business there. This for grown folks. My pa saw them one night, and he fought him. I don't know what really happen. Maybe his heart hurt so much he not think 'bout what he do. My pa was beat for two days before they send him back to us. I think he spirit broke. Then my momma had my baby sister, and she came out so light. The most beautiful baby I ever saw. More beautiful than any white baby I ever saw. I couldn't understand how she look so different than us, but when I got older, I understand that my sister's pa was my master. It was when I got away and was taught about women, I understand the truth. I know why my pa was never the same. I don't think he was allowed to touch my momma no more. I don't want to sound sad. I not sad just speaking truth."

"That's a hard thing to remember, Benjamin. I'm glad you didn't let a hard thing rule your life."

"I still do what the white man say, but I think the difference between me and a slave is I can leave when I want."

"So, who knows that you're a runaway slave?"

"Just other Negroes. White people can't be trusted, so I guess your words were as true as my words. I know God loves me, and I like what I do for work. I love giving water to horses. They like me. They don't care I Negro. They don't unlike each other because one had spots and the other don't. Or one bigger than the other, so they don't like each other. I wish people was like that in this town."

"I think there are people in this town that don't care if we are Negro. It was hard for me to see, especially with a few people that truly scare me, but I can say that I do have friends here. They are my miracle; an answer to my prayers, even though I have lost a lot. I often think about my friend, Judy Mays, and her husband. She taught me how to read and how to speak good English. She helped me become bold and even protected me while we were growing up."

Benjamin's eyes widened. "So, Judy Mays was a white girl!"

"See, there is more to you than you think. You were able to make a good guess without me telling you everything about her."

"Why, thank you, Miss Sasha. Nobody never said that I was smart."

"You're welcome. I think everyone needs to hear something good about themselves."

"If it don't bother you me asking, why you not married?"

Annabelle sighed and looked away from Benjamin. "I believe in marrying people out of love. I don't believe in marrying someone because of social status, blood, or because someone says I have to marry them. So far, I haven't been found by a man that I'm in love with."

"You would not marry a rich man because he rich?"

"That's right. Now, I do know someone who probably would say yes to a man because he is rich, but I don't see anything special in that."

While they strolled, Annabelle looked at Benjamin's face to see his reaction. A small smile appeared on his face, and he started to strut confidently.

Annabelle withheld her excitement as she learned more about him.

"So, what is something that you enjoy besides giving water to horses?"

"When I wake up in the morning, I like to watch the sunrise. Sunrises are the most beautiful things to me. I feel close to God when I watch them, and I feel hope."

Annabelle chuckled a bit and said, "That's funny, coming from someone who used to be a slave. I would think the sunrise would remind of you of not having a choice but to wake up."

Benjamin replied, "I guess that one of the things that no matter where I be, it reminds me of love."

"I can't stand sunrises. To me, the rising of the sun reminds me of the things that are out of my control."

"I remember watching my pa as he got ready to work, and most of time, I could see he wanted more."

Annabelle scrunched her eyebrows. "I don't ever want to be in a position of want, or not being fulfilled in the life God has given me. There was a scripture my friend, Judy Mays, would always read to me when we were children. Seek first the kingdom of God, and things will be added onto you. So to heal and become stronger, I would always tell myself to seek God, and eventually, the good times will come. I still hate the sunrise, but I love sunsets because they remind me of things that are to come."

Benjamin and Annabelle arrived at Annabelle's home.

"Thank you for escorting me home, Benjamin. It was a pleasure to spend some time with you after all."

"Why, thank you, Miss Sasha. If you like, we walk together again another day?"

Annabelle smirked. "Sure. The next time I see you, if I have time, you can walk with me."

Benjamin gave a big grin.

"You have a good day, Benjamin."

"You too, Miss Sasha. Enjoy your sunset."

Annabelle grinned and turned around to go up the stairs, thinking Ruthanne might have been right.

"Sasha!" Marilyn said.

Annabelle turned around and saw Marilyn in a new yellow dress trotting toward her.

"I'm glad I saw you, dear. Do you have this tall man under your consideration?"

"Oh no, Marilyn, he happened to see me and walked me home," Annabelle said.

"Nice to see you again, ma'am," Benjamin said.

Marilyn's sensual emerald green eyes fixed on Benjamin. "That's right, Benjamin, you were with us at the festival. It is a pleasure to see you again as well. Such a handsome Negro." Marilyn gasped. "That's right...you need to see Hansel again. It's nice to see that Sasha is making more friends."

Annabelle replied, "He was leaving. Have a good day, Benjamin."

"Miss Sasha, I will see you later. Miss Marilyn," Benjamin said.

Benjamin left, and Marilyn watched him, riveted and grinning. She looked at Annabelle.

"Why are you looking at me like that, Marilyn?" Annabelle asked.

Marilyn replied, "Because somebody likes you, and I think you like him too!"

Annabelle rolled her eyes and began to go up the stairs to her home. Marilyn followed her.

"Don't be that way. Don't deny that he is a sweetheart and handsome."

"You're making this so hard for me. All he did was walk with me back to the house."

The women entered the house while Ruthanne entered the living room.

"Sasha is back, Elizabeth," Ruthanne said. "Hey, Marilyn!"

"Hello, Ruthanne. I just saw something quite special," Marilyn said.

"Don't listen to this crazy woman, Ruthanne. She is clearly imagining things. I think she's coming from the saloon," Annabelle griped.

"What denial I hear, Sasha," Ruthanne said.

"I witnessed Sasha talking to that handsome Negro man named Benjamin," Marilyn said.

"Do tell, Marilyn. I'd like to know if Sasha kept her promise."

"It was so cute, Ruthanne, seeing those two together."

Annabelle rolled her eyes and escaped into the bedroom.

"The way he smiled at her, and they looked like such a cute couple."

"Did it look like she was giving him a hard time?" Ruthanne asked.

"No, it looked like she was actually enjoying his company. It was so cute."

Elizabeth popped her head out of the kitchen. "So their courtship went well today?" she asked.

Marilyn replied, "I think it did, Elizabeth. Sasha is being so private about it."

"Come out and talk about it, Sasha. Tell us how it went. Don't be a coward now," Ruthanne said. "Don't make me come in there and drag you out now."

"You're a sore, Ruthanne!" Annabelle screamed, but she came out of the bedroom with an agitated smirk.

"I've done it now, ladies. I pressed for the truth, and now, somebody is mad at me. Come on out and have a seat before Marilyn starts coming up with more ideas of what she thinks happened," Ruthanne said.

Annabelle sat down next to Ruthanne and unenthusiastically looked at the two women. She replied, "He's okay, and he is polite."

Ruthanne scoffed. "That can't be all you have to say."

"I agree with Ruthanne. I'd say the way you looked at him showed you would not mind seeing him again," Marilyn said.

Annabelle glared at Marilyn and tilted her head a little. She stood, clutching her hands. "Okay, he is a good man—better than I thought he was—and I hate that I think he is handsome!" Annabelle fell back onto the couch, groaning.

Marilyn clapped her hands and giggled.

"Now that wasn't so hard, was it? You even got Marilyn excited," Ruthanne said.

"What did I miss, Ruthanne?" Elizabeth asked.

Ruthanne replied, "Sasha said that she thinks Benjamin is a handsome man!"

Elizabeth rushed into the living room, giving Annabelle a kiss on her cheek, and rushed back into the kitchen.

"So when is the next time you'll see him?"

"I don't know, Ruthanne. I said I would see him again," Annabelle answered.

"So the next time you see him, if he offers, then you better say yes."

"This is so exciting," Marilyn eagerly said.

Annabelle scoffed and shook her head as she looked at Marilyn. "Well, I think I'm going to check on Elizabeth in case she ruins dinner again."

Annabelle entered the kitchen while Marilyn and Ruthanne watched.

Marilyn frowned. "Did I say something wrong, Ruthanne?"

"No, you didn't. Sasha does not have the greatest history with men, and that makes it hard for her," Ruthanne said. "You may not understand, but the past can be hard to let go of. Even when a wound is healed, a scar can still be present."

"I never thought of Sasha being frail. She always seems so strong."

"She is strong. The fact that she gave Benjamin her time is a big step for her because he is the first man she has willingly shown interest in."

Marilyn pressed her lips together as she looked at Ruthanne. "I feel bad now for pushing her."

"Don't feel bad. I've been the main instigator, and sometimes, even strong people need a nudge in order to move forward in this life. So, are you going to stay for supper?"

"That sounds great to me. I need some rest from cooking for my papa. He should be fine. I baked his favorite bread today, and there's some soup left in a pot."

Ruthanne lifted an eyebrow. "Sounds like you made plans to stay out of the house before coming here."

Marilyn lightly clenched her teeth. "I may have purposely left the store as soon as it was time to close."

Ruthanne's eyes widened while she looked at Marilyn.

"Yup," Marilyn said.

The ladies got off the couch and went into the kitchen, watching Elizabeth's continued struggle to cook while Annabelle coached her. The rest of the joyful night was spent with the women looking at a full moon and the constellations.

Marilyn went home, realizing that the time she had spent with the ladies was an authentic friendship, not just a dinner engagement or fancy gatherings to promote her father's store.

Marilyn entered her home exhausted from the long day, and she began to go up the stairs.

"So, where have you been all this time, Marilyn?" Mr. Pots asked.

"Papa, I would have thought you would have gone to bed. It is late," Marilyn said.

Mr. Pots scowled. "Go to bed when I have no idea where my youngest daughter has run off to?"

Marilyn's eyes began to narrow. "I'm seventeen years old, father, and I will be turning eighteen in fourteen days."

Mr. Pots growled. "You're still living in my house, and you're to live under my rules."

"Maybe I would follow them if you didn't treat me like a child every day," Marilyn said with a frustrated tone. "Furthermore, I told you I was going to Elizabeth's."

Marilyn began to stomp up the stairs to her room with her fists clenched.

"Don't you walk away from me, Marilyn. Don't you walk away from me!" Mr. Pots yelled.

Marilyn slammed the door and lay on her bed.

Mr. Pots shook his head and mumbled. He went to their living room and sat in his chair, looking to the ceiling. "God, help me. I feel that her anger is more than losing her mother, and I don't know how to reach deeper." Mr. Pots soon fell asleep in his chair.

CHAPTER 14
Opening Hearts

TWO WEEKS HAD PASSED SINCE the young ladies had spent the evening together, and Mr. Pots began to pray for help. The season of fall had arrived, and some of the trees began to change along with hearts. Annabelle, Rebecca, and Ruthanne had spent much time together. They discussed Annabelle's past and helped her heal from it.

In the second week of October 1845, Rebecca had the ladies come over while Allen was at a town meeting.

"I've been praying more than I ever have, not only for myself but for you ladies as well," Rebecca said. "I believe that's something that God has put in the hearts of all three of you. After reading this Bible, I've realized I should pray for all three of you. Do all of you accept me praying for you? If not, I won't be angry at any of you, nor will it affect our friendship."

Ruthanne said, "I accept receiving prayer from you."

Rebecca's eyes widened, and her eyebrows slightly lifted when Ruthanne stood before her.

"I don't know how to fully express myself or let go of the guilt I feel. I have people I love, but my guard remains high even toward them. I look at the slaves, and I feel disgust."

Ruthanne began to cry. "I still hear the whips and the screams, and I feel the evil of my own household. I don't know how to deal with people that you love but who live wrong. I've read the scriptures, and I'm amazed by how Jesus treated those who hated him."

Rebecca placed her hand on Ruthanne's shoulder while Annabelle and Elizabeth watched. Rebecca began to pray, "God, thank you for reaching Ruthanne's heart. Heal her heart in a way that no human can. Free her from her past, and free her from the core of what makes her rebel against authority. Through your power we pray and agree, amen."

Sobbing, Ruthanne hugged Rebecca, and the other two women came up behind her and gave Ruthanne a hug.

"Okay, who is next for prayer?"

The women cheerfully giggled while Ruthanne cleared the tears from her eyes and sat down.

"I will go next," Elizabeth said. "I've been shown so much love, and I can't repay it. I'm ready for you to pray for me, Rebecca."

Rebecca placed her hand on Elizabeth's shoulder. "God, show Elizabeth that she is worth far more than she realizes. Correct the wrong thoughts that go through her mind. Set her free and give her boldness to trust you and trust your ways. In Jesus's name, amen."

Elizabeth smiled. "Thank you, Rebecca. That meant so much."

"Of course, it was a pleasure. Annabelle, are you ready? Do you want me to pray for you?"

Annabelle replied, "Yes, I'm ready to let it all go and be completely free. I've tried so long to do it alone, and it has never worked."

Rebecca placed her hand on Annabelle's shoulder. "God, thank you for what you will do here today. Thank you for the courage you have given these women to ask for healing and guidance through you. Father, we ask that you reveal to Annabelle the roots of her past that make it hard for her to love those who love her. Give her confidence in your ways. May your love fill her and teach her more about herself so she can be a blessing to others, loving those who hate her. In Jesus, we pray, amen."

Annabelle gave Rebecca a hug, and the other two women put their arms around them. Rebecca felt the baby kick with excitement, and Annabelle felt the baby as well.

Rebecca laughed. "It looks like the baby agrees with all the praying as well."

The women laughed and felt Rebecca's stomach.

"Years ago," Rebecca said, "I wouldn't have imagined marrying Allen. He wasn't exactly my first pick. He always came off as quiet, sweet, and shy. One day, when we were sixteen, I was on a swing. This boy, Micah Jefferson, came up to me and asked if I would dance with him at the town dance. I politely said no, largely because I didn't even know him well, but he wouldn't take no for an answer. I told him I would rather dance with a friend.

"I told him I would like to get to know him first, and we can dance at another dance together later on. Then he started yelling at me, calling me spoiled. He said I would be lucky to get married if I kept my attitude. I told him, 'And this is exactly why you're alone now.' I started to leave, but he grabbed my arm really hard. I tried to pull my arm free, but he wouldn't let go. I told him to let me go. Out of nowhere, Allen came down the road, and I called for him. He ran right over and told Micah to let me go.

"Micah was bigger than Allen. I was afraid he might hurt Allen if I didn't cooperate. Before I could say anything, Allen told Micah to let me go, and that was the only time he was going to ask him. I was thinking that I hoped his bluff worked because Micah was scaring me, and Micah laughed at him. It made me feel so bad that Micah thought nothing of Allen. I looked at Allen, and I'd never seen him look so serious. With a smile, Micah told Allen he had no chance of beating him or being with me. He told Allen to leave. I was about to tell Allen that it was okay and to leave, but before I could, he punched Micah in the stomach so fast.

"Allen hit Micah so hard, he let go of me, and Allen gave Micah two more punches in his face. He grabbed my hand, and we ran off to my house. It was such a rush, and I understood how he really felt about me. When we got back to my house, the soft-spoken boy returned with that same smile. I learned that normally, Allen would have passed my house, but the strangest thing had happened. A bird stole his hat from him, and he followed the bird until it dropped his hat. I truly believe God had the bird take Allen's hat so he would walk down the road at the right time and open my eyes to who he really is.

"He is more than a soft-spoken man. He's God-fearing, and he's a protector. So my advice to you ladies is if something seems to be going wrong, trust God because nothing stops his plans. After we moved here, we never saw Micah again."

The ladies were inspired by her story. Annabelle realized this was what true love was supposed to be, and it reminded her of the relationship her parents had with each other. The women spent the evening together enjoying each other's company, then separated to prepare for the next day.

The next morning, Annabelle and Ruthanne traveled from their home to Mr. Boston's store to begin work. On their way to the store, they saw Benjamin and greeted him while he gave water to the horses. The women continued while Benjamin tried to quickly give the horses water.

"Miss Sasha, I was wondering if you would want me to walk you home after you get done working for Mr. Boston?" Benjamin asked.

Annabelle happily looked at Benjamin and answered, "Sure, Benjamin, I would not mind your company today if you see me walk by."

The corners of Benjamin's mouth curved into a big smirk. "Well then, I hope to see you later too, Miss Sasha. You ladies have a blessed day."

"You as well," Ruthanne said.

The ladies continued to travel to Mr. Boston's store as Benjamin returned to the horses, twirling his ladle in his right hand. Later in the day, the ladies finished working for Mr. Boston. On their way home, they passed the horse stalls where Benjamin normally worked, but he wasn't present.

"Is that disappointment I see on your face, Annabelle?" Ruthanne asked.

"Please, why would I be disappointed? I'm enjoying the day as it is," Annabelle said.

Ruthanne giggled as the women went past the different buildings.

"Hello there, Ruthanne and Annabelle, what a splendid day it is! You ladies are obviously enjoying it," Allen said.

"Hello, Mr. Keys. I'm surprised you're not at the town hall talking to businessmen and politicians," Ruthanne said.

Allen chuckled. "Ruthanne, even I have a limit to how much corruption I can deal with in a day."

Ruthanne laughed. "The truth is a powerful thing."

"I hope all is well at Mr. Boston's store for both of you."

"Things have been quiet, Mr. Keys. Far better than I expected," Annabelle said.

As Mr. Keys nodded, acknowledging their positive report, the loud pouring of water attracted their attention to one of the town's saloons. It was Benjamin, pouring water into the horse troughs.

Benjamin waved and moved toward them, passing men going into the saloon. "It is good to see you today, Mr. Keys," he said.

Allen replied, "Benjamin, always a pleasure. Are things going well for you?"

"Why, yes, sir. They is going well, thanks be to God. Miss Ruthanne and Miss Sasha, it is a pleasure to see the two of you again."

Ruthanne grinned and said, "You as well, Benjamin. I'd say without you taking care of those horses, many of these businesses would not be doing so well."

Ruthanne glanced at Annabelle. "Anyway, Mr. Keys and I

have some business to attend to as preparation for the new baby he and Mrs. Rebecca are expecting."

Mr. Keys looked at Ruthanne with a blank stare, and a crease formed between his eyebrows.

"Please escort Sasha home for us. We shouldn't be too long."

Benjamin replied, "It would be my pleasure, Miss Ruthanne, to do as you ask."

Mr. Keys looked at Ruthanne, understanding what she was attempting to do. Mr. Keys tipped his hat toward Benjamin and left with Ruthanne, leaving Annabelle alone with Benjamin.

"You're quite the clever woman, Ruthanne. Does Sasha find interest in him?" Allen whispered.

Ruthanne whispered, "We will see, Mr. Keys. We will see."

"Well," Annabelle said, "I'm a keeper of my word. I said I would not mind if you walked me home."

Benjamin smiled, and the two slowly went to Annabelle's home, sharing more stories of their experiences. In her heart, she held back, wanting to see more of who Benjamin was as a man. However, Benjamin was so open to Annabelle that she saw it wasn't desperation in him, but the willingness to be content with what he had and wanting to do better. The two arrived at Annabelle's home and continued to talk to each other as people passed them. Ruthanne and Rebecca watched from a window in Rebecca's house, unnoticed by the two.

"Well, Benjamin, thank you for taking me home. It was appreciated," Annabelle happily said.

"Why, thank you, Miss Sasha. I don't understand what 'appreciated' means, but it sounds nice," Benjamin said.

Annabelle giggled as she said, "It means that what you did was valued or noticed."

"I never thought such a nice word means that."

"You have a good evening, Benjamin. You can escort me home the next time you see me."

Benjamin beamed in disbelief. "I will be ready to take you home the next time, Miss Sasha. Have a good dinner."

Benjamin left as Annabelle watched, seeing a humble man.

Ruthanne and Rebecca excitedly followed Annabelle once she had entered the upstairs. For the first time, Annabelle had felt completely comfortable spending more time with Benjamin. The others beamed while she described the discussions she had with Benjamin.

That night, dim moonlight lit Rebecca's bedroom. Rebecca, in her white nightgown, lay in her bed, staring at the ceiling with a grin. She glanced over at a sleeping Allen, the boy she'd met so long ago was now a man.

"Maybe now is your time to find happiness, Annabelle," Rebecca whispered.

Benjamin and Annabelle continued to meet with each other while the days of October passed. Ruthanne had also become fond of Benjamin, and she purposely left Annabelle alone half the way home by making an excuse. Sometimes, she visited the church to see Peter, unknown to everyone else. Ruthanne had been inconsistent with her visits, sometimes only passing by the church to watch Peter help those who came. Ruthanne smiled as she watched him do things for others and pray for people. The times she would allow him to see her, their conversations increased her interest in him, and Ruthanne would occasionally have good laughs with Mr. Jefferson.

As October ended and November began, Annabelle had not only spent time with Benjamin but also with a few of the other Negroes. In late November of 1845, Annabelle agreed to Benjamin's request to visit his home. She was surprised by their homes. They looked very similar to the slave houses. Even though the Negroes were free, the conditions for most of them were harsh. Most houses were made up of boarded old wood, and most had uneven roofs.

"Well, this is my home. I know it not the most pretty, but it is home," Benjamin said.

Annabelle replied, "It's not too bad. I have seen worse."

"The other Negroes will come here a lot, so we have fun and talk about many things."

Benjamin went past the kitchen table, accidentally bumping

into an old oak cupboard and knocking down a book hidden on top of the cupboard.

Annabelle picked up the book and saw that it had partial burns on the cover of it. She opened the book and saw the title was *The Three Musketeers*.

"I thought you couldn't read well."

"I can't. I was saving it for when I can read, and I can only read two of the words on the first page."

Annabelle smiled as she stared at the book. "The name of the book is *The Three Musketeers*. Where did you get this book from?"

"Not long ago, one the houses around here burned to the ground, I found the book and tell nobody. I was scared the white people do something bad to me because I have it. White people probably kill me for it. I sound like a fool dying for a book that not important to white people maybe. I see evil in they hearts when we get smart, and they want death as the answer."

"I think that's brave of you, holding on to a book that could get you into a lot of trouble."

Annabelle put the book back on top of the cupboard and reached for Benjamin's hand. He held hers gently as he smiled.

"Sometimes, we have to take chances in life," she said.

Suddenly, Annabelle let go of Benjamin's hand when Daniel knocked on the door excitedly.

"Hope I wasn't interrupting. I came for music time, Benjamin," Daniel said, entering the house.

Annabelle sharply replied, "You didn't interrupt anything, Daniel. Move out of the way." She exited the house hastily.

Daniel lifted his shoulders and looked at Benjamin, who frowned.

The two men went out of the house with Daniel, shouting. "Let's celebrate! We not slaves by law, and God love the Negro man like the white man."

Most of the other Negroes in the shack houses came out to celebrate. Annabelle frowned because their celebrating reminded her of the slaves dancing around the campfire. Half of the Negroes didn't have jobs, and those that did were given jobs that mimicked the tasks done by a slave.

Sally, watching Annabelle, came up behind her and scowled. "So why you look at them so sad?" she asked. "You too good to dance with other Negroes?"

Annabelle turned around as she inhaled and forced a smile. "No, I'm not too good to dance with the others. I was enjoying watching them dance. Is that a problem?" she asked.

"No, you see yourself so special. Born free in white man's eyes."

"I think you need to let go of how I grew up. I don't see me as better than you or the others."

Sally scoffed, "But you talk with them white folk like it nothing. I see you with the redhead woman. I seen white girls take black women they like. Comb hair, watch them cook, play the clapping games, sing to Jesus, but they toys for them. Nothing but living dolls, so they not sad when master go. But you different. They don't need you but like you, and let you go when you want. It like they think you free like them, but you ain't nothing but a pretty nigger that can talk like them. The chains you have just sing different than us. I think them chains even shiny."

Annabelle's smile dropped while she glared at Sally's provocative smirk. "Sally, don't you ever think that I haven't suffered or don't understand what it means to be a Negro," Annabelle angrily said. "I haven't had it easy. Not every white person in this town likes me, and I thank God every day for how far I have come. The redhead's name is Ruthanne, and she is a great friend. She has been there for me through some hard times and has helped me get over so much. I'd love to introduce you to her."

Annabelle stepped closer to Sally, looking into the other woman's dark brown eyes. "I will ignore you insulting me this one time—just this once—but if you ever in your life accuse me of not understanding suffering again, I will choke you, and it will take Jesus himself to pull me off. God bless you, dear."

Sally stared at Annabelle with her eyes wide. Her nose began to crinkle as her breathing became heavy, and she began to sweat. Annabelle turned around and moved toward Benjamin when Sally let out a yell and lunged at her, tackling her to the ground. Sally shook her and tried tearing her dress, but Annabelle slapped her. Sally fell to the ground, stunned, while the others watched with their mouths open.

Sally quickly got up again, and both of the women screamed while they grabbed each other, attempting to throw the other to the ground. When Sally attempted to grab Annabelle's dress again to rip it, Annabelle slapped her to the ground. She got on top of Sally and slapped her again. Quickly rubbing her hand in dirt, she slapped Sally once more. Benjamin and Esther pulled Annabelle off of Sally as Daniel picked Sally up.

"You want to be a nigger now? You look like a nigger, Sally," Annabelle yelled.

"What has gotten into the two of you?" Esther said.

"Esther, white people watching us. We need go inside," Daniel said.

"I'm alright. I need to go home, Benjamin. Can you walk me home?" Annabelle asked.

"Yes, I can walk you home. I don't think it good to leave you two together right now," Benjamin said.

Esther escorted a dirty Sally into Daniel's house while Daniel and Benjamin began to figure out why the two women had fought. Annabelle stood, waiting for Benjamin.

A white boy approached Benjamin, tugging his shirt. "Mister, is there going to be more fighting between the two ladies? Me and my friends want to make bets," the boy asked.

"I sorry, but there will be no more fights, sir," Benjamin said.

"Okay, well, have a good day. My pa says you take good care of my horse when he using him to pull the carriage. Later, mister."

"Well, Miss Sasha, I see you again," Daniel said.

"Goodbye, Daniel," Annabelle said.

Annabelle and Benjamin traveled to her home, and during their stroll, she explained what had happened between the two women.

By the time they arrived at Annabelle's home, Benjamin had a crease between his eyebrows.

"I is sorry for what happen. She was wrong, and I don't know how to say it no other way," Benjamin said.

"Don't worry about it. She has many problems," Annabelle said with a blank face. "I probably shouldn't have threatened her like I did. I also have a temper I have to control."

"Do you want me to take you home tomorrow?"

Annabelle approached Benjamin in her dirt-covered green dress and smiled. "Only if you stop calling me Miss Sasha and call me Sasha."

Benjamin chuckled as he stared into Annabelle's elegant brown eyes. He leaned over and kissed her. At that moment, Rebecca, who had just left her home carrying her tea tray, saw them. Rebecca's eyes became big while she dropped the tea set on her porch. The two snapped out of their romantic moment, and Rebecca scrambled to pick up the pieces of her tea set.

"I think it be time for me to go. I'll see you tomorrow," Annabelle said, taking a step back from Benjamin.

"Yes, ma'am. I will see you tomorrow. I hope you having a good day, Mrs. Keys," Benjamin said, smiling.

"Hello, Benjamin, it is good to see you," Rebecca cheerfully said.

"Goodbye, Sasha."

Annabelle gave a quick smile, and Benjamin quickly departed, waving bye to her with a smile. She waved back with her hand close to her chest. She turned around, her gaze toward the ground, avoiding eye contact with Rebecca as she walked over to help pick up the teacups and pieces of the teapot that had broken. Rebecca looked at Annabelle, smiling.

"Was that the first kiss I saw, or was I seeing things, Annabelle?" Rebecca asked.

Annabelle replied, "I think the sunshine is too bright today. You know that the sun does things to pregnant women."

Rebecca laughed and gave Annabelle a hug. "You're so cute when you're embarrassed."

The ladies entered the house, and Annabelle explained what had happened earlier that day.

"I'm glad that for the most part, you have clearly had a good day, but be careful around this Sally woman. She is obviously jealous of you, and jealous people can be some of the most dangerous people. Try being nice to her, but don't take your eyes off her because even snakes can be nice for a moment before striking."

Annabelle took Rebecca's advice, and by the time she left the house, Rebecca had pursed her lips. Annabelle went to the upstairs quarters to see the others, and she told them what she had said to Rebecca.

"I've met women like her. The next time you see her, she might smile in your face, but she will be waiting for the first chance she gets for revenge," Ruthanne said.

"I agree with Ruthanne, Annabelle. Don't take your chances with her," Elizabeth said.

"I won't, you two. I promise to try to stay away," Annabelle said.

"Let's get ready for tomorrow. I have a feeling we will need a good night's rest. Mrs. White is scheduled to return to the store tomorrow," Ruthanne said.

Annabelle rolled her eyes while she headed into the bedroom to pick out an outfit.

Elizabeth replied, "While you ladies do that, I'll clean up the dishes and make a list of some supplies we will need soon."

Ruthanne replied, "Elizabeth, don't forget to put nuts on the list."

Elizabeth grunted, "Why do I need to do that? You're going

to work tomorrow, and there is a big old barrel full of them. You need to get them yourself."

Ruthanne grunted and began to aggressively put on her nightgown.

That night, Annabelle prayed, "God, thank you for the new things you brought me in my life, but please protect me from my enemies. I haven't remembered any dreams lately, and I'm worried about what Constance told me."

Annabelle woke up the next morning, strangely optimistic. She helped Elizabeth cook breakfast as Ruthanne sat at the breakfast table, watching with her eyes somewhat squinted. She pressed her lips and fiddled with her fingers. After eating breakfast, Ruthanne and Annabelle went down the stairs and glanced at the remarkable sunrise. For the first time in a long time, Annabelle enjoyed seeing it.

The ladies worked, dealing with the norm of a grumpy Mrs. White and the usual customers.

The walk home was different for Annabelle this time. She was filled with expectation and excitement. Instead of the usual greeting of nodding her head at Benjamin, she welcomed a hug from him before he escorted her home, holding her hand. This continued for three weeks. During this time, they strolled home together and talked more about their lives.

When the first light snow fell, they took their time going to Annabelle's home. The day was a special moment for Annabelle because she had never seen it snow before.

"This is something else I tell you, Sasha," Benjamin said. "This crazy. It so warm, but it snow anyway. God tease us. He think he funny. I think he funny, but I hoping it won't get real cold yet."

Annabelle replied, "I can get used to this sense of humor. I think this town needs every bit of fun it can get. Thank you for walking me home again."

Benjamin grinned. "It is always my joy."

He leaned forward to give Annabelle a kiss, but she placed her fingers on his lips to stop him.

"Did I do something wrong?" he asked.

Annabelle smirked. "No, you didn't, but I want to tell you something. I've been thinking a lot, and if you would let me, I would like to teach you how to read."

Benjamin's eyes widened. "You want to teach me how to read!"

"Well, I believe it is the least I could do to make life easier for you."

Benjamin gave Annabelle a hug while he cheered. "God truly good. You the best thing in my life, Sasha."

"There is one thing. You must remember that the white people cannot know how well you can read. That will bring a lot of bad attention on both of us probably, so be careful when I get done teaching."

"With you, how can I make that mistake?"

Annabelle beamed at Benjamin, giving him a hug and a kiss on the cheek.

"Don't wait for me tomorrow. Ruthanne and I have some girl time to catch up with."

"Okay, well, I come look for you on Saturday."

"Mrs. Rebecca is actually doing a dinner party on Saturday, so I will ask her if I can bring you. How does that sound?"

Benjamin's eyebrows rose a little. "I never been to a dinner party. That sound good."

"Okay, I'll see you Saturday, handsome."

Benjamin blushed as Annabelle went upstairs to enjoy dinner with Elizabeth and Ruthanne.

The next day, after working in Mr. Boston's store, Annabelle and Ruthanne walked their typical distance with each other before Ruthanne did her usual encouragement for Annabelle to walk home with Benjamin.

Annabelle giggled and said, "You know, you have to stop leaving me alone with him."

Ruthanne smirked, replying, "Please don't act as if you would not want Benjamin here. Go show off that pretty smile."

"I will be right behind you, as always."

Ruthanne went on her way as Annabelle watched, hiding behind a carriage that had stopped. Annabelle continued to follow her friend. She watched Ruthanne reach the doors of the church and look around to see if anyone was watching her. Ruthanne cracked the church door open a little, peeked into the church, and slid inside. Annabelle's forehead creased, and an eyebrow went up as she watched Ruthanne sneak around.

Annabelle immediately followed an old couple inside. She thought, *Why is she being so sneaky when she's only going to the church?*

As Annabelle started to go up the stairs to the balcony, Mr. Jefferson approached her.

"My dear," he said, "there is no scheduled service, but you're welcome to sit in the main sanctuary. I recognize you, young lady. Even though Negroes are only allowed to sit in the balcony, you still come to the Lord's house. You're always with Ruthanne and the blonde young lady."

Annabelle replied, "Yes, sir, it is a pleasure to meet you."

"I'm Mr. Jefferson, and what is your name?"

"My name is Sasha, Mr. Jefferson."

"A pleasure it is to finally speak with you after all this time. I assume you have come here looking for Pastor Avail?"

"Actually, I was looking for Ruthanne, if that's not a problem."

Mr. Jefferson chuckled and said, "My dear, if you're looking for Ruthanne, then you will also find Pastor Avail. They're at the front of the sanctuary. In all my years, I've never seen a couple in so much denial about their feelings. It's like watching two children who secretly want to play with the same ball, but one child watches, anxiously waiting for an invitation."

"How do you know they like each other, Mr. Jefferson?"

"Ruthanne has been coming here for the past couple of weeks, mostly in the shadows, watching and listening from the balcony. I only noticed three or two weeks ago, so I don't know how long she really has been coming to the church. The way she watches him, it's with admiration and understanding.

I wouldn't say that she loves him, but she certainly has her eyes on him in a good way." Mr. Jefferson sighed and continued, "Peter, on the other hand, has been a bit oblivious, or he is scared to act. He is the pastor of this church, in charge of this congregation, and some of the people may be worried if he started a relationship. However, I think it would be about time for that man to take what God is putting in front of him. Fear and stubbornness can cause one to be disobedient—not to say that they're meant for each other—but sometimes, it's good to court and for it not to work out. It tells the individuals about themselves and allows them to see more of what they need. It's childish to believe that the first time is a charm, when—in fact—it's the failures that strengthen a person in life. I hope it does work for them, if only Peter would say something to Ruthanne. I believe Ruthanne isn't the kind of woman to chase a man, am I right?"

"I believe you're right. I think Ruthanne would rather grow old than be the first to admit feelings."

Mr. Jefferson began to cackle, lightly tapping his brown cane on the floor.

"How about we pay those two a visit while Peter continues reading some scriptures, shall we?"

Annabelle's mouth opened a bit. "Oh no, I shouldn't. Ruthanne would become upset with me."

Mr. Jefferson pressed his lips. "Now, why would she become upset with you, my dear?"

"I thought she had been behaving a little weird after we worked at Mr. Boston's supply store for the past couple of weeks. She may not take it lightly that I followed her here."

"Well, in that case, no worries. You're welcome to stay and listen though."

Annabelle said, "It's quite alright. I think I will be on my way home."

Mr. Jefferson nodded. "Well, alright, dear. I look forward to seeing you on Sunday with the girls."

As Annabelle turned around, two women in their ruffled

Victorian dresses strolled through the pews and heard Annabelle and Mr. Jefferson.

"Mr. Jefferson, who are you entertaining?" one of the women asked.

"My dears, this is Sasha. She is one of our attending Negroes. Such a lovely young lady," Mr. Jefferson said.

The two women looked at each other with scowls on their faces.

"Lovely? I'd never known a nigger to be lovely, Mr. Jefferson. We are in the church. There is no need to lie," one woman said.

The other woman maliciously laughed while the first woman fanned herself with a smirk.

"Now, ladies, we are all children of God. I think our Father would be quite disappointed in you, referring to your sister in spirit as a lesser person."

"How can you say such a thing, Mr. Jefferson?" the other woman said.

"Enough of your foolish behavior. We are in the house of the Lord. She is here every Sunday, loyal to God's commandment to keep the Sabbath holy, and here you two crows are squawking away, brainless."

The two women became upset with Mr. Jefferson and charged toward the church doors, furiously glaring at Annabelle.

Mr. Jefferson, watching the women, shook his head. "Sasha, I apologize. That should never happen in the house of the Lord. It seems as time continues on, the division among us continues to grow, and a hidden hatred seems to have settled into the entire country. As I grow older, I see it even clearer, or maybe God has opened my eyes to the truth."

"What do you mean, Mr. Jefferson?" Annabelle asked.

Mr. Jefferson sat down on a stool and took a deep breath. "Slavery is actually corrupting our society. This country is built on blood, power, enslavement, and a false form of freedom. The truth is it will take a miracle to break the country out of the economical use of slaves. May God forgive us for being filled with pride and self-righteousness.

Annabelle's eyes were wide. "I don't know what to say."

As Mr. Jefferson shook his head, he frowned and said, "There's nothing to say, my dear. The truth can be cruel, but if it's never spoken, no form of true healing can ever occur. I guess you will be on your way before Ruthanne sees you."

"Why, yes, sir. It was a pleasure to finally speak with you."

Mr. Jefferson smiled. "Have a blessed day. I will be looking for you on Sunday."

Annabelle walked out of the church, various things trickling through her mind as she marched home.

As Annabelle approached her home, Ashley ran up to her and gave her a hug, wearing a pink dress.

"Miss Sasha, you feel so warm. How are you doing today?" Ashley asked.

"I'm doing quite well, Ashley. It looks like somebody is enjoying this weather," Annabelle said.

Ashley smirked. "Yes, I love this weather. I want to see it snow again and dance in the snow."

Annabelle giggled and said, "Well, that's a beautiful way to look at life."

"You looked like you were thinking, Miss Sasha. What was it?"

Annabelle looked at Ashley's big eyes and said, "I was thinking how excited you must be to become a big sister."

Ashley grinned widely while she held her hair and twisted side to side.

"I really hope Mommy has a girl so I can comb her hair while Mommy combs my hair. Do you have sisters, Miss Sasha?"

"No, I don't. I had a brother. I haven't seen him in a long time, but I still love him."

Ashley hugged her as a few people passing by gave confused looks, noticing the affection the little girl gave Annabelle.

Ashley replied, "I think he still loves you too."

Annabelle sighed while she smirked. "I think he does as well. What is your mommy doing right now?"

"She is making dinner for Daddy, and she said it's a surprise."

"That sounds like your mommy wants to make you smile."

Ashley giggled, thinking of what her mother might be cooking.

"Well, how about I sit down with you while your mommy makes dinner?"

"Okay, that sounds like fun."

They sat down on the hammock, which was moved to the front of the house. While sitting down, they watched the clouds pass in the cool weather. As they sat together, Annabelle noticed how some people stared angrily as they went past the house, but she knew Ashley was oblivious to the attention. She wondered how long Ashley would remain innocent. While they continued to swing on the hammock together, she noticed Ruthanne coming home. She giggled when Ruthanne came closer to the house, and Ashley leaned to see where Annabelle was looking.

Ashley jumped off of the hammock and ran toward Ruthanne. Her arms open, she gave Ruthanne a hug.

"Miss Ruthanne, you look so pretty today," Ashley said.

"Why, thank you, Ashley. You look adorable in your pink dress," Ruthanne said.

Ashley skipped back to the house with Ruthanne following, and she sat down on the hammock. Annabelle stood up and approached Ruthanne.

"I thought you would've had Benjamin with you," Ruthanne said.

Annabelle replied, "Oh no, not today. I figured a day without him would be a good thing. It gives me the space to observe other things that are occurring instead of becoming focused on me."

Ruthanne calmly replied, "Well, that's quite wise. What have you been focusing on?"

Annabelle gave a suggestive smile. "A lot of different things. I think you could maybe think of one."

Ruthanne raised an eyebrow, asking, "Me think of something you're focusing on?"

"I'm sure you could, Ruthanne."

Ruthanne scoffed. "My dear, your mind is complex, and even someone like me would have difficulty."

Annabelle slightly bit her lip as she smirked and asked, "Where have you been going the past couple of weeks when Benjamin escorts me home?"

Ruthanne gave a blank stare as her green eyes widened and her eyebrows lifted. "I go to numerous places when I leave you to spend time with him. Sometimes, I visit Marilyn. Sometimes, I walk to other parts of the town. It gets boring going the same direction, and I even read my Bible on my way home to slow me down."

Annabelle squinted her eyes. "Is that what you did today, Ruthanne?"

Ruthanne shifted her gaze off Annabelle to the house. "Well, not exactly. I had some interesting conversations with some new people I've met who adore Marilyn's work."

"So, you went to visit Marilyn today."

"Oh no, I haven't seen her today, but I recognized a few women that are constant customers of the store."

"If you say so. I find it hard to believe you suddenly developed a love for people."

Ruthanne crossed her arms and sharply replied, "Are you accusing me of lying?"

"I would never do such a thing. What would you have to hide?" Annabelle struggled not to smile as Ruthanne glared at her.

Suddenly, Rebecca came out of the house. "Ashley, it's time to prepare the dinner table," she said.

Ashely replied, "I'm coming, Mommy."

Ashley ran into the house to help her mother.

"I swear, that girl is getting faster every day." Rebecca chuckled. "What are you two talking about?"

Annabelle replied, "We were discussing Ruthanne's recent adventures over the past couple of weeks."

Ruthanne squinted her left eye a little while she glared at Annabelle, and Rebecca nodded at Annabelle with her lips pursed.

"Mommy, I think the chicken is done cooking," Ashley yelled.

Rebecca grunted and said, "I will let you two continue to understand each other better before my daughter burns the house down."

Rebecca quickly entered the house as Annabelle attempted to go upstairs.

"Hold it right there, Annabelle," Ruthanne growled, her teeth clenched and nose somewhat crinkled. "I want to know what you know."

"I don't know that much. I'm guessing that you may not know those scriptures that well," Annabelle said, shrugging her shoulders.

"What does that mean?" Ruthanne snarled.

Annabelle jogged up the stairs, and Ruthanne gave chase. As they entered the house, Ruthanne's eyes dilated, and her face began to scrunch.

"What do you mean by saying I may not know scriptures that well?"

"I'm just saying that your interests may not only be the good book."

Ruthanne stared into Annabelle's passive face and scowled.

"I can't believe you!" Ruthanne yelled. "You followed me into the church. You...you clever, unbelievable thorn in my side. Why couldn't you focus on something more important, like you were supposed to?"

Annabelle's brown eyes widened while she lifted up her hands to her chest. "I never thought you were going to the church, but I noticed that you became more excited to leave me alone with Benjamin than usual the past few weeks."

Ruthanne pointed her finger at Annabelle. "You cannot tell Elizabeth. That's the last thing I need."

A crease formed in between Annabelle's eyebrows.

"I don't understand. It's clear that you like him, so why not spend time with him alone?"

Ruthanne sighed and said, "He is a pastor, Annabelle. It isn't that easy. I don't feel like dealing with the pressure right now."

"Please believe me. There is no pressure coming from me. If the two of you do court, it does not necessarily mean that you will get married to him."

"That's true, but the truth is my concern is people in this town wanting me to change in some way because I have Peter's interest."

"You called him Peter! You really have some feelings for him."

Ruthanne sighed as she stared at Annabelle, then rolled her eyes. "I'm done. I don't want to talk anymore about this for the rest of the day."

She stormed off to the bedroom, and Annabelle tossed her hands in the air and sat down on the couch. Elizabeth later entered their home, excited as she carried in vegetables and a cut-up chicken.

"Elizabeth, did you come from Mr. Boston's store?" Annabelle asked.

Elizabeth answered, "Why, yes, I did. It was a nice little journey after I had stopped by to see Marilyn."

Annabelle replied, "How is she doing?"

"She is having some more issues with her father, but no need to worry. She said it comes and it goes. Where is Ruthanne?"

Annabelle scoffed, "She's in the bedroom planning her next move in life."

Elizabeth rolled her eyes and smacked her lips. "That sounds like her. She can never just enjoy the moment."

"Shut up, Elizabeth, nobody asked for your opinion," Ruthanne sharply said.

Elizabeth responded, "Well, pardon me for being honest. I will start cooking dinner. There is no reason for me to continue in a pointless argument. So, you know, Ruthanne, we're having chicken again. It will be another wonderful masterpiece."

"Elizabeth, you're still burning the chicken when you cook. A masterpiece for dogs is what it will be," Ruthanne growled.

Elizabeth approached the bedroom door and kicked it. The door swung open enough for an aggravated Ruthanne, sitting on her bed, to roll her eyes at Elizabeth. Elizabeth grunted as she walked into the kitchen to attempt to cook the food she'd purchased.

Later on, the women ate their dinner together. Elizabeth talked most of the time about her day and how she didn't understand how people tolerated the cold weather. Elizabeth was so focused on her day, she didn't notice that Annabelle kept smirking at Ruthanne, who stared back with her eyes somewhat narrowed and her lips pressed.

Later that night, Ruthanne insisted that she would blow out all the Argand lamps while the other two women slept. She entered their bedroom and changed into her nightgown, staring at Elizabeth and making sure she was asleep. She tiptoed to Annabelle and placed her arms on her bed.

Ruthanne whispered, "We need to talk."

Annabelle opened her eyes and said, "Okay, as long as you don't have your revolver on you."

Ruthanne sarcastically replied, "Well, it's on the counter. I figured that for this, I wouldn't need it."

"So, you really want to talk. I assume it's about Pastor Avail."

Ruthanne nodded, her calm eyes locked on Annabelle.

"I promise I won't tell anyone about your feelings for him."

"It's not that I don't trust you, but I have a better deal if you're interested."

Annabelle lifted her head, "What is the deal?"

"I will stop intruding about you and Benjamin unless you ask, and in return, you don't pry on me when I visit Peter."

Annabelle quietly giggled. "You sound so cute saying his name. You have a deal."

Ruthanne smirked. "So, it's a deal."

The women shook hands, smiling at each other, and Ruthanne went to bed.

CHAPTER 15
Expressed Love

THE WINTER COLD GREW STRONGER, and bonds became stronger as well. As Rebecca's pregnancy progressed, the Keys had more gatherings with the three women. Mr. Boston and a few other neighbors, along with Marilyn and Benjamin, were recurring guests. The men sometimes sat together, talking about politics or their families, while the women sat down to talk about events in their lives. Other times, they would sing songs together while the fire burned, and hot tea kept them warm.

For Annabelle, the experience she was gaining from the gatherings revealed to her a true difference between white people and the slaves. A lack of fear was present. There were no thoughts of separation or fear of undeserved punishment. She thought to herself how blessed she had become by hiding in the carriage of two women and barely escaping slavery. She watched Rebecca playing with Ashley and couldn't help but smile. Hope filled her heart that one day, she'd also have a daughter.

Annabelle also became more comfortable with the neighbors, the Williamson family. Though the Williamsons supported slavery, they welcomed Annabelle's presence. More importantly, she watched Benjamin when he came by. Even though he struggled with being comfortable, he stood out on his own. Benjamin tried to show love and respect to everyone, displaying strength with kindness.

Despite being a runaway slave, he was different than the others who were unwilling to learn more. He always asked questions and was happy to give his opinion about topics that came up. Annabelle began to admire a man who was willing to love people, even if they didn't understand him.

November passed, and December arrived with a peaceful snowfall, more than Annabelle had ever seen. The sound of the fireplace and the early morning sunshine raised her hopes even more. During one of the gatherings the Keys hosted, Annabelle noticed how much larger Rebecca had become. It was puzzling because she had seen pregnancies numerous times. It made her excited to see the baby. Ashley was far more interested in the baby than anyone else. The mystery of how a baby ended up in her mother's belly astounded her, and the new baby was something new to love.

Annabelle and the others enjoyed watching Ashley put her head on her mother's belly in hopes of feeling the baby kick. Ruthanne sat down next to Annabelle and grinned at her.

"What's going through your mind?" Ruthanne asked.

Annabelle answered, "Nothing, I'm enjoying watching how well Ashley is accepting becoming an older sister. Her pure happiness makes me happy."

Ruthanne looked at the grin on Annabelle's face as she held her tea.

"Truly, there is something more to it than that," Ruthanne said under her breath.

As the two women sat together and continued their conversation, Benjamin noticed Annabelle's glance at Ashley and Rebecca. He looked down at his cards, smiling a little at the conversation between the men as Allen and Mr. Boston dominated the conversation. The night ended with Allen escorting Marilyn home while Mr. Boston went home.

Elizabeth and Ruthanne left and said goodbye to Benjamin, but Annabelle stayed behind.

"I guess I will see you tomorrow. It looked like you really enjoyed yourself today," Annabelle said.

"I did, but I think you had a greater time than me," Benjamin said. "You wouldn't stop smiling at Mrs. Keys. I guess pregnant women make other women smile a lot."

Annabelle giggled and shrugged. "It was cute to me. That's the only way I know how to explain it to you."

Annabelle went up to Benjamin and gave him a kiss on the cheek as she touched his face.

"I'm happy, Benjamin. I really am happy right now." She climbed the stairs and looked back at a beaming Benjamin. "Will I see you tomorrow?"

Benjamin cleared his throat. "Why, yes. After I work them horses, I look for you."

"Okay. Bye, Benjamin," Annabelle said.

"Bye, Sasha," Benjamin said with a big grin.

Annabelle turned around and continued her way upstairs while Benjamin went home.

On Christmas day, they all went to Pastor Avail's special sermon, celebrating the birth of Jesus Christ. It was a cheerful sermon that surprised some of the congregation. It touched Annabelle's heart as she sat with Benjamin and the other Negroes.

The sermon started with celebrating the miraculous birth and ended with Pastor Avail's emphasis that Jesus died for all people. It seemed this was one of the few moments he felt comfortable to put pressure on his white congregates to treat their Negro brothers and sisters as equals.

The day continued with a large dinner at the Keyses' home, which was decorated with evergreens and mistletoe. The celebration of Christmas was major at the time. The Williamson family, along with Benjamin, Mr. Boston, and Marilyn, ate dinner with the women and the Keys family. It was an extravagant event for Annabelle because this was the first Christmas dinner she wasn't forced to serve or eat leftovers. A new year was on the rise, and Annabelle's past had seemingly been left behind.

However, with the full moon's light shining through the

bedroom window that night, she couldn't help but wonder about her family's wellbeing. Annabelle thought, *I can't return for now, but I hope that in the future, we'll see each other again.* She fell asleep that night, guilty and unable to know the fate of her family.

One day in January of 1846 was unique for a winter day. The sun had melted all the snow, and a certain warmth was felt in the air. Annabelle and Ruthanne had left that morning for Mr. Boston's store. After finishing their work, the women began to march home.

"Are you going to see your secret love today?" Annabelle asked.

"That was completely unnecessary, Annabelle," Ruthanne complained. "I've decided that today, I will spend time with one of my favorite people. I never told him that I would be at the church today. It is good to be missed at times."

"I guess you're right." Annabelle stopped in the road, and a carriage with two white horses walked by slowly. "I haven't talked to Benjamin in three days."

"Well, that's what normally happens when courting. At first, they are trying to touch you everywhere, and you become that special woman in their heart. Don't worry about it. It just means those horses have been keeping that man busy."

The women continued advancing when they heard someone running on the wet road.

"Sasha, please wait!" Benjamin yelled.

"Benjamin!" Annabelle said with wide eyes and a smile.

Benjamin replied as he tried to catch his breath, "I lose time warming the water for the horses. Hello, Miss Ruthanne."

Ruthanne replied, "Hello, Benjamin. You seem in a hurry."

"I knew today I needed to see Sasha."

Ruthanne smirked. "I'll go ahead while the two of you converse."

Annabelle scoffed. "You had me worried that something bad happened today."

"I is sorry for the confusion. I really wanted to see your pretty face today," Benjamin said.

Annabelle blushed while trying not to show her joy. Benjamin gently grabbed her hand, and they traveled to her home, talking about their past gatherings. Ruthanne moved ahead, listening with a smile. When they were across the road from Annabelle's house, Benjamin stopped walking.

"Sasha, I need to ask you the most important thing I ever ask anyone."

Ruthanne stopped by a light pole, hearing what Benjamin said.

"I want to be better for you. You make me want to do better," Benjamin nervously said. "I would never believe Mr. Keys would welcome me in his home when he did. For Mr. Boston and Mr. Williamson to speak to me as a man, I never would believe it, but because of you, it true. You warm my heart and speak the truth. You love God with all you are, and somehow, you gets even the white people to love you. It something so special about you no man can take from you, and I love you. I love you from deep in my heart. The woman you is and will turn into. I believe God gone do something big with you."

Tears trickled down Annabelle's face, and she began to breathe heavily. Ruthanne watched with her hands over her mouth.

"Sasha Williams, will you do me the honor of spending the rest of your life with me as my wife?"

A tear went down Ruthanne's face, waiting to hear Annabelle say yes. Annabelle's eyes widened as her breathing became heavier. She abruptly turned around and ran to the house, accidentally knocking down a white man.

Ruthanne ran up to the white man and helped him stand up, calming him down while downplaying Annabelle's actions. Afterward, Ruthanne quickly ran up to Benjamin and placed her hand on his shoulder.

"Benjamin, I need you to walk with me," Ruthanne said.

"What did I do wrong? I see the white men do it all the time," Benjamin asked.

Ruthanne sighed, "I don't think you did do anything wrong. Walk with me to the stairs and wait."

Benjamin followed Ruthanne across the street, and she placed her hand on his face soothingly.

"Don't worry about it. Wait right here."

Ruthanne jogged upstairs and into the house, only to see Annabelle pacing back and forth.

"Annabelle, what's wrong? I saw it in your eyes. You were ready to say yes."

"I can't marry him. I'm not the person he thinks I am," Annabelle said. "I can't live a lie. I can't do that to him."

"What do you mean, Annabelle?"

"All this time, and he has no idea I used to be a slave...or my real name. He has no idea."

Ruthanne's face showed happiness, and she hugged Annabelle. "I think it's time for someone else who is in your circle to see the whole picture of who you are."

"How do I know he won't walk out of here and never speak to me again or not tell anyone?"

"If he truly loves you like he said he does, then he'll be able to understand," Ruthanne said before going out of the door and inviting Benjamin upstairs.

"I want to first apologize for running away like that. I know I hurt you, but there is more to me than I told you," Annabelle said, locking eyes with Benjamin. "I haven't told you everything. I'm a runaway slave from Mississippi. That's how I know Ruthanne and Elizabeth. I was a house slave, and I had become friends with the master's youngest daughter when we were children."

Benjamin sat on the couch in shock. "Who else knows you really not free other than Miss Ruthanne and Miss Elizabeth?" Benjamin asked.

"Rebecca knows the truth, but Mr. Keys doesn't know. And

my real name is Annabelle Brown, not Sasha Williams." As she wiped tears away from her face, she felt her heart continue to pound.

Benjamin stood up and approached her. He reached out, held both of her hands, and looked into her brown eyes. "I still love you, and you raise my spirit even more now."

Annabelle laughed, and tears covered her face as she gave Benjamin a hug. "Yes," she said, "I would love to be your wife, Benjamin."

The two kissed as Ruthanne grinned and watched, holding back tears. Smiling, Ruthanne went up to the couple and gave them a hug.

Benjamin strolled home, excited to tell the other Negroes the great news.

As Annabelle and Ruthanne talked to each other in the living room, Marilyn and Elizabeth entered their home.

Marilyn noticed that Annabelle was radiantly smiling, and she stood at the door with a slight smirk and a crease forming between her eyebrows. "Sasha, your smile...it's contagious," she said. "Why are you so happy?"

Annabelle replied, "Benjamin has asked me to be his wife, and I said yes."

Elizabeth and Marilyn screeched as they ran over to give her a hug.

Marilyn asked, "When did this happen?"

Ruthanne answered, "It happened just a moment ago."

Elizabeth began to cry while she beamed at Annabelle. "I'm so happy for you! It warms my heart so much," she said. "Ruthanne, were you here the whole time?"

Ruthanne grinned. "I was here the whole time. It was special."

Elizabeth clutched her hands to her chest while she smiled and laughed. "I know what I can do to make this a true celebration!" she said. "I'm making a cake for you, Annabelle!"

The other three women were speechless as Elizabeth rushed into the kitchen to get ingredients.

Marilyn and Ruthanne rushed behind Elizabeth to slow her down.

"Let us help you! It would be a great way to celebrate Sasha's engagement," Ruthanne said.

"Well, alright. I think a vanilla cake will be adequate."

Elizabeth looked at Annabelle, who nodded in agreement.

"Why did you call her Annabelle?" Marilyn asked.

Ruthanne scowled at Elizabeth and shifted her gaze to Marilyn. "I guess we have no choice since someone can't keep a secret," she said as Elizabeth frowned.

"Annabelle is my real name."

Marilyn looked at Annabelle with her emerald green eyes wide open.

"I don't understand," Marilyn said.

"Annabelle was being abused by a man. We took her away from him to save her," Ruthanne said. "It's why she took the name Sasha. Sorry we didn't tell you earlier, but really, only Rebecca and us know to protect her."

Marilyn inhaled while she frowned. "I'm so sorry, Annabelle. You're such a kind spirit. I couldn't imagine a man hitting you."

Annabelle said, "It's okay, I'm free from him now, and I gained some friends."

Marilyn beamed. "Yes, you did. I will keep your secret. I promise."

Marilyn looked at Ruthanne. "Alright, let's bake a cake."

Marilyn and Ruthanne began to help Elizabeth prepare the cake. Annabelle sat down on the couch, still trying to grasp how the day had turned out so unpredictably.

Ruthanne helped organize the ingredients and mumbled, "I'll be damned before I let Elizabeth cook a cake for this girl. The next thing we know, we'll all be poisoned from her mixing stuff wrong. It's bad enough she told Annabelle's secret."

The women celebrated the night together. Afterward, Ruthanne offered to escort Marilyn down the stairs.

"I'm glad you were able to join us, Marilyn," Ruthanne

said. "You were unexpected, but I think you being around only warmed Annabelle's heart even more."

Marilyn replied, "She is an amazing woman in my eyes, Ruthanne, and the best news to end a month. I admire her strength, to be honest. I look at myself as a Christian woman now. As I look around in this town, I feel ashamed at times. Even though I'm able to smile, my smile is fake for fake people. I couldn't imagine being a Negro, especially a woman that's Negro. I was a hypocrite, singing hymns to Christ but cursing my brothers and sisters because they have a different skin color. Who am I that I choose to only love our white race and call myself righteous? Five years ago, I would have told Annabelle to clean the dirt off my shoes."

Ruthanne's head slightly tilted, and her eyes widened.

"I'm grateful now that God has opened my eyes to my pride and hypocrisy." Marilyn sighed. "Because I work the store, I believed I had to learn how to read, to my father's dislike. The only book I could get ahold of was a Bible. At first, I hated it, but the more I learned about Jesus and the sacrifice that was made for every man and woman, I wept. I'm blessed to witness Annabelle's happiness. It lifts my spirit so much. It is something truly special about her. I see all four of you as extended family of mine; my new sisters."

"All four of you... Well, what about me, Marilyn?" Rebecca said.

Marilyn and Ruthanne turned around, surprised that they hadn't noticed Rebecca when they went down the stairs.

"How long have you been there, Rebecca?" Marilyn asked.

Rebecca replied, "I was right here the whole time, watching the stars since the night isn't that cold today. And the stars are absolutely stunning."

"I guess the conversation was that interesting for us not to notice you." Marilyn looked up into the sky before looking back at Rebecca. "Yes, I see what you mean."

"So, both of you seem extremely happy. What has both of you so delighted?" Rebecca asked.

"Benjamin has asked for Annabelle's hand in marriage, and she said yes!"

Rebecca shrieked while holding her belly. "That's marvelous news! I remember how much joy I felt when Allen proposed."

"Well, I must be off before my father begins to worry. Goodbye, my lovely sisters. Till we meet again."

"Um, before you go, you said 'Annabelle' instead of 'Sasha.'" Marilyn smiled at Rebecca. "Ah, I see. Well, now we all are connected, aren't we?

"Have a good night, Marilyn."

Marilyn replied, "You too. Bye, Ruthanne."

Ruthanne replied, "We'll talk tomorrow."

Rebecca and Ruthanne watched Marilyn go home, greeting a carriage that passed her by.

"I can't even truly express the amount of joy I feel for Annabelle," Rebecca said. "We must be careful with this though."

Ruthanne faced Rebecca with a somewhat scrunched face, her arms crossed. "What are you talking about?" she asked.

Rebecca replied, "Slaves are not allowed to get married in this state. It is for certain that if one of the officials in this town finds out the truth about Annabelle, they will find her previous owners. Only free Negroes' marriages are acknowledged, and even those can be troublesome. We need to find a priest that will ask few questions and won't request a double-checking of their records."

Ruthanne smirked. "I know someone who will do it for them."

"Are you certain you know someone who will support their marriage?"

"I believe I could even convince him to allow them to have a ceremony in the church instead of a home. I have seen many Negro unions in the south, and all of them beneath what they deserved. Some of them dance as a celebration, many jump a broom, and some seal it with a long kiss, but none of them are even close to the elegance of a white wedding. I hope to at least give Annabelle half of what white people would get."

"I think it may be best to keep it a secret from Annabelle, so she can focus more on her happiness than the law."

"I agree with you, Rebecca."

Rebecca stretched her arms. "For now, we can focus on the fun part, and keep Annabelle excited for her new beginning. I think it will be wise if we meet later this week and develop a plan to keep Annabelle unaware of the danger."

Ruthanne gave a curious look. "What did you have in mind?"

Rebecca crossed her arms and lightly tapped her chin with her finger. "For now, I'm not completely sure, but I do have some favor in high places, thanks to Allen's involvement with the city officials. I will have to pray on it and see if God gives me more insight on what needs to be done."

"That sounds like a plan to me. I better return upstairs before they become worried."

Rebecca replied, "I should do the same. I will see you tomorrow."

Ruthanne smiled. "Yes, indeed."

The two women grinned at each other and went their separate ways. Rebecca entered her bedroom, where Allen was lying in the bed, reading. She put on her cream-colored nightgown and lay next to Allen, staring at him contentedly. She placed her hand on the book, slowly pushing it down from his eyes while she smirked.

"Don't act like you have no interest. This child in my belly is more than enough proof."

The two laughed as they kissed each other, and she sat on his lap. She placed her hands on his chest and pressed her forehead against his with her eyes closed.

"Do you remember when you proposed to me?"

"I remember it was under that old willow tree, and we were watching that pair of foxes playing with each other," Allen said.

Rebecca giggled while rubbing her hands on Allen's chest. "You don't remember which day it was, do you?"

Allen could feel his heart begin to race while his wide eyes looked at Rebecca, and he gulped. "I'm sorry, I don't remember that day, but I at least remember our anniversary."

Rebecca giggled. "The look on your face. I was hoping you wouldn't lie. The reason I asked you was because we need to get prepared for a wedding that will occur soon."

"Oh! Well, who are the lucky man and woman in this occasion? Is it Theodore Meyer and Joyce Jakes? It would be about time for them to take their courting more seriously."

"Yes, well, that would be nice, Allen, but you're completely wrong. The amazing couple we must be careful with is Sasha and Benjamin."

Allen's jaw dropped, and his eyebrows shot up as he stared at Rebecca.

"Dear, that blank stare is making me quite uncomfortable," Rebecca said.

"I can't believe it! I mean, I'm happy for them. It's that it has been so long since we've had a Negro couple married. It's been at least five years to my knowledge. Do they know which priest they want to ask to marry them?"

"I would assume they will ask Pastor Avail. Both of them have been going to the church consistently. I think he'll do it for them. He is the most open priest we have in this town. Ruthanne said she knows someone that will, and I believe she meant Pastor Avail."

Allen smiled and nodded his head. "It sounds like you and Ruthanne talk a lot now."

"We do, my lover. Are you jealous?" Rebecca joked.

"I might be a tad bit jealous, my lady, but as you said, this beautiful belly of yours says something on its own," Allen said, lifting an eyebrow and smiling.

Rebecca cackled while she smacked Allen's chest. "Only in certain matters am I a lady. I thought you would have learned this lesson by now."

Rebecca slipped down the upper part of her nightgown, blew out the candle by their bedpost, and they passionately made love.

The morning brought great promise. Annabelle woke up, still excited by her choice. She couldn't stop beaming. As the women enjoyed their breakfast together, it seemed that Annabelle's happiness warmed the kitchen. Elizabeth and Ruthanne seemed anxious to leave the house to take care of errands. While the two left, Annabelle followed them down the stairs to tell Rebecca the great news. Annabelle came up to the door, and before she could knock, Rebecca opened the door.

"The smile on your face says it all," Rebecca said.

Annabelle replied, "Benjamin has asked me to marry him, and I said yes!"

Rebecca gave Annabelle a hug, causing her to smile from ear to ear.

"I heard last night about the great news from Ruthanne and Marilyn. They were so happy for you that they couldn't keep it to themselves."

As the two separated, a tear went down Annabelle's face, and Rebecca wiped the tear away.

"Careful now, or you'll end up making me cry too."

Annabelle sighed. "I'm sorry. I don't know why I'm so emotional."

"It's joy, Annabelle. It's joy. Did you want to sit with me on the hammock since this weather is getting warmer?"

"Sure, I need to ask what planning a wedding is like anyway."

As the two sat down together, enjoying the morning rays, Elizabeth and Ruthanne had already begun making preparations for Annabelle. While Elizabeth had gone to the clothing store, excited to ask Marilyn to prepare something new for Annabelle, Ruthanne had gone to the church.

CHAPTER 16
Silent Storms and Nightmares

ELIZABETH ENTERED THE STORE, SMELLING the perfumes Marilyn liked to spray in the morning air.

"Marilyn, are you available?" Elizabeth asked.

Marilyn answered, "Just a minute, Elizabeth. I'm with another customer. I'm getting her fitted."

Marilyn and the woman later came to the front of the store with an astounding red dress.

"I will be back tomorrow to pick up the dress once you have finished the final sewing, Marilyn," the woman said.

"That will work fine, Mrs. Hanson. Have a great day," Marilyn said.

Mrs. Hanson replied, "You as well."

"Well now, you seem to be excited, and you haven't said a word," Marilyn said as Mrs. Hanson exited the store.

"I feel so happy for Annabelle. I can't help but smile," Elizabeth said.

"I understand what you mean. Just the thought of going to a wedding for her is grand."

Elizabeth nervously looked at Marilyn. "Would you have time to make a new dress for her?"

"Well, I don't know. Have they set a date for the wedding?"

"I don't believe they have, but surely it will be about a

month before preparations are completed. They don't have a lot of people that they could invite."

Marilyn shook her head. "A month isn't a lot of time to make a wedding dress, Elizabeth, but I believe you're right. I don't think Benjamin has any family left. Now that I think about it, he did have a cousin who died two years ago."

"How sad. I know it will be hard to have Annabelle's parents attend."

Marilyn pouted. "Why? Jefferson City is only a half a day away."

Elizabeth's eyes shifted off Marilyn, and she began to fidget with her fingers.

"Annabelle said that her father is quite ill now, so travel would make it worse. Don't bring it up, Marilyn. She's tried so hard not to worry about him."

"Okay, I won't mention it. I believe it would be sad if they're unable to see their happy daughter. I suppose you want to keep this dress a secret. What kind of design are we talking about?"

Elizabeth replied, "I'd say a beautiful purple dress would be practical."

Marilyn looked at Elizabeth with a blank stare as she sneered a little.

"You don't have to look so disappointed with me. If you have something better, please say so."

Marilyn tilted her head as she held her hands together. "I think we need to do this in a way it sends a message, like Queen Victoria."

Elizabeth's eyes somewhat widened. "There is no way you would be able to make something so extravagant in such a short amount of time."

"Not as extravagant, but yes, a beautiful white dress with a white corset, since they're becoming more popular. I can even supply the ring for them, I bet. However, I will have to be creative with that part of the surprise. If Papa finds out about the ring and who it's for, there is no possible way I could get them."

Elizabeth asked, "How much will this cost?"

"I would say twenty dollars will be sufficient," Marilyn answered.

"Are you sure that's all you want? This dress will take a lot of time."

Grinning, Marilyn gave a dismissive wave of her hand. "I already have received a new shipment of material, and I'm excited to use it. So that will be the main part of this wonderful event to come; her walking into the church with an astonishing dress. Imagining the smile on her face makes me want to get started now."

Elizabeth's face showed excitement. "Well, that sounds great!"

"Remember that while my father is around, there will be no mention of it. If he finds out about the dress, he will continue to ask who it is for. So before anyone else comes in the store, I have some perfumes I must show you."

"By all means, entice my senses with something new."

The women moved toward the back shelves, holding a new variety of perfumes.

"My word, Marilyn, you will end up keeping me in this store forever. I must make sure I get these letters to the mail carrier."

"Who are those for?" Marilyn asked.

Elizabeth sighed. "They are letters for both Ruthanne's and my families, so they know what we have decided, though I doubt they will be pleased. Their responses were harsh when the first three letters were sent by Ruthanne. This was supposed to be a trip of ours to see Mercy and get out of Jefferson City for a while. Who would have ever believed that we would fall in love with this town."

Marilyn grinned as the two continued to experiment with the new perfumes.

Ruthanne had her own priorities. She traveled through the town, greeting townspeople. She couldn't help but smile, still excited for Annabelle. She approached the church, pausing to allow a carriage to go by her, only to have her arm grasped.

Ruthanne turned around, her eyebrows lifting and eyes

widening when she looked at Mad Moe, who wore a malicious leer with his brown eyes locked on her.

"Mm...I can smell your body. It's like a sweet flower," Mad Moe said. "I bet your skin is smooth, like them silk cloths them rich folks love."

Ruthanne snatched her arm away as she scowled. "I guarantee you'll never have the pleasure of getting close enough to smell me again," she said.

"I must disagree with you, redhead. I'd never been too fond of the women that let me take it. It becomes boring, but the fighters like you...that's a treat. Where is your nappy-head friend? She's a fighter too. My boys would like her."

Ruthanne squinted, and a crease formed between her arched eyebrows. "No need to concern yourself with her." Ruthanne marched away quickly.

Mad Moe stared at her, tightening his hand into a fist. "You may walk away from me today, but there will come a day you won't have all these eyes saving you," Mad Moe growled.

Ruthanne continued to ignore Mad Moe. While she walked away, he followed her, his eyes blazing. As he continued to pursue her, he pushed a man out of his way abruptly.

"Excuse me, sir, but please be courteous while walking," the man said.

Mad Moe turned around and approached the man aggressively. "What makes you think I want to be courteous?" he asked.

Ruthanne heard the commotion and looked back, seeing Mad Moe confronting the man, so she quickly hurried away.

The man replied, "I believe any good and respectable gentleman is capable of courtesy."

Mad Moe scoffed. "Sir, I guarantee you that respect is even given to men who are not gentlemen."

The men stood face to face, while those walking by tried to ignore the commotion.

"I'll show you that you'll give me the respect I demand," Mad Moe hissed.

With a quick punch to the nose, Mad Moe knocked the man down. The townspeople passing stopped, looking in shock. Mad Moe climbed on the man, hitting him two more times before three men stepped in, pushing Mad Moe off him.

"Do you fools want a beating too?" Mad Moe yelled.

The injured man stared back at Mad Moe with big eyes and a bloody nose.

"Like I said, you'll give me the respect I want. Tell me to be courteous again, and I guarantee my pistol will be the last thing you hear."

The three men helped the injured man up. Mad Moe realized he didn't see Ruthanne. Mad Moe grunted, squeezing his hands into fists. He marched to the injured man and was about to punch him again when the three men held him back, and he screamed. The three men let him go, and he stopped struggling. Mad Moe walked off, growling and kicking the dirt on the street.

Ruthanne arrived at the church, huffing once she looked back and didn't see Mad Moe. She entered, noticing nobody was inside. "Pastor Avail, are you here?" Ruthanne shouted.

Peter walked from his office while he stretched. "Hello, Ruthanne. You missed everyone else. I believe they decided to have lunch together at Mr. Jefferson's home," Peter said. "I'm sure they would have been thrilled to have someone young join them."

Ruthanne smirked. "I came here for you, Peter."

Ruthanne's abruptness made Peter's heart drop, and his eyes locked with hers as he blushed. Peter cleared his throat. "Please don't address me like that here, Ruthanne. It feels too personal."

"So is spending time with me not personal?"

"Well, it is personal, but my main focus is to go over scripture with the community, not just you."

Ruthanne scowled a little while her eyes dilated, but she quickly closed her eyes and inhaled. She opened her eyes and forced a smile. "So, since we are in the house of the Lord, I expect nothing but the truth from you. As I will be truthful with you, I came here to ask a rather large favor."

Peter replied, "As long as it is within the realms of the church, I'll do it for you."

"Benjamin Mosely has asked Sasha to marry him, and she said yes."

Peter half-smiled as he put his hands in his pockets.

"Please marry them. I doubt either of the other two churches in the town would have the courage to do so."

"Ruthanne, that's an enormous thing to do. In this state, even though it is legal, the idea of two Negroes marrying isn't popular."

"I'm not asking for them to have a huge ceremony. I'm asking for you to uphold what is right. Why should their happiness be put on hold, when it isn't even scriptural to say no to them?"

Peter sighed, "I will have to pray on this."

Ruthanne narrowed her green eyes. "How dare you!"

Peter looked away from Ruthanne while she tried looking into his troubled brown eyes.

"Don't you dare turn away from me, you hypocrite."

"Don't call me a hypocrite. I have stood for many things the others in this town won't, including having a Negro and white congregation," Peter yelled.

Ruthanne yelled, "Standing for one right thing and yielding to standards set by society makes you a hypocrite. You have made Sasha and the other Negroes feel comfortable to come here to the point that this is their sanctuary. You know this is the truth."

Peter scowled while he shook his head. "I have enough pressure from others, including many town officials, because I allow Negroes to come. A Negro wedding could cause an uproar."

Ruthanne's green eyes blazed while she pointed her finger at Peter and scowled. "Don't try to tell me about uproars. I have heard the slave master's whip across the backs of slaves. I grew up hearing their cries and the songs they sing out in those fields. You have lived in areas where hypocrisy rules, and as a result, when the real pressure appears, you cave to their demands."

Peter shook his head. "You're asking me to put the congregation at risk. If the two of them want to live together and establish a family, it will be acknowledged here that they're married, and therefore, not living in sin."

"You still would not be giving them justice! All that would be needed is for a small ceremony to be given here. Their parents won't even be able to join us. We are the closest thing to family that either of them has in this town."

"Like I said, I need time to think about this."

Ruthanne growled, "You need time! Okay, let's talk about time. The time we spent together during the festival before Miss Sierra Nicole appeared. Was that more than a nice conversation?" Ruthanne stared at Peter, hands on her hips.

Peter remained unresponsive, trying to avoid eye contact with Ruthanne.

"Forget it, if you can't give me an answer. However, I'm asking you to show me who you really are in this moment. Can you please not follow this path of fear? Do you think I do everything in my life without any thought of consequence?"

Peter sighed as he put his hand on his forehead. "Ruthanne, it isn't that simple. You act like it will go unnoticed, and everyone will go on happy, living their lives. God help me, I'm happy for the both of them. I don't know what to do."

Ruthanne stared at Peter angrily. "If you truly want to serve God, then you would not care so much about what people think. When on Earth did God ever object to a marriage because of race?" Ruthanne grabbed a Bible sitting on a pew and shook it at Peter. "Tell me, where in these pages does God say only one race of people can be married, or there should be no mixing of the bloodlines? I only see scripture that says don't marry if they don't follow God."

"I know you grew up with Sasha, and you care for her a lot."

"I more than care for her. She is one of the most authentic people I have ever known in my life. She is one of my best friends next to Elizabeth."

Peter's gaze went downward. "I can't divide this congregation up even more over a marriage. I sincerely support acknowledging their bond, but creating tension in this town does not prove your individual strength or love for her."

"Because of what God has done in my life, that's why I'm strong. Something I have learned this past year is that God allows problems to arise in our lives to remind us we need help. We need to seek him. If you're unwilling to truly demonstrate true love and trust to a congregation that's as sensitive as you describe, then in my opinion, you have failed as a leader."

Ruthanne dropped the Bible on the pew and stormed out of the church, holding back tears. *Never again will I shed a tear for a man,* she thought.

Peter frowned as he watched Ruthanne leave. He returned to his office, where he wept. "God, give me strength. Please give me strength. Open my heart more to be strong and trust you more."

Ruthanne moved through the town, focusing on maintaining her composure as she held back her tears. *Jesus, please walk me home through this. I was so hopeful that I would have wonderful news for Annabelle,* she thought. She continued her walk home with a fake smile, acknowledging some of those who passed by her. Seeing the horse carriages walk by bothered Ruthanne. It reminded her of how hard Benjamin worked. Upon her return home, she saw Annabelle and Rebecca sitting on the hammock talking together. Ruthanne sighed while waving her hands at the ladies.

The two women smiled, waving back at Ruthanne.

"Well, how did your journey through town go?" Rebecca asked.

Ruthanne replied, "It was okay, Rebecca. Nothing special to really talk about. I do have great news that Elizabeth and I decided recently. We are going to live here, possibly permanently, instead of returning to Mississippi."

Annabelle was overjoyed and gave Ruthanne a hug.

Rebecca chuckled. "So this town sucked both of you in."

"I would say that for now. It has Rebecca, and having Annabelle here adds to it. Though this weather is a joke compared to the marvelous south, the people here trump the weather."

The ladies laughed together as the day passed and enjoyed lunch together.

"I need to go to the outhouse again. When you ladies have the opportunity to experience pregnancy, you will understand."

Ruthanne joked, "I won't complain, especially if I don't get as big as you."

Rebecca entered the outhouse while the other two watched the townspeople, but suddenly, they saw Peter coming to the house. Ruthanne tried to remain calm while Annabelle was ecstatic to see Peter.

Annabelle stood from the hammock to greet him while he approached the house.

"Pastor Avail, how are you doing today!" Annabelle shouted.

"It's a blessing to see you today, Sasha. My day has been a bit eventful," Peter said.

"How so, Pastor?" Annabelle asked.

Peter quickly glanced at Ruthanne. "No need to worry. It was taken care of properly."

"That's good to hear. I also need to tell you that Benjamin asked me to marry him yesterday, and I said yes!"

Peter happily looked at Annabelle. "What a blessing! I can see that 'excited' would be a weak choice of words to describe your happiness. I'll congratulate Benjamin when I see him. I have actually come here to speak with Ruthanne. I will be happy to continue this lovely conversation with you, maybe on Sunday."

"Why, of course, Pastor Avail." Annabelle moved past Ruthanne, smirking while Ruthanne pursed her lips and quietly sighed. She climbed up the stairs, entering the upstairs quarters of the house, unaware of the tension between Ruthanne and Pastor Avail.

"Peter, before you say anything, please keep in mind that I have a pistol in my purse," Ruthanne said.

"I understand greatly and accept that you have every right to be upset with me," Peter said with a nervous tone. "At this time, I will admit that as I said before, I'm happy for Sasha, and I'm terrified at the idea of giving them a ceremony. However, who am I to stand in the way of what God is showing me? How can I be an example of Christ when I won't even try to stand for what is right? I would be pleased to give them a ceremony. A small one, I believe, won't belittle their symbol of love."

"It's nice to see that you've chosen to show some strength."

Peter shrugged. "Making this decision has taken all of my strength, and the source of my strength is God. I have nothing left on my own."

Ruthanne's happy face began to turn annoyed. "How can you have nothing left? Have you not seen these people suffer before?"

"I have lived most of my life in Indiana. Even in this state, I have never been on a plantation. I fear the very thought of even seeing the evil."

Ruthanne's voice began to rise. "But isn't that the problem? Too many men with the power to put things right have let greed and hate be their god. What good is a shepherd if he won't speak the truth to those he is responsible for?"

Peter crossed his arms while he scowled a little. "Don't disrespect me. You still speak to me like this is something easy."

"That's because it is, despite what my ancestors did and how my family continues to live at this moment. I have made the choice to reject such hypocrisy, as a woman who is trying my hardest to be a Christian. What good am I if I can't speak against anything that's morally wrong?"

"You still don't understand the political power that's key to these issues, and you're a woman."

Ruthanne put her hands on her hips while her eyes narrowed. "Don't underestimate me because I'm a woman. I was present with my father when he made most of his financial dealings. I learned how to gain knowledge and remain silent."

"Once money gets involved in the matters of making decisions, the right decisions are often not what's priority."

Ruthanne scoffed, and her arched eyebrows shot up. "Then I suggest you go out there to those plantations to hear the whips crack on the backs of your brothers and justify it in your mind, since you're a man of faith. You want to know more of the secrets of the south?" She approached Peter. "I know of five plantations in Mississippi alone that still have Indians as slaves. The 'full-blood savages' is what we called them. Most of those are old and dying now, but there are plenty of mixed-blood niggers and Indians. Their long durability is what the masters love. The strength and intelligence of an Indian and African resistance to illness is a sought-after combination. Redskins, grass niggers, or prairie niggers is what we've called Indians and their mixed-brood children. How about that for vulgarity?"

Peter pouted and took off his black top hat. "Please don't speak in that manner around me!"

"You fear seeing what it's like on a plantation? Why not hear the words that arc spokcn on a plantation?"

People walked by, staring at the two.

"I don't need those images to know our people are wrong!"

"Then how can you reach those who grew up like me? You know something my father used to tell me when I was a child? The better we keep these niggers stupid and away from their kin, the stronger we become."

"That's a common belief, unfortunately."

"My father also said that because the Indian is so focused on keeping his land, they have forgotten about their own family still shackled in our fields. So, please don't come and tell me you have no more strength left when you have never even lived the life."

Peter was dismayed with Ruthanne's aggressiveness. "Is

growing up owning slaves and hating it the thing that has pushed you so strongly against slavery?"

"No, it is because I asked God to show me truth, even if I didn't want to believe it myself. I was a queen on my plantation—adored—having them bow their heads to me, but I've decided not to return because I can't free them."

Peter gasped as he looked away from Ruthanne. "Very well, I will keep my word and give them a ceremony once they are ready. The next time we meet, I would ask that you would be much more courteous. I understand you're upset with me at this moment, but I must still demand your respect."

Ruthanne nodded her head. "As a reminder, there are no Negro churches here. You're it."

"I understand."

"Good. I can admit that I still need work. I will try harder to be respectful."

"Thank you, Ruthanne." Peter put on his top hat tilted and left with his heart still racing.

Ruthanne watched him leave while she tried to calm down, hoping her words reached him.

Rebecca exited the house and placed her hand on Ruthanne's shoulder.

"How much of that did you hear?" Ruthanne asked.

Rebecca answered, "I heard enough, and I'm pleased with the results. However, I think we may have to make it clear to the Williamsons we're not crazy. Nor is there anything special between you and Pastor Avail. The two of you argued like a married couple."

Ruthanne scoffed and bit her lip. "I have no intention of marrying that man."

"I understand that feeling quite well. How about some cake?"

"Cake sounds like a good idea."

The ladies continued the evening together, discussing how to do Annabelle's wedding ceremony. The entire argument between Peter and Ruthanne escaped Annabelle's knowledge, and Ruthanne decided not to tell Elizabeth.

A week passed as Annabelle's excitement had calmed down, and Benjamin had asked some of the other Negro men to help him fix up his home. Benjamin was determined to make Annabelle comfortable. One evening, Benjamin came over to Annabelle's home to spend time with her and talk about the wedding. Annabelle noticed he wasn't his normal cheerful self while he stared at the sunset through the window.

"Benjamin, what's on your mind?" Annabelle asked.

Benjamin replied, "Nothing, I happy to be here with you."

"Benjamin, don't lie to me. You have barely spoken a word," Annabelle said as she sat down on the couch.

Benjamin stopped looking at the sunset and sat down next to her.

"I know I could never get you a home like this. You deserve a home like this...pretty."

"Your love is the main thing that matters to me. I have lived in a shack worse than what you're living in now. You work hard taking care of those horses, and I'm proud of you."

The couple kissed and watched the sunset together. Benjamin went home, more encouraged hearing Annabelle's response.

The next day, the Keys family and the young women traveled to church, enjoying the warmer weather. As the sermon ended, they socialized, and Ruthanne noticed Peter trying to signal for her. Reluctantly, Ruthanne passed through the congregation while Rebecca watched curiously. During her approach, Mr. Jefferson approached Peter, shaking his hand and talking about the sermon. She stopped, patiently waiting for Mr. Jefferson to end his conversation.

"Mr. Jefferson, can we continue our conversation in a moment? I need to talk with Ruthanne," Peter said.

Mr. Jefferson looked at Ruthanne and said, "By all means, take all the time you need." He approached Ruthanne, leaning into her ear the moment she leaned down to accommodate him. "He needs all the time in the world he can get with you, dear." Mr. Jefferson cackled.

Peter looked with a little confusion, unable to hear what Mr. Jefferson said. The smile that appeared on Ruthanne's face made him nervous.

Ruthanne approached Peter in her blue floral dress, the sunlight amplifying its beauty.

"How are you doing?" Ruthanne asked.

Peter answered, "I'm doing quite well. How are you?"

"I'm doing well enjoying this warming weather."

"I figured since you left immediately after last week's sermon, to look for you throughout the week would've been a bad idea."

"You were wise in your decision. I may have continued to say some harsh words toward you. I assure you, I'm far more even-tempered as of recently."

"I'm glad to hear of such progress. Have you and the ladies determined which day you want the ceremony?"

"We haven't discussed an exact date yet. We're having a new dress made for Sasha, and Benjamin insists on not going through the legal proceedings until he has finished fixing his home."

"I see. Well, how much longer do you believe this will take?"

"It will probably take a month from now, to be honest. I'm unsure as to how soon the dress will be completed, but I know it will be astounding."

"If you don't mind me asking, who is making the dress?" Peter asked.

Ruthanne calmly answered, "The maker of the dress is being kept secret to avoid a family feud. I'm sure you can understand."

"I understand, but please let me know soon so I can make sure none of our deacons that would oppose the ceremony will be present in the church."

"You will get what you need soon, Pastor Avail."

"By the way, what did Mr. Jefferson say to you that made you smile?"

Ruthanne whispered, "I assure you, Peter, it isn't anything for you to be concerned about."

Ruthanne left with a smirk as Peter pursed his lips, scanning the sanctuary.

Mr. Jefferson cackled as Ruthanne went by. "I enjoy your ferocity, my dear. Such strong beauty," Mr. Jefferson joked.

Ruthanne smirked, hearing Mr. Jefferson's instigation.

"Peter," Ruthanne said in an indulgent tone.

Mr. Jefferson continued to cackle and stare at Peter, whose eyes widened as a few confused church members noticed the upheaval.

Peter shook his head and mumbled, "Mr. Jefferson is either going to be the death of me or drive me insane."

Ruthanne glanced at Rebecca with a smirk and went toward the doors.

"Ruthanne, what was that about?" Elizabeth asked.

"Nothing big. Everything is working as planned," Ruthanne answered.

Elizabeth smiled as she followed Ruthanne out of the church.

Over the next two weeks, Annabelle, Elizabeth, Rebecca, and Ruthanne sat down together to discuss the preparations for the wedding ceremony. They explained to Annabelle that the ceremony would need to be kept secret to avoid any unnecessary problems. Annabelle reluctantly agreed to the arrangements. Annabelle understood keeping the peace in the church to protect her. She thought about when she had told Mr. Boston the good news.

"There isn't anything better than seeing true love in its rawest form and the happiness on your face," Mr. Boston had said.

"Thank you, Mr. Boston. That means a lot to hear you say that," Annabelle had said.

"The best moments to see true love are when a mother gives birth to her child and the union between two people who love each other. If you have a ceremony, please inform me when you intend to do so?"

"I will be glad to inform you when we have decided on a date."

The thought of their conversation made Annabelle question if she would be wise to tell Mr. Boston of the ceremony. Through the preparations, Annabelle believed her dark blue and white dress would work fine for the ceremony. Rebecca also insisted that Annabelle and Benjamin wait a bit longer to wed so flowers would be in bloom by then. Annabelle agreed, wanting not only flowers at the ceremony, but she also wanted to give Benjamin more time to improve his house.

As the bond between the four women grew, Rebecca's belly also grew. The other three women were excited, both by her pregnancy coming to an end and planning the wedding.

On March 4, 1846, Annabelle sat down with Rebecca, going over the final wedding plans.

"So, we have a final date of March 20, and invitations are sent," Rebecca said. "Mr. Boston, the Williamsons, and some of the other Negroes in town will be our dinner guests, while myself, Ruthanne, Elizabeth, Marilyn, Allen, Daniel, and Esther will be present at the ceremony."

Annabelle replied, "Thank you so much for helping me with all of this."

Rebecca smiled. "It was my pleasure, Annabelle. I have already gone through one round of this, so it was my pleasure."

Annabelle put her hands underneath her chin. "I wish I was able to learn from Judy Mays when she was preparing, but Mrs. Regina wouldn't let me stay around when they were planning things."

"Well, that's what the others and I are here for. Elizabeth and Ruthanne have really taken a liking to this town. The more I see how much time has gone by, it amazes me. Elizabeth has found a companion who loves clothes and perfumes to the degree she does. Ruthanne has found someone who interests her, even though she doesn't want to admit it."

"What is it between her and Pastor Avail? I see how the two of them look at each other. Did something happen between them that she hasn't told me?"

"There's nothing for you to worry about. Stubborn people can sometimes have the hardest time expressing their feelings, and that's Ruthanne. What I do know is I need to have this child right now. My feet are swollen, my back aches half the day, and if I see any food, I want to eat it."

The women laughed, and Rebecca stood up to stretch.

"The baby is kicking again. Feel how strong this child kicks."

Annabelle stood and felt the baby kick. "That baby is moving, Rebecca. Maybe you should have had this one before Ashley."

"Please don't say that. That girl is a handful. Don't curse me by saying this one will be worse."

The two laughed while Annabelle continued to feel the baby kick.

"Wow, the baby kicked with both feet. How often does that happen?"

"At first, not that often, but now one kick is shortly followed by another most of the time. I think after this, I'm reading my Bible some more. I think that was my mistake with Ashley."

Annabelle beamed as she looked at Rebecca's stomach.

"Well, I know we need more flour upstairs, so I will be on my way to Mr. Boston's store."

"Okay, stay out of trouble. We've been doing well so far, and it has felt quite relieving."

Annabelle replied, "I agree."

The two women gave each other a hug, and Annabelle left for Mr. Boston's store, eager to greet him.

"Good afternoon, Mr. Boston," Annabelle said.

Mr. Boston replied, "Ah, Sasha, how are you doing on this beautiful day?"

"I'm enjoying it quite well. I need to get some flour today. I told Elizabeth I would get it for her."

"You and Ruthanne work this store four days a week. She could have come herself."

Annabelle sighed. "She has been spending more time than normal at Pots's Garments. I suppose that she must be helping Marilyn with something in order to keep herself busy."

Mr. Boston's mouth curved into a grin. "Your kindness is a strong point, Sasha. Don't ever lose it."

Abruptly, Sierra Nicole entered the store and placed her reticule on the counter.

"Mr. Boston, there has been a mishandling of dates due to the foolishness of my house slaves," Sierra Nicole said. "I need three whole chickens so they can be prepared in time for my guests."

Mr. Boston replied, "That's not a problem. One moment, please." He turned around to get a bag of flour for Annabelle.

Sierra Nicole glared at Annabelle. "Did you not hear my needs, nigger? I have already been inconvenienced by one of your kind, and I refuse to let it continue today."

Annabelle scowled as she heard Sierra Nicole's demeaning demand.

"Sierra Nicole, I have told you before, please don't use that word in my store," Mr. Boston said. "Furthermore, Sasha isn't working today, so she won't be getting any chickens for you. I will."

Sierra Nicole's cold blue eyes glared at Annabelle while she clutched her reticule. "I bet if she had gotten some whiplashes as a child like the rest of her kind, she would be grateful about where she stands now," Sierra Nicole snarled. "It's detestable how much freedom we give you."

Annabelle rolled her eyes and turned to face Mr. Boston.

Abruptly, Sierra Nicole slapped Annabelle. Annabelle's anger erupted, and she slapped Sierra Nicole, causing her to drop her reticule and hit her head on the counter. Sierra Nicole's eyes widened while she held her cheek and stared at Annabelle. Her pupils dilated, and she shrieked.

Sierra Nicole grabbed Annabelle's collar and slapped her again. "You have no right to put your filthy hands on me!"

Annabelle pushed Sierra Nicole away, struggling to maintain her balance. "You have no right to call my hands filthy when they're the hands that have cleaned off chickens for you!" Annabelle yelled.

Mr. Boston shouted, "Ladies, that's enough! There will be no more of this foolishness! Annabelle, take this flour and go home."

Annabelle began to approach Mr. Boston when Sierra Nicole lunged at Annabelle, pushing her into an aisle and spilling several spices on her. Annabelle pushed Sierra Nicole back, knocking her into an aisle and causing her to fall. Annabelle jumped on top of Sierra Nicole, pinning her to the ground and slapping her. Mr. Boston pulled Annabelle off Sierra Nicole and escorted her behind the counter. Mr. Boston approached Sierra Nicole, helping her up while she held her bruised face.

"You think he can save you?" Sierra Nicole growled. "I will make sure you realize how unsafe you really are in this town."

"Calm down, Sierra!" Mr. Boston yelled.

Sierra Nicole grabbed her reticule and stormed out of the store, screaming into the cool air, "Where is Sheriff Shepard?"

People walked past Sierra Nicole, curious about her screams for the sheriff. One man walked up to her and said the sheriff was a block over. She ran, yelling at people to move out of the way. During this time, Annabelle had begun to move away from Mr. Boston's store.

Sierra Nicole found the sheriff, waving her hands and screaming for him.

"Sierra Nicole, why are you making such a commotion? You have all these townsfolk looking at you as if you found a dead body," Sheriff Shepard said.

Sierra Nicole screamed, "This nigger woman put her hands on me in Mr. Boston's supply store. Look what she did to my face."

"Where is she now?" Sheriff Shepard asked.

Sierra Nicole pointed toward Mr. Boston's store. "She's still at the store this moment!"

"Okay, we're going to settle this now!"

Sierra Nicole followed Sheriff Shepard while his horse trotted to Mr. Boston's store. He began to get off the horse when Sierra Nicole tugged on his arm.

"There she is now. She left the store already."

The sheriff cracked the reins of the horse, prompting it to move quicker and cutting off Annabelle's path. She stopped fearfully, looking at Sheriff Shepard. He got off his horse as Sierra Nicole followed him. He approached Annabelle, holding his holster and clearing his throat.

"I'm surprised by what I see here today," Sheriff Shepard said. "Miss Sierra Nicole tells me that you and she had a disagreement, resulting in you putting your hands on her. Now, I know she has a temper, but please tell me she's lying. Because no Negro in their right mind would touch a white woman."

Annabelle replied, "She attacked me in Mr. Boston's supply store, Sheriff. I didn't want to touch her, but she would have kept hitting me."

Sheriff Shepard replied, "So what she tells me is the truth, I take it."

Annabelle gulped. "It is part of the truth, Sheriff Shepard."

"I don't see much bruising on you, but on her beautiful skin, I see marks. I think I need to take you and see what the court has to say."

"Please, Sheriff Shepard, she isn't as innocent as she seems," Annabelle said.

"I'm no fool, but for you to be bold enough to hit her back is a problem. What's going to stop the other Negroes from acting out? What's to keep them from saying they have the same rights because they're free?" Sheriff Shepard stepped forward and slapped Annabelle, knocking her to the ground.

Most people who were passing continued by, only quickly glancing at what they had seen while a few watched in the background. Annabelle stared back at the sheriff, her eyes slightly narrowed as her body trembled.

"I should let Iron press his hoof into your head."

"You should do it, Sheriff. She has no place here," Sierra Nicole coldly said.

"I see it in your eyes. You want to fight back," Sheriff Shepard said. "Well, I'll make sure you will think twice before you act."

Sheriff Shepard stepped forward to grab Annabelle while Sierra Nicole watched with a vindictive leer.

"Sheriff Shepard, what is the problem here?" Mr. Boston asked.

"Ah, Mr. Boston, you saved me from having to come to your store later today," Sheriff Shepard said. "I'm about to take this nigger in for attacking Miss Sierra Nicole and resisting capture."

Mr. Boston slightly frowned. "It didn't look that way to me, Sheriff. It looked like you got a clean hit on her, and she did nothing. What is to become of Miss Sierra Nicole? I assume she'll be charged as well."

Sheriff Shepard squinted. "On what grounds should I charge this woman?"

"Why, she destroyed my store attacking this Negro woman. Sasha was attempting to get flour when Sierra Nicole decided to engage Sasha, and in the process, she damaged my store."

Sheriff Shepard became agitated with Mr. Boston defending Annabelle. "I expect both of you women to wait right here. Mr. Boston, please show me this so-called damage to your store."

"It would be my pleasure, Sheriff Shepard."

The two men went to the store, talking to each other. Annabelle stood up, trying to hear the conversation.

"You know they're going to come back, and you'll still have to stand before the judges for what you did to me," Sierra Nicole said. "The audacity you have to still behave as if you did nothing to me."

"This bruise on my face didn't come from me hitting myself, and you call yourself a Christian," Annabelle bickered while she narrowed her brown eyes. "Maybe it's the gap in your teeth that makes you so nasty."

Sierra Nicole gasped as she covered her mouth, but her eyes dilated while she stared at Annabelle. Sierra Nicole's face began to turn red, and she clutched her hands into fists.

"You're a fool to think the law is on your side. Like I said, a trip to a plantation would do you some good."

"I have faith that God will see me through this. Even if the sheriff takes me away, I know God will save me."

Sierra Nicole snarled, "Giving you niggers sanctuary is Pastor Avail's biggest mistake."

"No, the biggest mistake is all that hate you hold onto, and you have the audacity to call yourself Christian. You can't even show your sister in spirit any form of love," Annabelle said as she shook her head.

Sierra Nicole's eyes remained locked on Annabelle, and she sneered while beginning to rub the horse's black mane.

Mr. Boston and Sheriff Shepard soon exited the store in what appeared to be a casual conversation. The two men stopped and continued to talk, and Sheriff Shepard crossed his arms. Annabelle stepped in front of the horse as Sierra Nicole stared at the two men with a lopsided grin, waiting for the men to approach them while she petted the horse's mane. The two men ended their discussion and continued their march to the women. The sheriff approached the women and sighed.

"It appears to me that the two of you engaged each other like you were both men," Sheriff Shepard said. "The damage to the store is undeniable, and I have made a decision that I won't waver on."

"Good, she needs to be punished like the nigger she is," Sierra Nicole said.

Annabelle held back tears while her heart rate increased.

Abruptly, Sheriff Shepard grabbed Annabelle's collar. She gasped while Sheriff Shepard slapped her hard five times and let go of her.

Annabelle put her hand on her sore cheek.

"Sasha, this one time, I won't take you to the court based on the accounts of Mr. Boston," Sheriff Shepard said.

Sierra Nicole gasped, and her blue eyes bulged.

"Sierra Nicole, you have attempted to use me in a way I find quite undignified. Therefore, you will appear before the court today. I see it best that you work the store under Mr. Boston's supervision for two weeks and help clean up the destruction. That's what I will recommend."

Sierra Nicole began stomping her feet on the ground and shrieking. "That nigger put her hands on me, and you're going to do nothing?" she yelled.

Sheriff Shepard replied, "I have already given her the one and only warning that she'll get. Now, if you hadn't destroyed Mr. Boston's store, the outcome would be different. However, the winner of stupidity today is you, Sierra Nicole. Mr. Boston, please report to me if she does not show up to help you clean up the store."

Mr. Boston replied, "I will do as you ask of me."

Sheriff Shepard shifted his eyes to Annabelle. "Sasha, I expect you to know your place in this town. Do you understand?" he asked.

Annabelle replied, "Yes, sir. This won't happen again."

"It better not. I doubt few others would come to your aid like Mr. Boston did." Sheriff Shepard mounted Iron, brushing the horse's mane.

"I'll make sure my father hears of this outrage, Sheriff Shepard," Sierra Nicole yelled.

"If you feel the need to use your father to fight your battles, by all means, do so. Keep in mind that your father is a property owner, not a judge or member of Congress," Sheriff Shepard said.

Sierra Nicole growled while the sheriff cynically trotted off to another block, greeting other townsfolk.

Mr. Boston walked next to Sierra Nicole as she looked at him. "If your sentence is to begin work tomorrow, I open the store at 8 a.m. Please arrive a bit earlier to help me clear the rest of the mess," Mr. Boston said.

Frowning, Sierra Nicole replied, "How could you? How could you do such a thing to me?"

"You were willing to tell a partial truth in order to have Sasha punished for your own satisfaction. How could you be so cruel? I suggest you ask God to show you how you were wrong."

Sierra Nicole stared back at Annabelle while Annabelle held the bag of flour.

"She is nothing, but you defended her because you pity her."

"No, I defend her because she needed to be defended. You represent the sickness of our country."

Sierra Nicole gasped. "How dare you call me a sickness!"

Mr. Boston replied, "If you were allowed to vote at elections, would it be fair for Annabelle to also be allowed to vote as well? Both of you are women, after all."

"Why should she share my rights when she is beneath me?"

"I suggest you remember what Jesus did for every human being, regardless of color. You take pride in your privilege, but the privilege corrupts your soul. It turns you into a beast that feels pleasure from watching your brothers and sisters suffer; tempts you to curse their name and dare them to challenge you. If this isn't a sickness, then I'm truly terrified of your idea of what a sickness in this day is."

"My great-granddaddy, my granddaddy, and my daddy owned slaves, and I will never see her as an equal!" Sierra Nicole screamed. "If I be wrong, then God can strike me down!"

Mr. Boston shook his head and went past a furious Sierra Nicole. "Then I will see your scornful spirit tomorrow, more than likely. For the next two weeks, Miss Deeds," he said. "Sasha, you enjoy the rest of the day. Don't worry about anything."

Annabelle nodded. "You too, Mr. Boston."

Annabelle left, and Sierra Nicole angrily watched her. Sierra Nicole inhaled as she stared at the back of Mr. Boston moving further away, pouting before she went home.

Annabelle later arrived at home, still trying to calm down. She decided not to tell the others about her incident. She let the day pass, attempting to enjoy dinner with Benjamin and the others.

CHAPTER 17
An Extra Miracle

On March 10, 1846, the sound of a rooster carried through the morning, awakening the women. They enjoyed their breakfast together and prepared for the day. Elizabeth looked out the living room window to see Mr. Keys leave the house, whistling down the street and checking his golden pocket watch.

"I'm excited to go see Marilyn today. She is supposed to be getting some new silk fabrics in," Elizabeth said.

"Elizabeth, I do believe you're addicted to how silk feels on your skin now," Ruthanne said.

"That's untrue. I appreciate the nice smooth feeling of silk. It makes me feel some kind of way."

Ruthanne rolled her eyes, going back into the kitchen and clearing the table of her plate.

"Annabelle, what do you think of silk? Ruthanne is no fun."

Annabelle replied, "I've never put on anything that was silk before, but it sure does sound nice."

Elizabeth proudly responded, "Thank you, Annabelle. Someone in this house has some taste."

As Ruthanne cleaned the dishes, she heard a faint sound from downstairs. Her eyes widened, so she lowered her ear to the floor while Annabelle and Elizabeth continued in conversation. Again, Ruthanne heard a slight cry or moan.

"Both of you, quiet it down. I hear something from downstairs," Ruthanne said.

The two women looked over the couch, watching Ruthanne. Again, Ruthanne heard a moan. She quickly stood up, ran for the front door, and flung it open while she rushed down the stairs.

Annabelle and Elizabeth gasped. Their eyes widened when they saw Ruthanne's quickness, and they followed her path into the Keyses' home. Annabelle could feel her heart pound while she rushed into the house with Elizabeth.

The women saw a scared Ashley. She held her mother's arm while Rebecca squatted against a wall. Ruthanne helped her off the wall while Annabelle and Elizabeth watched.

"I'm okay, ladies. I had a few contractions unexpectedly," Rebecca said. "I had a few two days ago, but they were weak, so I guess this means I'm finally getting rid of this baby soon."

Rebecca began to giggle, causing the other women to calm down.

"Mommy, are you sure you're okay? You looked sad," Ashley asked.

Smiling, Rebecca replied, "I'm fine, dear. This is normal. Sometime, in a few days, you will have your baby brother or sister."

Ashley smiled, delighted by the idea of having a sibling. Again, Rebecca felt the pain of the contractions, but she took a deep breath to counter her pain.

"Rebecca, are you sure you're okay? Do we need to get the doctor?" Ruthanne asked.

Rebecca answered, "Oh no, Ruthanne. The contraction is small. This is just the beginning, and besides, I've been consulting with Catherine Wilson. She is my midwife. She has only lost a few children in fifteen years. I think that's a good qualification, don't you?"

"I think that's amazing, but are you sure we don't need her now?"

"Ruthanne, when you go through one pregnancy, you never forget that instinct of knowing."

The women reluctantly began to leave the house with Rebecca behind them. A pop was heard, and amniotic fluid hit the floor. The others turned around, gasping as the fluid rushed down Rebecca's legs.

Rebecca experienced a stronger contraction, and she squatted in pain.

"Elizabeth, get Catherine!" Rebecca shouted. "She should be at home five houses down. Please hurry!"

Elizabeth ran out of the house, rushing to find Catherine, as Annabelle and Ruthanne rushed toward Rebecca.

"Ashley, dear, I need to you to sit on the couch. Don't leave that couch unless an adult tells you to."

Ashley sat on the couch, excited by her mother's reaction.

"Where do you want us to help you sit?" Ruthanne asked.

"My bed. Help me to the bedroom."

They entered the large sunlit bedroom as Rebecca experienced another contraction, and she subconsciously squeezed Annabelle's and Ruthanne's arm. Annabelle and Ruthanne looked at each other with big eyes, and jaws dropped the moment they felt the strength of Rebecca's grip. They tried to help her on the full-sized bed.

Rebecca groaned. "No, wait! Rip the sheets off."

Ruthanne replied, "I don't think we have time for that."

"Ruthanne, I said rip off the bedsheets! They're my favorite set, and I won't have them ruined by afterbirth! Now rip them off!" Rebecca growled.

A terrified Annabelle and Ruthanne ripped the sheets off the bed and grabbed another set of sheets, putting them on the bed quickly. The contractions continued as Rebecca continued to try to take deep breaths, running her hand through her hair. Rebecca could feel the baby's movements and became scared that she would have to start pushing.

"Look and see if you can see the baby's head."

Annabelle and Ruthanne looked at each other with their

hearts pounding. They looked as Rebecca pulled back her gown a little.

"I'm not sure what to look for, Annabelle," Ruthanne said.

Annabelle replied, "It's okay. If the head is there, it will be obvious."

The women looked, and Rebecca sat in the lithotomy position.

"No baby head, but you're opening up, Rebecca."

"Thank you, Annabelle. It's not as bad as I thought," Rebecca said.

"How do you know that?" Ruthanne asked.

Annabelle replied, "I have helped four of Judy Mays's cousins give birth to their children before, and you don't forget stuff like this."

The contractions continued while Rebecca realized she might have to try to deliver without Catherine present.

A young woman with rounded eyebrows suddenly entered the front doorway, winded and staring at a small puddle of amniotic fluid on the living room floor. Rushing to the home caused Catherine's twin bun style to become partly undone, exposing the frizzy nature of her black hair. Being Marilyn's height, she carefully stepped over the amniotic fluid. Her round face turned toward Ashley.

"I'm here, Rebecca!" Catherine shouted. "Ashley, where is your mother?"

Ashely replied, "She is in the bedroom with Miss Ruthanne and Miss Sasha."

Catherine rushed to the bedroom, entering with her brown eyes wide.

"Oh, thank God, Catherine! You made it," Rebecca said.

"Are you having labor pains constantly?" Catherine asked.

"Yes, I'm ready to get this over with."

Catherine calmly replied, "Okay, let me take a look and see how ready you are. My goodness, Rebecca. I think with the next labor pain, you need to push."

"Oh no, I wanted Allen to know when the baby was being

born," Rebecca said, her voice full of emotion. "Ruthanne, he's at the city hall. Please hurry and get him."

"I'll get him as fast as I can," Ruthanne replied. Running out of the house to the barn, she took one of the carriage horses and rode to the city hall.

"Who is this you have helping you?" Catherine asked, glaring at Annabelle.

Rebecca replied, "Catherine, I would like to introduce you to Sasha. She is quite the interesting lady."

Annabelle replied, "It is a pleasure to meet you finally, Mrs. Catherine."

"Nice to meet you too. Do you have any experience in delivering a baby?" Catherine asked.

"Yes, I have helped with four babies in the past."

"Well, that makes life easier. Please get those wrapping cloths off the couch. I had sent those over in preparation for this. I never thought she would go into labor so quickly."

Rebecca chuckled. "I didn't think I would either."

"Trust me; if you ever want to make another woman envious, tell them how quickly you went into labor."

The women laughed while Annabelle got the wrapping cloths and came back into the room. The contractions continued as Elizabeth returned and entered the bedroom. Rebecca began to push, and the baby's head began to appear. The women became more excited.

"Rebecca, you stubborn log, you must've been going through labor since early this morning. Why didn't you tell Allen to tell me?" Catherine yelled.

"Now isn't the time, Catherine!" Rebecca shouted.

"I thought you were old the way she talked about you," Elizabeth said.

Catherine replied, "That sounds about right. She always speaks of me like I'm an old maid. You would never think I was thirty-two years old, the way she describes me."

Rebecca became frustrated as the contractions and pain increased.

"Yes, that's it! Push!"

Allen rushed into the house with Ruthanne behind him, hearing the strong cry of a baby. Allen slowly opened the bedroom door to see Annabelle cleaning off an infant, and he began to weep as he smiled.

"It's a girl, Mr. Keys. Another beautiful daughter," Annabelle said.

Rebecca smiled at Allen, but she felt more pain. "Catherine, something is wrong," she murmured.

"What's the matter, Rebecca?" Catherine asked.

Rebecca moaned, "I still feel pain."

Catherine's eyes widened. "Oh my God! Rebecca, push again!"

"Push what!" Rebecca screamed.

"I'm telling you to push again!"

Allen quickly stepped out, and Annabelle and Elizabeth gasped as they saw another baby head being pushed out.

"Ah, they're twins! All this time of feeling around, and the other twin was hiding in there!" Catherine happily said.

Tears of joy covered Rebecca's face as the baby made subtle sounds while Catherine cleaned the baby off.

"Rebecca, I would like to introduce you to your first son."

Allen came back into the room, smiling as tears streamed down his face.

"You're amazing. I can't thank God enough for placing you in my life," Allen said.

He kissed Rebecca and placed his hand on his son's head. Then he went over to Annabelle, and she handed the baby girl to Allen. He approached Rebecca, holding his daughter so she could see her brother. Rebecca grinned, although tears flowed down her face when she saw her daughter. Allen placed his daughter in Rebecca's other arm. Rebecca beamed as she nestled her children. Allen left the room, and the women were awed by the newborns. He returned, holding Ashley's hand.

"Honey, I want to introduce you to your new little sister and little brother," Allen said.

A giant grin appeared on Ashley's face while she slowly approached her mother.

"Ashley, now you're fully a big sister," Rebecca said.

Ashley replied, "Mommy, they're so small."

"Well, yes. At first, they will be, but they will grow fast like you did. You can hold their hands."

Ashley held each of their hands as the newborns calmly stared back at her.

Ashley kissed both of them on the head and gave her father a hug. "They seem so happy, Daddy."

"I'm sure they understand they have a great mommy. Let's give mommy some time to rest," Allen said.

Allen and Ashley exited the room holding hands, and a cheerful Ashley began skipping.

"So, I know you were only thinking of one name, but we need to figure this out," Catherine said.

Rebecca replied, "Now you bring this up? I just gave birth to two children when I was expecting one."

"What names were you thinking of?" Ruthanne asked.

"To be honest, I was hoping for a son to make Allen happy, and I know he didn't want me naming our son after him," Rebecca said. "I was thinking of John or Alexander, but after this double blessing, I think I know. How about I name my new princess Esther, and my sweet boy will be named Elisha? So in the town, they will be known as the E twins," Rebecca humorously said.

"Come now, that isn't funny. It is slightly cute, but that isn't funny," Catherine said.

"You pull every moment of joy from me," Rebecca said, pouting.

"I think the names are beautiful, but let's not push the E twins, if the town starts calling them that, so be it."

"I also believe the names are lovely. It fits them well," Ruthanne said.

Rebecca replied, "Thank you, Ruthanne."

Annabelle and Elizabeth nodded their heads with approval.

"My beautiful Esther, I expect great things from you, my angel."

Esther let out a cute grunt as the women giggled at the baby.

"Well, it's time for us to try to get them to nurse, so it's not a fight for you in the middle of the night," Catherine said.

"I guess I will need as much practice as I can get," Rebecca said.

"I think that's our cue to give you all the rest you need," Ruthanne said.

The edges of Rebecca's mouth curved into a big grin. "Thank you to all of you. I appreciated having you all here to help me."

The women beamed and left the room, feeling excited about Rebecca's new beginning. Benjamin arrived at the women's home later that day, and he was overjoyed with the baby news. The news made him even more excited about his future with Annabelle. For Annabelle, looking into the eyes of the newborns reminded her of what true love is: unconditional.

CHAPTER 18
Becoming One

THREE DAYS WENT BY, AND everyone was adjusting to the sounds of twin infants in the late hours of the nights. Ashley became even more enthusiastic with the twins, looking to aid her mother in any way. The Keys had received congratulations from the church.

Meanwhile, Sierra Nicole had begun working in the store with Mr. Boston. Sierra Nicole struggled with the duties in the store and hated Mr. Boston's cheerful spirit. Annabelle and Ruthanne began their normal work schedule, and Sierra Nicole refused any advice from Annabelle. The two women would move past each other in the aisles, spitefully glaring each other down.

Sierra Nicole's worst occupation was helping Annabelle with the chickens because she feared being bitten. The week was approaching its end when Ruthanne approached Sierra Nicole.

"The amount of anger you have shown throughout this whole week surprises me," Ruthanne said.

Sierra Nicole replied, "How so? Wouldn't you be upset to be forced to do duties that are hard or unpleasant?"

Ruthanne slightly tilted her head, "I would, but I've also learned to accept responsibility for my actions. God doesn't like ugly."

Sierra Nicole scoffed. "You only say that because you pity

the nigger. You grew up with her, with nigger-loving parents that threaten our way of living."

Ruthanne deeply inhaled and exhaled. "Just so you know, my life didn't start in Missouri. It started in Mississippi, and no, my parents don't favor Sasha that much. I remember a stronger form of mistreatment you don't see in this town. You have slaves at your home, but I guarantee you the slaves I've seen in the Deep South would be glad to trade places with your slaves."

"I treat my slaves like they should be treated. Rewarded for obedience and disciplined for disobedience. How is that any different than the Deep South?"

"Have you ever seen a slave whipped so much you can see bone? I have. I have even seen a slave get his foot cut off because he kept running away."

As she heard Ruthanne's words, Sierra Nicole's eyes quickly shifted around the store and back onto Ruthanne, attempting to hide her discomfort.

"You need to learn to take advice from Sasha about those chickens because I won't be the one to show you."

Sierra Nicole gave Ruthanne an angry glare. "What on earth can a nigger show me?"

"She can teach you how to approach chickens so they won't try to attack you, or even better, how to be humble and respect someone who's different than you."

Ruthanne walked away, and Sierra Nicole began to angrily sweep the store floor.

Two days before Annabelle's wedding, Sierra Nicole showed up early that morning, exhausted. The night before, she had sat in her bed, unable to sleep because she was frustrated. She hated Ruthanne's politeness and Annabelle's more recent acts of kindness. Sierra Nicole had begun to pay more attention to her own slaves. Watching the friendship between the two women had worn on her. Sierra Nicole tried to adjust her twin bun hairstyle when tears suddenly started to flow down her cheeks as she looked at the sunrise. She placed her head on her knees and wept.

"God, why do I feel this pain in my heart? I don't think I understand myself anymore," Sierra Nicole said.

Sierra Nicole continued to weep, and she heard a soft voice say, "You need to love yourself before you can truly love others."

She felt someone place their hand on her shoulder. She turned around but saw nothing. Those words warmed her heart, but knowing it wasn't her conscious mind scared her.

That day, Sierra Nicole worked alongside Annabelle and Ruthanne silently for most of the day. While she worked with Annabelle in the chicken coop, she sighed, "Please show me how to work with these disgusting birds."

Annabelle replied, "It would be my pleasure."

Annabelle showed her how to work with the chickens.

Sierra Nicole glanced at Annabelle. "I heard that you are getting married."

"Yes, it's true."

"How exciting that must be for you. Are you having a ceremony?"

Annabelle gave a soft sigh. "No, we are receiving a license and having a dinner celebration."

Sierra Nicole pressed her lips. "Well, I'm sorry to hear that you're not having a ceremony, but a dinner is better than receiving the license."

Annabelle nodded. "That's true. Thank you for saying that. It makes me feel a lot better about getting married."

Sierra Nicole beamed, and the women continued to work the rest of the day. It was the last day of Sierra Nicole's mandatory work agreement, and she said her farewells to Mr. Boston and the two women.

Annabelle and Ruthanne strolled home as Annabelle became more excited about the coming wedding. At home, the three women were enjoying their dinner that evening when they heard a knock on their door. Elizabeth opened to door and was greeted by Rebecca with the twins.

"Look how adorable they are!" Elizabeth said with a grin.

"There are the little monsters that have been keeping me up at night," Ruthanne said.

The women cackled while Rebecca carried Esther and Elizabeth carried Elisha. Ashley followed behind her mother, beaming when she saw the women. The women sat together, playing with Ashley and the twins for a while. There was another knock at the door.

Ruthanne went to the door and opened it.

"Your ability to get things done is astounding," Ruthanne said.

Marilyn walked in the door, carrying an astounding white wedding dress. Annabelle gasped and put her hands over her mouth. Her brown eyes widened, and everyone else looked at the dress in amazement.

"I have something special for you, Sasha," Marilyn said.

Annabelle stood up and began to cry. Elizabeth came up to her and gave Annabelle a hug.

"Y'all treat me so well. I can't repay any of you. There's no way I can repay you," Annabelle said.

Marilyn approached Annabelle, smiling and wiping tears from her eyes.

"People that love you don't expect payment for acts of kindness."

Marilyn placed the dress on the couch and gave Annabelle a hug as tears of joy covered her face. Rebecca and Ruthanne looked at each other with satisfaction, knowing their plan to give Annabelle the wedding she deserved was coming into existence. Annabelle tried on the dress with Marilyn's help, and she glanced into the mirror, trying to hold back tears.

Marilyn had also brought the dress that she herself would wear the next day. She got into Elizabeth's bed once the young women were ready to go to sleep. They were so excited, they barely slept. Annabelle stared at the ceiling, smiling while she listened to the others talk.

The wedding day arrived, and the upcoming joy and excitement of the ceremony went through Annabelle's mind. Ruthanne pulled up the carriage. Annabelle carried the dress into the carriage to hide it while Elizabeth and Marilyn followed her. The Keys had left earlier to meet them at the church. Annabelle and the others arrived at the church before Benjamin and the other Negroes, giving her time to change. During this time, Ruthanne looked for Peter to ensure that he would not change his mind.

"Peter, are you ready for this special day?" Ruthanne asked.

Peter replied, "Please, address me as Pastor Avail while we are here, Ruthanne."

Ruthanne smirked when she saw Peter wipe sweat from his forehead.

"I'm ready, so let's make this special for them."

Peter and Ruthanne exited his office, greeting the others. Benjamin and the other Negroes, including Daniel and his cousin, Mary, entered the church, greeting the others.

"Benjamin, I'm pleased about this union between you and Sasha. I'm excited for your future," Peter said.

Benjamin replied, "Thank you, Pastor Avail. I can't use many big words, but I'm a blessed man here."

Peter grinned at Benjamin, feeling the joy coming from him.

The back doors opened, and Annabelle appeared in the middle of the doorway with Marilyn at her side. The women beamed as the men stared with wide eyes at the elegance and beauty that shone off Annabelle. Marilyn went down the aisle, holding Annabelle's hand. Annabelle's white dress was fitting, and two yellowish-orange flowers from the California poppy were placed in her hair.

Peter leaned over to Ruthanne, whispering, "How did you get her a dress like that? She looks stunning."

Ruthanne replied, "Marilyn is the reason we were able to do this. She made the dress for Annabelle. She started on the dress the day after she found out about the engagement and managed to hide it from her father."

"I see. Well then, let's continue to keep Mr. Pots in the dark."

Ruthanne quickly stood in the front aisle and watched Annabelle come forth with Marilyn. Annabelle stopped in front of Peter and Benjamin, who stood in front of the oak pulpit as Marilyn stood next to Ruthanne. Benjamin struggled to hold back tears of joy while he stared into Annabelle's beautiful brown eyes.

"I don't deserve you," Benjamin said.

Annabelle smiled and placed her hand on his face. "I feel the same way about you," she replied.

Peter beamed, witnessing the love between the two.

"What a glorious day it is today for this wedding ceremony, and I'm pleased to bless this union in the eyes of God," Peter said. "Sasha, Benjamin, please turn to me. Everyone else, please take a seat."

Peter began to go over Bible scriptures on the importance of marriage and what it symbolizes.

Daniel playfully nudged the olive-skinned Mary. "I never seen pastor smile so much, Mary," Daniel said.

"What you think, he gone frown in such a nice ceremony?" Mary replied, exhibiting a soft, mature southern voice.

"Well, no, but with a Negro couple, I never think I see him so happy. Sasha so pretty, I know you jealous. She make white women look bad right now, so I know you jealous."

With her hazel eyes, Mary glared at Daniel with a firm look. "I ain't jealous. She beautiful like us mulattos." Mary scoffed and shook her head, "Jealous."

Daniel smirked. "You say that, but you can't wear no dress like that. I know pastor would cry if he see you in that."

Mary scowled when Daniel continued to joke, and she hit him with her reticule while he quietly giggled. "Shut up and watch, Daniel."

"Well, okay, Miss Jealous," Daniel giggled.

Peter continued to explain to Annabelle and Benjamin the benefits and challenges of marriage. "Now remember this, Sasha, you are to be submissive to Benjamin and trust him, but also, Benjamin, you're to love her as Christ loves the church,"

Peter said. "I know submission may not sound good, but it does not mean you're lower than him or his servant, but that you're to let him lead. I know you will state your opinions, but let him lead." The others in the pews giggled.

Annabelle replied, "I understand my role, Pastor Avail."

"Benjamin, I'm beyond proud of how much you have grown in Christ, so remember, Christ sacrificed and served the people just as much as you need to do for Sasha," Peter said.

Benjamin replied, "I understand, Pastor Avail."

"May I have the ring?"

Ruthanne handed the ring to Peter and sat down.

"This ring symbolizes your marriage to the people, and may God bless you with more and more." Pastor Avail placed the ring on Annabelle's hand and held her hand.

"Ladies and gentlemen, I would like to introduce you to Mr. and Mrs. Mosely."

Everyone stood up and clapped, screaming shouts of joy as they came up, hugging the bride and groom with happiness filling the church.

"Everyone, I would like to have your attention," Rebecca said. "We will continue this celebration immediately at Allen's and my home for the entirety of the day. We look forward to seeing you there."

Everyone began to exit the church while Elizabeth and Marilyn made sure Annabelle got into the carriage without being seen, and Benjamin sat next to her.

Ruthanne began to leave the church when she stopped and turned around to Peter. "Thank you for doing this, Peter," she said.

Peter replied, "It was my pleasure. Thank you for convincing me."

"You had a choice, no matter what I said. You had a choice, and I'm glad you chose to do something pleasing in God's eyes. Hope I see you at their celebration sometime today."

The two friends smiled at each other, and Ruthanne left the church.

Annabelle and the others arrived at the Keyses' home, and the celebration began. Mr. Boston and the Williamsons arrived to join in the celebration. The celebration continued throughout the day with singing and dancing. Most of the Negroes Annabelle had met showed up, although Sally refused. Peter arrived later in the afternoon, surprising most of the guests. Ruthanne smirked at Peter once he did arrive.

"Pastor Avail, what a pleasure to see you here," Mr. Williamson said.

Peter replied, "Well, I had to come give my blessings to Sasha and Benjamin. I'm pleased with this union, Stephen."

"Well, Marjorie and I will be on our way. Again, congratulations, Sasha and Benjamin."

The Williamsons left the party, only to have their path blocked by a man. He wore a black top hat, black trousers, and a black frock coat. A marvelous green cravat wrapped around a high-collared red shirt. It was covered by a fancy dark green vest, which contained a gold pocket watch. He moved forward, clutching his black walking cane.

"Mr. Williamson, how nice it is to see you and Mrs. Williamson on this glorious day," Mr. Hildebrand said.

"Well, hello, Mr. Hildebrand. It has been a while since we have talked to each other," Mr. Williamson said.

"Yes, it has been. I've been a busy man lately. Where are you coming from? It sounds like a joyous occasion."

"Why, yes, we are coming from celebrating the marriage between two Negroes, Sasha and Benjamin, the horse cleaner. Their marriage was acknowledged today, and since we know both of them, we decided to congratulate them."

"Well now, what an interesting world this is turning into. When the marriage of two niggers is glorified—"

"Mr. Hildebrand, may I remind you that since they're both free by law, they're able to gain marriage licenses."

Mr. Hildebrand cringed, and the Williamsons stared back at him uncomfortably.

"It was a pleasure to see both of you. I best be on my way," Mr. Hildebrand said politely, tilting his black top hat.

"Good day, Mr. Hildebrand," Marjorie said.

The Williamsons walked off, and Mr. Hildebrand watched them, a spiteful expression marring his face. He crept toward one of the windows of the Keys home, but he was unable to see Annabelle or Ruthanne, so he stormed off.

"I'll see them soon. I'll make sure that they know their place," Mr. Hildebrand said.

As the party continued and the evening arrived, everyone departed. Marilyn gave Annabelle a hug and went home after the others had left.

Annabelle left the house, staring at the sunset.

"This is going to be so weird, Annabelle, waking up and not seeing you," Elizabeth said before hugging her.

"I will miss it too, Elizabeth," Annabelle replied.

Elizabeth smiled at Annabelle and climbed up the stairs. Benjamin came out of the house and placed his hand on Annabelle's shoulder.

"Are you ready to go home?" Benjamin asked.

Annabelle smiled and placed her head on Benjamin's chest. "I think I am," Annabelle said.

"Now, hold on a bit," Ruthanne said.

Annabelle slightly pouted and replied, "Ruthanne, what is it?"

Ruthanne smirked. "Were you going home with this handsome man without saying goodbye to me?"

Annabelle grinned and approached Ruthanne, giving her a hug.

Ruthanne whispered in Annabelle's ear, "Now, go enjoy yourself."

Annabelle looked at Ruthanne, and Ruthanne gave her a wink and a smirk.

"Why can't you be more proper like Elizabeth?"

Ruthanne laughed. "Benjamin, you can begin walking. She'll be right behind you."

Benjamin replied, smiling. "Yes, ma'am, Miss Ruthanne. I know I not going to win against you."

Ruthanne smiled back as he began to leave.

"What are you doing?" Annabelle asked.

Ruthanne answered, "Hush, go enjoy yourself, Annabelle. There's nothing proper about what you will be doing in a little while."

Annabelle grunted. "Okay, I'm leaving before you surprise me more."

Annabelle began to walk off when Ruthanne patted her on the butt. She looked back, embarrassed as Ruthanne began to cackle, before she went after Benjamin, shaking her head.

Annabelle and Benjamin arrived at their new home, and she beamed, noticing how much work Benjamin had put into improving the small shack. Almost all of the wood had been replaced, and two plates had been set on the dinner table.

"Miss Marilyn found our home and gave me these nice plates and forks," Benjamin said.

"I'll have to thank her tomorrow. She has such a good heart," Annabelle said.

"I still think you have the strongest heart of them all."

Annabelle grinned at the moment Benjamin came to her and placed his hand on her cheek, leaning over to kiss her. She wrapped her arms around his neck and kissed him back as they stumbled into the small bedroom. The passion between them elevated as they caressed each other and began to slowly undress one another.

Warmth spread through Annabelle's body as her eyes remained locked on Benjamin, and she helped him take off his shirt. The two smirked at each other and continued to passionately kiss. Annabelle stopped and stared into Benjamin's affectionate brown eyes.

"I love you, Benjamin."

"I love you too, Annabelle."

"This will be the first time I will be with a man when I want to, and I couldn't be happier."

"I belong to you, and you belong to me. You make me forget my problems; make me want to do better."

As the young couple was about to lie down on the bed, Benjamin noticed the seven scars on Annabelle's back. His eyebrows lowered, and he frowned while he touched her skin. "Is these scars?"

Annabelle exhaled with a blank face. "There are parts of my past I'll never escape."

"I never known nobody that heal like you. They smooth with no bumps."

Annabelle gave a lopsided smile. "Yeah, it's crazy."

Benjamin smirked. "I say special because that what you are…special."

Annabelle smirked as she kissed him, and they lay down on the bed as the heat of their passion took ahold of them. Her body craved his touch, and they made love throughout the night. For the first time, Annabelle felt in control of something in her life by being vulnerable and giving herself to a man she loved.

The next morning, the two woke up together, smiling at each other, kissing and cuddling. Annabelle made their breakfast, and they both left home to go to church, holding each other's hand. The two arrived at the church with a radiant aura of joy. The other Negroes sitting in the balcony happily congratulated them, and they were excited that Pastor Avail had approved of their union.

Annabelle briefly spoke to Marilyn, thanking her for everything. Annabelle was so excited to spend more time with Benjamin that she forgot to greet the others, rushing out of the church holding Benjamin's hand. Elizabeth, Rebecca, and Ruthanne watched them leave the church, gazing into each other's eyes and smiling.

Rebecca said, "God, please continue to send your angels to protect them. I have never seen this side of Annabelle."

Annabelle and Benjamin spent the rest of the day together, expressing their love for each other.

The next morning, Annabelle arrived at Mr. Boston's store, unable to stop smiling.

"Good morning, Sasha," Mr. Boston said.

"Good morning, Mr. Boston," Annabelle said.

"I must say, that was a great celebration for you and Benjamin. I can't help but to rejoice for your marriage."

"Thank you, Mr. Boston. That means a lot. Has Ruthanne arrived yet?"

"No, but I'm sure she'll be here any minute."

Annabelle went to the chicken coop and began to work. Ruthanne arrived at the store and went to greet Annabelle when she heard the other woman humming.

Ruthanne happily watched Annabelle work joyfully as she hummed and petted the chickens.

"Since when do you hum while working with chickens?" Ruthanne asked.

Annabelle was startled by Ruthanne and dropped one of the eggs.

Annabelle replied, "What are you talking about? I always do this with them. It keeps them calm."

"You have never done it that loud, but I know why you hum."

Annabelle stared back at Ruthanne, embarrassed as Ruthanne walked away, giggling. Ruthanne began working and returned to the chicken coop.

"I may pick on you, but I love you and Benjamin so much! I want to see the two of you remain happy."

Annabelle gave Ruthanne a hug. "I love you too."

The women continued to work together as the day continued.

Benjamin's joy was obvious. His boss liked seeing the man happy, as it seemed to have a positive effect on other employees.

"Boy, if I had known you getting married would give you more reason to be happy, I'd have paid one of those Negro women to marry you," Mr. Stone said.

"Why, thank you, Mr. Stone, but I sure I got the best one." Benjamin chuckled.

Mr. Stone laughed, and he hobbled back into the saloon. Mr. Hildebrand suddenly approached Benjamin with a mud-covered horse, and he held out the reins of the horse to Benjamin.

"Clean him up good, nigger, and make it fast," Mr. Hildebrand said.

Benjamin replied, "Yes, sir. I clean him soon as I finish giving the others they water."

Mr. Hildebrand scowled. "I said you need to get started on him now, boy."

"Is there a problem here, Mr. Hildebrand?" Mr. Stone said.

Mr. Hildebrand replied, "Mr. Stone, I think your nigger can't hear properly. I told him he needs to clean my horse, and he tells me what he's going to do first instead."

"Mr. Hildebrand, the policy here is first come, first serve. Now, if he dropped what he was doing, he would be disobeying my policy, and I don't tolerate that. He has always been a respectful Negro, and well-prized, so don't belittle him."

"I do believe you give this Negro too much praise, but if that's how you run your business, I will respect it."

Mr. Stone nodded. "Thank you, Mr. Hildebrand."

Mr. Hildebrand glared at Benjamin with his cold blue eyes, and he moved past Mr. Stone.

"Go ahead and get the water for those horses, and clean up Mr. Hildebrand's horse good," Mr. Stone said. "Don't worry about anything. You did the right thing here."

Benjamin replied, "Yes, sir, Mr. Stone. I get it done."

Benjamin took care of the horses and took special care to clean Mr. Hildebrand's horse. The day went on, and Benjamin continued to offer people water who passed by the saloons and take care of the horses. Mr. Hildebrand exited the saloon while talking to another businessman, watching Benjamin brush and pet the horses. The men ended their conversation, and Mr. Hildebrand marched up to his horse and checked its coat.

"Not bad, Negro, not too bad at all," Mr. Hildebrand said.

"Thank you, sir," Benjamin said.

"I suggest you remain grateful to Mr. Stone because any nigger can be replaced with a white man worth far more than you."

"Would you like some water before you go on your way, Mr. Hildebrand?" Benjamin asked.

"I believe I would, Benjamin. You seem to know how to serve well and know your place. I wish your wife, Sasha, had the same attitude. I suggest you learn how to tame her. She is quite outspoken for a Negro woman. I believe she has learned unfortunate things from that redhead—Ruthanne, I believe her name is."

Benjamin approached Mr. Hildebrand and handed him the ladle.

"Miss Ruthanne is a good woman, sir. She always treat me nice, and she love Sasha. She a good Christian woman."

Mr. Hildebrand scowled as he heard Benjamin's remarks defending Ruthanne, and he tossed the water into Benjamin's face. Benjamin began to choke on some of the water while he coughed it out.

"Is there a problem here, gentlemen?" Sheriff Shepard said as he slowly rode up on Iron.

"Sheriff Shepard," Mr. Hildebrand said. "Why, no. This clumsy nigger can't hand me a simple ladle of water."

Benjamin bickered, "Sheriff Shepard, I do nothing wrong. Mr. Hildebrand threw water on my face after I give him the ladle."

Sheriff Shepard glanced at Mr. Hildebrand while Mr. Hildebrand's face somewhat sneered.

"Now, look here, boy. I suggest you not lie. Otherwise, the last thing you will see is a rope noose," Mr. Hildebrand said.

"On whose call? What is the justification?" Sheriff Shepard asked. "Don't overstep your bounds here. I've known this boy for quite some time. The evidence here I can see looks more like he is telling the truth. Go to the well and clean up the ladle before other customers want water, Benjamin."

"Yes, Sheriff Shepard," Benjamin said.

Benjamin went to the well to clean off the ladle, nervous of the accusations.

"Lay off the boy, Victor. He is a good Negro."

"I think you're too soft on these free ones. They should all have chains on them and be sold to the highest bidder," Mr. Hildebrand said as he shook his head.

Sheriff Shepard raised his eyebrows. "Well, that's why we have laws here in this state. I suggest you follow them before I have to have a noose put around your neck."

"Keep showing these Negroes favor, Sheriff. It will do us no good."

"Go home back to your store and wife, Victor. I have low tolerance for you today."

Mr. Hildebrand clenched his teeth, got onto his horse, and rode off murmuring. Benjamin returned from the well with the cleaned ladle, glad to see that Sheriff Shepard and Mr. Hildebrand had left.

"Where'd you go?" Daniel asked.

"I went to clean off this ladle. You done cleaning them horses down there?" Benjamin asked.

"Yeah, I saw the sheriff talking to Mr. Hildebrand. Mr. Hildebrand looked mad. I guess sheriff told him to go."

"Good. He a scary white man."

Daniel nodded. "Yeah, I stay away from him. I see someone else riding up. I take care of this horse."

"Alright, I stay right here."

Benjamin watched Daniel greet the white man on his horse, and he waited while he petted a horse that was drinking from a water trough.

The day went on, and Annabelle and Benjamin continued to enjoy each other's company once they arrived at home. He decided not to tell her about the incident because he didn't want her to worry. He lay in the bed, staring at the ceiling as Annabelle slept. He thought, *Jesus, I know I is a Negro, but please help me where I need it. Thank you for protecting me today.*

Annabelle rolled over, feeling that Benjamin was not sleeping. She stared at his emotionless face while he remained unaware that she was awake.

"What's wrong, Benjamin?" Annabelle asked.

"You awake. I sorry I wake you," Benjamin said.

"No, you didn't wake me up. I could feel that you weren't sleep."

"Oh, well, I was just 'bout to sleep. Just had thinking to do because I'm happy."

Annabelle smiled and placed her arm over his chest as the two fell asleep.

Two months passed as the couple adjusted to living with each other and having frequent visits from Elizabeth, Marilyn, and Ruthanne. For Benjamin, it was welcome attention, but for Annabelle, it was a bit of an annoyance because some visits were near suppertime. She felt obligated to cook more if they visited near suppertime, but she did enjoy cooking with her friends if they stayed for supper. The loving sarcasm of Ruthanne and the carefree attitudes of Marilyn and Elizabeth made Benjamin's days easier. Benjamin realized this was a family. Even though he might never again see his enslaved family, he had been blessed with new people in his life who genuinely loved him.

One day in June of 1846, Marilyn arrived at the Moselys' home to give Annabelle a small perfume bottle Annabelle had said she liked. Benjamin opened the door and welcomed Marilyn.

"How are you doing today, Benjamin?" Marilyn asked.

"I is doing quite well today, Miss Marilyn. How are you?" Benjamin asked.

"I'm doing well, Benjamin. Is Annabelle home?"

"Oh no, she and Miss Ruthanne went to get some supplies. They wanted their woman time."

Marilyn giggled and showed Benjamin the perfume. "Alright, I had brought this over for her because she said she liked it."

Benjamin smiled. "I will make sure she get it."

"I know you will," Marilyn cheerfully said.

Marilyn was about to place the perfume on the table when Daniel abruptly walked inside. Being startled, she dropped the perfume, and it shattered on the floor.

"I so sorry, ma'am," Daniel said.

Benjamin yelled, "Daniel, you fool. That was a gift from Miss Marilyn. I told you 'bout not knocking."

Marilyn replied, "No, it's okay. I can actually get another. We have more at the store. Where is there a washing cloth to wipe this up?

"Oh, Miss Marilyn, no need to worry about it. Daniel can clean up the mess."

"Again, I sorry. It was an accident," Daniel said.

"Told you that knocking on the door matters," Benjamin said.

"We've met before. What was your name again?" Marilyn asked.

"Daniel, ma'am. I was at they wedding in the back of the church and work with the horses."

"That's right. I knew I knew you from more than one place."

"That smells really nice. It must be expensive."

"It's not that expensive, but I think it is best. I'll go back to the store and get another."

"If it is alright, can I come by to the store? I would like to get my cousin, Mary, something for her birthday."

Marilyn showed off her dimpled grin. "Sure, you can actually come with me now if you want."

"Thank you so much, Miss Marilyn. Let me clean this mess."

Daniel quickly cleaned up the perfume and placed the cloth on one of the chairs. "I'm ready when you are."

Marilyn began to leave the house, and Daniel excitedly followed her. Benjamin shook his head as he grabbed the water bucket to wash out the cloth. Daniel and Marilyn strolled through the town, talking about their day.

Marilyn had known of Daniel for years, but Benjamin was

the only Negro man Marilyn had acquainted herself with, and she was eager to learn more.

"We've never really talked before," Marilyn said. "So, how many of your family members do you have in the town, Daniel?" Marilyn asked.

"It just me and my cousin, Mary. She my heart," Daniel answered. "We grew up together since we was children. My momma and her momma was sisters."

"That must've been a great bond you had with her. So you have no brothers or sisters?"

Daniel calmly exhaled, and his expression became saddened. "I did. I had two brothers and two younger sisters. Mary had three sisters long time ago."

Marilyn frowned, "I'm sorry to hear that, Daniel. What happened?"

"Well, my Auntie May had become ill, and my momma thought it was just fever. But she got worse, and doctor came over and say it was smallpox."

"Oh my, that must've been terrible."

"I remember it well 'cause next two days, she not do too good, but on third day, she got much better. We children was not allowed to see her. Then Auntie May boss, Mr. Muldon, come over so angry and say a lot of bad words 'cause Mrs. Muldon had got sick too. He say so much and was crying because she died. He blamed my auntie for her death, calling my momma and auntie half-breed niggers. My momma yell at him to leave and never come back. See, my grandma was Sara Mallory, and she was white.

"We not see a lot of her when we was young. They never talked about they daddy, but say he died young and never tell us how. She gave my grandpa three good children, one boy and two girls.

"We was told not to talk about it a lot, but my momma and auntie was able to get hired easier than my pa or uncle. That night, my uncle and pa heard a horse outside, so they went out, and we heard two gunshots. My momma rushed us to the back of the house, and we heard two men yelling for us to come out. I know one of them was Mr. Muldon, but I hear it in his voice. It was full of anger and sadness. They shoot through the windows for a while, but they quiet, but then fire was on the door. My momma tried to hurry to get my auntie up, but she say 'no, take the kids.' My momma try to open the back door, but they block it."

"My goodness," Marilyn said, her emerald eyes wide open.

"She scream to get it open but couldn't, so she break the shutters and tell us to jump out. We jump out, but they waited for us. My momma tries to remove the junk they put on the door, but they start shooting her, and she fall down. She tell us to run to grandma, so we start to run, and then I hear nothing but guns and hear my cousins fall. I couldn't cry for them...I was so scared. I see my older brother, Timothy, run and try to grab the rifle from the other man wearing a straw hat. 'Cause he had try to put more bullets in the rifle, but he shook him off and hit him in the head. We keep running across the field. He and Mr. Muldon take more shots, and my brother, Paul, pushed me down.

"He fell to the ground, dead. He saved me. I tell my sisters and Mary to keep running. I don't think they see me. They shoot my sister, Emily, in the back. Mr. Muldon take aim at my sister, Emma, but then my momma grabbed the rifle, and he miss her, but the other man shoot her. My momma screamed when it happened. My brother, Timothy, got up and hit Mr. Muldon, but the other man knock him down again. He put the rifle in his face, but momma kicked it, and the shot miss.

"Mr. Muldon punched my momma, and she looked at me and tell me to run after Mary. Mr. Muldon yell at the other man to shoot me, but he point his rifle at my brother, killed him there. I ran, looking back. All I could see was they hitting my momma. I ran so fast. I found Mary, and she was scared, so we run to grandma as fast as we could. I tell grandma everything, and she get my two big cousins, Jeffery and George, 'cause they was white. They brought my momma back, but she died when they was bringing her to my grandma.

"My cousins say all she ask was me and Mary safe. They tell her we got them, and she smiled and say 'Tell them I love them, and my momma too. And I love y'all too.'"

Marilyn had a saddened gaze. "How did your family deal with it?"

Daniel shook his head and said, "My family told the courts, but they don't want to hear nothing from half-breed children. My grandma used to cry so much at first, but as we get older, she got better."

"I couldn't imagine it, Daniel. I've already lost my mother, but to lose all of my siblings also in one day. It takes a lot of courage to continue in life after that."

Daniel smiled. "Thank you. That means a lot."

"How did Mary deal with it?"

"She do much better now. See, she was seven when it happen, but I was nine. We bury them in the church cemetery. The pastor say evil never wins, but that day, it feel like evil did. It was a long time before Mary smiled again, but I don't think she want children or husband. I think it hurt her too much."

"Everyone handles pain differently, Daniel, but I've learned as long we trust Jesus and forgive, then we can really heal."

"Our cousin, George, he not take they deaths well. He shot Mr. Muldon, and they put him in jail ten years because Mr. Muldon didn't die. If it was me that done it, they would have hanged me. That the most justice we got for my family."

Marilyn frowned as her eyebrows lowered with her gaze, and she thought about Daniel's loss. She realized that Daniel was speaking the truth about the imbalance of the law. Marilyn and Daniel entered Pots's Garments.

"Here we are. Is this your first time in a fabric store like this?"

"Yes, it is. I go past this store all the time. It so pretty."

"Thank you, I did most of the displays, but my papa helped me with some."

"He must be a good man to raise someone like you."

Marilyn grinned at Daniel while she reached into a crate filled with perfumes. "He has his good moments, but still, there is a lot about him I pray about."

"Well, we all need prayer. That something I learn from Pastor Avail."

Marilyn raised her arched eyebrows. "That's true, Daniel."

"This bottle here is so pretty. Can I smell this perfume?" Daniel asked.

Marilyn smirked. "Sure, you can have a sniff."

"Wow, this smell so good. Mary would love this. I know this expensive, but if I have five dollars, is that enough?"

"Let me see the bottle, and I can tell you how much it will cost." Marilyn realized it was the jasmine perfume and would have cost him ten dollars. "I think this is a good choice for your cousin, Daniel. Most women love the smell of this lilac perfume, and it will last for long time."

"That's good. She need things that will last a long time. Is the five dollars enough?"

"Yes, that's actually the full amount that's needed to buy it."

"Praise to God, it take a long time to save that 'cause I clean the horses with Benjamin."

"No need to worry then. You're a blessed man."

Daniel grinned at Marilyn. He handed her the money, and she gave him the perfume.

"Well now, let's get back to Benjamin. I have what I need."

As they were approaching the door, Mrs. White entered the store in her purple dress with puffed sleeves.

"Oh, good, Marilyn. I'm pleased to have caught you instead of your father," Mrs. White said.

"Good afternoon, Mrs. White. What can I do for you?" Marilyn said.

"Did you get the shipment of the new blue dress I ordered from New York City?"

"Yes, I did. I was expecting you yesterday."

"Well, my dear, when you get married and have children, you will find that things never go as planned."

Marilyn replied, "I will have to go upstairs to get your dress."

Mrs. White dismissively waved her hand.

"Why are you getting it, dear? Have the Negro get it for you."

"No, Mrs. White, he isn't a worker here. He actually bought a nice perfume for a relative just now."

Mrs. White fixed her gaze, and her eyes widened. "How could he afford such a thing?"

Daniel replied, "I clean the horses for Mr. Stone's businesses, ma'am."

"I can believe that. You smell like it," Mrs. White snobbishly replied.

"Mrs. White, please don't insult the other customers," Marilyn said.

Mrs. White grunted in response.

Marilyn rolled her eyes and went up the stairs to get the dress and quickly grabbed it. The moment she hurried down the stairs, she heard Mrs. White continue to ask Daniel questions, and he replied politely.

"I have your dress, Mrs. White, and it is as adorable as I told you."

Mrs. White put her hand on her chest. "Oh my, that is quite adorable. So, this Negro tells me he is waiting for you, Marilyn."

"Yes, he knows a good friend of mine, and I was taking a perfume to her."

"Well now, do I have to keep educating you? Don't lower yourself with these Negroes. You give the wrong impression that they matter. He is quite the specimen of their race though."

Mrs. White moved closer to Daniel while he leaned back a bit and avoided eye contact with her.

"Oh my. His eyes—they're hazel. Why, he's a mulatto. Marilyn, why didn't you correct me? I mean, I should have known."

Marilyn was shocked as she listened to Mrs. White's change in demeanor. "I didn't think it would matter to you, Mrs. White."

"Well, not so much, but it explains so much with his mannerisms. Look at his strong build and light brown hair. Quite a specimen. So, was it your mother who was white or your father, boy?"

Daniel replied, "My mother's mother was white. She raise me most of my life."

Mrs. White replied, "Hmm, amazing you came to look so good. These mulattos seem to keep growing in number, Marilyn, thanks to these whores in the saloons. Those harlots in New England are also harming our race too. Do you agree, boy?"

Marilyn glared at Mrs. White with her blazing, emerald green eyes.

"Yes, ma'am, in some way."

"Ah, see, these mulattos are a smarter breed. I can't decide who would make better slaves, them or the Indians." Mrs. White chuckled as Marilyn approached her, handing her the dress.

"Always a pleasure doing business with you, Mrs. White, but I must be on my way. If you need anything else, my father is in the back," Marilyn said with a fake smile.

"No, dear. I believe that's all I need today. You have a good day," Mrs. White said.

"You have a good day as well."

As she left the store and stepped into her carriage, Marilyn turned to Daniel. "I apologize for that. I have to be careful with Mrs. White."

"I understand, Miss Marilyn. I not mad at you," Daniel said. "I feel little good. She say I look good. I never hear that from a white woman before."

Marilyn laughed, and they left the store together. Unknown to Marilyn, her father had watched them leave the store. Mr. Pots scratched his head while he strolled into the back room of the store. Daniel and Marilyn continued to talk to each other, oblivious of the stares the other townspeople were giving them. They arrived at Annabelle's home, and Marilyn stepped up to the door, on which she enthusiastically knocked.

The door opened, and Ruthanne was in the doorway.

"Hello, Marilyn and Daniel," Ruthanne said.

"It's good to see you as well, dear," Marilyn said.

"Good afternoon, Miss Ruthanne," Daniel said.

Ruthanne replied, "It is always good to see good friends. Come in."

"I have something for Sasha that I had brought over earlier."

"Ah, yes. Benjamin was complaining about Daniel."

Annabelle entered the kitchen with Benjamin behind her.

"Marilyn, how are you!" Annabelle said.

"I'm doing quite well today. I had Daniel here escort me back to the store, so that was fun," Marilyn said.

Annabelle put a hand on her hip. "Yeah, well, he should have walked you back after what he did."

"I did apologize to her, Sasha," Daniel said.

Annabelle replied, "Hush, Daniel. She wouldn't have been forced to go back if you paid more attention."

"Don't be so harsh on him. He's a gentleman," Marilyn said. "Well, here is the perfume you kept talking about."

"Thank you. I have been eager to get my first bottle of perfume," Annabelle said.

Marilyn smiled at Annabelle while she looked at the designs on the bottle.

"I need to get back to the store. I will certainly see all of you soon."

Annabelle smiled. "Thank you again, Marilyn."

Marilyn beamed. "Of course, Sasha, we ladies have the right to our beauty."

"I need to be leaving too," Ruthanne said.

"What do you have planned, Ruthanne?" Annabelle asked.

"Nothing much. I'm going to go back home and relax."

Annabelle went up to Ruthanne and gave her a hug. "Well, as long as you're staying out of trouble."

Ruthanne giggled while she hugged Annabelle. "The only time I get into trouble is when I'm around you," Ruthanne joked. "Keep taking care of her, Benjamin."

Benjamin replied, "Yes, ma'am. I will do my best."

Marilyn and Ruthanne moved toward the door. "Have a great day, Daniel," Ruthanne said.

"Thank you, Miss Ruthanne. You have a good day too," Daniel replied.

Marilyn turned and smiled at Daniel. "Goodbye, Daniel. I really enjoyed our conversation. We'll have to talk some more."

"I enjoyed your company too, Miss Marilyn," Daniel said with a smirk.

Daniel and Marilyn waved bye to each other as Marilyn left the house. Daniel kept smiling, even though Marilyn had gone, and turned to see that Annabelle and Benjamin were staring at him. He quickly stopped smiling and took a seat.

"She's a... She's a nice woman."

Annabelle rolled her eyes and went to the stove to start cooking.

"Is Mary cooking for you, Daniel, or are you joining us today?" Annabelle asked.

Daniel replied, "I forgot she did say she making my favorite today. I best go now before she get mad. I see you two later."

"You have a good day, Daniel."

Daniel cheerfully replied, "Thank you, Sasha."

"Take your time, my friend. I don't want to see you trip leaving my house," Benjamin said.

Daniel replied, "You have a lot to say, Benjamin. You clumsier than me." The two friends smirked at each other as Daniel left the house.

"I think he like Miss Marilyn," Benjamin said.

Annabelle replied, "I think he thinks that she is cute, but I think it's too early to say there are feelings there. Besides, I don't want to see either of them get hurt."

"But you know Daniel mulatto."

"It's still not allowed. It's not Marilyn that concerns me. It's Mr. Pots. I will never forget how that old man acted toward me when I first met him. If something was to grow between Daniel and Marilyn, it would be a mess, so let's not encourage anything like that between them. I'm sure Marilyn was being nice to him. You're the only Negro man she has as a friend, Benjamin, so it wouldn't surprise me if that's her focus."

Benjamin nodded. "Alright, I say nothing."

"I didn't say don't say nothing. I said don't let Daniel believe there is something special between them."

Benjamin pouted. "Why I have to say something?"

"You don't have to say anything. Keep that man in his place. You're being complicated. All you have to do is keep Daniel from seeing Marilyn as someone interesting."

Benjamin shrugged. "I can't stop him from liking who he like."

Annabelle scoffed. "Oh, yes, you can. The moment he asks you what do you think about Marilyn, say nothing that would get his thinking to say it might work."

"Forget it. I want nothing to do with this. He mulatto. He going after whatever he want."

Annabelle pointed a wooden spoon at Benjamin. "If you want to eat, you're going to keep him in his place."

Benjamin sat down at the table and reached for a plate.

"That's what I thought. Supper will be a ready in about ten minutes."

Benjamin stared out at the windows, knowing he wasn't going to win the argument. The two ate dinner together as they watched the sunset. That night, Annabelle couldn't help but think about what Benjamin had said. It bothered her that she'd also noticed that Daniel was attracted to Marilyn, but she wasn't sure about Marilyn. She decided to let it go instead of stressing out about it.

Two weeks passed, and at Pots's Garments, Elizabeth had been entertaining Marilyn, explaining to her that two of her brothers and one of Ruthanne's brothers were coming to see the town.

"That must be exciting for you to have your brothers come to this town," Marilyn said.

Elizabeth replied, "I'm a bit excited, but I'm more interested in learning what has become of Robin. It's been so long since I've seen her. I miss her greatly."

"It must be a different feeling you have for her now. Knowing the truth that she really is your own kin."

"In a way, yes, but I think being raised to love a slave makes it different because I already loved her, but now I would never allow her to be treated unfairly."

"I think my father would go insane if my family had any Negro blood in our family."

"I often wonder if my father did lose his mind temporarily when my cousin became pregnant. The pregnancy must've been hard for her."

The doorbell rang, and the two women turned around to see Daniel entering the store. He wore a short top hat and beige shirt, along with a blue vest and brown trousers.

"Hello, Daniel, I wondered when I was going to see you again," Marilyn said.

Daniel replied, "Good afternoon, ladies. I wanted to come by during my lunchtime to say thank you, Marilyn."

Marilyn beamed. "You're welcome, Daniel. I appreciate you coming by."

"Anytime, Miss Marilyn, and good afternoon to you, Miss Elizabeth. I don't mean to ignore you."

Elizabeth replied, "Oh no, you're fine, Daniel. I know you came by to visit Marilyn."

"I guess I need to get back before Mr. Stone get upset. I'm happy to see you both."

"I'm happy to see you too, Daniel. You should come by more often," Marilyn said with a smirk.

Daniel held back his smile. "I may try to do that. Have a good day, Miss Elizabeth."

"You too, Daniel. Take care of yourself," Elizabeth said.

Daniel left the store to continue his work, and Marilyn watched him attentively through the store's windows from where she stood by the cedar counter.

"He is such a nice Negro man. I understand why he and Benjamin are good friends," Elizabeth said.

Marilyn replied, "Oh, he's mulatto."

"That isn't surprising. He doesn't look too different from Robin in some ways. I think we need more men like him in this town. There are too many men looking to prove something. Daniel seems so confident that he's always relaxed from what I've noticed."

"How do you know that, Elizabeth?"

"Before they got married, Benjamin decided to fix up his home some more for Annabelle. Ruthanne and I would sometimes go by the house to see how he was doing, and every time we came by to check on Benjamin, Daniel was there, helping him without complaint. Always cheerful, making light of anything that may have gone wrong, but seeing those two together is quite interesting."

Marilyn continued to watch Daniel walk further away while Elizabeth continued to talk.

Elizabeth noticed that Marilyn had begun to daydream. "What are you looking at?" she asked.

Marilyn inhaled and looked at Elizabeth. "I wasn't looking at anything. I'm a little tired."

"Well, alright. I guess I can give you some space. Oh, and this Saturday, Rebecca wants you over for some tea and muffins."

Marilyn smiled. "That sounds like fun. I'll be there."

"Great! I will see you later."

"Goodbye, Elizabeth."

As Elizabeth went home, Marilyn pulled out some paper and began drawing a dress.

On Saturday, the young women met at Rebecca's home. Annabelle had become excited about the gathering, and she looked forward to seeing the twins. The women enjoyed each other's company. A lot of the attention was directed toward the twins and Ashley. Annabelle noticed that Marilyn wasn't social like she normally would have been.

"Marilyn, what is on your mind? You seem like you want to say something," Annabelle said.

Marilyn casually responded, "Oh no, I'm actually quite fine. I'm enjoying this moment with all of you. It's good for me to get away from the store sometimes, and this is something I need. Thanks for asking, Annabelle."

"You know to speak up if something is wrong," Ruthanne boldly said.

Marilyn smiled, amused by Ruthanne's boldness.

"Of course. I know better, especially around you ladies," Marilyn joked.

The women cackled and continued the day, experimenting with making different muffins. As Annabelle and Marilyn said their goodbyes, Annabelle felt that Marilyn hadn't told them everything.

While Marilyn went home, she heard a horse nay. She looked over to see Daniel putting water into a horse trough. She strolled toward him. By that time, he began to brush the horse.

"Hello, Daniel," Marilyn said with a playful tone.

"Hello, Miss Marilyn. I'm surprised to see you," Daniel said, smiling.

"I was spending time at the Keyses' home for a while."

"I think they one of my favorite families. Mrs. Keys always nice, and Mr. Keys always speak to me."

"Yes, I've grown quite fond of them myself over time. They're like a second family for me."

Daniel stopped brushing the horse and looked at Marilyn. "Do you have a big family?"

"I do have several cousins all over the country, but I have four sisters, and I'm the youngest."

"My goodness, it amazing your daddy alive. He had to live with six women at one time."

Marilyn laughed, and she brushed her ringlets back. "I'm sure there were times death seemed like a choice in his mind."

"I'm sure your momma treat him good though."

Marilyn huffed with a blank face. "My momma died five years ago. She had gotten sick and never recovered."

Daniel frowned as he nodded his head. "I'm sorry. I did not mean to bring you bad memories."

"No, it's okay. You didn't know, and it's been five years. Five years is quite different than five days. Well, I don't want to get you into trouble with Mr. Stone, but you should stop by the store sometime later."

"I might do that."

Marilyn grinned and left while Daniel watched her. He turned to the horse he was cleaning and scratched its mane.

"She know she is a pretty thing. Did you take a good look at her, Samson? I bet you seen some good-looking mares, but not as pretty as her." The horse made a low nay as Daniel brushed him. "Yeah, I thought I was right."

Benjamin walked around the saloon, carrying two water buckets.

"What you smiling for?" Benjamin asked.

"I just enjoying old Samson here, that all," Daniel said.

"I heard someone when I was in the back. Who was you talking to?"

"Ah, nobody important. Just a nice little talk."

Benjamin looked at Daniel, squinting his eyes as he put more water into the horse troughs.

Benjamin went home that evening, meeting Annabelle at the front door.

"I think it nothing between Daniel and Marilyn," Benjamin said.

"Why do you believe that?" Annabelle asked.

Benjamin answered, "This afternoon, I know he talking to someone, and I know it was a lady. I ask him what he was smiling for, and he say nothing."

Annabelle gave an unconvinced glare. "How are you sure it wasn't Marilyn?"

Benjamin slightly tilted his head. "She didn't sound like Marilyn."

Annabelle exhaled and rolled her eyes as she entered the house. "I know something was on Marilyn's mind lately."

"Why not leave them alone. They both grown folks. They know it not safe for them here to even spend time together."

Annabelle threw her brown reticule on the dinner table and put her hands on her hips as her gaze focused on the bedroom doorway. Benjamin came up behind her, placing his hands on her shoulders.

"I ask him...if it bothers you so much."

Annabelle turned around and placed her hand on his cheek. "It's 'I will ask him if it bothers you so much.'"

Annabelle began to giggle when Benjamin gave her a hug.

"I'm trying, my love."

"I know, but maybe tonight, we can spend more time helping you read through *The Three Musketeers* than playing around."

Benjamin's eyebrows lifted while he shrugged his shoulders. "We can do both later tonight."

Annabelle twisted her mouth. "You always fall asleep afterward."

"I don't. I swear I can make it as long as you keep reading."

Annabelle chuckled as she turned to the stove to finish their dinner.

"I guess tonight, we can try for that."

Benjamin kissed Annabelle on the cheek and sat down at the table to watch the sunset.

July 19, 1846 was the next Monday. While Benjamin and Daniel worked, Benjamin approached Daniel while he was brushing a horse.

"So why were you smiling so much?" Benjamin asked.

Daniel replied, "It was no real reason. I was enjoying the day."

Daniel continued to brush the horse, but Benjamin crossed his arms as he looked at Daniel, unconvinced.

Benjamin asked, "Who is she?"

Daniel looked at Benjamin with his mouth agape. "Is it that easy to see?"

"Well, yes, it is. You acting the same way I did when Annabelle finally gave me time."

"She don't really know I want to see more of her," Daniel said while he beamed and continued to brush the horse.

"I heard a woman talking, but I knew it wasn't business. You looked too happy."

Daniel stopped brushing the horse as he lifted his hands to his chest. "I didn't know what to say when you asked me. I couldn't get her off my mind."

"So, you like this already, and she don't even know?"

Daniel scoffed. "I know it sad. I know it is."

"I bet I know who it is."

Daniel's eyes became big while he looked at Benjamin.

"That was Jean talking to you, wasn't it?"

Daniel's eyes relaxed, and he smiled, shifting his eyes from Benjamin. "Your mind amazes me."

"I figure you was going to try for someone Mary got along with. So, I know Sally was not someone you wanted to put time into."

Cackling, Daniel strolled to the back of the saloon for water.

"You know me well. I sure wouldn't put no time into that woman. It amazing she doesn't catch on fire. Sally always complaining, never happy. I don't want anyone like that."

Benjamin replied, "I understand how you feel."

"How are things with you and Annabelle?" Daniel happily asked.

Benjamin smiled. "Things are real good. We started reading this book, *The Three Musketeers*, and I like it a lot. She sometimes reads some stuff over because I fall asleep, but I think I'm getting better at not falling asleep."

"Sounds like a good house to me."

"It is, and I thank God every day for it all."

The two continued with the day while Daniel held onto the truth about his feelings. Benjamin later confirmed with Annabelle that Jean was the woman who Daniel had a current interest. Annabelle was satisfied with what Benjamin had discovered and let go of the situation.

A week passed as Annabelle and the others continued their normal schedules, but Mr. Pots noticed a change in Marilyn. After Elizabeth finished her typical afternoon visit, Mr. Pots came to the front counter.

"I feel that sometimes, I don't tell you enough how proud of you I really am," Mr. Pots said.

"Papa, what would make you say that?" Marilyn asked.

"I noticed how much happier you seem now. You have always been a smart and loving child. You remind me so much of your mother, and I'm grateful for that." Marilyn smiled at Mr. Pots as he continued, "I wish your other sisters had more of those things in them, but I fear your sisters are too passive. Don't make that mistake. You do what God puts on your heart, dear."

"I think I'm doing what's been put on my heart, Papa."

"I'm sorry for how I have treated your friend, Sasha. She and the others seem to have brought a new light in you."

Marilyn grinned. "They really are great people if you get to know them."

Mr. Pots nodded. "I believe you. I need more time to work with God. I don't want to leave this world a bitter or hateful man. I also don't want to leave you alone."

"Papa, I will find someone. I need you to open your heart to whomever I might bring home someday."

"What do you mean by that?" Mr. Pots asked, a crease forming between his eyebrows.

"Well, what if he doesn't make a lot of money with the job he has? I can't say who God will bring into my life, but I do want your approval when the time comes. I don't want to be rushed into anything."

Mr. Pots smiled at his daughter and nodded. "Like I said, you really are a smart girl, and I'm working on changing for the better."

Marilyn beamed at her father as he returned to the back of the store.

"By the way, what are we having for dinner today?"

"We're having beef stew today, Papa," Marilyn enthusiastically said.

"Ah, my favorite dish. Sounds great, dear."

Marilyn continued to sort boxes cheerfully. The encouraging talk with her father made her more hopeful.

A month passed as something new was occurring in Annabelle. After speaking with Rebecca, Annabelle discovered that she had become pregnant. The new change excited her, and she started thinking of names for the baby. Annabelle arrived at her home and entered into the bedroom, looking at Benjamin attempting to read *The Three Musketeers*. She sat next to him, smiling, and he looked at her curiously.

"What has you so cheerful?" Benjamin asked.

Annabelle answered, "You're going to be a daddy."

Benjamin gasped with wide brown eyes. "I'm going to be a daddy?"

Annabelle's grin became bigger. "Yes, you're going to be a daddy. I'm pregnant."

Benjamin jumped up, shouting with joy, and gave Annabelle a hug. "I love you with everything I am."

"I love you too, but you need to calm down."

"I can't. It going to be a little me or you in our home!"

Tears of joy began to stream down Benjamin's face while he gave Annabelle another hug. He rushed out the house, screaming that he was going to be a father. Annabelle sat down in the bed, dumbfounded by his excitement. The news spread with the others, congratulating Annabelle and Benjamin. Annabelle quickly gained attention from the others next to Rebecca's twins. Catherine agreed to be Annabelle's midwife, while Marilyn kept insisting on making the baby some clothes.

Pastor Avail also gave his blessings to the couple. Mr. Boston was so overjoyed for Annabelle that he began to include extra food supplies along with her payment and wouldn't allow her to refuse his offers. She was almost overwhelmed but was grateful knowing this wouldn't have occurred if she was in Mississippi.

Three months into her pregnancy, Annabelle had felt ill, unlike the other days. During the time she continued her way to work, she felt more intense cramps and sharp pains. In a panic, she rushed to Catherine's house while trying not to attract the attention of the townspeople. Annabelle arrived at Catherine's home, so focused on bearing the pain, she didn't notice Catherine had seen her.

Catherine rushed out of the front door and tried to help Annabelle stand.

"It hurts so bad, Catherine. Something is wrong," Annabelle cried.

Catherine noticed a small trail of blood behind Annabelle. "How long has this been going on?" Catherine asked.

"It started this morning," Annabelle cried.

"Come on. Let's get you inside."

During this time, Ruthanne had become concerned as she waited for Annabelle, and she traveled toward the Moselys' home. Ruthanne was unable to find Annabelle and began to rush to Mr. Boston's store, hoping she had somehow missed Annabelle. Ruthanne arrived at Mr. Boston's store with her normal greeting.

"Sorry I'm running late, Mr. Boston. I was looking for Sasha, but I missed her," Ruthanne said.

Mr. Boston replied, "Sasha hasn't shown up to the store."

"Are you sure she's not in the chicken coop?" Ruthanne asked.

Mr. Boston frowned. "I was just in there."

"Something is wrong, Mr. Boston. I'm going to go look for her."

"Inform me when you find her."

"I will."

Ruthanne rushed home to inform Rebecca that something was odd, and she didn't want to alarm Benjamin.

Meanwhile, Catherine was trying to help Annabelle, but her worst fear was realized as she left the room where Annabelle rested.

"It's a miscarriage." Catherine sighed.

Catherine had her older daughter, Kristen, hurry to Rebecca to tell her the news and to ask her to come to help Annabelle cope. Kristen arrived and told Rebecca the dire news. Rebecca rushed from her house with her children, asking God to help her say the right words to Annabelle.

Catherine continued to comfort Annabelle, withholding the truth from her until Rebecca had arrived. Rebecca arrived at Catherine's home, greeting her with a hug.

"She's in the back room lying down," Catherine said. "Do you want me to tell her?"

Rebecca replied, "I think you should. Right now, I don't know what to say to her."

Catherine entered the room with Rebecca behind her.

"Hey, Rebecca. Catherine, you didn't have to get Rebecca. I'm feeling so much better now," Annabelle said.

Rebecca replied, "Well, she had Kristen run and bring me over. It's not an inconvenience. This is what friends are for."

Rebecca held Annabelle's hand while the two women smiled at each other.

"Sasha, dear, there is more that you need to know," Catherine said.

"What is it?" Annabelle asked.

"The reason you were experiencing the pain so bad today is because you had a miscarriage."

Annabelle gasped, and her eyes widened, "I what?"

"Sasha, dear, you lost the baby today."

Heartbreak came over Annabelle in a way she had never felt before. "Are you sure?"

Catherine frowned. "Yes, dear, I'm sure. I'm so sorry."

Annabelle broke out in a silent cry as Rebecca knelt next to the bed and hugged Annabelle. Annabelle clutched onto Rebecca while she cried uncontrollably. Catherine grabbed a cloth to wipe Annabelle's tears, and she knelt next to the bed and hugged Annabelle along with Rebecca. As Annabelle continued to cry, the two women cried with her.

"What did I do wrong, Catherine?" Annabelle bawled.

"I have seen you do nothing wrong throughout the pregnancy. Sometimes this happens. It wasn't meant to be."

Annabelle continued to cry while the women consoled her. During this time, Ruthanne had arrived home, but no one was there. Ruthanne became increasingly worried. She walked past Catherine's red brick home, seeing Kristen in her polka-dotted yellow dress on the porch.

"Hi, Miss Williams. How are you doing today?" Kristen asked.

"Hello, Kristen," Ruthanne replied. "I apologize, but I'm in a rush to find Mrs. Keys."

"She is inside with my mother this very minute. I just came outside because the twins were sleeping."

"I'll come right in. I need to speak with her." Ruthanne entered the house as Kristen escorted her to the room, and she could hear crying. She moved in front of Kristen and slowly opened the door.

"Sasha? Rebecca? What is going on?" Ruthanne asked.

The feeling of sadness was overwhelming in the room as Annabelle broke into more tears.

"I lost my baby, Ruthanne. I lost it," Annabelle cried.

Ruthanne's heart dropped when she approached the bed and gave Annabelle a hug.

"I don't know what to say. When did this happen?"

Catherine replied, "It happened this morning. She fell near my porch. I knew something was wrong, but I never thought it was this bad."

Ruthanne replied, "I'm sorry. I have no words to comfort you."

"It's okay. The three of you here right now helps," Annabelle said.

The women sat around, and Annabelle calmed down. Ruthanne had opted to escort Annabelle home later that day, and Elizabeth was told to tell Mr. Boston and Marilyn of the terrible news. Ruthanne and Annabelle went through town, ignoring all of the townspeople. Ruthanne began to coach Annabelle so she could tell Benjamin the news.

Benjamin arrived at their home with his normal positive attitude.

"I guessed you was kidnapped by Ruthanne," Benjamin said.

Ruthanne replied, "Hello, Benjamin. It's good to see you."

"Always good to see you too, Miss Ruthanne. Annabelle, why you so quiet?"

Annabelle took a big gulp as Ruthanne placed her hands on her shoulders.

"Something bad happened today when I was on my way to Mr. Boston's store," Annabelle said.

"Did someone give you trouble today?" Benjamin asked.

"No, Benjamin, it wasn't that." Annabelle's body began to quiver while she looked at Benjamin.

"I promise I talked to Daniel, and he said it Jean he likes, not Miss Marilyn."

Annabelle began to sob, and Ruthanne reached for her hand to help calm her.

"I lost the baby," Annabelle cried. "I lost the baby today on my way to work."

Benjamin gasped. He began to walk in a small circle, trying to hold back tears.

"I'm so sorry I lost our baby."

Benjamin came up to Annabelle and gave her a hug as she cried in his arms.

"It wasn't Annabelle's fault. These things do happen," Ruthanne said. "Catherine said it will be a while before the two of you should try for another baby."

"So, Mrs. Catherine say we can still have children?" Benjamin asked.

"Yes, but wait a while for Annabelle's body to heal." Ruthanne nudged Annabelle while she wiped her tears. "I love you both, so don't let this pain ruin who you are."

"I'll try not to," Annabelle replied.

"No, you do it, Annabelle. You're a strong person with a loving heart," Ruthanne firmly said, giving Annabelle and Benjamin a hug. "I will be praying for you two tonight, and don't worry about working for now, Annabelle. You need to heal."

"Thank you, Ruthanne. It means a lot that you walked her home," Benjamin said.

Ruthanne replied with a half-smile. "That's what friends are for, Benjamin."

Ruthanne left the house while Benjamin took Annabelle to their bedroom to comfort her.

As December of 1846 arrived, Annabelle fell into a deep depression, and the others noticed Annabelle's broken spirit. One day, Rebecca left the children with Elizabeth to search for Benjamin before he arrived at work. Rebecca saw him and cut through the morning crowd as she approached him.

"Good morning, Benjamin," Rebecca said.

"Good morning, Mrs. Rebecca," Benjamin said. "I was on my way to work at Mr. Stone's saloons."

"Yes, I know you must get there on time. I wanted to know if Annabelle had become better."

Benjamin frowned. "She still quiet sometimes but started to cook again. She still won't smile though. Just wants to hug next to me at night."

Rebecca sighed. "I see. I will go and speak with her."

"That may be what is needed at this time. Anything you can do to make her better. I will be in your debt." Benjamin's discouragement appeared on his face. "I don't know what to do with her, Mrs. Rebecca. At first, it was anger, but now it nothing but sadness."

"Then I will try to help her change that."

"Thank you." Benjamin nodded and went away to Mr. Stone's businesses.

Rebecca arrived at Annabelle's home and knocked on the door, and Annabelle opened it.

"Well, there is a face I haven't seen in a couple of days," Rebecca said.

"Hi, Rebecca. How are you?" Annabelle asked.

"I'm doing well, but how are you?" Rebecca curiously asked.

Annabelle sighed while she avoided eye contact. "I don't know how I am."

Rebecca entered the house and sat down with Annabelle.

"Annabelle, there isn't anything wrong with having a season of mourning, but you can't allow this to define who you are."

"I don't know how. I failed as a mother."

"You cannot hold on to this pain. There was nothing you did wrong. There is something I need to tell you. Allen doesn't even know. Ashley was not the first child I was pregnant with."

Annabelle's eyebrows shot up when she heard Rebecca's secret. "Why didn't you tell him?"

"I was young, and we had only been married for a month. At two months, I was trying to figure out a way to tell him I was pregnant. Then I kept bleeding and experiencing pain, so I rushed to Catherine. I didn't take it well, just as you didn't. It made my marriage to Allen harder. So much ran through my mind. Did I do something wrong? Maybe I didn't eat enough. Why would God let me go through this? I had to get prayer from Pastor Avail. Then, by allowing Allen to love me and not letting my pain take over my life, I gave the pain to Jesus. I saw the real darkness of my reality grow stronger the more I let myself be alone."

Rebecca sighed and continued, saying, "I was mad at God. I didn't want God's peace or pity. I wanted an answer. Why give me a taste of what it would be like to be a mother and then take it from me? The moment I let go, gave my pain away, and opened my heart again, I felt God's love in me. It's far different than the joy you can give yourself. So I'm here to tell you, Annabelle, it is time to let go."

Annabelle began to bawl while Rebecca held her hand.

"Please, Annabelle, for the sake of not only your life but the people that love you, will you accept me praying for your healing?"

Annabelle replied, "Yes, I accept it."

Rebecca prayed for Annabelle, and she accepted that she wasn't responsible for losing a child. Rebecca spent the rest of the day with Annabelle, and she left before Benjamin arrived back home. Annabelle chose to keep reciting in her heart, "This is the day the Lord hath made. I will rejoice and be glad in it." She soon began to heal, emotionally and spiritually.

Over the next three months, into March of 1847, Annabelle's true nature returned with the spring. Over time, Annabelle became strong again, and new changes had started to occur with the others.

Ruthanne's and Peter's relationship began to grow, though the two of them still struggled to admit it. Sierra Nicole continued her pursuit of Peter, and her relationship with Ruthanne had formed into a rivalry.

Annabelle had also noticed that more Indians had begun to come in and out of the town. Annabelle and Ruthanne even began developing friendships with a few Indians because they favored Mr. Boston's store and were welcomed there.

The Indian, John Lightning, had become a more frequent customer over the months. Mr. Boston believed John became more of a frequent customer because of the loss of his wife. Annabelle felt sorry for John and constantly spoke to him throughout the month, and John thanked her for trying to lift his spirit. On March 24, 1847, John returned to Mr. Boston's store, and he seemed even sadder to Annabelle with his upward slanting eyebrows and deep frown.

"Good afternoon, John," Annabelle said.

"Hi, Sasha," John said.

Annabelle replied, "It's a slow day today."

"Is that right? Well, there are days like that."

"Yeah, but a smile can go a long way."

John nodded his head, "Yeah, smiles help."

Annabelle sighed. "I can see the pain in your eyes, John. She's deep on your mind today, isn't she?"

John gulped, and he gazed at the floor and back at Annabelle. "I'm trying, but last night, all I kept thinking about was the last time I hugged her. The last time I kissed her. The last time I looked into her beautiful eyes. I feel lost. I can't even put into words how much pain I feel."

Annabelle frowned. "I understand the pain. I've lost a lot."

John crossed his arms while he frowned. "What have you lost?"

"I lost my baby a few months ago." Annabelle shook her head. "I didn't even get a chance to hold my own baby, but I felt the life leave my body. So yes, I do understand your pain."

John closed his eyes and shook his head, looking back at Annabelle. "I'm sorry if I sounded like it wasn't possible for you to understand. I couldn't imagine losing a child."

"Yeah, it's hard. It's very hard, but God gives me the strength to move forward. I pray every day for strength because I know without it, I'd break. I'd fall right back into the sadness."

"Asking for strength that isn't your own. I should've prayed for such a thing."

"Are you okay for me to pray for you?"

"From you, I'd accept prayer. My older sister prays."

Annabelle smiled. "I hope this is good enough for you to return back to Indian Territory when you're ready."

Annabelle prayed for John, and after she finished, John grinned at her.

"I didn't expect to get a smile," Annabelle said.

Continuing to smile, John replied, "A smile can go a long way." He grabbed a sack of seeds. "I will see you later, Sasha."

"It's always good to see you, John."

John moved toward Mr. Boston and bought the sack before leaving the supply store. As Annabelle's and John's friendship grew, Annabelle expected to see John over the weeks.

Throughout this time, the relationship between Marilyn and her father also improved. Mr. Pots became a happier man, even greeting Annabelle when she was in the store. Marilyn had begun to develop a stronger friendship with Daniel, and he and Marilyn frequently saw each other during their lunch breaks. Daniel started to become a welcomed visitor in the Keyses' home as well. Allen had developed an unforeseen friendship with both Benjamin and Daniel. Yet, at times, he still kept his distance from them to maintain a strong voice in the town's political scene. Allen had revealed to Rebecca that some of his most joyous times were spending time with the two men who were more like brothers than friends.

Unfortunately, Mr. Hildebrand continued to give Benjamin a hard time as he worked, waiting for an opportunity to confront Annabelle alone. Annabelle's happiness was a poison to Victor, as she represented the possible future of Negroes. The greatest threat Mr. Hildebrand felt was that more of the townspeople had begun to change their feelings and views toward slavery. Therefore, Mr. Hildebrand continued to live his life, determined to keep the hierarchy. However, Annabelle's focus was on her loved ones. The threat of Mr. Hildebrand and Casey Bones had left her mind.

Annabelle had also discovered that she was pregnant again. The news of the pregnancy spread quickly, but she held back her excitement, worried about another miscarriage. The others were far more hopeful for Annabelle and the baby.

CHAPTER 19
Ruthless Motives

THREE MONTHS PASSED WITH THE late arrival of two of Elizabeth's brothers and one of Ruthanne's brothers. The men arrived in a two-horse carriage, and Elizabeth ran down the stairs as Ruthanne slowly followed.

"Billy! Frank! It is a blessing to see you both!" Elizabeth happily shouted.

"Little sister, it's good to see you," Frank said.

The two men, blue-eyed and blond like their sister, walked up and gave Elizabeth a hug. Frank had an average build. He wore a frock coat, black striped trousers, and a white high-collared shirt with a blue cravat. A blue vest that held a gold pocket watch completed the look. Billy wore almost the same outfit, having a red plaid cravat instead of blue, a silver pocket watch, and a hefty build with a beard.

"I was expecting you both last summer, but the letters you sent read that things had become difficult." Ruthanne continued to come down the stairs in her green ruffle dress with a blank expression.

"Well, Ruthanne, I see you haven't changed. Still an angry redhead," Billy said.

Ruthanne replied, "It's good to see you too, Billy Goat."

Ruthanne's brother, Ruben, jumped down from the carriage. Ruben, with his curly brown hair and green eyes, wore a brown frock coat, brown striped trousers, a brown shirt with a green cravat, and he covered it with a dark green vest. His gold pocket watch had the word 'Williams' engraved on the back.

"Ruben, my brother, it's nice to see you're not moving around like an old man."

Ruben laughed as he marched toward his sister and gave her a hug and a kiss.

"It took you boys long enough to come see us."

"We would have come a year ago, but these two were obsessed with helping to figure out this Underground Railroad," Ruben said. "It's been costing a lot of the plantation owners' time and money."

Frank replied, "We gave up for now, once pa yelled at us because you ignored his demand to return home, Elizabeth. This June weather don't make it easier either."

"Frank, a lot has been going on in this town. Ruthanne and I have met great people here," Elizabeth said.

The front door opened, and Rebecca emerged from the house, holding Esther.

"Well, hello there. Who are these gentlemen, Ruthanne?" Rebecca asked.

Ruthanne replied, "Rebecca, this is Billy and Frank, two of Elizabeth's brothers, and one of my brothers, Ruben."

"Pleasure to meet you, ma'am," the men said.

Rebecca replied, "It is nice to meet all of you on this beautiful day. I was baking some cookies. You men are welcome to some of them."

"I would love some. I wish Ruthanne was that polite," Ruben said.

"I'm polite. I'm just not your servant, Ruben," Ruthanne bickered.

Ruben scoffed. "You have never taken a liking to serving when that's what women do."

Ruthanne rolled her eyes. "Keep it up. I serve when it is necessary."

Billy replied, "We will take some home cooking too. Our little sister here doesn't have the skills."

Elizabeth put her hands on her hips and said, "For your information, I have recently improved greatly in my cooking."

"Now, because you stopped burning stuff doesn't mean it tastes good."

Elizabeth's nose crinkled. "Shut up, Billy. I promise I've gotten much better. You will see tonight when I cook dinner."

"She has actually improved far more than I thought possible," Ruthanne said.

"If Ruthanne says she has gotten better, that's good enough for me," Frank said.

"Well, come on in for some cookies," Rebecca said.

The men, Elizabeth, and Ruthanne followed Rebecca inside her home. They enjoyed each other's company while the men discussed their lives and learned more about the town of Mercy.

During this time, Annabelle had visited Catherine, nervous about the pregnancy. Catherine encouraged Annabelle, telling her the pregnancy was going well.

Annabelle left to see Elizabeth and Ruthanne, excited by the news. She arrived and knocked on the door.

"It's Sasha!" Elizabeth said as she opened the door. "Come in, dear. We were just eating some cookies. I know you must be hungry."

Annabelle went inside, but she was met with judgmental stares from the three men.

"Who is this nigger?" Billy said.

"Billy, don't call her that!" Elizabeth said harshly. "This is Sasha."

Billy's eyes widened. "You mean the sweet woman you ladies have been talking about this whole time has been her?"

"Billy, you need to watch your mouth," Ruthanne snapped.

Ruthanne approached Annabelle and sat her down next to her.

"Ruthanne, you've turned into a nigger lover. No wonder you didn't want to come back home," Ruben said.

"Shut it, Ruben. Is it that much to ask?" Ruthanne snarled.

"I'm sorry, sister. I'm surprised by all this. Like when you surprised Harold by stealing the carriage and leaving him in Mississippi."

Ruthanne gulped as Ruben looked at her, but she maintained her stubbornness. "Sasha, I would like you to meet my brother, Ruben, and two of Elizabeth's brothers, Frank and Billy."

"It's nice to meet you," Annabelle said.

The men seemed stunned by Annabelle's speech.

"Where are you from, Sasha?" Ruben asked.

"I'm from Jefferson City."

Ruben sat back in his seat. "My, how the world is changing. She speaks so well. No wonder you like her, Ruthanne."

"Hush, she is a great woman," Ruthanne replied.

"I bet she is a great woman, and she's got a little baby there with her."

Ruthanne's tone began to become more aggravated, "She's married, Ruben."

"Wow, that's a rarity. Well, congratulations are in order then," Frank said.

Billy stared at Annabelle, his lips pressed together.

"I swear she looks so familiar though," Ruben said.

"How can she look familiar to you, Ruben? She's always been here, and this is your first time in the state, fool," Ruthanne snarled.

"You see, that attitude there is why you can't get married. Pa is going to go into the grave before you find someone."

Ruthanne grabbed a cookie and threw it at Ruben, who picked the pieces of the cookie off his vest and ate it.

"Pa wants you home. He's mad at you for ditching Harold. Being a woman out here all by yourself."

"I'm not alone. I have Elizabeth."

Ruben put another piece of the cookie in his mouth and said, "A woman."

Ruthanne sneered. "I see nothing has changed about you."

"Anyway, enough of this questioning stuff. It's different in this state, and that's the end of it," Frank said.

Rebecca replied, "I agree. Would you young men like some more cookies?"

Frank smiled. "Why, yes, Mrs. Rebecca. I would love more of your cooking."

"Elizabeth, come help me."

Elizabeth got up and helped Rebecca prepare the next batch of cookies.

"I just don't like it," Billy said. "I don't care what my sister or Ruthanne says about you. You should be out working those cotton fields, not walking into people's homes like you matter, getting married, and feeling free to speak to me."

"Billy, we've known each other since we were children, but if you say something else like that to her, I will make sure that when they get done baking those cookies, you choke on them," Ruthanne growled.

Billy sat back in his chair, and Annabelle avoided eye contact with him.

"Well, that's the end of that," Frank said.

"So, what do you do in this town, Sasha?" Ruben asked.

Annabelle replied, "I work at a supply store."

"That's right. My sister did say she works with you. I'm not too surprised that my sister found someone that was willing to give her a payment. My sister is a smart woman. I think there is much you can learn from her. I wish she would learn something from you so she can get married."

Ruben began to cackle with the other men. Ruthanne grabbed another one of her cookies and threw it at her brother.

"I miss you too, Ruthanne."

Elizabeth and Rebecca finished the next batch of cookies while Frank and Ruben continued to tell stories. Ruthanne later took the men around town and introduced them to Peter, Catherine, and the Williamson family. Annabelle returned home to Benjamin with another batch of cookies.

Elizabeth later cooked dinner for her brothers, surprising

them with her improvement. The men stayed in a hotel while visiting Elizabeth and Ruthanne for a week. During this time, Elizabeth introduced them to Allen and Marilyn. Marilyn decided to keep her distance from Billy after he kept flirting with her.

As Ruthanne and Ruben spent time together in the hammock, Elizabeth asked her brothers about Robin. Frank informed Elizabeth that her family had found a lawyer in Pennsylvania who saw Robin as a beauty. Frank explained they never believed they could find her someone in Mississippi, even though Robin was a beautiful mulatto. Elizabeth was also pleased to learn that the man had visited Mississippi a couple of times to meet Robin, and she liked him. Elizabeth's brothers also tried to convince her to return to Mississippi at the request of their father, but she refused. Billy became upset with Elizabeth's rebellion, but Frank reluctantly accepted it, leaving her more money. The men agreed with Elizabeth to return in two months, keeping in closer contact with their sister, and Ruben instructed Ruthanne to write every week.

Ruthanne wasn't excited about the idea, but Elizabeth was happy that she would see more of them. Annabelle had kept at a distance from the men. Before the men got on their carriage to leave Mercy, Elizabeth approached her brothers and gave them hugs.

"You boys be safe getting back home," Elizabeth said.

"Little Elizabeth, you keep writing us," Frank said. "Don't wait so long like last time now."

Elizabeth grinned. "I will, Frank."

Billy replied, "You know, pa isn't going to be happy about you staying here, but after talking with Frank, I understand."

Elizabeth replied, "Thank you, Billy."

Ruthanne hugged her brother as the others got into the carriage.

"You keep those two in check," Ruthanne said.

"I see you still struggle with saying goodbye," Ruben replied.

Ruthanne smiled. "You'll be back in two months. Why make this a sad moment?"

Chuckling, Ruben moved back toward the carriage.

Allen came out of the front door with a pie. "Ruben, please wait. Rebecca made this for you all," he said.

"Why, that's quite kind of your wife. I see why my sister is happy with staying here in this town," Ruben said.

Allen handed Ruben the pie. "I'm sure the ride won't be too bad going back to Jefferson City."

"Oh, no. We're from Mississippi. That's where we are going, so we have quite a ride ahead of us."

"Oh...well, my mistake, Ruben, but it was a pleasure to meet you."

"You too, Allen, and it truly was a pleasure."

Ruthanne was unable to hear the conversation between them and gave her brother one last hug before he left on the carriage. The men left the town, but Ruthanne felt an unease she couldn't distinguish. Two months passed, and life in the town continued.

One day in August of 1847, Annabelle entered Pots's Garments, surprised to see Daniel talking with Marilyn.

"Good afternoon, Marilyn and Daniel," Annabelle said.

Marilyn was excited to see Annabelle and gave her a hug.

"Look at you, Sasha. You're really starting to show!" Marilyn said.

Annabelle scoffed. "I know. Please don't remind me."

"Daniel and I were just having a talk."

"Hey Sasha, I was on my break, so I stopped by the store," Daniel said.

Annabelle replied, "Oh...okay. I wanted to know if the new perfumes had come in, Marilyn."

"Oh no, the crates haven't arrived yet, but maybe tomorrow," Marilyn replied.

"That sounds good. I'll be back tomorrow then."

Marilyn grinned. "That works. You know I'm mostly here, so come back when you can."

Annabelle put her hand on her back. "I will, and goodbye, Daniel."

"I'll see you, Sasha," Daniel said.

"When does your break end, Daniel?" Annabelle asked.

Daniel looked at the cuckoo clock in the store. "I have about five minutes before I need to be back. I guess I should leave to be there on time."

Marilyn frowned as she lightly tapped her fingers on her thigh. Annabelle stood in the doorway while she looked at the two standing next to each other. The moment became awkward when Daniel hesitated to leave.

"I'm sorry I'm blocking the door, so much is on my mind." Annabelle went out the door, and Daniel followed her.

Annabelle glanced back, witnessing Marilyn and Daniel waving to each other flirtatiously. Annabelle's eyes slightly narrowed, realizing that either Benjamin was wrong or Daniel's feelings toward Jean had changed. Annabelle marched home with swollen feet and a slight frown.

After Daniel left the store, Marilyn joyfully organized some new clothes in the store windows. At this time, Mr. Pots came to the front of the store.

"Marilyn, you seem a lot happier than usual, dear," Mr. Pots said.

Marilyn giggled, "Papa, I'm in a good mood most of the time."

"No, no. This is more than you being you." Mr. Pots sat down in the chair behind the front counter. "What is going on between you and that mulatto boy?"

Marilyn scoffed, "Nothing, Papa. There isn't anything inappropriate between us."

Mr. Pots shook his head. "I don't believe you. Every time he comes into this store, you're like a different person."

Marilyn's eyebrows rose, and she stepped closer to her father. "He's a good man, Papa. Am I wrong for treating a good man politely?"

"I have watched both of you for the past few months now. What goes on between the two of you is more than a friendship.

I'm working on accepting the Negroes in this town, but don't make it harder on me by letting your feelings steer to a Negro."

"He's a mulatto, Papa, and even if he was as dark as your shoes, I would still treat him the same," Marilyn said, her tone furious.

Mr. Pots began to breathe heavier. "Don't let your feelings fall for that man, even if he is a good one. You can find a better white man that can provide for you. If you allow this to continue, you will only make life harder for both of you."

Marilyn's face scrunched, and her eyes narrowed. She began to sniff and hold back tears. "If I were to have children that were half white, would you love them?"

Mr. Pots began to go to the back of the store.

"Daddy, please tell me. If I gave you grandchildren that were not all white, would you love them as I love you?"

Mr. Pots turned around, his gaze avoiding Marilyn's eyes. "You would shame our family with such a selfish choice."

Mr. Pots marched to the back of the store as tears shimmered in Marilyn's eyes. He continued to make shoes while he bit his lip and mumbled to himself. As he worked, he stared at a picture of his family and frowned as he tapped his foot. The next day, he went to the church to talk with Peter. He went into deep prayer, asking for help to love what he had been taught to hate. Mr. Pots left the church, starting to feel a reassurance of change.

Later in the week, Annabelle shared her concern about Daniel and Marilyn with Rebecca and Ruthanne. They both agreed a relationship between them was dangerous. The women agreed to keep Elizabeth in the dark to keep pressure off of Marilyn, but they felt that Marilyn should be warned. Annabelle continued to pressure Benjamin into finding out more from Daniel, but Daniel continued to avoid the topic. A week passed, and one morning, Annabelle and Benjamin had a fight about the situation, causing Benjamin to promise he would get the truth from Daniel. Benjamin understood the danger of Daniel and

Marilyn becoming romantically involved, but he didn't want to ruin it.

As Benjamin and Daniel worked at the businesses, they had their joyous conversations. Mr. Hildebrand arrived at a saloon on horseback with Casey Bones.

"Now, clean him up good, nigger," Mr. Hildebrand said.

"Yes, sir, Mr. Hildebrand. We get him nice and pretty," Benjamin said.

"Benjamin, I mean his coat better shine like a foal's coat. I also have five dollars in this sack, and when we get out, five dollars better be there."

Casey lifted the small sack hanging on the saddle, showing it to Daniel and Benjamin. Casey opened it up, counting it in front of them before closing the sack. Unknown to Benjamin and Daniel, there was a small hole in the bottom of the sack, and Casey forced out a quarter eagle and walked off with the gold piece. Mr. Hildebrand and Casey entered the saloon to socialize with the other business owners.

Benjamin and Daniel gave water to the horses while they cleaned them.

"That Mr. Hildebrand sure has an eye out for you, Benjamin," Daniel said.

Benjamin replied, "I know, but I do my best, so at least Mr. Stone is happy. Now you tell me, is there something between you and Miss Marilyn?"

Daniel continued to clean one of the horses as his face stayed emotionless. "The past few months, I have been visiting her on my breaks."

Benjamin crossed his arms. "So, all those times you say you was going to Mr. Boston's store or taking a walk, you was visiting Miss Marilyn."

Daniel kept his eyes on the horse. "Yes, but don't get mad now. It really is something about her. She is always happy to see me, and she makes me laugh. She is a lively woman."

"Now all that talk needs to stop, Daniel. The two of you need to stop or…keep it quiet. My wife already keeps bringing it up. She know something special between you and Miss Marilyn."

"What makes you think that the wrong people have noticed us? I don't think they do. I only see her in her store."

"That's her father's store, and the things I have heard about him… I think you must be careful. That man would have you hanged for even looking like you're interested in his daughter."

The two men continued their conversation while Benjamin listened to understand the relationship.

Meanwhile, Mr. Pots had left Pots's Garments, and with a smile, he looked around the busy town.

Once Benjamin and Daniel finished with Mr. Hildebrand's and Casey's horses, they began to work with horses from other customers. Mr. Pots arrived at the saloon, slightly exhausted from the travel, and marched up to Benjamin and Daniel.

The men were caught off guard. Unsure of Mr. Pots's intentions, Daniel felt his chest tighten as Mr. Pots got closer.

"Good afternoon, boys. I'd like some water," Mr. Pots said.

"Of course, Mr. Pots," Daniel said.

Annabelle was almost at the saloon, bringing Benjamin his lunch, when she saw Mr. Pots at the saloon and felt something was wrong. Annabelle dropped Benjamin's lunch and hurried to the Keyses' home.

Mr. Pots replied, "Wow, it seems you boys have been doing a good job out here."

Benjamin replied, "Yes, sir, Mr. Pots. We know if customers not happy, we not doing our job."

"That's a good standard, Benjamin. What do you think of that, Daniel?" Mr. Pots asked.

Daniel nervously replied, "I agree, sir. If the customer isn't happy, then something needs to improve."

Mr. Pots nodded his head with his lips pursed. "So you're a man of integrity."

Daniel could feel his throat tighten. "Yes, sir, I am."

Mr. Pots grinned. "That's good to know."

As the men continued to talk to each other, Mr. Hildebrand

and Casey Bones exited the saloon. The men were slightly intoxicated and laughing.

"Well, niggers, those horses better look flawless," Mr. Hildebrand said.

"We have them ready for you, Mr. Hildebrand," Daniel said.

"Shut your mouth, Daniel. I was talking, boy...to Benjamin here. Ah, Mr. Pots, how are you on this glorious day?" Mr. Hildebrand slurred.

Mr. Pots replied, "I was doing quite fine, Victor. It seems you and your friend had a few drinks."

"My apologies. This young man here is Casey Bones, my assistant at my store."

"It is a pleasure to meet you officially, Mr. Pots," Casey said.

The men moved over to the horses with a slight stumble. Casey Bones reached for the reins of the horse while Victor reached for the money sack on the horse's saddle.

"Now wait a minute, Casey. Something doesn't feel right," Mr. Hildebrand said.

Mr. Hildebrand opened up the sack and started to count the money. Benjamin and Daniel looked at each other worrisomely.

"Now, I know good and well these niggers didn't steal from me."

Casey put the horse's reins back on the post and confrontationally marched up to Benjamin.

"Where is the money, nigger?" Casey asked.

Benjamin answered, "Mr. Bones, we haven't taken anything from the money sack. We watched you count it and then go inside."

Casey sneered. "You think we're stupid, don't you?"

Casey reached for his revolver, but Mr. Pots stepped in front of him.

"Now hold on. How much was in the sack?" Mr. Pots asked.

"It was five dollars in the sack," Mr. Hildebrand said.

"How much is in there now?"

Mr. Hildebrand scoffed, "Just two-fifty."

Casey pushed Benjamin hard, and Daniel hesitated to step forward.

"Was you going to do something, nigger?" Casey asked.

"Enough with these fruitless arguments. Now Daniel, did you or Benjamin take money from Mr. Hildebrand's money sack?" Mr. Pots asked.

"No, Mr. Pots, we didn't," Daniel said.

Mr. Pots stepped in front of Daniel, wearing a slight frown and a crease in between his eyebrows.

"Daniel, I'm going to ask you one more time as a man of integrity. If my daughter was standing here right now, and she asked you for the truth, what would you tell her?"

Daniel boldly replied, "We didn't steal from Mr. Hildebrand."

Mr. Pots went over to Mr. Hildebrand and petted the horse. "I do believe that man is telling me the truth, Victor."

"You're a fool, Mr. Pots," Mr. Hildebrand said. He approached Benjamin and Daniel aggressively. "I know it was one of these niggers right here."

"What currency are you missing, Mr. Hildebrand?" Mr. Pots asked.

"I'm missing a quarter eagle."

"Then surely they would have one in their pockets if they stole it."

Mr. Hildebrand nodded his head. "That's true, Mr. Pots."

Mr. Pots folded his arms. "If you boys have done nothing wrong, there isn't anything to fear here."

Daniel nodded at Mr. Pots reassuringly while Mr. Hildebrand marched up to Benjamin to begin checking his pockets. Before he did so, Mr. Pots looked at the money sack and noticed a loose thread on it. He moved the sack slightly and noticed a small slit in the money sack, but decided to wait and see if they found anything on Benjamin or Daniel. He watched closely while Mr. Hildebrand checked Benjamin, and he watched Casey approach Daniel. Casey checked one of Daniel's pockets and reached over to check the other pocket with his other hand.

However, there was a slight shine from a coin in Casey's hand from the sun.

Mr. Pots's eyes widened. He marched up to Daniel right as Casey was about to place the coin in Daniel's pocket. Mr. Pots smacked Casey's hand the very moment he reached for Daniel's pocket, and the coin fell on the ground.

"You low-down animal. You were trying to frame these two men for thievery!" Mr. Pots yelled.

Out of anger, Casey pushed Mr. Pots, knocking him down.

"Don't put your hands on me, old man," Casey yelled.

Daniel went up to help Mr. Pots up when Casey kicked him, causing Daniel to fall. Annabelle and Ruthanne returned just in time to see the incident, and they began to run to them, pushing townspeople out of the way. A few of the townspeople paid attention, assuming it was a drunken argument. As Annabelle and Ruthanne raced to stop the incident, Daniel lunged at Casey, startling one of the horses and causing Mr. Hildebrand to take a step back. Daniel began to punch Casey, and Casey hit him back to stand up. The two grappled each other, causing the townspeople to take notice.

Ruthanne made Annabelle slow down and raced down the street, screaming for the men to stop fighting. Casey scooped up dirt, tossing it in Daniel's face, and grabbed the ladle, hitting Daniel with it. Benjamin was about to stop Casey when Mr. Hildebrand pulled his revolver on Benjamin, making him stop. Daniel managed to grab Casey's hand and punched him, causing Casey to fall. Daniel grabbed the ladle and was about to swing when Mr. Hildebrand took aim at Daniel. Mr. Pots used all his strength to push Daniel out of the way when Mr. Hildebrand pulled the trigger, and Mr. Pots was struck by the bullet. Daniel turned to Mr. Pots with wide eyes, seeing that Mr. Pots had risked his life for him.

Annabelle's and Ruthanne's eyes bulged as their jaws dropped, and they ran over to Mr. Pots. Some of the townspeople stopped what they were doing and began to hurry over to the commotion. Mr. Hildebrand took aim at Daniel again, but Benjamin knocked him down with a punch. Benjamin continued to punch Mr. Hildebrand as Casey stood.

"You're nothing but a hateful man!" Benjamin yelled.

Benjamin hit Mr. Hildebrand again, but there was a sound of thunder. Suddenly, Benjamin felt his strength begin to leave his body, and he fell on his side.

Mr. Hildebrand crawled on the ground, trying to regain his composure. Annabelle screamed in agony as she ran over to Benjamin. Mr. Pots lay on the ground, unconscious, while Ruthanne and Daniel tried to wake him up. Annabelle tried to drag Benjamin away from Victor and help him stand, but he began to cough up blood. Annabelle's heart pounded heavily, and she cried as the townspeople watched in awe.

"Annabelle you...you listen to me," Benjamin said. "I'm so happy to have you in my life."

"Benjamin, why are you saying those things?" Annabelle cried.

"Somebody, get the doctor!" Ruthanne yelled.

Mr. Stone rushed out of the saloon and ran over to Benjamin.

"Benjamin, who did this to you, son?" Mr. Stone asked.

Benjamin pointed over to Mr. Hildebrand as he washed off his wounds.

"Mr. Hildebrand! This is inexcusable! You shot this man on what grounds?" Mr. Stone shouted.

Mr. Hildebrand replied, "Those niggers are thieves. They stole from my money sack I left on my horse."

Mr. Stone scowled. "That doesn't sound like either of these men."

"It's true, Mr. Stone. They were sneaky niggers today," Casey said.

"How did Mr. Pots get shot, Victor?" Mr. Stone asked.

Mr. Hildebrand callously answered, "That old fool got in the way because that nigger, Daniel, tried to knock my revolver away when I pulled it on him. It was the old man's fault."

"This is a real mess you two fools have caused here."

Benjamin began to lose consciousness as Annabelle held him.

"Benjamin, is it true? Did you and Daniel steal from Mr. Hildebrand?" Annabelle asked.

Benjamin shook his head.

"I saw what happened," Annabelle said with a furious tone. "For whatever reason, Daniel and Mr. Bones got into a fight, and Daniel was being hit with a ladle. But when Daniel was about to return the beating, Mr. Hildebrand was about to shoot him. Mr. Pots took the bullet instead. Benjamin protected Mr. Pots and Daniel, but Mr. Hildebrand shot him too. You're an evil man, Mr. Hildebrand."

Mr. Hildebrand pushed Mr. Stone out of the way. He was about to grab Annabelle, but he was met with Ruthanne, who placed her revolver at his temple.

"Please give me a good reason to pull the trigger," Ruthanne said.

"Now you think real careful about what you doing, Miss Ruthanne," Mr. Hildebrand said.

"I'm thinking far more clearly than I have in a long time. I suggest you think carefully," Ruthanne snarled.

Fire was in Ruthanne's green eyes, causing Victor to feel like she was staring into his soul. Mr. Hildebrand slowly backed up, realizing Ruthanne would kill him given the chance.

"Ma'am, you need to put down the revolver," a man said.

"I'm defending myself and my friend," Ruthanne said.

The man replied, "That weapon isn't meant for a lady."

The crowd continued to watch the standoff and talk among themselves.

"Sorry, but this is my weapon of choice."

Elizabeth was on her way back home when she saw the crowd. She was anxious to get home and decided to ignore it when, in the corner of her eye, she saw Ruthanne holding her revolver at Mr. Hildebrand's face. Elizabeth panicked and rushed through the crowd to see Mr. Pots and Benjamin severely injured. Tears began to stream down Elizabeth's face.

"Ruthanne, what is going on?" Elizabeth cried.

Ruthanne replied, "Mr. Hildebrand shot them both!"

Elizabeth gasped, "Oh no, is Mr. Pots dead?"

"His breathing is weak, and he won't wake up," Daniel said.

"I have to go get Marilyn," Elizabeth said.

Elizabeth ran off, pushing the townspeople out of the way while she hurried to reach Marilyn. Smiling, Benjamin lifted his hand and caressed Annabelle's face.

"None of this is fair, but God with us," Benjamin said.

Annabelle replied with tears flowing down her cheeks, "I know. Hold on, please! Hold on!"

"Where is the doctor?" Ruthanne shouted.

"Two men left to get Dr. Wilson. They should be back shortly, and a few left to find the sheriff," a man shouted.

"That's good to know," Ruthanne said.

Benjamin stared into Annabelle's brown eyes. "I don't cling to life sufficiently to fear death."

Annabelle began to rock Benjamin as she frowned.

"Never fear quarrels, but seek hazardous adventures," Annabelle said.

Benjamin let out a weak chuckle. "All for one and one for all, united we stand and divided we fall," Benjamin murmured.

Annabelle forcefully smiled, and she kissed Benjamin. "Love is the most selfish of all the passions."

Benjamin smiled again, and Annabelle waited for a response as she rocked him, but only silence was there. Annabelle shook Benjamin, but there was no response. Dr. Wilson pushed through the crowd with his apple-shaped body and medical bag.

"I'm here now. Who are the injured?" Dr. Wilson asked.

"Oh God, no!" Annabelle howled.

Ruthanne pulled Annabelle away to give the doctor room. The doctor tried to revive Benjamin, but Dr. Wilson looked at Annabelle and Ruthanne with his brown eyes and frowned.

"I'm sorry. There is nothing that can be done for this man. I need to tend to Mr. Pots."

Annabelle broke down in tears as her spirit fell apart, and Ruthanne held her.

Mr. Pots regained consciousness while Dr. Wilson worked on him, but he was weak. The doctor explained to Mr. Pots that he had a mortal wound.

Sheriff Shepard arrived at the scene. Ruthanne and Mr. Stone explained the situation to him when Annabelle knelt down next to Benjamin. The sheriff told Mr. Hildebrand and Casey to stay where they were and marched over to Mr. Pots.

"Mr. Pots, time is running short in this undeniably miserable situation," Sheriff Shepard said. "Did these Negroes steal from Mr. Hildebrand, or did these Negroes tell the truth?"

Mr. Pots widened his eyes and breathed with determination. He said with a raspy voice, "Those boys didn't do what that man says."

"Thank you, Mr. Pots. That's what I needed."

Sheriff Shepard returned to Ruthanne and Mr. Stone, looking at a mourning Annabelle.

Marilyn abruptly pushed through the crowd and rushed to her father, Elizabeth behind her. She suddenly noticed Benjamin lying on the ground lifeless, next to a crying Annabelle.

"Oh no, Annabelle!" Marilyn said with wide eyes.

"My sweet little girl, there you are," Mr. Pots said.

Marilyn's face twisted, and tears poured down her cheeks.

"Papa, I don't understand. What happened?"

Mr. Pots held Marilyn's hand. "Those two men over there... you make sure you stay away from evil like them. I'm sorry."

Marilyn shook her head. "No, there is no need to apologize, Papa. Save your strength."

"Ma'am, I'm sorry, but there isn't anything more I can do for him," Dr. Wilson said.

Marilyn's heart wrenched as she held her father's hand, realizing her father was going to die. Daniel watched, powerless, trying to hold back his emotions.

"Please listen, Marilyn, please," Mr. Pots said with a raspy voice. "Daniel defended me. He did. He is a good man."

Marilyn's voice was filled with sorrow. "I know he is. I kept telling you."

Mr. Pots let out a weak chuckle. "I need to whisper something in your ear."

Marilyn leaned her ear to her father's head.

"I know God has done something in my heart," he said. "Even though I didn't get to live long in it, I'm grateful. You asked me could I love your children if they were half white, and my answer is yes. But if that's the plan God has for you, please be careful, my sweetheart."

"Oh, Daddy." Marilyn wept, becoming overwhelmed with both joy and sadness. She kissed her father on his forehead. She held him, and he placed his other hand on top of hers.

Mr. Pots groaned. "Daniel, I appreciate your integrity. Stay that way. No matter how bad things get, don't turn to evil. Do things the right way in God's sight."

"I will try my best, Mr. Pots," Daniel said.

Mr. Pots grinned. "I know you will. Ruthanne, Elizabeth, I enjoyed you both. I know both of you have bright futures ahead of you."

Ruthanne nodded, and Elizabeth began to cry.

"Sasha, I'm sorry what happened to Benjamin, and I'm sorry for how I treated you. You're a good woman."

Annabelle's tears continued to gush down her face while she looked at Mr. Pots. "Thank you, Mr. Pots, you raised an amazing woman," Annabelle said.

Mr. Pots looked back up at Marilyn and beamed. "My sweet angel, how much you've grown. I truly was a blessed man," Mr. Pots murmured.

Mr. Pots gazed into his daughter's emerald green eyes one last time with a smile.

"Papa! Papa! Daddy, don't leave me!" Marilyn wailed.

Marilyn bawled while she held her lifeless father. Dr. Wilson had men help him take Benjamin's and Mr. Pots's bodies to his office to be cleaned up.

"That was a tough old bird," Mr. Hildebrand said.

With an outburst of rage, Annabelle stood up and punched Mr. Hildebrand. Casey began to approach Annabelle when Ruthanne pulled her revolver out again.

"That's enough!" Sheriff Shepard yelled.

As the others turned their attention to the sheriff, Mr. Hildebrand advanced and kicked Annabelle in her stomach. It was such a blinding pain that she howled and collapsed to the ground.

"What have you done! She's pregnant!" Ruthanne shouted.

"The nerve of that nigger even touching me is beneath me," Mr. Hildebrand said.

Ruthanne punched Mr. Hildebrand with her full strength, knocking him to the ground, unconscious.

"Oh no, something is wrong. Where is Dr. Wilson?" Annabelle asked as she held her stomach.

"He's gone already. Is something wrong with the baby?" Elizabeth asked.

Annabelle continued to hold her stomach when she tried to stand.

"We're taking her to Catherine, Sheriff Shepard," Ruthanne said. "Which horse is Hildebrand's, Casey?"

Casey reluctantly answered, "The black horse is his."

"Mr. Stone, is there a wagon we can use?"

"I have one. The wagon should still have a horse. They just brought in supplies," Mr. Stone said.

Daniel and Ruthanne sprinted to the back of the salon. They got on the one-horse wagon. Daniel grabbed the reins, and once he brought the wagon to the front of the saloon, they helped Annabelle onto the wagon. They rode it over to Catherine's, and Annabelle's pain continued to get worse.

Meanwhile, Marilyn approached the sheriff calmly, wiping tears from her face.

"I will be pressing full charges against both of these thugs, especially the one that has his face in the dirt where it belongs," Marilyn said.

"Everything will be processed through the courts, Miss Marilyn. Only then can charges be known," Sheriff Shepard said. "I'm very sorry for your loss."

"I will be looking to hear from you soon, Sheriff."

Marilyn and Elizabeth hurried to Catherine's home, hoping Annabelle's condition had improved.

Annabelle's pain greatly increased, and Catherine realized the blow had possibly caused Annabelle to go into early labor. Ruthanne aided Catherine while they tried to prepare for Annabelle to give birth. During this time, Elizabeth ran to the Keyses' home and informed them of what had happened. Marilyn and Daniel waited outside Catherine's home.

The Keys family quickly rushed over to Catherine's home to comfort Annabelle. Allen had decided to go to the sheriff's office to find out how long it would take before the case would be heard.

Four hours passed, and Annabelle went into labor. Another two hours went by as Annabelle kept pushing, and Catherine delivered the baby. She was relieved once the baby had been delivered, but she noticed a heartbroken expression on Catherine's round face.

Catherine stared at Annabelle with a frown and said, "Annabelle, she doesn't have much time."

"What do you mean? Give me my baby!" Annabelle yelled.

Catherine continued to clean her and then handed Annabelle her daughter. Annabelle noticed her daughter's labored breathing.

Elizabeth left the room feeling completely helpless, and she broke down in tears. Annabelle calmly rocked her struggling daughter as she stared at her. Catherine, Marilyn, Rebecca, and Ruthanne watched Annabelle, speechless with tears in their eyes.

"Isn't she beautiful? Such an adorable little girl. My beautiful baby girl." Annabelle continued to rock her daughter, staring into her daughter's brown eyes when a tear fell down her face.

Rebecca came up to the bed and wiped the tear away. "She is something else," Rebecca said.

Annabelle grinned at Rebecca and began to weep. Marilyn's heart broke again while she sobbed. She approached Annabelle, giving her a kiss on the forehead, and exited the room as she began to hyperventilate.

Marilyn went onto the front porch where Daniel was standing. Daniel stared at Marilyn and walked up to her. Abruptly, Marilyn embraced Daniel and began to cry again.

"She's going to lose the baby. Oh God, she's going to lose the baby," Marilyn bawled.

Daniel began to cry as he held Marilyn tightly. During this time, Ruthanne sat down on the bed next to Annabelle, who hummed to her daughter. Ruthanne placed her hand on the baby's smooth head.

"Look at her. She's at peace, Annabelle," Ruthanne said.

"She is peaceful, isn't she?" Annabelle said as tears fell from her face.

"Did you and Benjamin already start to think of names?"

Annabelle looked at Ruthanne with her bloodshot eyes. "No, he wanted to wait. I'm not sure what to name her."

Ruthanne saw the question increased Annabelle's misery, and she thought deeply. "How about these two names: Pacífica and Benita?"

"That sounds beautiful. Do they mean something?"

"Pacífica means 'peaceful' in Spanish, and I thought of Benita in honor of Benjamin."

Annabelle nodded with approval as she cradled her fragile daughter.

"My little Benita, I wish you could've at least seen your father."

Benita opened her brown eyes while Annabelle tried to keep her composure. Catherine stood up and went over to a small desk and picked up a Bible. Catherine sat back down, held Annabelle's hand, and read.

"Peace I leave with you, my peace I give unto you: not as the world giveth, give I unto you. Let not your heart be troubled, neither let it be afraid. John 14:27."

Annabelle smiled at Catherine as she felt more comforted in her spirit. By sunset, Annabelle had lost her husband and daughter. She spent the night in Catherine's home.

Elizabeth, Rebecca, and Ruthanne returned home, heavily troubled by the trauma. The friends comforted Marilyn, and Daniel later escorted her home. Marilyn and Daniel arrived at the store, and the moment she unlocked the door, she felt a lifeless atmosphere that was new to her.

Marilyn turned around to Daniel, staring into his hazel eyes. "Are you alright?" Marilyn asked.

Daniel replied, "I'll be fine. I was more worried about you because you lost your daddy today."

"I did. You also lost your best friend today." Daniel turned his head away when Marilyn gently put her hands on his face. "Don't hide from me. Please don't hide."

A tear went down Daniel's face, and Marilyn wiped it away. "I feel that some of this is my fault. If I hadn't come to your store so much, your daddy wouldn't have come to talk with me and—"

"Stop it!" Marilyn boldly said. "My papa left the store to learn more about you. You did nothing wrong. If anything, you showed my papa the good man you really are. Never call me Miss Marilyn again."

Marilyn slowly stepped forward and kissed Daniel. Daniel gazed into Marilyn's emerald green eyes and kissed her back, leading to their emotions breaking free. Tears of desire began to go down Marilyn's face. Daniel closed the store's door behind them while they slowly went inside, where Marilyn led them to her room.

The two made love with each other as they held hands and caressed each other. Marilyn had given herself to a man for the first time as mixed emotions of love, pain, and lust dominated her and Daniel's minds. In Daniel's arms, Marilyn felt secure that night, but while he slept with her head on his chest, she thought, *I'm sorry I didn't do things your way. God, please forgive me. I'm in so much pain, and I know he loves me.*

The next day, the two of them agreed not to speak of their moment to anyone. The others coped with the tragedy in other ways. Rebecca struggled to sleep. Allen stroked her head to help her relax. Ruthanne spent the night calming down a distraught Elizabeth when all her emotions came out throughout the night, leaving Ruthanne no time to cope.

The next day, the news of the tragedy shot through the town. When Peter learned of the news, he immediately went over to the Keyses' home to find Annabelle.

Ruthanne explained the entire story to him. They went over to Catherine's house, and he spent time with Annabelle, praying for her. After spending hours with Annabelle, Peter went to Pots's Garments and comforted a distraught Marilyn. Peter later went to the prison to confront Mr. Hildebrand and pray for him and Casey. Mr. Boston visited Annabelle. He brought Mr. Fluffs with him to bring Annabelle comfort.

Two weeks passed. During this time, the others continued to help support Annabelle and Marilyn through their loss. A funeral was held for Benjamin and Benita in the Keyses' home. Annabelle, in a black dress, was comforted by her friends when she saw Benjamin's lifeless body. It had been placed in a wooden coffin, and he was dressed in one of the few outfits he had. A tear hit his coffin as Annabelle stared at his lifeless body. She slowly reached to touch Benjamin's lifeless shoulder but pulled her hand back. She deeply exhaled as tears covered her face.

Annabelle turned to Benita's wooden coffin, which had a few flowers placed around the baby. However, seeing Benita in her small coffin and red checkered dress caused Annabelle to hyperventilate. Quivering, she was unable to form words and began to wail uncontrollably. The young women immediately escorted her upstairs to mourn and consoled her. She was too heartbroken to attend their burials, overseen by Peter.

Mr. Pots's funeral was held at Pots's Garments the next day. Annabelle went with Ruthanne to give her condolences to

Marilyn before others were let inside. Mr. Pots's funeral was massive, with many paying respects to Marilyn and her sisters. Marilyn stared at her father's lifeless well-dressed body. She clutched his golden pocket watch, holding a handkerchief in her hand as tears glistened on her face. Many attended his burial, overseen by Peter.

During this time, Ruben, Frank, and Billy returned to visit. Ruthanne and Elizabeth told them of the incident. Frank and Billy reacted with sympathy, but Ruben expressed little concern, which bothered Ruthanne. Rebecca offered to have a special dinner for them since it was their first day back. The men appreciated the offer and accepted it. Later in the day, Allen arrived home.

"Good to see you, Allen," Frank said.

Allen replied, "Welcome, gentlemen. It is good to see you three again."

"They are staying for dinner, Allen," Rebecca said.

"Yes, dear. I'm sure you will have something special in mind," Allen said with a grin. "It's certainly been quite a week."

Rebecca noticed the slight frown on Allen's face.

"What is it that you wanted to say?"

Allen looked at Rebecca with a blank stare. "The courts have released the charges on Mr. Hildebrand and Mr. Bones. Mr. Hildebrand is being charged with the accidental death of Mr. Pots, but not Benjamin's murder. They're calling it self-defense. The judge will also not accept any charges involving Annabelle losing the baby because there was no way of telling if the baby was healthy in the first place."

A wave of nausea hit Rebecca, and she dropped a plate she was holding.

Ruthanne felt tightness in her gut while she clenched her teeth, and Elizabeth stood up, squeezing her hands into fists.

"There has to be something we can do to have the charges changed for Benjamin!" Elizabeth yelled.

"There's nothing that can be done with these charges," Allen said. "They're not going to charge him in the death of a Negro.

It's illegal for a Negro man to forcibly hold down a white man, and his lawyer used this law to aid in no charge being given."

"Makes sense. We would have done the same in Mississippi," Billy said.

"Yeah, I've never seen any Negro win a court case. I suggest y'all stay low for a while," Frank said.

Elizabeth stormed out of the house, grunting once she heard her brothers' comments. Allen sat down in his chair as Ashley greeted her father and sat in his lap. Ruthanne was upset, but she was still bothered by her brother's reaction. Ruthanne could see the sympathy in his face. Elizabeth left to invite Marilyn to dinner to make sure she wasn't alone. Marilyn agreed to come to dinner, but she wanted Daniel to join them. Elizabeth reluctantly agreed because she dreaded her brothers' reaction to Daniel.

The dinner was grand, with Rebecca and Ruthanne cooking a feast of roast chicken, rolls, green beans, corn, and an apple pie. Daniel sat at the edge of the table next to Marilyn, with Ruthanne facing him. The conversations were serious, and Daniel said little. Allen, Ruben, and Ruthanne were the main topic drivers. Unfortunately, Billy constantly stared at Daniel, expressing his animosity.

"It's Daniel, right? That's your name?" Billy asked as he put down his fork.

Daniel replied, "Yes, sir, that's my name."

Elizabeth stopped eating and stared at her brother.

"How are you so free that you can eat at this table with us?"

Her blue eyes furious, Elizabeth shouted, "Did you really just ask him that question!"

Billy replied, "He is a grown man. He can answer the question."

Daniel boldly replied, "If you must know my background, sir, I was born free. My mother was a mulatto, and I am too."

"So, your granddaddy was white?"

"No, sir. My grandma was white, and she was a wonderful woman."

"Not if she was a nigger lover."

Elizabeth reached across the table and slapped her brother, causing everyone's eyes to widen.

"I guess that puts an end to that," Frank said.

"You surprise me. Being Elizabeth's brother, your rudeness is sickening," Marilyn said.

Billy replied, "No, I think what is sickening is you sitting next to that mulatto mutt."

Marilyn put down her utensils and stared Billy down. "He is a good man. Ten times what you could ever be," Marilyn snarled.

The others looked at Marilyn, speechless.

"Billy, if you have such problem with Daniel, you're free to eat outside," Allen said.

"Well now, I believe that really ends this talk," Frank said. "Allen, after this, I believe I will be ready for another game of poker."

Allen chuckled while he continued to eat his food. "I think that sounds like a good idea, Frank. September seems to bring out the best and worst."

The light exchange was enough to ease in other discussions, but Elizabeth continued to sneer while keeping her gaze on Billy. Ruthanne remained bothered by her brother's unusual nature, so she politely left early and went upstairs. Marilyn and Daniel soon left their friends, but they left separately so they wouldn't attract any more negative attention. The night continued as the men played poker, and Elizabeth, still angered by her brother, went upstairs.

The next day, Elizabeth strolled around town with her brothers as Ruthanne and Ruben stayed back. Ruthanne, wearing a green and blue dress, sat on the couch next to Ruben.

"I know there is more than this being a simple visit," Ruthanne said.

"What are you talking about?" Ruben asked.

"Ruben, don't take me to be a fool. The moment we told you about the incident, I saw it in your face. Sympathy. When have you ever shown that for any Negro? It was like all of a sudden, you had such a strong change of heart."

Ruben scoffed. "I don't know what you're talking about."

Ruthanne's nose crinkled, and she marched over to Ruben's trunk and began to open it. Ruben rushed over to Ruthanne and grabbed her as she continued to try to force her way. Ruben tried to hold his sister down, but with one hand, she grabbed a handful of his clothes and tossed them at him. She grabbed more of his clothes and tossed them on the floor. When she looked down in the chest, she saw a piece of paper. She reached for the piece of paper, but before she could turn it over, Ruben forced her to the floor as he hugged her.

Ruthanne struggled to break free of his hold.

"You don't want to read that," Ruben said.

"Let me go! I said let me go!" Ruthanne shouted.

Ruben grunted. "Stop fighting me. You won't understand."

"What are you hiding from me?"

Ruthanne continued to struggle with her brother as she elbowed him in his side, causing him to let go. She reached for the paper again and grabbed it, but the moment she attempted to turn it over, Ruben grabbed her again. Ruben tried to hold her down, causing his silver pocket watch to fall out of his vest and shatter. Ruthanne lost her grip on the paper, and it drifted in the air and landed on the ground. She stared at the paper as her jaw dropped, and she saw the top of the paper read "Reward."

Ruthanne began to cry while Ruben held her.

"How could you? How could you put so much effort into being so cruel?"

Ruben released Ruthanne, allowing her to read the reward letter for Annabelle. Ruthanne let go of the wanted poster.

"How did you figure it out?"

"As you read the description of her, it was very specific, but I guess if you're looking for someone to blame, that would be Mr. Keys. He first made a statement about Jefferson City, and I thought he confused our home with Annabelle's. But then he made the same mistake again, and Annabelle's wanted poster is all over Mississippi. They want her back bad. Frank and Billy are in on the plan too."

Ruthanne looked at Ruben with tear-filled eyes.

"So...what? You were going to kidnap her while we were asleep or something?"

Ruben sighed. "It isn't kidnapping. She is someone's property."

"You have no idea how hard she fought to make it this far for freedom. The things that have been done to her on that plantation... I won't let you take her back. I saw it in your face. It bothered you. How can you still even consider putting chains back on her after all of this?"

"It is the law—our way of life," Ruben said with a stern voice.

Ruthanne replied with a sharp tone, "It is no longer my way of life."

Ruben crossed his arms. "You spit on our family, your own blood, for one woman?"

"I don't spit on our family. I love you and everyone else. It breaks my heart how we treat these people now. God has opened my eyes to the evil."

Ruben shook his head and walked out, but Ruthanne immediately went after her brother.

"Where are you going, Ruben?" Ruthanne yelled.

"I'm going for a walk. No need to worry about your Negro for now, sister."

"You disappointment me, brother. I always saw you as a better man than this."

Ruben began walking away, but he turned his head.

"You have one day to get her out of town."

Ruben continued to walk away, and Ruthanne gripped the stairway railing, balling her other hand into a fist. She promptly marched downstairs and informed Rebecca of the situation. Rebecca and Ruthanne talked about the seriousness of the situation and concluded it would take three days to get Annabelle to Illinois. She hadn't been taught how to ride a horse properly, and Ruthanne's horse, Marley, was only familiar with her owner. Rebecca suggested that maybe hiding Annabelle with Peter would be a temporary solution. Ruthanne disagreed, realizing she had shown Ruben the church. Mr. Boston seemed like the only logical place where they could hide Annabelle.

Rebecca and Ruthanne left the children with Catherine, then rushed over to Mr. Boston's store, where they explained Annabelle's origin to Mr. Boston. Mr. Boston was shocked but understood the urgency of the situation, and he agreed to hide Annabelle until they could get her out of the state. Rebecca and Ruthanne planned to bring Annabelle to Mr. Boston that night. As the women left the store, they noticed that the Indians had returned to town. Rebecca and Ruthanne greeted John and told him of the tragedy, but they didn't tell John about getting Annabelle out of Missouri. John was greatly saddened by the news and gave his condolences.

Rebecca and Ruthanne rushed back to Catherine's home. During this time, Casey Bones had returned to the jail to visit Mr. Hildebrand.

"I haven't seen the nigger at all, Mr. Hildebrand," Casey said. "She been very quiet, but I have seen Miss Pots doing her normal things."

Mr. Hildebrand replied, "I know who can find her and have her taken care of."

"Who can do that?" Casey asked.

"Get a hold of Mad Moe and his thugs. It won't be hard to find them. Check every saloon and ask every whore. Mad Moe and those fools won't be hard to find, and regarding payment, there is thirty dollars in the money sack, hidden in the cupboard behind the front desk of my store. Mrs. Hildebrand knows where it is. I won't be able to get out of here to see that nigger die, but the news of it will be glorious."

Casey nodded. "I will get it done."

Meanwhile, the news of Annabelle's identity being revealed filled Rebecca with fear. Rebecca spoke with Catherine, knowing Catherine was still unstable on her stance with slavery.

However, Annabelle's tragedy had softened Catherine's heart, and Catherine agreed to tell the men that she didn't know of Annabelle's whereabouts if they were to come to her home. Rebecca and Ruthanne decided not to tell Elizabeth, believing that she wouldn't be able to contain her emotions.

That night, Elizabeth and Ruthanne cooked for their brothers. Ruthanne attempted her best to be herself as Ruben watched. During their dinner, Rebecca rushed to get the children to bed earlier. Rebecca told Allen the entire truth of the situation, and he became furious.

However, Rebecca calmed him down and explained to him that Ruthanne believed it would be best to pretend that only she and Elizabeth knew the whole truth about Annabelle. Allen was greatly bothered by them making the decision without him, but he understood the decision was to keep his family safe. Allen agreed to play dumb, but he decided that he would be the one to take Annabelle to Mr. Boston's store. Ruthanne was trying to maintain the peace, so she didn't run the risk of angering the men. During the dinner, she told everyone she wanted to look at the stars for a moment.

Ruthanne went outside, waiting for Rebecca.

"Ruthanne," Allen said.

Ruthanne looked down and saw Allen, so she went downstairs.

"I know everything, and I must say I'm impressed with how well you hid Annabelle. I will gladly help get Annabelle out of the state, but please, no more serious secrets. I'm the head of my family, and it is my right to know," Allen said with a somewhat stern look.

Ruthanne calmly replied, "Thank you, Mr. Keys. I know this is a lot to take in a short amount of time."

"It is a lot, but I believe this is how God really tests our character. I will walk with you to Catherine's quickly, and I will take Annabelle to Mr. Boston. I think it's best that you're not out here for so long. Your brother may become suspicious."

"I agree."

Allen and Ruthanne rushed over to Catherine's home.

They greeted Catherine, and Catherine gave Annabelle one of her blue plaid dresses, hoping it demonstrated her sympathy and would help comfort Annabelle in some way. Ruthanne reassured Annabelle she'd be safe while she held her hands. Allen took Annabelle to Mr. Boston as Ruthanne hurried back to the Keyses' home. Ruthanne arrived and had begun to ascend the stairs when Ruben opened the front door.

"You had me worried, Ruthanne," Ruben said.

"I told you that I was watching the stars. Don't you trust me, Ruben?" Ruthanne said.

"It's not a matter of trust. I think you're too smart for your own good sometimes."

Ruthanne scoffed. "I think you need to learn how to gain more sympathy."

"I'm being very sympathetic. I'm letting you make a plan. You may disagree with the laws, but that doesn't make what you're doing right."

"What if the laws we make don't follow God's ways?"

"We will always make mistakes, but there will always be a dominant race. It will never be fair between the Negroes and us—or the Indians, for that matter—so why even fight for them?"

Ruthanne tightened her hand into a fist. "We are all God's children, but we've made the mistake in creating a division that was never meant to exist." Ruthanne moved past her brother, closing the door behind her.

In the meantime, Allen and Annabelle continued to Mr. Boston's store. When they arrived, Allen gave Annabelle a hug when Mr. Boston opened his door.

"I wish we could've done more for you, Annabelle," Allen said.

"I think you're doing a lot for me right now," Annabelle said, her eyes tearful.

"It's the least I can do to honor Benjamin. He was my friend."

A tear went down Annabelle's face. "Thank you."

"Mr. Boston, I'm leaving her with you."

"I'll make sure Annabelle is taken care of," Mr. Boston said.

"I know. Have a good night, Annabelle; Mr. Boston."

"Good night, Allen."

"Good night, Mr. Keys," Annabelle said.

Allen left while Annabelle entered Mr. Boston's store.

The next day arrived, and Ruthanne started the day as if it were normal. Ruthanne went to work at Mr. Boston's store, but she was concerned her brother would follow her. She took different streets than she normally would and kept looking back. Ruthanne anxiously arrived at Mr. Boston's store and began to work her normal shift.

Later that day, Sierra Nicole entered the store. "Good morning, Mr. Boston," she said.

"Good morning, Miss Sierra Nicole," Mr. Boston said.

"I was wondering if Sasha had begun to work here again?"

Mr. Boston's eyebrows shot up when he heard her question. "Why, no. She is still in mourning."

"What a shame. That's why I'm here."

Ruthanne approached the other woman.

"Hello, Ruthanne."

"Hello, Sierra Nicole," Ruthanne replied.

Sierra Nicole pulled out a card and handed it to Ruthanne. "The card is for Sasha. I cannot imagine the pain she is in." Sierra Nicole's eyes became watery as she put her hand over her mouth, and she sighed. "Not only did she lose her husband, but she also lost her child in the same day. No woman should ever experience that. Will you please make sure that she receives that card?"

Ruthanne smiled. "I will."

"Thank you, Ruthanne. Mr. Boston, it is always a pleasure."

Sierra Nicole left the store. Ruthanne returned to the chicken coops, lifted the cellar door in the coop, and handed

Annabelle the card. Staring at the card, Annabelle was touched by Sierra Nicole's kindness.

Ruthanne left the supply store early to go to Marilyn's store and tell her about Annabelle. She arrived at Pots' Garments and spoke with Marilyn, who was shaken by the news and vowed not to tell Elizabeth, agreeing that she wouldn't be able to handle the truth.

Ruthanne returned home, seeing her brother resting on the hammock.

"Time is almost up. Tomorrow morning, we are leaving with her," Ruben said.

"You sicken me," Ruthanne said, her tone harsh.

Ruben tilted his head, and he briefly lifted his eyebrows. "You can change all of this by giving her to me now."

Ruthanne growled, "How dare you make someone's life a game."

"No, you're making this a game by making whatever plan you're making. I think the wiser thing is to leave her at that midwife's home so you don't waste my time."

Ruthanne scowled. "You're willing to ruin that woman's life again for money. I think you want this to be a game. Does this make you feel like a man, brother?"

Ruben stood up and approached Ruthanne. "We will see who outsmarts who by the next morning."

Ruben pointed behind Ruthanne, prompting her to turn around. She saw that the one of the traces on her carriage was cut, and the carriage axial was cracked, showing Ruben had sabotaged her carriage.

Ruthanne stomped her foot and stormed upstairs with her hands balled into fists. Ruben followed right behind her.

"Ruthanne, Elizabeth doesn't know, does she?"

Ruthanne turned her head and stared at Ruben. "No, she doesn't know."

Ruben smirked. "You're playing the game well."

Ruthanne angrily slammed the door as her brother chuckled.

Ruben left, strolling through the town and arriving at the sheriff's office. Ruben alerted Sheriff Shepard about Annabelle's status, but he negotiated with Sheriff Shepard. Ruben wanted to break Ruthanne's pride, and he felt that would be enough to keep her in line. An angry Sheriff Shepard agreed, believing that Ruthanne and Elizabeth were the only ones who knew Annabelle's origins. Ruben was returning to the Keys' home when he saw Elizabeth and decided to follow her.

Elizabeth greeted other townspeople as she moved through the town. As she greeted one woman, she noticed Ruben watching her and waved at him anxiously.

Ruben approached Elizabeth and greeted her.

"What are you doing, Ruben?" Elizabeth asked.

Ruben replied, "I was exploring a little more of the town. Ruthanne seemed tired. Where are you going?"

"I was about to go to Mr. Boston's store and then to Marilyn's. I know Ruthanne didn't remember the flour. She almost never remembers to bring it home with her."

"Did she tell you she was going for supplies earlier today?" Ruben asked, his voice calm.

"No, silly. She was in such a rush this morning, we didn't even have a real conversation at breakfast. Ruthanne works for Mr. Boston. That's where she's been getting money. The supply store is right over there. Mr. Boston is a kind old man," Elizabeth said, pointing at the store.

Ruben smirked. "I bet he is. Well, I will let you continue. I will see you at supper."

"That sounds good." Elizabeth saw Mr. Boston walk out of his store with a broom, "Oh, and there he is, sweeping up."

Ruben tilted his top hat. "I best go now."

"Okay, Ruben."

Elizabeth strolled over to Mr. Boston. "Good evening, Mr. Boston," she said.

"Good evening, Elizabeth," Mr. Boston said. "Who was that man you were talking to?"

"Why, that was Ruben, Ruthanne's older brother."

Mr. Boston felt fear run through his body as he realized that Annabelle might be in danger. "What did he want with you?"

"Nothing out of the normal. I didn't realize Ruthanne didn't tell him she was working for you. She probably felt it unnecessary, so no worries."

Elizabeth entered the store, got her supplies, and headed for Marilyn's.

Mr. Boston felt in his spirit that danger was coming, and he felt compelled to pray for guidance. He went into deep prayer, asking for wisdom. He felt a presence of peace that didn't come from him and heard a whisper.

"John," a calm voice said. "Give her to John. Trust in God's plan, and give her to John." Mr. Boston realized it was the Holy Spirit. He was shaken by the experience, but he knew he needed to search for the Indians.

Several hours later, Mr. Boston was about to leave his store. When he opened his door, John and Samuel stood there. Mr. Boston's mouth unhinged, and he dropped his black cane. Becoming winded, he fell back, but Samuel caught him.

"Thank you, Samuel. I'm sorry, I don't mean to worry you. I'm okay. Just surprised. Y'all's timing right now confirms what I needed to know."

"What do you mean, Mr. Boston?" John said with a raised eyebrow.

Mr. Boston replied, "Time is short, but I must ask this of you. It's no coincidence that you boys are here now."

"Please explain, Mr. Boston," Samuel said.

Mr. Boston sat the men down and explained Annabelle's situation to them. He further explained what he believed God wanted him to do. Samuel was reluctant to take Annabelle with them. John, on the other hand, felt connected to Annabelle, and he felt a duty to help her remain free. Samuel was scared of being chased by the sheriff, and he tried to make John realize the danger that taking Annabelle would put them in. John continued to talk with Samuel and convinced him that they could take her to Indian Territory with them.

"John, I trust Annabelle. She has always shown us kindness. Just remember, this was your idea," Samuel said.

John replied, "We can do this easily without getting caught. If it is true, these men will be looking for Annabelle. They will track everyone she knows to find her. They don't know us, and that gives us a lot of time to take her away from here."

Samuel nodded in agreement.

"I'm glad you men believed me. I had no idea how else I could explain it," Mr. Boston said.

"Our Creator has many ways to talk to us, and I agree that our timing is no mistake," John said.

Mr. Boston inhaled as he smiled. "Thank you, John, and thank you, Samuel. When did you want to take her?"

"We need to take her tonight. If Ruthanne's brother is as smart as you say, he may not wait until tomorrow morning. This will be hard for her. She won't be able to say goodbye to the others."

Samuel replied, "Maybe in a few months, they can come to the Cherokee territory to search for us. We will also keep returning for supplies, so when we return next, we can take any letter they want her to have."

"I think that will work," John said. "We will be back when the sun has gone down, and she must be ready to go immediately."

"I understand, John, and thank you," Mr. Boston said.

The men got into their carriage and rode off. Mr. Boston locked his doors and went to open his cellar in the chicken coop. He explained the change in the plan to Annabelle while they ate. She was reluctant but understood the rush.

Night came, and Ruthanne reluctantly ate dinner with Ruben, knowing she wouldn't be able to leave their dinner without suspicion. She said nothing at the dinner table while everyone else acted normally.

During this time, John and Samuel arrived at Mr. Boston's store. Mr. Boston unlocked the door and let them in.

"Annabelle, it is time for us to go," John said.

"I'm ready, but there is one thing I need to get from my home," Annabelle said. "It is a book that means a lot to me. Please let me get it."

"Okay, but we must leave now."

Annabelle gave Mr. Boston a tight hug and nervously got into the carriage. John signaled the two horses and drove the carriage away as Mr. Boston watched with a frown.

Annabelle, John, and Samuel arrived at her home. Her eyes started to become watery as she arrived, reminded of everything Benjamin had given her. Annabelle entered her home and walked toward the bedroom with the moonlight guiding her. She saw Benjamin's book on the bed and picked it up, holding it to her chest as she fought back tears.

Annabelle was about to leave when she saw her Bible on her desk and grabbed it, but while she walked toward the door, she felt a shiver down her spine. She turned to her right and was struck, causing her to fall to the ground as both books slid toward the front door. A lamp was lit, and although stunned from the blow, Annabelle's eyes widened as she saw Mad Moe.

"I've been waiting for you," Mad Moe said. "I knew your feelings would betray you since you lost your husband and all. I was hoping I would make you one of my puppets, but someone wants you dead bad. Don't worry, girl, I won't touch you. It makes this job easier."

"It was Mr. Hildebrand, wasn't it?" Annabelle asked as a tear dropped from her eye.

"Smart woman, but no. It was Casey Bones that gave me the money. Mr. Hildebrand will be in the jail for a while because of Mr. Pots's death, but he wants you dead. I tell you what. I'll make your death quick. This isn't personal."

"I'll do anything you want. Please, I'm leaving town now."

"Now, I told you I can't do nothing physical now, as tempting as it is. I don't need the—oh, what's that word?—attachment.

And to let you go will cause people to question me. If you had the ability to pay me more, I could consider changing my mind, but we both know you don't have fifty dollars on you. Maybe I'll come across another nice Negro girl. Well, at least I'll still have the redhead."

Mad Moe approached Annabelle while he adjusted his red cravat and reached for her, but she quickly kicked his ankle, causing him to fall back and knock the lamp over. A fire began as the cloth on the wooden table caught fire. Annabelle scrambled to grab the two books, and she ran for the doorway, but Mad Moe grabbed her shoulder.

Mad Moe slammed her against the wall as she screamed.

"I was going to make it a quick death, but you had to mess up my leg! You dumb nigger! Now there has been a change in plans."

Mad Moe pulled out a knife, and Annabelle screamed. Samuel ran into the house, abruptly catching Mad Moe off guard, and punched Mad Moe, knocking him down. Samuel pulled Annabelle out of the house.

Mad Moe shouted as the fire grew stronger, "What the hell is going on?" Mad Moe stumbled out of the house with his revolver drawn.

Mad Moe took aim at Annabelle while she tried to enter the carriage, but Samuel pulled her down as the gun fired. John fired a shot back at Mad Moe, who took cover in the house's doorway. Samuel had Annabelle crawl under the carriage to take cover. Mad Moe took another shot but missed, and Samuel returned fire as the horses neighed. The fire and smoke grew, forcing Mad Moe to rush out of the door, taking another shot at John. John returned fire with his rifle, hitting Mad Moe in the shoulder. Mad Moe screamed in agony, dropping his revolver, and began holding his shoulder as he rolled on the ground.

Annabelle crawled from underneath the carriage and squatted on the other side of it. She noticed a glowing figure, and she believed it was Constance.

John grabbed Annabelle's hand and coaxed her into the

carriage. He looked at Annabelle and said, "No one will ever hurt you like that again."

She sat down in the carriage holding the two books as Mad Moe continued to moan in pain.

Mad Moe's thugs suddenly showed up and helped carry Mad Moe away as Samuel kept aim at them with his rifle. The Negroes began to turn on their lamps while John and Samuel got into the driver's seat and rushed the carriage toward the edge of town.

When the carriage rode past the houses, Annabelle saw people were being awakened. Lamps turned on as they passed. It weighed heavy on her heart that she didn't get a chance to say goodbye to her friends.

John and Samuel looked at each other, smiling as the pounding of heavy horse hooves awakened the people.

CHAPTER 20
Uncertainty

THE NEXT DAY, RUTHANNE AWAKENED in a panic when she heard nothing but silence in her home. She quickly put on her clothes and rushed downstairs, then ran to Catherine's house, asking Catherine if Ruben had come to the house. Catherine told Ruthanne no, but she assured her that she would keep her word. Ruthanne began to march toward the church, hoping to run into her brother, but she felt someone touch her shoulder. She turned around in a panic, her green eyes wide.

"Daniel, it's you," Ruthanne said.

"I'm sorry I scared you, Miss Ruthanne, but something bad has happened," Daniel said.

Ruthanne's arched eyebrows lowered. "What has happened, Daniel?"

"Annabelle's home caught on fire last night, and some of the other Negroes are sure they heard gunfire."

Ruthanne huffed. "Daniel, I promise you that Annabelle was not there. She is safe. That's the most I can tell you right now."

"Okay, I trust you."

Ruthanne placed her hand on Daniel's face convincingly and walked away, but she quickly turned back around. "Who told you her name was Annabelle?"

Daniel paused as his eyes shifted from Ruthanne, and he slightly gulped.

Ruthanne's eyes narrowed. "Marilyn... Okay, but you keep that to yourself, Daniel."

Ruthanne marched off and reached the church. Ruthanne asked Peter if he had seen her brother. Peter told Ruthanne that he and Elizabeth's brothers had been by, but they left shortly afterward.

Ruthanne rushed back home, but she didn't see them in the area. Elizabeth was going downstairs when she noticed Ruthanne's face.

"What's wrong, Ruthanne? You don't seem like yourself," Elizabeth said with a worrisome tone.

Ruthanne replied, "I was looking for my brother. I can't figure out where else he would go."

"Maybe he is viewing the other parts of town. I saw him yesterday as I was going to Mr. Boston to get supplies. I thought it was weird, but he seemed like himself, and I was surprised you didn't tell him you worked there."

Ruthanne's heart dropped. She gasped and took off running.

Elizabeth's eyes widened as she shouted, "Ruthanne, what are you not telling me?"

Ruthanne pushed townspeople out of the way with her heart racing. Tears flowed down her face. She came in view of the supply store and saw Ruben and Elizabeth's brothers standing outside the entrance. Ruben saw his sister and began to approach her arrogantly, adjusting his brown frock coat and black top hat.

"Ruthanne, you truly are clever. Maybe, just maybe, it would have played to your advantage if you would have also told Elizabeth," Ruben said.

Ruthanne replied, "I don't know what you're talking about."

Ruben chuckled, and he entered the store. "One of these days, you will learn, baby sister."

Ruthanne snarled, "Leave Mr. Boston alone. He has nothing to do with this."

"Your plan has failed you, and I suggest you know your place. The sheriff now knows you've been sheltering a slave."

Ruthanne followed her brother with her hands clenched into fists. The men entered Mr. Boston's store while Ruthanne took a deep breath.

She stood in the doorway, and they went through the supply store. Ruben entered the chicken coop and saw nothing, but he noticed a handle covered by hay. Ruben pulled up the cellar door, and as Ruthanne heard it open, she crouched down to her knees. Her lips began to quiver, and she broke down into tears. She heard the men coming to the front door and wiped her tears away. Her eyes narrowed, and she scowled.

Ruben and Elizabeth's brothers exited the store.

"Thank you for your time, Mr. Boston. We may pay you a visit back later," Ruben said.

"You boys take care of yourselves," Mr. Boston said.

Ruben came up to his sister with rope in his hands. "I don't know whether to smack you or pat you on the back," Ruben said. "Where did you hide her?"

Ruthanne replied, "As you said, brother, I turned this into a game, so keep on looking."

Ruben scowled at his sister. "Alright, boys, let's keep looking. She can only be in so many places in this town."

The men walked off, grumbling as they continued to look for Annabelle. Ruthanne entered the store in a panic.

"Mr. Boston, where is she?" Ruthanne asked.

Mr. Boston answered, "The Indians, Ruthanne. I gave her to the Indians so she could get out of town."

Ruthanne put her hand on the back of her neck. "Which ones took her?"

"The Cherokees, John and Samuel, took her away last night. I felt something was wrong when I saw Elizabeth talking to your brother. He is a smart man, but I give credit to God. I felt the Holy Spirit speak to me so powerfully when I prayed, asking for guidance. None of us could have planned it so well. I'm sorry you didn't get to say goodbye, but at the right time,

I'm sure you will see each other again. At least in the Indian Territory, it will be hard to find her."

Ruthanne was overcome with emotion. She gave Mr. Boston a hug and cried tears of joy and sadness.

Three days passed as Annabelle, John, and Samuel arrived in Indian Territory. In this time, the cheerful nature of John and Samuel helped Annabelle calm down, though she was filled with uncertainty.

"Annabelle's ride to Indian Territory was harder for her than hiding away in Elizabeth's chest," Albert said. "She was silent most of the time, listening to the men, but they understood her pain and silence. All she had fought for was destroyed. She knew getting caught wouldn't lead her back to Judy Mays. It would've led her back to Mr. Brown."

Albert picked up a thick old photo album from the large wooden chest and placed it on his lap.

"There's nothing like the wind being against you," he continued. "She did continue her fight and her journey. Her walk of faith was just getting started. Into the Indian Territory they took her...a land of uncertainty."

Albert wiped the dust off the album and opened it to continue Annabelle's story.

TO BE CONTINUED

I hope this adventure was an enjoyable experience for you and that you will visit your favorite retailer to leave a review because your feedback is priceless!

ABOUT THE AUTHOR

Hi, everyone! I'm Marcus, from the south side suburbs of Chicago. I have two degrees in zoology, love the Olympic games, and I am into Native American history, especially regarding issues that have divided families. Some of the stories I enjoy creating focus on parts of history rarely talked about and revolve around genealogy and interracial relationships, particularly between African American and Native American communities that cause us to reflect on the choices we make especially in our teenage and young adult years. This focus is to help young adults see the bigger picture earlier in their lives. God's greatest commandment is to love each other. I hope to fascinate your minds, to educate, to make you think about your family, and make you reflect on your own choices in life.